Greater Love

Greater Love

A Novel
By Carol Kinsey

Greater Love
Copyright © 2015 by Carol Kinsey
Published by Breautumnwood Publishing

First Printing – October 2015

ISBN-13: 978-1505827583

ISBN-10: 1505827582

Edited by Rachael Woodall
Cover design: special thanks to Autumn Kinsey and Seth Ringwalt
Special thanks to my team of proofreaders—I appreciate all your help and encouragement.

Other books by Carol Kinsey:

Under the Shadow of a Steeple
Published in 2013
Until Proven Innocent
Published in 2014

Coming soon:

Witness Protection
Special Ops and the Grace of God

Dedication

To my Lord Jesus Christ. May You be glorified.

To my wonderful family. It's so much fun reading to you!
I love you.

"Whatever you do, do your work heartily, as for the Lord rather than for men, knowing that from the Lord you will receive the reward of the inheritance. It is the Lord Christ Whom you serve."

Colossians 3:23-24

Chapter 1

"You have a date?"

Rainey Meadows grinned at her college roommate and shrugged. "I know. Kind of crazy, isn't it?" There was a twinkle in her blue eyes and she bit her lower lip to keep herself from smiling too big. "You've got to help me find something to wear." She grabbed Clarissa's arm and practically dragged her through their living room to the small bedroom at the back of their apartment.

"Who is this guy? Where did you meet him?" It was clear that Clarissa wasn't ready to jump in and help Rainey get dressed until she understood more of the situation. In the three years that Clarissa and Rainey had been friends, Rainey rarely dated. Not that there weren't opportunities. With her long brown hair, winning smile, and naturally tan skin, Rainey was a beautiful woman and turned the eyes of many young men at Pepperdine University. But Rainey was selective. She told Clarissa that she wanted a man of integrity who was sold out for Jesus.

It was after three in the afternoon and Rainey explained that her date was coming to pick her up at five. "Just help me pick something out and I'll explain." Rainey threw open her closet doors and stepped back to assess her choices. "I met him at the Bible study I've been going to on Thursday nights. His name is Matthew Westerly and he's a senior."

Clarissa sat on Rainey's bed and pulled her legs up under her. "Is he cute?"

Rainey pulled a soft beige sweater out of the closet. "Amazingly so." She held the sweater up to herself. "It might be cool tonight. How about this one?"

"Too plain." Clarissa shook her head. "How long have you known him?"

"He's been coming to Bible study for about a month. He just transferred to Pepperdine from a Christian college in Ohio."

"I've never seen you like this." Clarissa crossed her arms. "I'm not sure I approve."

Rainey shoved the beige sweater back into the closet and pulled out another. This one was a light blue cardigan with hand made ceramic buttons. Rainey designed and knit the sweater herself and made the ceramic buttons in one of her college classes. As a fashion design major, Rainey had lots of resources in the art department. "Is this too... out there?"

"For my granola-loving hippie friend? Never." Clarissa chuckled. "I love that sweater. It's you."

With a nervous sigh, Rainey pulled out a plain white shirt to wear under the sweater and a knee length flowing skirt that matched the sweater beautifully.

"So, when did he ask you out? This is totally spontaneous—and you aren't a spontaneous person when it comes to guys."

A slight chuckle escaped Rainey's lips. "It's not that spontaneous. We've talked quite a bit at Bible study and we've sat together at chapel a few times. He also came with the Bible study group when we all went out to dinner last weekend. You should have come, then you would have met him."

Clarissa smirked. "I don't do the Bible study thing. It's bad enough that I have to attend chapels." She nodded her approval of Rainey's outfit. "So, when did he ask you out?"

"Today after chapel. We're going down the coast to Casa Sanchez."

"That's a nice restaurant." Clarissa stood up and pulled a pair of earrings off Rainey's dresser. "These would look adorable with that sweater."

Rainey pulled out the small ruby studs she was wearing and put in the silver hoops.

"Why didn't you tell me about this guy before?" Clarissa sat back down and watched Rainey brush out her hair.

2

It was hard to explain. Rainey looked at herself in the mirror and thought it through. "I guess I didn't know if he'd ask me out or not and I didn't really want to get my hopes up by talking about him."

"You're so funny, Rainey." Clarissa shook her head. "As if any guy wouldn't sell his right arm to go out with you. I'm impressed he had the nerve to ask."

Rainey sat down at her desk chair and turned to face Clarissa. "He's so nice. Wait 'til you meet him. He's amazingly polite, incredibly sophisticated and smart." Rainey let herself daydream about him for a second. "And he's totally in shape… Like, I think he works out more than I do."

Clarissa laughed. "That's hard to believe."

One of the joys of attending Pepperdine University was its proximity to the Pacific Ocean. Running on the beach was something Rainey enjoyed at least four days a week. "Okay, so I know what I'm going to wear. Now I need to get a shower and do my hair." Rainey stood up and spun around in her room. "I can't believe he asked me out!"

***

Trey Netherland ran his fingers through his sandy brown hair and leaned back on his beige living room sofa. The Bible sitting across from him on the coffee table seemed to be glaring at him, if a Bible could glare. He'd read through the book of Philippians three times to make sure he'd have something spiritual to talk about with this religious young lady. This was the most unusual undercover job he'd ever taken.

Get her to fall in love with you. Be everything she could ever want in a man and more…

Trey's boss' words rang through his ears and he shook his head.

This case was a bit out of his league. Rainey wasn't some international criminal or strung out drug lord. This was a pleasant, attractive, young woman who hung out in conservative Christian circles and Bible studies. For all the rumors he'd heard about religious nuts, Rainey and her group of friends were some of the nicest people he'd ever met. Being undercover around such genuinely good religious people seemed like a sacrilege.

Tonight was his first actual date with Rainey Meadows. Was that really her name? It made him smile when he first heard the job. *Come on, who comes up with the name 'Rainey Meadows'? Did she come up with it or did her parents?*

But this case was nothing to smile at. Rainey Meadows was quite possibly a link to something far greater and this case went far deeper than him pretending to be a transfer student from a Christian college.

When he'd first agreed to the case, he thought it would be easy. Surely Rainey's fanaticism was only a front. Brilliant actually. Who would believe the daughter of two top ethno-biologists working for one of the world's largest illegal drug producers would be attending a Christian college in Southern California? What a great place to hide their daughter—who would ever suspect it? But what if they were wrong? What if this Rainey Meadows was not who they thought she was?

Trey glanced at his cell phone and saw that it was getting close to five. How was he going to play this girl? Did all the spiritual talk he'd been feeding her truly impress her? Was it really his supposed interest in the Bible that attracted her attention? It almost seemed real. But Trey was convinced it couldn't be.

I'll play your game. Trey picked up a picture of her he'd been given when this assignment fell in his lap. It was one of several photos taken of her around campus to familiarize him with her. *You want a nice Christian man... I'll give him to you. But what will you tell me in return?*

Chapter 2

"I've heard the food here is wonderful," Trey said as he pulled out a chair for Rainey. They'd been seated on the deck, overlooking the Pacific Ocean. "Have you been to Casa Sanchez before?"

"Only once. I was with a group. We took one of our professors here when he retired a couple years ago." Rainey watched as Trey took a seat and let her eyes roam to the ocean. "We definitely didn't have this nice of seating."

Trey grinned. "What did you order?"

"I don't even remember." Rainey picked up the menu and read through several of the meals. It was a nice diversion from the nervous butterflies in her stomach. "It all looks good."

"Can you bring us some queso dip?" Trey asked the waiter. "And extra chips." Trey smiled.

After ordering their meals, Trey asked Rainey if she minded if he asked the blessing.

"Sure." Rainey was pleased that he asked. How many young men would think to thank the Lord for their meal and their time together? When he finished his short prayer, Rainey looked up and found his eyes on hers. *He has the darkest eyes I've ever seen...* Rainey smiled. There was something about his large brown eyes that made Rainey feel safe around him.

"Thank you." He grinned. "So…" Trey reached for his water. "Tell me about yourself." He took a sip and set the glass back down. "At Bible study you mentioned living in several places around the world. I bet you have some good stories."

Rainey shrugged and twirled her straw around in her drink. "My parents are biologists. Their jobs took us all over the place. I was actually born in South America. My birth certificate says Bolivia."

"Wow." Trey moved his napkin to his lap when he saw the waiter bringing his food. "Are you not an American citizen then?"

"I am. I had to choose my citizenship when I turned eighteen. I don't even remember Bolivia. I was very young when we lived there."

"What do your parents do?"

Rainey licked her lips and chose her words carefully. "They study rare plants." Rainey glanced down at the meal placed in front of her. "This looks amazing." She smiled.

They both took a few bites of their meal and remarked on the wonderful flavors.

Trey watched Rainey for a moment and smiled. "So how do you like the Bible study?"

Rainey's eyes lit up. "I love it!"

"I've really enjoyed it too. I like how Andy focuses on digging into the scriptures." Trey used his best Christian lingo.

"I do too, and Philippians is one of my favorite books."

"Mine too."

"When I was in high school, I attended a Bible study on Philippians," Rainey reminisced. "Philippians 3 talks about our citizenship being in heaven. That really helped me a lot because we traveled around so much sometimes I felt like I didn't have a home. Thinking of my citizenship being in heaven really puts things in perspective for me."

Trey nodded. He remembered reading those verses.

"What have you found most meaningful in Philippians?"

Trey considered her question for a moment. "I guess Philippians 4 where Paul talks about learning to get by with humble means. Although, I confess it's not always easy being content in all those situations."

"I agree." Rainey fidgeted with her fork. "That's why the following verse is so important. 'I can do all things through Him who strengthens me.'"

There was a moment of awkward silence. Trey took a sip of his drink. "So you lived in Bolivia. Do I get to hear the rest of your story?"

Rainey tilted her head to the side and tucked a long hair behind her ear. "We lived in Colombia for a while."

"Colombia? That must have been somewhat dangerous for Americans."

Rainey nodded. "It was. That's why my parents sent me away for my four years of high school. They didn't feel Colombia was safe for me. They sent me to a school for missionary children in Europe."

"Missionary children?" Trey took another sip of his water. "But you said your parents were biologists, not missionaries."

Rainey shook her head. "You don't have to be missionaries to send your children there. Actually my parents are not even Christians. I wish they were." Rainey's eyes grew somber. "They chose it because there really weren't a lot of options for me. Most of the children at the school were from Christian homes. While not all of them shared their parents' faith, many of them did, and because of that, I heard the gospel for the first time in my life and put my faith in Jesus Christ."

"How did your parents respond?" Trey asked.

Rainey grinned. "They weren't exactly happy about it. Especially when I started talking to them about their need for a Savior. Don't get me wrong—I love them dearly. But more than anything, I want to see them get saved."

Trey nodded. "I understand. I'll be praying for them."

"Thanks." Rainey appreciated Trey's understanding. "Now I want to hear your story. Where are you from?"

"I'm from Illinois. I went to school in Ohio for a while. Now I'm here." Trey gave the simple version of his life story.

"Are your parents believers?" Rainey asked.

"They were." Trey paused. "My parents both passed away a few years ago."

"I'm so sorry." Rainey's tone was sympathetic.

Trey glanced outside at the soft blue sky where it met the dark blue ocean. "Don't feel bad. I've had time to heal."

Rainey opted not to ask what happened to them. She wasn't sure how much he wanted to share. "What made you switch to Pepperdine?" She kept the question less personal.

"I just needed a fresh new place to live. Pepperdine caught my attention. Living near the ocean and the mountains was something I couldn't resist."

That was easy for Rainey to understand. Going to a Christian college was a priority for Rainey, but the mountains and ocean were what drew her to California. "I've never been to the Midwest," she confessed. "I've always wanted to travel across the country and see the U.S."

"There are a lot of beautiful places in the U.S." Trey took a few minutes to share with Rainey some of his favorite national parks.

After dinner, Trey suggested they take a walk along the coast. Rainey was happy to comply.

There was a gentle breeze off the water and Rainey pulled her sweater close around her shoulders. She glanced at Trey out of the corner of her eyes. His strong biceps and masculine chest showed through his black t-shirt. She didn't know many young men built as well as him. It embarrassed her to notice and she turned to watch the waves.

She felt Trey's eyes on her for a few minutes before he spoke. "So you said you went to a Christian school for high school." He kicked off his flip-flops. "Where did you go to school before that?" He picked up his shoes and watched as Rainey did the same with hers. Freshly painted pink toenails dug into the sand as she walked.

"When I was really young my parents homeschooled me. As they got busier they eventually hired tutors for me."

"How was that?" Trey asked.

Rainey considered how to reply. "It was good for the most part." Rainey wasn't sure how much she should share. She didn't know this man very well. How would he handle her answers? "I never developed the scientific mind my parents have," she shared. "But when the world is your classroom, you realize there's so much to learn about everything."

Trey watched her tan face against the slowly appearing pinks in the sky.

"I was the little kid who would carry her schoolbooks out to the beach and let my mind drink in the scenery instead of drinking in my science and math books." Her eyes twinkled. "I'd sneak my watercolors with me and spend the afternoon painting when I should have been memorizing my elements." She pushed the sand around with her feet. "I'd write a poem instead of a report."

"You're a creative thinker." A genuine smile crossed his lips.

Rainey shrugged.

"Where were your tutors?"

"Sometimes they came with me. Other times I begged them to let me do my school alone outside and they'd comply." Rainey and Trey slowed down and sat on a large rock. "My parents didn't always hire the most reliable teachers. That's another reason they sent me away for high school. I think they hoped the discipline of a traditional classroom would restore my focus on the more important aspects of my education." She did air quotes around "important" and Trey smiled.

"Did it?" he asked.

"Well, creation made a lot more sense to me than evolution, so I guess it did." Rainey confessed. "I think my parents regret the Christian school more than any of it." She picked up a shell and tossed it toward the water. "Okay—now tell me about Ohio."

***

"How was your date?" Clarissa was still up when Rainey slipped in at midnight. She glanced at the clock and gave a disapproving shake of the head.

"It was wonderful." Rainey spun around and let her skirt twirl. "Matthew is amazing."

"He must be to keep you out past twelve." Clarissa snatched her bottle of water off the table and leaned back in her chair. "I was actually getting worried."

Rainey chuckled. "Why? It's not like I've never stayed out this late with friends before."

"Well, I don't know this guy and I've never seen you like this before." She tried to hide her grin. "I admit he's hot. Really hot. But you're my best friend and this was only the first date. He didn't kiss you did he?"

Rainey flopped down onto the couch and laughed. "No, we just talked. I think we must have walked ten miles on the beach tonight. It was the perfect night." There were more stars in Rainey's

9

eyes than she saw on their walk. "He asked me to go hiking with him in the Santa Monica Mountains tomorrow afternoon."

"A second date already?"

"Yeah."

"Don't you have school work to do?" Clarissa held up the textbook she'd been studying.

Rainey leaned back and closed her eyes. "I've got time. I think I just want to daydream right now." She thought about their long walk along the beach. Matthew was so easy to talk to. They had talked more about the Bible study, which Rainey loved. They also got into a long conversation about their interest in the outdoors. "Matthew has hiked the Appalachian Trail." She opened her eyes to tell Clarissa. "I've always wanted to hike the Appalachian Trail."

"Where is he from?"

"He's from Illinois and went to school in Ohio for a few years." Rainey got up and walked to the refrigerator to grab a bottled water. "We have so much in common, it's crazy."

Clarissa listened while Rainey chatted on about her date with Matthew Westerly.

***

Trey's apartment was unlocked when he turned the knob. His instinct told him to reach for his gun, but he'd left it at home tonight. He stepped inside where he was met by the strong smell of cigar smoke. He closed his eyes for a moment and let out a deep breath.

"I've told you not to smoke in my apartment." He turned on the light and walked into the living room.

Carlos Velasquez glanced up from Trey's leather sofa and held up a cigar with one hand and a glass of wine with the other. "It's about time you got home." His thick accent met Trey with little warmth.

Trey walked across the room and opened the door to the balcony. "Get outside with that thing."

Carlos followed Trey to the deck and they both sat down outside. "There's more wine inside if you'd like a glass."

"I don't plan on staying up much later." Trey ran his fingers through his hair. "How did you get into my apartment?"

"I make it my point to get into apartments, Mr. Smith." Carlos leaned back and took a long draw from his cigar. "What did you learn?"

The soft sounds of the ocean could be heard from Trey's apartment and Trey let their rhythm steady the beat of his heart. "It's her. I'm sure of it." His tone was cold and level.

Carlos' lips curved into a sinister smile. "Bueno." He set the cigar at the edge of the table and finished his glass of wine. "Now we learn what she knows. What did she tell you?"

"Nothing of value. It's going to take some time."

"Enrique wants results." Carlos took another puff of his cigar and studied Trey's face intensely in the dim light of the moon.

It was all Trey could do to keep himself from throwing the cigar off the porch. "You knew when you hired me that this could take time." Trey crossed his arms. "I'll get the information—and she'll hand it to me on a silver platter."

Carlos steadied the cigar on the edge of the table. "You are good, Mr. Smith. I will give you that. Slow, but good." He narrowed his eyes on Trey. "But we want to find them before they move again."

"Their daughter is in college. There have to be trails. She doesn't live in that nice apartment and attend Pepperdine University on her own dime." Trey kicked off his flip-flops and stretched his long, muscular legs out before him.

"California beach boy is a good look for you." Carlos chuckled. "I like the Bible on the coffee table too… is that part of your cover?"

"I have to be convincing." Trey glanced through the patio door toward the coffee table. "She plays her part real well." His brown eyes hid any warmth Rainey might have seen in him. "I told you I'd call you next week. You didn't need to check on me tonight."

"Enrique likes to keep a close eye on his employees—to make sure they are not doing any moonlighting." Carlos took one last draw from the cigar and put it out on the glass table.

It was late and Trey was tired. His gun was hidden on the other side of the apartment but he was sure that Carlos was wearing one. Trey was in no position to defend himself should Carlos decide to turn on him. "Is it necessary to do so at one in the morning?"

11

"Sometimes unexpected visits are the most telling."

"Did I pass?" Trey was sure Carlos could not have found anything in the apartment that would condemn him.

"You did." Carlos rose to his feet. "Although I could not figure out why you would leave your gun at home. Do you have more than one?"

"I have several." Trey stood up. "But I didn't feel a need to wear one when I'm undercover with a slim little brunette in a dress."

Carlos cocked his head. "I wouldn't let that be your motivation. You don't know for sure she is innocent."

Trey agreed. But for whatever reason, Rainey was putting on a good show of her own and Trey suspected that her show would not permit the use of guns on her person.

"We're going to need to search her apartment." Carlos watched Trey walk to the edge of the balcony.

"She's got a roommate. Be careful." Trey stared out at the moon for a moment. "Let me know if you find anything. I'll try to get at look at her cell phone."

Carlos stood up. "I'll be in touch."

Trey walked Carlos to the door and bolted it behind him.

***

Trey and Rainey hiked at a steady pace through Malibu Creek State Park. They started off hiking the four-and-a-half mile trail to the site where the MASH television series was filmed in the 1970s. It was an easy trail that traveled along Malibu Creek and wound past a grove of old-growth oak trees.

"Did you ever watch MASH reruns?" Trey asked as they walked past an old Jeep, reminiscent of the production of the show.

Rainey shook her head. "I rarely watched television growing up. I guess I was pretty sheltered." She stopped to read a sign about the site. "I've heard of it though."

"Well, I'd say that was a good warm up." Trey handed Rainey a bottle of water from his backpack. "Ready to try a more challenging hike?"

"Absolutely." Rainey let Trey lead her toward a more obscure trailhead.

This trail was rugged and took them up some steep, rocky

climbs. They hiked vigorously for almost an hour. They'd seen very few people in this section of the park. Trey climbed over a large boulder and was rewarded with a view of the ocean. He extended his hand to Rainey and she followed him up.

"This is gorgeous." Trey breathed in the fresh air. "I'd say this is where we need to have dinner." He turned to Rainey and watched her rapturous expression as her eyes scanned the panoramic view.

"I can't get over it." She scanned the horizon. "God's creation is so amazing and so vast." Her blue eyes almost matched the sky.

Trey nodded. "Which reminds me..." He unzipped his backpack and pulled out a small Bible. "I brought this." He sat down and opened the Bible to Psalm 100. "I thought this would be an appropriate way to spend our date. 'Shout joyfully to the Lord, all the earth...'" Trey began reading the five verses and Rainey sat down, leaned against a rock and listened with her eyes on a drifting white cloud.

"Thank you." She glanced over at him with a radiant face. "Can you read something else?"

Trey began flipping to Philippians. It was the only other book of the Bible he knew well enough to find.

"How about Romans 1:19-22?" Rainey leaned back and closed her eyes.

Flipping helplessly through the Bible Trey tried to figure out where Romans was. *Would that be in the Old Testament or the New Testament?* Trey did his best to make a guess. He knew Rainey would expect him to know where Romans was... this was not good. He glanced in the table of contents and quickly found the page number. Rainey didn't seem to notice.

"'Because that which is known about God is evident within them; for God made it evident to them,'" he began. "'For since the creation of the world His invisible attributes, His eternal power and divine nature, having been clearly seen, being understood through what has been made, so that they are without excuse. For even though they knew God, they did not honor Him as God, or give thanks; but they became futile in their speculations, and their foolish heart was hardened. Professing to be wise they became fools.'" Trey let the words sink into his mind. He thought maybe he felt something stir inside him.

Neither of them spoke for a few minutes. *Since the creation of the world God's power has been seen through His creation...* It was a new thought for Trey. He glanced out at the ocean beyond the mountains and considered those words.

"I read that verse to my parents once." Rainey sat up and wrapped her arms around her knees. "They didn't appreciate being called fools."

Trey closed the Bible and put it away before Rainey could make him look up anything else. *I need to memorize where the different books are...* He'd done his best to avoid asking too many personal questions so far on their date because he didn't want her to become suspicious. He figured the best thing he could do right now was earn her trust. Once she trusted him, he hoped she would tell him everything he wanted to know.

"That verse makes me think about all the people in the world who refuse to see God's hand in His creation." Rainey was still lost in the verse. "It must hurt God deeply to have those He created reject Him. Everyone loves His creation – but how many love the Creator?"

Trey watched Rainey's expressive eyes and listened.

"Psalm 19:1 says, "The heavens are telling of the glory of God; and their expanse is declaring the work of His hands.'" Rainey glanced up at the sky. "I can't imagine not believing in Him. You know what I mean?" She turned to Trey.

Her question caught him off guard. He could imagine unbelief quite well. He lived it.

"There would be no hope…" she continued.

That was a harsh statement for Trey. Was she saying he had no hope? *I have hope. How can she say that? Of course she doesn't know she's talking about me...*

"Are you ready for some food?" Trey broke his silence.

"I would love some. What did you bring?" Rainey crossed her legs and watched Trey unpack their dinner.

"I cut up a bunch of fresh vegetables and fruit." Trey pulled out a couple plastic bags. "And made sandwiches." He handed one to Rainey. "These look wonderful." Rainey snuck a peak inside the bread and moved a tomato around.

14

"Would you like to ask the blessing this time?" Trey asked.

"Sure." Rainey closed her eyes and folded her hands. "Father," her tone was soft and reverent. "Thank You for this beautiful place. Thank You for the opportunity to come here and take in your amazing creation and study Your word together. Thank You for the hope we have because of Your Son, Jesus. Help us, Lord, to cling to that hope and to grow in our walk with You. Please bless our food and our fellowship to Your glory. In Jesus' name, amen."

It was the first time Trey ever heard Rainey pray. While at Bible study, he'd heard Rainey interject a few words as the group prayed around the circle, but this time seemed different—more personal. She actually prayed for him. It was a strange thought to Trey. This was definitely the most unusual undercover job he'd ever worked.

Chapter 3

It was difficult to get herself back into the school mode Monday morning. Rainey sat in front of the bolt of fabric she'd ordered for her spring semester finals project and ran her hand over the silky teal blue organza. It was exactly what she wanted.

She designed the pattern for a modest ruffled organza party dress and now it was time to turn the pattern into reality.

I wonder what Matthew would think of the dress? Rainey tried to picture herself wearing it around him and smiled.

After their wonderful afternoon hiking in Santa Monica, Matthew showed up at her church on Sunday and they went out to lunch together following the service. Matthew told her he'd been looking for a good church in the area since transferring schools. She was glad he chose to visit hers.

She wondered how much she'd get to see him this week. She figured that as an engineering major, he would be pretty busy with school, but she knew she'd see him at chapel Wednesday and at Bible study Thursday night.

The dress… get back to the dress… Rainey glanced over her pattern and read through her measurements. Her professor was helping a first year student with some sewing machine problems and Rainey pulled out her earbuds and opted to listen to some praise music while she worked. *Maybe this will get my thoughts back on task.*

Rainey worked most of the morning and headed off to another class after lunch. She met up with some of her friends from Bible study after her last class of the day and headed to the gym.

Having friends who shared her faith was important to Rainey. Even though Pepperdine was a Christian college, not everyone who attended took their faith seriously. Her sophomore year of college, Rainey started attending a Bible study led by one of the professors and his wife and found the kind of fellowship she longed for.

Rainey was a little older than many of the young women in her Bible study. After high school, she had a falling out with her parents. It was a difficult situation for Rainey. She'd taken a couple years to travel around Europe, trying to deal with the broken relationship, mostly staying with the missionary families she'd met through the Christian school. When she finally decided to go to college, Rainey chose to accept an offer from her Uncle Jack to attend Pepperdine.

Her friends were already in the weight room when Rainey arrived. Clare, Ali, and Macy greeted her while Rainey set down her gym bag and pulled out a bottle of water.

"So I heard you had quite a weekend." Clare pulled her hair back in a hairband and gave Rainey a mischievous grin.

"Where did you hear that?" Rainey wondered how many of her friends actually knew she'd gone out with Matthew.

"I saw Clarissa in the computer lab." Clare began stretching and Rainey followed suit.

As much as Clarissa wanted nothing to do with the Bible study Rainey attended, she was more than willing to talk to them about Rainey. "I went out with Matthew this weekend." Rainey grinned. She really didn't mind these friends knowing. She just hoped they wouldn't stare at her and Matthew on Thursday night.

"That really cute guy who just started coming to Bible study?" Ali piped in.

Rainey nodded.

"I knew he liked you!" Ali elbowed Clare. "Didn't I say those two would end up going out?"

"You called it." Clare chuckled. "So what's he like? He's so quiet at Bible study."

"He's not a bit quiet." Rainey walked with her friends to the free weights. "He's really nice." She began sharing the details of their first couple dates.

Macy was a little less enthusiastic about the young man in discussion. "I hate to be a downer here, but be cautious." She warned her friend. "Mark said Matthew is really private and doesn't seem to want to get together with the other guys."

Everyone knew Macy's fiancé, Mark, was big on trying to get the guys together for fellowship and accountability.

"I think Matthew just doesn't know them yet." Rainey strained a little as she lifted a weight above her shoulder with her left arm. "Tell Mark to keep trying."

"He's tried quite a bit." Macy sat down on a yoga mat and crossed her legs. "You know Mark. He's always putting together social events."

"Matthew came with us when we went out for pizza." Clare defended him for her friend.

Macy stretched out her long slender legs. "I'm just saying be careful." She pushed a short red hair behind her shoulder and shrugged. "He may be a wonderful guy—I don't know."

Rainey lifted a weight with her right arm and closed her eyes to count reps. *Mark shouldn't judge Matthew just because he doesn't hang out with the other guys.* She tried not to let it bother her.

***

"How was the gym?" Clarissa glanced up from her donut and watched Rainey drop her gym bag on the floor.

"It was good." Rainey fluffed her wet hair. "Clare said you've been talking."

Clarissa laughed. "I just think it's funny, that's all." She took a sip of her iced cappuccino and picked up her pencil. "You never date and then suddenly you go out with a guy three days in a row."

"Whatever."

"And he sent you flowers." Clarissa motioned to the bouquet sitting on the kitchen table.

"Matthew sent these?" Rainey walked into the kitchen and grabbed the sweet smelling bouquet. There was a little card attached and Rainey read it with eager eyes. "Thank you for the wonderful weekend." She held the card against her chest. "Can you believe he sent me flowers?"

"No. I can't actually." Clarissa shook her head. She watched Rainey dance around the living room with her flowers and tapped her pencil on the desk rhythmically. "Did you get started on your dress today?"

"Yes, my material came in over the weekend. It's perfect." Rainey set the flowers down and sat across from Clarissa on the couch. Their conversation shifted to school and Rainey let herself focus on her responsibilities.

***

Bible study was perhaps the most difficult part of this undercover mission for Trey. At church he could go through the motions—sing the songs, take notes, and close his eyes to pray when needed. But Bible study was interactive. It required input and interaction with other people who knew more than he did about the Bible.

Being the expert was part of Trey's responsibility as an agent. It gave him the upper hand. These Bible study people seemed leaps and bounds ahead of him and it almost intimidated him.

"Matthew, can you read Isaiah 41:9-10 for me?" Andy asked and continued requesting other readers from the group.

After his last intimidating experience of not knowing where a book was in the Bible, Trey had spent time memorizing the books of the Bible and found Isaiah without a hitch.

It still bothered him that Rainey caught him off guard with the book of Romans on their second date. Their short discussion about the verses from Romans still lingered in his mind. He'd worked through the verse in his mind so many times that he almost had it memorized. "*For since the creation of the world His invisible attributes, His eternal power and divine nature, having been clearly seen, being understood through what has been made, so that they are without excuse...*" *So apparently God has made Himself so clear through His creation that I'm a fool if I can't see it—I have no excuse.* Why did the Bible make him feel so defensive?

When his turn to read came, Trey placed his finger on the verse and began to read. "You whom I have taken from the ends of the earth, and called from its remotest parts, and said to you, 'You are My servant, I have chosen you and not rejected you. Do not fear, for I am with you; do not anxiously look about you, for I am your

God. I will strengthen you, surely I will help you, surely I will uphold you with My righteous right hand.'"

His eyes lingered on the verse while others read their verses. They were strange, new words to Trey. *You are my servant. I have chosen you.* Trey tried to process the feelings he was having. The words were so personal, so intimate, as if God was speaking to Trey directly. *Chosen by God...*

"God knows us personally. There is no other religion in the world that gives us the hope that we have through Jesus Christ. It's incredible to me that the God of the universe seeks to have a personal relationship with us. " Andy's words interrupted Trey's thoughts. "John 10:14 tells us that He is the good shepherd, Jesus says, 'I know My own, and My own know Me...' He knows us. He knows who we really are."

Trey glanced at Andy to see if the older man was looking at him.

"From the conversations I've had with many of you, I'd say most of us in this Bible study profess to have that personal relationship with Him. I pray this is the case with all of you. But only you know your hearts—do you know Him? Are you His child?"

Andy's eyes scanned the room and Trey looked down.

"If you are a follower of Jesus Christ, you will not be rejected. He will protect you. He will use you for great things—far greater than anything you could ever dream or imagine. But it all begins with entering into that relationship with Him by accepting the free gift of forgiveness that He gives us through His Son, Jesus."

There was a moment of quiet and Trey stirred uncomfortably. *Why am I letting this get to me? Why am I even listening to this? I'm undercover—this isn't real. None of this is real.*

***

Over the next three weeks, Rainey and Trey went out several times. A couple times during the week they met for a walk on the beach. They also had dinner together before Bible study. On the weekends, Trey took Rainey on several creative dates and Rainey couldn't believe how much she enjoyed spending time with him.

"I've never felt this way before." She sat with her Bible study leader's wife at a small café off campus. "Is this what it was like when you met Andy?"

Jamie took a sip of her frozen lemonade. "I had a wild crush on him from the day we met." She grinned. "But our situation was different. We started dating in high school."

Rainey pushed a sweet potato fry around on her plate. "We're going to Santa Barbara on Saturday."

"That's a nice drive. Have you been to Santa Barbara?"

"No. That's why Matthew wants to take me there. I've heard it's beautiful." She popped a fry in her mouth.

"Andy went to college at Westmont, which is in Santa Barbara. We love it up there."

Rainey was quiet for a moment. "Have you noticed that Dylan hasn't been to Bible study since Matthew and I started dating?"

"I've noticed." Jamie nodded.

Rainey watched a few college students walk past to take a table at the back of the restaurant. "I know Dylan liked me. But I only saw him as a friend."

There was sympathy in the older woman's eyes. She placed a comforting hand on Rainey's arm. "You can't force feelings that aren't there."

Rainey turned her face toward the window. "I know. I just feel bad that he's shut me out as a friend all of a sudden."

"I think it's just too difficult for him to be your friend when you're dating someone else."

Rainey and Dylan had been friends since their freshman year. It was no secret that Dylan had feelings for Rainey. He'd been asking her to go out with him for years. Dylan was all about having fun and enjoying life—more into surfing than his education. It was a wonder to Rainey that he was passing any of his college classes.

Several of her friends thought Rainey should date him. He was tall, well built, and handsome. He had sandy blonde hair, always just long enough to show off soft wavy curls, and light blue eyes. A tattoo of the waves encircled one of his muscular arms and one of a seagull spanned the back of his neck. Dylan told Rainey they were emblems of his love for the water. He started attending the Bible study about a year ago, but seemed more excited about seeing her

21

each week than studying the Bible. Rainey enjoyed her friendship with Dylan, but she didn't want to date him.

It saddened her that Dylan was avoiding her. She missed his friendship. "Has Andy talked to him?" she asked.

"Not really." Jamie admitted. "Dylan doesn't seem to want to talk."

Rainey nodded. She didn't really know what to say. She'd been careful over the years not to lead Dylan on. She'd also been honest with him about her own feelings. But Dylan was convinced that some day she'd realize he was the right one for her.

"Andy and I wanted to see if you and Matthew would like to come over for dinner on Sunday." Jamie changed the subject.

"I can ask him." Rainey thought it would be nice to have dinner with this other couple. It would be nice to have Jamie and Andy get to know Matthew. She was sure they'd all get along.

***

"When can I open my eyes?" Rainey clutched Trey's arm as he led her toward a park bench on the beach. "I can hear the ocean. You're not going to throw me in are you?"

Trey let out a dry chuckle. "Okay. Sit down carefully." He opened a bag and set something in her lap. "Open them."

Rainey glanced down and her eyes lit up. "Roller blades!" She held one of them up and smiled. "Did you buy these?"

Trey sat beside her and pulled out his own pair. "I did. And I got myself a pair."

"This is why you told me to wear shoes with socks." Rainey began to unlace her running shoes and pulled the roller blades on. "How did you know my size?"

A smile crossed Trey's lips. "I have my ways." He winked.

Rainey gave him a playful slap. "Seriously—how did you know?"

"I asked Clarissa."

"You're sneaky." Rainey held out her legs and studied her new blades.

You have no idea. Trey grabbed both of their shoes. "You wait here. I'll take these to the car." He rollerbladed to the car, pleased with her enthusiasm with his gift. When he returned, Rainey rollerbladed toward him and greeted him with a hug.

"Thank you, Matthew."

It wasn't the first display of affection Rainey had shown, but it caught Trey off guard. He wrapped his arms around her and pulled her close. The smell of her soft perfume met his senses and he moved back to see her face. Her blue eyes seemed to bore into his and he ran his hand gently across her soft face, brushing a long brown hair from her eyes. "You're beautiful."

Rainey's full pink lips curved into a smile and impulsively Trey pulled her close to him and kissed her.

The kiss lasted only a moment, but there was something beautiful and pure in her kiss and Trey felt suddenly guilty. She wrapped her arms around him and rested her head against his chest. Trey ran his hand over her long soft hair. *Was that her first kiss?* His heart beat just a little faster with the feel of her lips still lingering on his own. He cleared his throat and tried to ward off his uncomfortable feelings.

"Are you ready to roll?" Trey rollerbladed backwards and reached for her hands.

Rainey let him lead her to the start of the trail. He held her hand as they bladed along the beach path.

"Just be careful not to hit any piles of sand," he warned. "If you do, your roller blades will stop immediately, but you won't."

They couldn't have picked a better day to spend in Santa Barbara. An arts and craft fair was going on at one end of the beach, and they spent a couple hours exploring the various artisans after they finished rollerblading on the beach.

It seemed natural to hold Rainey's hand now, but he refrained from another kiss. For some reason, Trey knew that a kiss meant a lot to Rainey. She was different than other women he'd dated. *Of course I'm not really dating her...* Trey watched her pick up a handcrafted bead necklace at a jewelry-maker's tent.

"Your beads are beautiful," she spoke encouragingly to the artisan. "Have you ever made buttons?"

The lovely Mexican woman nodded. "Yes. But I don't have any of them with me today," she said in a soft Spanish accent.

"Do you have a card?" Rainey asked.

The woman handed Rainey her business card and Rainey thanked her. "Your work is very unique."

"We'll take the necklace." Trey handed the woman a couple of twenties.

Rainey glanced at him with appreciative eyes. As they stepped away she expressed her thanks. "You didn't have to buy me the necklace."

"I wanted to." Trey watched her put the necklace over her head. "It looks better on you than it did on her table anyway."

"You spoil me." She took his hand and they continued their walk through the other booths toward the beach.

After a light dinner, they returned to the beach. A large swing set drew Rainey's attention and the couple sat on the swings and talked while the sun set across the water.

"This has been a perfect day." Rainey spoke with her face toward the ocean.

"I agree." Trey watched her as the wind blew through her hair. This was part of his job… but he enjoyed spending time with Rainey. She was intelligent and attractive, not shallow like many of the women he knew. They'd spent a lot of time together over the past four weeks. Trey knew it would take time for Rainey to open up to him. Perhaps the kiss provided the intimacy Rainey needed to share those secrets he was sure she had. He still needed to find out where her parents were. She'd been tight lipped about her parents. It was time to give her a story that might help her open up.

"Come on." He stood up and reached for her hand. "Let's go sit on the sand."

***

Rainey walked along beside him to a quiet place on the beach and sat beside him. Her heart trembled and she licked her lips. He leaned over on his elbow and seemed to study every part of her face.

"I didn't mean to kiss you earlier… without asking first I mean." He brushed her hair away from her face.

Rainey lowered her eyes shyly. "I didn't mind." She glanced back up at him.

"Then… may I kiss you again?"

Rainey nodded and Trey moved closer for another, even more intimate kiss. Her heart raced with feelings she'd never known. *Is this love?* Her eyes opened when he pulled away. *Can I possibly feel this way for a man I've only been dating for a month?*

He reached for her hand and played with her fingers. She leaned forward and kissed him. She blushed. The feeling of his lips on hers tingled.

Trey grinned. He leaned back on the sand and looked up at the sky.

What am I doing? Rainey's mind raced with emotion. Matthew was wonderful. It felt good to care about someone this way.

"Rainey." Trey sat up and ran his hand along her arm. "I know I haven't talked much about my family—my parents." He began softly.

Rainey could tell by his tone that Trey was about to share something personal.

"It's not easy for me to talk about." He glanced toward the water. "I wasn't very close to my parents when they died. I regret it. I loved them. But we were so different. Even though they were Christians, they did a lot of things I didn't agree with. We argued before they died…" Trey's voice drifted off. He clenched his teeth. Rainey could tell something was bothering him, but Trey stopped talking. He shook his head and stood up.

***

You're the biggest jerk in the world. Trey moved slowly toward the water. Even as the lies rolled from his lips Trey hated himself. He knew he needed to show some kind of vulnerability with her if he hoped to get her to open up to him. But Rainey was being so real. *Those kisses were real.* Trey licked his lips.

Rainey approached and touched his arm.

"I'm sorry, Rainey." Trey was apologizing for more than she knew.

"I'm glad you opened up." Rainey reached for his hand. "Don't apologize."

Trey shook his head.

"I'm not that close to my parents either." Rainey began to share.

This was it. Trey knew Rainey was about to open up. But his conscience told him that he'd only tricked her into her vulnerability. The fictitious story about his Christian parents who had died in an automobile accident was one big lie orchestrated to tug at her heartstrings and manipulate her to accomplish his goal. *What if she knew my real story? What if I'd been truly vulnerable and told her about my mother who ran off with another man and my father who turned to alcohol? What would she say if she knew my mother abused drugs when I was young and that her boyfriend abused me?* Trey hated his childhood. *But Rainey doesn't want to hear a story about that man. She wants to hear about her nice Christian boyfriend who grew up with strong Christian values and can be a spiritual leader in her life—her Christian boyfriend who doesn't exist.*

They walked back to their place on the beach and sat down while Rainey began.

"Things began to change when I went away to school." Rainey pulled her knees up and wrapped her arms around them. "But it got worse after I became a Christian. I spent a couple summers with some of my high school friends and their missionary families. It was so different than my home life. I began to question some of the things my parents did. They were pretty liberal about their lifestyles." Rainey kept herself vague.

Trey watched her intently.

"After I graduated high school I moved back home and started observing their lives. I made a few accusations that upset my parents—my father especially. It got ugly." She shook her head. "After that, my parents told me they thought it was best if I found my own way in the world. I was eighteen—they told me it was time to cut ties."

"They kicked you out?"

"More like—they moved and didn't tell me where they went." Rainey turned her blue eyes onto Trey.

"You don't know where your parents live?" It seemed unlikely.

Rainey shook her head. "I traveled around Europe for a couple years – living with a couple of my high school friends and their families. It was actually a healing time for me to find so much love and acceptance from my Christian family."

"How did you end up at Pepperdine? This is a pretty expensive school." Trey narrowed his eyes and tried to process her story.

"My uncle, Jack." Rainey's eyes showed a glimmer of joy.

Uncle Jack? Trey tried to figure out how this uncle he didn't know about fit into her life. "Who is Uncle Jack?"

"He's the closest thing I have to family in this country." She brushed away a tear. "He's been paying for my college." She tucked a hair behind her ear.

Trey needed to know more. "Is he your dad's brother or your mom's?"

Rainey scrunched her nose. "He's more of an adopted uncle." She shrugged. "I've known him since I was a child. When I was little he always sent care packages from America. A couple times we met him in Europe when we were there and when I started attending the Christian school, he visited me every year."

"What about his wife?"

"Her name was Ruth. She died when I was young. I never met her. I think that's why Uncle Jack grew so close to us. They never had kids of their own so Jack kind of adopted me."

This was a side of Rainey's life Trey hadn't expected. She obviously knew something about her parents that she wasn't sharing. But she was more than generous with her story about Uncle Jack. Trey listened as she continued.

"Uncle Jack knew that things weren't good with my parents and he invited me to come to California. He paid for tuition and I've been able to pay for housing with my personal accounts."

"Accounts?"

"My parents had a couple bank accounts set aside for me in the U.S." Rainey explained. "In the event that something happened to them. Uncle Jack helped me access the accounts and has made sure I've been able to get by."

Questions ran through Trey's mind. Who was this guy? Did he work for the same people her parents work for? Does Jack know how to reach her parents?

"Maybe you can meet him sometime." Rainey interrupted his thoughts. "He lives in Santa Clarita."

Trey sat on the beach wearing a tight blue t-shirt, beach shorts and flip-flops and watched the tall slender blonde approach wearing a pair of pants and a suit jacket.

"It's been hard to get a hold of you." Tiffany Waterford sat down beside him and glanced with amusement at his choice of clothing. She tucked a short blonde hair behind her ear and put on a pair of sunglasses.

"That's the whole idea of undercover work."

"You're supposed to be updating us regularly. I've been getting heat from the top wanting to know if you're any closer." She cleared her throat. "And to make sure you're still alive."

Trey glanced at the water. "You could have dressed the part a little better. Let's hope I'm not being watched."

"You just met a sexy blonde taking her lunch break on the beach. Is that so unbelievable?"

Trey wasn't sure he would have used the word sexy to describe Tiffany, but he chose not to burst her bubble. Sometimes it was better to keep your boss happy.

"So what you got? You sent me the signal to meet you—it's taken you long enough."

Trey spread his legs out in the sand, letting the sun warm his skin. "It's taken me a while to get anything out of her. She's quiet about her life."

"Well?"

"It's her Uncle Jack who pays her college tuition and helps her with her bank accounts."

"Accounts, huh?" Tiffany raised her eyebrows. "They're apparently not under her name because we've looked for her source of income. Interesting." The blonde agent took off her suit jacket and sat on it. "What about her parents?"

"She claims she doesn't know where they are."

"The lying little brat."

"I'm not so sure." Trey shook his head. "She seems genuine."

Tiffany chuckled. "I seriously doubt that." She dismissed it with a wave of her hand. "But what about Carlos? Has he taken you into his inner circle yet?"

"No. I haven't met Enrique yet, but Carlos is keeping a close eye on me. I've had to be extra careful. He managed to get into my apartment a few weeks ago—he bugged my apartment. I can't leave anything there that could point me to you."

"Then don't." Tiffany sniffed. "Once you've met Enrique though, we need you to come to L.A. and identify his photograph. Parks thinks he's got something, but we can't be sure."

"I'll keep you posted."

"I'll look into this Jack fellow. No last name?"

Trey shook his head. "I didn't want to push." He turned toward a few people walking on the beach.

"So, have you hooked the girl yet?" Tiffany gave Trey a once over with an amused glance. "You're looking kind of hot there, college boy."

Trey didn't know how to respond. *Yeah, I've hooked her.* He licked his lips and thought about their kiss when he dropped her off at her apartment the night before. He was sure Rainey didn't give her kisses away liberally. Somehow her affection made him feel like he was stealing something not meant for him. "She said something about me meeting her uncle. The man lives in Santa Clarita."

Tiffany nodded. "That's good to know. We'll get right on this." She stood up and grabbed her jacket. "Text me. We really were getting a little worried. If Carlos finds out who you are, don't expect to live through it."

Trey was aware. He watched Tiffany walk away and scanned the beach to see if he'd been watched. *She really needs to learn to dress the part.*

Chapter 4

"We're so glad you two could come tonight," Andy welcomed Trey and Rainey at the door. "Jamie made my favorite meal." He shook Trey's hand and opened the door wide so his guests could step through.

Jamie walked from the kitchen wiping her hands on a towel and hugged Rainey. "I'm pleased you guys could make it!"

Trey followed Jamie and Rainey into the kitchen and Andy offered him a coffee.

"Sure. Thanks." Trey watched as Andy poured a cup and handed it to him. "I'll let you add the cream. Jamie says I never add enough. I drink mine black."

Trey poured in enough milk to turn his coffee beige.

"Do you guys like bacon?" Jamie asked as she pulled the meat out of the oven. "These are called bacon-wrapped chicken. They've got cream cheese in the middle. Andy loves them."

"Everything's good with bacon!" Andy wrapped his arm around his wife's waist.

Once Jamie got everything dished out, they motioned toward the table and everyone took a seat. Thick, handcrafted pottery plates sat at each seat with hand blown water glasses.

"Matthew, would you ask the blessing?" Andy asked.

"Glad to." Trey forced a smile and rattled off the best prayer he could think of, thanking God for the food, the fellowship and the beautiful church service that morning. He wanted to pat himself on the back for his eloquence but part of him felt guilty.

The conversation started out with an update about a women's retreat Jamie was planning for the ladies in the Bible study. She thought it would be fun to camp at Big Bear. "I know not all the women are into camping, so I might need you to help me convince them."

Rainey said she was more than willing. "But trying to sell Ali on camping might be a little difficult."

"So, Matthew," Andy began. "Do you like to camp?"

Trey nodded. "I do."

"Matthew has hiked parts of the Appalachian Trail." Rainey reached for her water and took a long sip.

"Really?" Andy sounded impressed. "What was that like?"

Trey shared some of the highlights of his trips to the Appalachian Trail and the others listened with interest. "I always wanted to actually hike the whole trail at once, but I could never get away for that long."

"What was your favorite part of the Trail?"

Trey considered this for a moment. "It would be a toss up between parts of Maine, New Hampshire and Vermont. They each had such unique appeal and I don't think I could narrow it down to a favorite."

"I've looked at pictures online," Rainey said. "And some day I plan to get out East and hike at least a portion of the Trail."

"Well, Matthew," Andy turned to look at Trey. "Would you be up for a guy's camping trip? I figured if the women get a retreat, we guys should too."

Trey was absolutely sure he would not want to go away camping with the Bible study guys, but instead he nodded quietly. "Sure. That might work." He took a bite of the delicious chicken and complemented Jamie on her cooking.

"Thank you, Matthew." Jamie smiled. "I'm glad you two were able to join us tonight."

Andy refilled his coffee. "It's been great having you join our Bible study. I've never gotten to hear how you came to Christ."

Trey was quiet for a moment. Was that a question? He took a moment to finish chewing and tried to come up with something to say. He'd been attending Bible study long enough to know that most people had some story that described a "moment" of salvation. It was different than what he'd always believed about Christianity. He always figured that you were just born into it.

His dad and step mom recently told him they had "gotten saved" and started attending church. They had said something about it being a "strong Bible teaching church." Trey never asked them to explain and they knew better than to push.

Trey cleared his throat and took a sip of his water. "Well," he began. "I grew up going to church but it never really meant anything to me. It was just a religion. Then I got saved and my parents and I started going to a strong Bible teaching church." Trey hoped that was good enough. Somehow it felt more deceptive coming up with a salvation story than creating a false identity. *Not that any of it is real anyway.*

"So, your parents are believers?"

Well, my dad and my step mom... Trey glanced at Rainey. "They were. They both passed away several years ago."

"At least you know you will see them some day," Jamie said.

Trey nodded. *Christmas probably. Unless I have to work.*

"I hope I get to see my parents again some day." Rainey lowered her eyes.

Jamie knew some of Rainey's story and reached to take her hand. "We'll keep praying."

The rest of the conversation stayed on safer ground and Trey forced himself to stay in his role.

***

"Thank you for lunch, Uncle Jack." Rainey sat forward on the smooth black wooden chair and smiled at the older man across from her. There was a cool breeze blowing from the ocean, but the oil heaters on the restaurant deck provided them with warmth.

Jack Peterson glanced at his grilled salmon and nodded. "I've been wanting to come here for a while. Judy came here with her sister and said the food is amazing."

Rainey listened as Jack shared about his girlfriend's sister and her recent visit to California. It was encouraging to hear about this new woman in his life.

"I think Judy wanted to see if her sister approved of me." His blue eyes twinkled with pleasure.

"Well, did she?"

Jack chuckled. "Lynn asked Judy when the two of us were getting married.... She approved." He took a sip of his iced tea. "I never thought I would be able to marry again after Ruth passed away." He shook his head at the memory. "It's hard to believe that was almost twenty years ago."

Rainey had no memory of Jack's wife. She died when Rainey was a child and she'd had little contact with her uncle in her early years. "Do you think Judy is the one?"

Jack watched a waitress struggle to carry drinks on a small round platter to the table next to them. "We definitely share something beautiful." Jack glanced at his plate. "She's been good for me."

Impulsively, Rainey reached across the table and grasped her uncle's hand. "I'm glad you're happy." Her eyes sparkled.

"Sometimes it's hard for me to imagine God blessing me with someone so wonderful. I definitely don't deserve her." Jack said quietly.

"Whose house would you move to if you did get married?" Rainey asked. She knew Judy had a lovely home near the ocean not far from Malibu, while her uncle lived in Santa Clarita.

"We would probably sell mine first. We actually talked about moving back east after you graduate from college." Jack watched to see how Rainey would respond. "I don't want to leave California while you're still here."

"Uncle Jack, you don't have to make decisions based on me."

"I'm all the family you have right now, Rainey. I'm not about to leave you." Jack put more sour cream on his baked potato. "And, quite honestly, it will most likely take a couple years to sell two houses."

Rainey widened her eyes. "You and Judy really have talked about all this." Rainey was glad to hear this dear man was looking toward a future with Judy. Rainey liked Judy. It would be easy to see her as the aunt she never had.

Jack took a bite of his salmon and nodded. "And now I want to hear about this young man you've been seeing." He drank his tea and motioned toward the waiter for a refill.

"His name is Matthew Westerly," Rainey began. She shared how they'd met and a little bit about Matthew's background.

"So he has no family, no siblings and he just started attending Pepperdine spring semester?" There was something mistrusting in Jack's tone.

"Leave it to you to bypass all the other things I said about him and find the details that cause you suspicion." Rainey grinned. "How hard is it to believe that he's alone in this world. Look at my situation."

"Your situation is exactly why I become suspicious when I hear about people like Matthew." Jack pulled out his iPhone and searched the name Matthew Westerly.

"What did you learn?" Rainey raised her eyebrows.

"There's a lot of Matthew Westerlys." Jack set his phone aside. "I'll have to do more research."

"I have an even better idea." Rainey set down her fork. "How about Matthew and I come out to visit you some time."

"My house?"

"Sure, or a restaurant. Either way works for me." Rainey leaned back with her iced coffee in hand and watched for her uncle's response.

It sounded good to Jack. "Why don't you come visit me Friday or Saturday?"

"Then will you give him a chance?" Rainey chuckled. "You're more protective of me than my dad." She clutched his hand. There was something so endearing about her Uncle Jack.

***

"I'd love to meet your uncle." Trey couldn't be more pleased by the offer. This was better than he could have hoped for—an opportunity to meet this "uncle" and see his house. Trey pulled out his smart phone and pulled up his calendar. He did his best to drown out the noise in the crowded coffee shop. "I can do Friday evening." He glanced up and waited for Rainey to give a response.

"Uncle Jack said Friday or Saturday were fine. He suggested five."

Trey nodded. "What's Jack's last name?"

"Peterson." Rainey watched Trey enter the time and day into his calendar.

34

"You're pretty close to your Uncle Jack, aren't you?" Trey sent out a quick text and reached across the table for Rainey's hand.

"He's all the family I've got right now." Rainey lowered her eyes and let out a heavy sigh.

"Family is important." Trey lifted his coffee to his lips. He studied Rainey's expressive blue eyes. How could a parent disown their child? Was Rainey being honest? Could she possibly be faking that look of hurt whenever she mentioned her parents? He was good at faking expressions. *It will be interesting to meet this Uncle Jack. How much does he know?*

Rainey finished her coffee and glanced at her phone. "I hate to hurry off, but I've got to get to class. Mr. Schumacher is grading our spring semester projects today."

"I can't wait to see it." Trey stood up and carried his empty coffee cup to the trash. "Call me when you're done for the day."

Rainey promised she would.

Trey pulled her toward him when they stepped outside and found her lips for a tender kiss.

Something sweet and vulnerable shone through Rainey's eyes. "Pray he likes my project."

"You'll do fine." Trey released her hand and watched her disappear across the campus, the feeling of her lips lingering on his. He felt his phone vibrate and glanced at the new text message. "Pier 4pm." It was from Tiffany. Trey glanced at the clock. He had two hours.

***

The teal blue organdy and silk was an attractive fit on Rainey's slender figure. She'd chosen to be her own model for her presentation in Mr. Schumacher's class. The color was right for Rainey's naturally tan skin and blue eyes. She glanced at herself in the mirror and said a quick prayer. Today's presentation would potentially open up opportunities that could positively affect Rainey's career as a fashion designer.

If Mr. Schumacher liked her design he would present it to several local specialty dress shops and prominent fashion design firms. For Rainey it was the local specialty shops that mattered most to her. Rainey had no aspirations of working for a big name in fashion; she hoped that her modest, stylish dresses would make it into the smaller, more unique market. Some day Rainey hoped to sell her own designs online and possibly own a small dress shop.

She tried not to be nervous as she watched her classmates present their projects. Some students hired models for their dresses. Others, like her, wore their own creations.

When Rainey's turn finally came, she stepped into the well-lit room and waited while her professor inspected her work.

It was a nice fit and Rainey knew her stitches were good. Each seam lined up perfectly.

"Tell me your favorite features of your dress," Mr. Schumacher said.

Rainey was ready for his questions. She smiled. "I love the flare of the skirt." Rainey did a little spin to show the movement of material. "The fabric is cool and comfortable, making it pleasant to wear. I also like the ruched rosettes, which I made using the same material as the dress." She touched the unique features and stood for her instructor to notice.

Her instructor nodded and took a few notes. "Thank you, Rainey." He gave an approving smile and watched her walk away while the next student approached.

The next stage would be an actual inspection of the dress. Rainey changed into her jeans and t-shirt and smoothed her dress over the dress form for the next phase of her evaluation. She was lucky to find a zipper that so closely matched the color of her organdy. She glanced over at some of the other students who looked just as nervous as her.

"Your dress is really nice," one of the young men said from his table.

"Thank you, Drake. I like yours too."

It seemed to take forever for Mr. Schumacher to begin inspecting dresses. He took careful notes as he made decisions for each student's final grade. Rainey hoped she'd meet his approval.

"I've seen some wonderful work today," Mr. Schumacher smiled at his class of upperclassmen. "I definitely have my favorites in style, but I'm impressed by the work represented here today. I will be evaluating my decisions and will have your grade posted on Monday." He dismissed the class and Rainey felt a weight lift from her shoulders. Whatever her grade was, she was finally done with what many of the fashion design students called the hardest class of the program.

**

"You're late." Tiffany barely glanced at Trey when he approached her on the pier.

"I'm a college student. Give me a break." Trey stood beside his boss, placed his arms on the pier and glanced out at the water. "Good choice on the clothes today," he added and glanced over her khaki shorts and white t-shirt. "But I think I need sunglasses for your legs."

Tiffany poked him hard with her elbow. "Not all of us have a natural tan like Rainey." She shook her head. "I'm afraid your expectations in women will forever be unrealistic after dating Rainey Meadows." Tiffany shook her head. "Please tell me you've found some physical flaws—some cellulite, a pimple, something. I hate women like her."

Trey chuckled. He was glad his boss felt free to joke with him. "So what you got?"

"Well, that name verified what our research showed us. It took a little digging. Her tuition information is well hidden through various accounts and payment information. We linked the name John Peterson to Rainey through her college payments." Tiffany passed Trey a sheet of paper with account information written on it. "John Peterson was a professor at Pepperdine University. He retired five years ago." She turned her eyes to Trey. "He went by Jack.

Trey listened curiously. "But what's Jack's relationship to Rainey?"

"Before he taught at Pepperdine, John Peterson was Margaret Reed's college professor in Connecticut twenty-six years ago." Tiffany handed Trey another sheet of paper. "Margaret Reed is Rainey's mother." There was a knowing gleam in Tiffany's eyes.

Trey rubbed his smooth chin. "So what are you saying?"

Tiffany crossed her arms and turned toward Trey. "You tell me… she's twenty-five years old, he was her mother's college professor twenty-six years ago, and he's paying for her college." Her tone dripped with sarcasm.

"But Rainey was born in Bolivia."

37

"Twenty-five years ago, Margaret Reed left the University of Connecticut. She finished her degree at University of San Andre's in LaPaz."

Trey considered Tiffany's words for a few minutes. *Could Jack Peterson be Rainey's birth father? If so—does Rainey know? She gave no hint of this idea. Why hide it if he was her father?*
"Rainey is taking me to meet her uncle on Friday. I'll see what I can piece together."

"What we need to find out is if Jack Peterson has a way to get in touch with Rainey's mother. This could be our link." Tiffany glanced over her shoulder. "Have you talked to Carlos lately?"

"I'm meeting with him Saturday night." Trey turned around and leaned on the railing, watching people stroll along the pier. A little girl walked past with her hand in her mothers and smiled at him. Trey returned the smile. "He wants more information, but I'm reticent to give him anything about Jack."

Tiffany nodded. "I agree. We don't want them getting ahead of us." She watched a boat pass by. "Who's the guy in the black Steelers shirt?" She hushed her tones.

"I've been watching him. He's been sitting there for a few minutes." Trey spoke softly.

Unexpectedly, Tiffany stepped in front of Trey and ran her hands over his muscular chest affectionately. "He followed you onto the pier." She whispered in his ear and pretended to be playful. "Let's give you an alibi in case you're being watched." Without warning Tiffany planted her lips firmly against his.

Trey knew what Tiffany was doing, but it caught him off guard. He quickly recovered and wrapped his arms around her waist and returned the kiss.

There was something aggressive and passionate about her kiss. Trey felt a strange kind of unfaithfulness in this moment of intimacy. "Watch your back heading home." He whispered into her ear and kissed her again. It was all a show—but it felt wrong.

"I'll hang out at the beach a while longer. You'd better go. See if he follows you." She took Trey's hand and they walked past the man in the Steelers shirt as they left the pier.

Trey almost hoped the man was watching him. It would justify this show of affection with his co-worker.

She reached her arms around his neck when they reached the beach and pressed herself into him for another equally passionate kiss. "I could get used to being undercover with you, Trey."

***

Trey watched the blonde walk away and headed toward his car. A quick glance around him revealed the man in the Steelers shirt climbing into a gray sedan only a few cars away.

The taste of Tiffany's lipstick lingered on his lips and Trey wiped his mouth on a napkin. *I'm glad Rainey doesn't wear lipstick.* He glanced in the rearview mirror to make sure he'd wiped away the evidence of Tiffany's kiss.

It was a strange kiss, more passionate than Trey would have expected for a show. The feel of Tiffany's hand over his chest still ran through his mind. It seemed natural for her to be forward. Either that or she was a better actress than he.

Music would be a good distraction. Trey turned on the stereo and Rainey's praise CD filled the car. Trey knew the songs pretty well by now—several of the songs they sang at their church and at chapel. Rainey left the CD in the car last time they'd gone out. Trey smiled when he thought about Rainey's beautiful voice. She wasn't afraid to sing out with these songs.

When I survey the wondrous cross, on which the prince of glory died. My richest gain I count but loss… Trey listened to the words and glanced out at the ocean along Pacific Coast Highway. *Oh the wonderful cross… oh the wonderful cross…* It was strange new music to him. Contemporary Christian, Rainey called it.

Tonight was Bible study. Trey was growing accustomed to his weekly schedule, but Bible study was difficult. Sometimes he felt like Andy could see right through him. It was necessary for Trey to continue attending the Thursday night burden. It was what made Rainey trust him most. But it was more and more difficult to study the Bible and not think about what he was hearing each week.

Last Thursday night Andy talked to the group about how to share their faith. "It's difficult to argue with someone who doesn't want to hear the truth," Andy had said. "So I find the best two things I can do is give my own personal experience—no one can argue your experiences. And secondly, ask them, 'But what if you are wrong?'"

39

Andy continued with Pascal's Wager. "If I have chosen to follow Jesus Christ and live my life in accordance with the Bible and I am wrong, all I have done is lived a good and fulfilling life, enjoying the hope of eternity. But if you have chosen not to follow Christ and you are wrong—you will be spending eternity in hell. Who has the greater risk?"

The question bothered Trey when he first heard it. How presumptuous of Andy to make such an argument. But after thinking about it, Trey realized that Andy's whole argument was that either the unbeliever was wrong or the believer was wrong—but the unbeliever had more to lose.

It was amazing to Trey how much hope and joy Rainey seemed to have. She prayed for her friends. She prayed for her parents. He never heard her speak ill of anyone. If Rainey was for real, she definitely had something worth looking into.

What if you're wrong? The words haunted Trey. His dad and step mom told him after they "got saved" that they had been wrong. "We thought it was just about religion," his dad's voice echoed in his mind. "But it's so much more. God is a personal and forgiving God. He loves us and wants us to know Him."

"That's nice, Dad." Trey remembered his response. "I'm glad you've found something to make you feel better." Trey knew he sounded sarcastic when he said it, but his dad's new 'faith' didn't make up for the years of heartache he'd caused in Trey's life.

Several miles up the highway, Trey noticed the gray sedan still behind him. He decided to play dumb. If it was someone Carlos hired, Trey figured he'd hear about it soon enough. It was better if he acted like he didn't know the man was there. It made his own story more plausible.

Chapter 5

The way Rainey's eyes lit up when he picked her up Friday evening made Trey smile. He felt compelled to pull her into his arms and kiss her. Was he trying to erase the feeling of Tiffany's lips? Rainey's were so clean and soft. He hugged her and breathed in the sweet smell of her shampoo. No hairspray. No lipstick. Just Rainey.

"I made some cookies for Uncle Jack." Rainey walked to the table and grabbed a glass container. "He loves snickerdoodles." She grinned.

"You bake?" Trey held the door open for her.

"I do." Rainey put her purse strap over her shoulder.

Clarissa caught them in the parking lot as she pulled in. "Headed out, huh?" She raised her eyebrows and shifted her eyes from Rainey to Trey. "You do know I rarely see my best friend anymore thanks to you."

Trey opened the car door for Rainey. "I would apologize, but I'm really not sorry." His eyes twinkled playfully.

"What are you doing tomorrow?" Rainey asked Clarissa. "Trey will be out of town and I have a whole Saturday open."

"Deal!" Clarissa pointed at her. "We'll think of something to do. Don't make any other plans." It sounded more like an order than a request.

Rainey agreed and buckled her seatbelt.

"I still haven't figured her out," Trey said as soon as they pulled away. "I can't tell if she approves of me or not."

"It depends what day it is." Rainey set her purse on the seat behind her.

"What's there to disapprove of?" Trey acted offended.

41

A few drops of rain hit the windshield as Trey headed west on Malibu Canyon Road. "Maybe we'll get that storm they've been predicting." He glanced through the windshield at the cloudy sky. Large billowing clouds hung above the mountains.

"We could use the rain." Rainey leaned back comfortably in Trey's car. "So how are your final exams going?"

"Not bad." Trey glanced in his rearview mirror. "I have one more on Monday and then I'm done." Was he being followed again? Trey tried to hide his consternation. "When do you find out about your dress?"

"Monday." Rainey crossed her fingers on both hands. "Keep praying."

The rain began to fall in earnest and Trey turned the wipers to high. It was difficult to see the car behind him, but he felt certain it was still there.

It was an hour drive to Santa Clarita. Trey reached for Rainey's hand and wrapped his fingers around hers. It seemed natural to hold her hand now. Trey found himself struggling with the line between the job and his genuine attraction for her. What man wouldn't be attracted to her? He glanced over at her long slender legs. She wore an orange and red skirt and Trey resisted the temptation to place a hand on the knee that peeked out from her skirt. He knew instinctively that Rainey would disapprove of such a show of affection.

He considered this in light of Tiffany. His co-worker had no problem rubbing his chest and running her fingers along his neck in order to put up a good show. Why did that bother him?

It went back to the question Andy asked the group. "What if you are wrong?" *I've been living my own way all my life.* He'd never considered the right and wrong of physical touch. *But what if I'm wrong? What if it is sin? What if God's standard is purity and I'm falling short of it?* Trey sighed.

Rainey caught the sigh and turned towards Trey. "Are you okay?" She rested her head on the seat and watched his expression.

"Yeah. Sorry. Just lost in thought."

"Care to share?"

Trey held back a chuckle. He steadied his hands on the steering wheel as the car hydroplaned across a large puddle in the road. "Lots of stuff really." He glanced at her, knowing she expected some kind of answer. "So, if you were telling someone why sexual purity was important, what would you say?"

Rainey considered his question for a few minutes. "There are a lot of verses that you could give a person showing that God created sex for marriage. God is very clear in scripture that fornication is sin. He also tells us to keep our minds on things that are pure and right and good."

Trey recognized her reference to Philippians 4:8.

"I know 1 Corinthians comes to mind," Rainey added. "It says that we are to flee sexual immorality. That every other sin is committed outside the body—but when we are sexually immoral, we sin against our own body." Rainey chewed on her lower lip. "Hebrews 13:4 talks about keeping the marriage bed undefiled." She was obviously deep in thought. "I don't have all the verses memorized, but it would be easy to find more. Have you been talking to someone about sexual purity?" she asked.

Trey realized he needed to have an explanation for his question. "Someone I should talk to…" He glanced at Rainey.

"If the authority of scripture is not enough for them, you could give them very good physical and psychological reasons for abstinence," Rainey continued. "When a person engages in a physical relationship with someone they become bonded to them through a chemical called oxytocin."

Trey listened while she talked. When had he ever heard her speak as such an expert?

"If a person bonds with someone and then someone else and then someone else, their ability to bond becomes skewed. Our health teacher in high school used tape as the example. She put tape on one of the students and then another and another. By the time we passed it around a few times, it was no longer sticky."

Trey nodded. *Interesting analogy.*

"And then of course there's all the sexually transmitted diseases. It's ridiculously high in this country. Europe is just as bad. We spent a whole week in health class on STDs. It was enough to make just about all of us want to stay abstinent, regardless of our relationship with God." She chuckled. "But for me, just knowing that I don't want to dishonor my God is enough to keep me on track."

Trey glanced quickly at Rainey and found her eyes on his.

"You're only the second man I've ever kissed…" Rainey blushed and looked into her lap.

Trey licked his lips and swallowed.

"When I was in high school, I dated a young man for a couple months. His name was David." She was quiet for a moment. "He's the only other person."

It seemed to bother her. Trey wondered if she felt guilty for kissing this other guy. "What happened between you and David?" He decided to keep the conversation going on her end to avoid talking about his past.

Rainey watched the wipers move methodically over the windshield. "He cheated on me and we broke up. It hurt at the time, but at least I got to see David for who he really was before I could really begin to care about him. I'm just glad a kiss was all I ever gave him."

Although unintentional, Rainey's words stung. *What would she think of me? I'm leading her on.* He clutched the wheel and glanced into the rear view mirror. Lights behind him told Trey they were still being tailed. He was sure it was the same car. As he turned onto the highway he watched the car to see if he could get a better glimpse. Was it the same gray car he'd seen yesterday?

Trey figured Rainey would like him to share more about his past, but he couldn't. The more stories he made up about himself, the more he played with her heart. Trey knew he could create a story about only having dated one other girl and regretting kissing her. He could even tell her that he'd crossed boundaries he regretted and keep it vague. But the truth was, until this conversation he'd never thought about regretting his past.

None of his dating relationships had been very serious. But Trey had crossed boundaries that he knew Rainey wouldn't approve of. It was always the fear of getting a girl pregnant that kept him out of trouble in high school and even college. But Trey could think of many situations that were not honoring to either him or the woman. *Or God.* Trey shuddered that he'd had that thought.

"Have you dated much?" Rainey asked the question he hoped she wouldn't.

Trey kept his eyes on the road. "Not really." He felt the warmth of her hand in his.

The rain picked up and Trey used it as an excuse to focus on his driving. The fact that they were being followed didn't seem to bother him as much as this topic of conversation.

***

When they finally reached Santa Clarita, the rain had slowed. Rainey gave Trey a few directions and they pulled up to Jack's large stucco and brick two story home. It was impressive. The large lot was meticulously landscaped and a BMW sat in the driveway. The house itself was well maintained.

Jack was at the door to greet them as soon as they knocked. He greeted Rainey with a huge hug and reached out to shake Trey's hand. "You must be Matthew."

Jack's blue eyes struck Trey immediately. *Just like Rainey's...* "Nice to meet you, sir."

"I was hoping the weather wouldn't cause you any trouble getting here." Jack motioned for them to follow him to the living room. "The lasagna needs a few more minutes."

"It smells delicious." Rainey exclaimed. "Do you need me to help you, Uncle Jack?" There was tomato sauce in his silver gray hair and she brushed it away.

"No. Italian is my thing. This is one of my mother's old recipes."

Judy walked in a few seconds later and greeted Rainey with a warm hug. "I'm Judy." She reached to shake Trey's hand.

"Judy is my fiancée." Jack placed an affectionate hand on the older woman's back.

"So it's official?" Rainey's eyes beamed and she reached to take both of Judy's hands in hers. "I'm so happy for you."

The expression in Judy's brown eyes was like a schoolgirl in love for the first time. Her face beamed radiantly. "We are thinking of getting married the beginning of July. That way my son, Wayne, and his family will be able to come out."

"How about Nicole?" Rainey asked about Judy's daughter.

"She and Bill can't get away from the mission field at this time, but they both approved." Judy reached around Jack's waist and gave him a hug. "And of course we'll have you here, and my sister plans to come back out. It will be a small wedding, but as long as we

45

have our families here, we're happy."

"Did you hear that, my girl? I've got my family right here."
Jack used his free arm to wrap around Rainey. "Can I get either of
you a drink?"

Trey was ready for a cup of coffee after the hour-long drive.
He watched Jack and Judy disappear into the kitchen and let his eyes
scanned the nicely furnished living room. Two lovely arts and crafts
bookshelves took up one wall and a matching coffee table sat in
front of the sofa. The colors were warm and neutral. Several unique
pieces of art graced the walls and shelves. Plush rugs and hardwood
floors spanned the living room and hallway. It was obvious Jack had
expensive taste.

"Here you go, Matthew." Jack handed Trey a mug of coffee
with cream. "I guess the lasagna is done. Judy just checked it. Why
don't you both come on into the kitchen?"

Trey followed Rainey into the large, recently remodeled
kitchen, sat beside Rainey at the solid oak, craftsman style table and
let his eyes take in the room. Jack's kitchen had it all; stainless steel
refrigerator, a stove built into a large island, black marble counter
tops, two ovens, and what looked to be brand new appliances on the
counter top.

Jack dished out the lasagna and placed a large salad in the
center of the table. "Matthew, why don't you ask God's blessing on
the food?"

Trey was getting used to being the one asked to pray when
they dined with other Christians. He rattled off his best prayer of
appreciation and blessing and looked up to find Jack's eyes on him.

"Thank you." Jack passed the salad to Rainey and asked how
her finals were going.

Rainey spent some time telling him about the last couple
days and thanked him and Judy for all their prayers.

Jack turned to Trey, as if he were assessing the younger man.
While his eyes were older, they were sharp as tacks. He rubbed his
clean-shaven chin and cleared his throat. "So, Matthew, Rainey tells
me you're an engineering major."

"Yes, sir." Trey nodded.

"I've stayed in touch with several of my colleagues from
Pepperdine. A couple of them were engineering professors. Do you
know Dr. Winningham?"

Trey nodded. "I just took his final this afternoon. It was my worst one." Trey was glad he didn't blow off these useless classes. While he had been an engineering major in school, taking classes at Pepperdine was purely part of his cover.

"How about Ben Hampton?"

"I've not had him as a professor, but I've met him." Trey nodded. "I wasn't at Pepperdine my first four years, so I'm still pretty new to the engineering department."

"Where were you before Pepperdine?"

"Cedarville University in Ohio."

"This is a big change for you then." Jack took a bite of garlic bread.

Was this man testing him or just being friendly? "It is a bit of a change. But that's what I wanted."

"I see," Jack said dryly.

Trey wasn't sure how to take the comment. Did this man disapprove of him? "I'm really enjoying Pepperdine though. I love the campus. There's nothing like it."

"Do you live on campus then?"

"No. I have an apartment." Trey glanced at Rainey.

"Alone?" The questions kept coming.

"Yes."

"Most of the fifth year students do live off campus." Rainey interjected. She seemed aware of Jack's rapid fire of questions. "Do you mind if I get a little bit of coffee?" She stood up with her mug.

"Oh, I'll get it for you." Judy stood up and took the mug.

"Rainey tells me your parents are both deceased." Jack continued.

This really was an interview. "Yes." Trey nodded.

"I'm sorry to hear that. What happened to them?" Jack missed the glance his fiancée gave him from across the table when she handed Rainey her coffee.

"They were in an automobile accident. They both died instantly."

"Tragic. And you have no siblings?"

"None."

"How old are you?" Jack shifted questions.

"Twenty-seven." Trey gave his real age without thinking.

Jack paused for a moment and considered Trey's age. "A little older than most of the seniors, aren't you?"

Trey realized his mistake. "I needed some time to adjust after my parents passed away."

Jack took a few minutes to take a bite of salad and Rainey used the opportunity to tell her uncle and aunt-to-be about the ladies retreat Jamie was scheduling. "I'm so ready for a break."

"Were you still thinking of taking summer classes?" Jack's attention turned to Rainey.

"I probably will for just a few classes. Because, like Trey, I waited a few years to go to college, I'm so much older than most of the other full time students. They're all finishing up and they're two years younger than me."

Trey listened as Rainey talked about summer plans.

"But now it looks like I'll be attending a wedding. I'm so excited. Tell me how Uncle Jack proposed." Rainey leaned into the table and listened while Judy shared their engagement story.

"He wrote me a book had it published online." Judy began. "He wrote it like a children's book. The story was about a couple named Jack and Judy and how they met and began to fall in love and finally how Jack proposed while on a rocket ship to the moon."

Rainey and Trey both laughed. "That's unique," Rainey said.

"The book is at home. I'll show it to you some time."

Jack took a sip of his coffee. "I always wanted to propose in outer space so I figured writing about it in a book was almost as good."

"It was perfect."

"So you're literally the first woman to get a marriage proposal on a rocket ship to the moon," Trey interjected.

"Yes. I believe I am." Judy leaned over and kissed her fiancé.

Jack seemed to suddenly remember that Matthew was there and returned his attention to the young man under the microscope. "What's your perspective on dating, Matthew?"

Trey knew this was a trick question. His mind raced with possible ways to answer. "I believe the purpose of dating is to find your soul mate."

"Is that all?" Jack set his napkin on his empty plate and relaxed with his mug.

"Of course, ultimately the purpose would be to marry that soul mate and live happily ever after." Trey purposely used a story ending, hoping Jack might catch the play on words.

"Hmm."

"Jack," Judy scolded playfully and slapped his knee. "I'm sorry, Matthew. He's not always like this."

Trey watched Jack's expression carefully and decided to throw in a wrench to see what kind of response he'd get. "It's not a problem; Jack's just being a good father."

Jack seemed startled at Trey's words and glanced with a troubled expression at Judy.

"Jack's my uncle, not my father." Rainey laughed. "But you're right… he is giving you the third degree right now."

"Of course. But someone's got to take on the father role in your life. I think it's quite noble." Trey lifted his coffee cup up like a toast and gave an innocent smile. "Every woman needs a father figure."

"I think I need refill on my coffee." Jack stood up and walked to the counter.

Trey figured from the older man's reaction that Tiffany's assessment was right on.

"Uncle Jack has definitely been like a father to me over these last several years." Rainey looked at the older man endearingly. "Quite honestly, I don't know what I would have done without you."

Jack seemed to have recovered and returned to the table. He placed a tender hand on Rainey's shoulder before he sat down. "You're my girl, that's for sure." His voice sounded just a little different and Trey caught it.

Rainey placed her hand on Jack's hand and smiled up at him. From her reaction, Trey thought it might be possible that Rainey didn't know. Either that or she's a very good actress. *Surely she would know… his eyes are just like hers.* The table conversation continued and Trey glanced at Judy. *She knows too… This is getting interesting.*

***

49

The two couples moved to the living room to enjoy their dessert. Trey noticed that Jack was quieter. Trey felt somewhat guilty that he'd put the older man in this situation. "What did you teach at Pepperdine?" Trey glanced at Jack, hoping to get the man to open back up.

"Biology." Jack leaned back in his leather chair and accepted the dessert plate from Judy.

Trey nodded. "I haven't had to take any biology classes in a while."

"Thankfully, I haven't either," Rainey said. "Uncle Jack knows if he starts talking science it goes right over my head." She motioned toward Judy. "Of course, Judy's a nurse, so she understands it all."

"Not all of it." Judy chuckled.

"So did I hear you mention you have a daughter on the mission field." Trey decided to draw from the woman's interests.

"Yes. Nicole and Bill are serving with Athletes in Action in Italy."

"Wow. Italy. That sounds exciting. What do they do?" Trey feigned his best 'interested' expression, all the while hoping he hadn't just blown it with Jack.

Judy spoke for a few minutes about Athletes in Action. "They use sports as a tool to share the gospel," she explained. "Nicole and Bill have also served in Germany and the United States. It's awesome what they're doing. But I miss them and the grandchildren."

"This was wonderful pie, dear." Jack finished his bite of Judy's lemon meringue pie and set the plate aside.

"Oh, I forgot to bring in my cookies." Rainey rose from her seat. "I made you snickerdoodles." She stood up and asked Trey for his keys.

"I can get them." Trey offered.

"No. I'll get them." Rainey took Trey's keys and hurried out to the car.

Things had grown awkward since Trey's question and Trey worried that this "father figure" did not approve. It concerned him. Trey knew that Rainey respected Jack and might possibly let the older man influence her dating choices. He decided to grab the bull

50

by the horn. "I fear that my joke may have offended you, Jack." Trey spoke directly. "I apologize for my teasing."

"No offense taken." Jack glanced at his fiancée and back to Trey. "I tend to be very direct with people and I form opinions based on the responses I get."

Trey nodded. "I understand."

"I can see that Rainey cares for you." Jack leveled his eyes on Trey and leaned forward in his chair. "I tend to be protective of Rainey. She's been hurt a lot."

Trey appreciated Jack's honesty.

Jack studied Trey for a few moments. "Rainey tells me you're a believer."

"Yes, sir." Trey nodded and did his best to seem sincere.

"Then tell me, what does the Lord Jesus mean to you?"

Rainey walked in with the cookies just as Jack asked the question. She set them down on the counter and sat beside Trey to hear his answer.

The question caught Trey off guard. It was a little bit different than Andy's question. It felt more personal. He glanced at Rainey and found her eyes on him. Trey knew a lot was riding on how he answered that question. Nothing in his training prepared him for a question like that. *What does Jesus mean to me?* For the first time in an undercover job Trey's mind was drawing a complete blank. *Think of something... think of something...* Trey cleared his throat and took a steadying breath. "I guess it all comes down to Pascal's Wager." It was the first thought that popped in his mind. He did his best to recall the argument. "If I live my life following Jesus and I'm wrong—I've lost nothing. I've lived a good life on earth and then I die. But If I live my life following Jesus and I'm right—I have everything to gain. I will live for eternity in heaven." Trey hoped he was making the argument clear. "On the flip side, if I don't believe in Jesus and I'm right—I've lost nothing. But if I don't believe in Jesus and I'm wrong... I have everything to lose. Following Jesus makes sense."

Jack stared at Trey for a moment as if processing what Trey just said.

Trey swallowed. He knew he'd rattled it off quickly. Did it sound right? Was that the kind of answer Jack wanted? *What does Jesus mean to me? How does anyone answer that?*

"Can I tell you what Jesus means to me?" Jack leaned back and chewed on his lower lip.

"Absolutely."

"I was a cynic. Christianity meant nothing to me. I was a biology professor at a respected university. The idea of God was ridiculous to me." Jack leveled his eyes on Trey. "Then my wife started getting sick. We hadn't been close for years. I was busy with the university and… students there. But my wife, she turned to Jesus. Suddenly, her sickness, which at first terrified her, no longer scared her. She changed. She had joy. She had hope. All the anger she had toward me… went away. I saw what a living God can do in the heart of a broken woman and I started to investigate what she had."

As Jack's eyes began to mist, Judy moved to the ottoman near Jack and placed a comforting hand on his arm.

"I began to see that nature itself declared God's glory." He glanced at the darkened window. "Suddenly, evolution didn't make sense. If we evolved from a particle of dust… why would we humans care about beauty? Why would we love? Why would we create? No other life form cares about beauty. Sure they notice colors—a male bird draws the attention of a female bird by his brilliance in appearance. But every male bird of his kind is the same. Why are humans all different? We're all unique." Jack brushed away a tear. "I began to really examine creation and evolution and I realized that… professing to be wise, I'd become a fool. It takes more faith to believe in evolution than it does creation. Nature itself declares His glory."

Trey was surprised to hear that verse again.

"So, what does Jesus mean to me?" Jack leveled his eyes on Trey. "I gave Him my life. Before my wife died, she held my hand and said, 'I'm going to go see Jesus. I can't wait till you join us.'" It was difficult for Jack to hold back his emotion. "She forgave me for things—for pain I caused her, and encouraged me to forgive myself. Only Jesus could do that. Some day I'll see her again. I'll get to introduce her to Judy. Only Jesus could take a heart like mine and change it as He has. Only Jesus could heal my hurts and brokenness in losing Ruth." Jack looked at Judy and continued. "Only Jesus could bring a beautiful, sweet widow and a crusty old widower together and help us build a friendship that doesn't have jealousy, a relationship that is built on love and respect." Jack nodded and took a deep, calming breath. "Jesus means everything to me. He saved me. He loves me. He's my friend. He brought me a dear friend here on earth." Jack reached for Judy. "And some day, I'll get to see my other friend." Jack's face showed a special kind of joy Trey hadn't seen in the older man earlier. "Jesus means everything to me."

It was a powerful answer and Trey knew his didn't compare. *But his answer is genuine.* Questions flooded Trey's mind. Questions he wished he could ask Jack. What made Jack turn away from evolution? What evidence did he find that made it easier to believe creation? But those questions would only reveal the truth about Trey and he didn't want to be found out.

"Thank you for sharing that." Trey didn't know what else to say.

Jack nodded. "I think there's a point in every believer's life when we have to face that question. 'What does Jesus mean to me?' Ultimately... Jesus should mean everything to the Christian."

Trey could no longer stand Jack's penetrating eyes. *It's like he can see into my soul. Stop it, old man. These Christians are getting to me.*

"I hope I get to ask you that question again some day." Jack winked at Trey and got up to get a drink. "More coffee?"

Chapter 6

Jogging on the beach was Rainey's special time. There was nothing more invigorating to her than running along the sand with the waves crashing beside her. She was glad that the sun was out today. As much as they needed the rain, it was nice not to have it while running.

Rainey found herself thinking about their evening with her Uncle Jack. She still hadn't talked to him to find out what he thought of Matthew, but judging from his questions, she knew her uncle was mistrusting.

Rainey knew that Matthew's answer about what Jesus meant to him was not satisfactory to Uncle Jack. *But Uncle Jack doesn't know Matthew's heart. I do. I've heard him talk about his faith. Why did Uncle Jack have to ask it that way? I might not have known how to answer.*

Rainey knew this wasn't exactly true. Ever since her parents disowned her, Jesus became everything to her. He was all she had. She was thankful that Jesus provided her with a 'father figure' as Matthew called Jack, and she was grateful that He provided her with other good friends, but Jesus was the One Who tied them all together.

I'm sure Matthew meant that. He just didn't know how to answer Uncle Jack. I should have warned Matthew that Jack might put him through the ringer with questions.

Rainey slowed her pace and eventually came to a stop beside the water. She placed her hands on her knees and took several slow, deep breaths to still her heart.

She straightened up and stretched, glancing out at the cool Pacific Ocean, watching the waves crash against the beach. She listened to the sound of the water as it pulled away from the shore. Was there anything more peaceful than this? Rainey sat on the sand and leaned back to let the sun warm her face.

The position of the sun told Rainey that it was getting close to lunchtime. She and Clarissa had plans together for the day and Rainey would never live it down if she were late. They planned to go shopping in Redondo Beach and then run over to Torrance to have dinner at Kings Hawaiian Restaurant. She knew Clarissa only wanted to go there for the bread, but Rainey loved their food. She would start with the Coconut Shrimp Skewers for an appetizer and get the Huli Huli Chicken for dinner. *Best food ever!*

***

"Take a seat." Carlos motioned to a red vinyl chair beside the window in his hotel room.

Trey wasn't sure he wanted to sit there, but Carlos didn't seem to be giving him an option.

"Before we get started, I'm hoping you can clear something up for me, Mr. Smith." Carlos picked up a manila envelope from the bed and pulled out several photographs. "Who is the blonde?"

Trey reached for the photo and studied the picture of him and Tiffany in a very intimate kiss. He'd wondered if this might be coming. "She's my girlfriend." He blew out a heavy sigh and flung the photo back on the bed. "Darleen has been feeling neglected. She knows I'm on a job right now, but she doesn't know what it is. I met her at the pier. Rainey had stuff going on that day—I knew she'd never catch us."

"What about one of Rainey's friends?" Carlos didn't sound amused. "If word gets out that you've been with this bimbo, it's going to get back to Rainey."

"No one saw."

Carlos held up one of the photos. "We saw." He pulled out another few photos. "And apparently, this guy saw."

Trey glanced at the picture and recognized the face. "Rainey's friend Dylan?" *Why was he taking our picture?*

"You know him?" Carlos asked.

55

"He used to go to the Bible study I've been attending with Rainey. I think he had feelings for her."

Carlos slammed the photos down. "Well, good thing we caught him."

"What did you do to him?" A small feeling of dread crept into Trey's chest.

"My guy roughed him up a little—took his phone and his wallet. Made it look like a robbery." Carlos sniffed. "Said the guy put up a pretty good fight though."

Trey leaned his head back on his chair. He was relieved that they didn't kill Rainey's friend. But what was Dylan doing taking pictures? "Sorry, man. It won't happen again."

Carlos walked to the small refrigerator in the room and pulled out a couple beers. "It better not." He opened the bottles and handed one to Trey. "What you got for me? Who is this 'John Peterson?' Why were you at his house with Rainey last night?"

They must have followed him there and searched the address. Trey hid his frustration. Jack was an important link and Trey did not want Carlos and his men getting ahead of the game. It was Trey's job to keep the FBI in the lead. "About that…" Trey stalled for more time. "What's with following me all of a sudden? Yes, we went to John Peterson's place last night—can you not wait for me to tell you about it? I don't like your mistrust."

"Enrique doesn't even trust me." Carlos took a long sip of his beer. "So who is John Peterson?"

"He's a close family friend. He's been taking care of Rainey's college education." Trey glanced at his full beer bottle and took a drink. "She calls him Uncle Jack."

Carlos seemed pleased with this information. "This might be something."

Trey hoped his agents would find out before Enrique. "Rainey claims she's been estranged from her parents for several years and doesn't know where they are living."

"Do you believe her?"

"She seems genuine. But it's difficult to know. She knows her parents are involved in something that conflicts with her beliefs. That's why they cut her off." Trey explained how Rainey's Christian school exposure changed her views and how this caused the rift with her parents. He finished the beer and watched Carlos walk across the room.

"Want another beer?" Carlos asked.

"No. I'm good." Trey hoped their meeting would be over soon. "Keep me in the loop. If you find anything out about John Peterson let me know."

Carlos nodded. "Enrique will be in San Francisco in a couple weeks. He wants to meet you."

This was good news. Meeting Enrique was vital to this investigation. Keeping a low profile, the seemingly invincible drug trafficker had not yet been identified by the FBI. They knew he existed but no one knew who he was.

***

Rainey climbed the outdoor stairs to her apartment Sunday afternoon, letting her hand run across the smooth wood railing. She had just returned from a lunch outing with several friends from church. For some of those friends, it was their last Sunday before returning to their homes for the summer.

Golden sunlight streamed across the porch leading to her front door. She jumped when she spotted Dylan sitting with his back against the door.

"Dylan! What are you doing?" She sounded more annoyed than pleased to see him. It caught her off guard to find someone there.

"I knew you'd be back soon." Dylan stood up and smiled apologetically. "Sorry I scared you."

Rainey pulled out her keys and opened the door. "Come on in." She opened the door and let him walk in behind her. "I haven't seen much of you lately. Andy said he tried to call you but your phone's been off."

"So you never bothered trying?" Dylan raised an eyebrow and feigned a hurt expression.

Rainey set her books and purse on the desk. "Is that a loaded question? Why aren't you returning Andy's calls?"

"My phone was stolen." Dylan shrugged and made himself comfortable on a plush living room chair.

57

Rainey sat across from him on the sofa. "Where have you been?"

Dylan sniffed. "Just around I guess. Finishing finals. Surfing. I wanted to see if you wanted to go out and hit the waves for a couple hours. I brought my extra board. They're down by the garage."

Rainey hadn't surfed in a while. She didn't consider herself an exceptional surfer, but she enjoyed it. Matthew wouldn't be home until late tonight and with the semester wrapping up she didn't have any homework. "Okay. Let me get changed." She got up and walked toward the hallway.

"Do you think your new boyfriend will mind?" Dylan called out to her.

Rainey changed quickly into a modest light blue one piece and threw on a pair of board shorts. She wasn't sure why, but she felt like she needed to talk to Dylan. She'd felt bad that he'd been avoiding her so much over the past month. They used to spend quite a bit of time together and she actually missed his friendship.

"Do you think you remember how to surf?" Dylan grabbed his board and Rainey followed suit.

"It hasn't been that long." Rainey glanced at the teal blue board he was carrying and wondered how many surfboards Dylan owned. "That is a new one isn't it?"

"Yeah. The one you're using is new too. It's a Rip Curl—it's sweet."

It amazed her how much money Dylan spent on surf equipment.

As they neared the beach, Rainey glanced out at the colorful dots out on the waves. Several surfers were scattered out on the water.

"The waves are really cranking! We'll start out on some ankle busters to get you warmed up," Dylan said as they walked across the sand.

Rainey appreciated Dylan's "surfer talk." The small waves, or ankle busters as Dylan called them, were less intimidating. She'd surfed on several occasions with Dylan, especially her freshman and sophomore year of college. But he would still consider her a "Barney," Dylan's lingo for an inexperienced surfer.

Dylan set his board down and pulled off his shirt, exposing his smooth tan chest. He sat in the sand and glanced up at Rainey. The sun was in his eyes so he closed one and studied her with a tilted head. "So tell me about Matthew."

Rainey sat beside Dylan and he opened his other eye. "He's really nice," she said casually. "We've gotten close."

Running his fingers through his sandy blonde hair, Dylan let out a sigh. "I'm nice too, you know." He handed Rainey some surf wax and began waxing his own board. "For two years I tried to get you to go out with me."

Rainey had wondered if this conversation was going to happen. She just didn't expect it so abruptly. Using circular strokes she applied the wax to the board, mainly focusing on the spots where she would be standing. "I can't explain it."

"Yeah. I understand. You're just hot on this guy. Whatever. I just thought I should tell you, I saw him with some blonde woman with his tongue down her throat."

"What?" Rainey shook her head. She stopped waxing and stared at Dylan. How dare he make such an accusation? That was ridiculous. "There's no way."

"I actually took pictures but someone jacked my phone." He glanced out at the waves, watching the movement of the other surfers. "I know it was him. He was wearing a sky blue Under Armor shirt—trying to show off his pecks or something." Dylan shrugged. "Ask him about it."

Rainey tried to hide her annoyance. Matthew did have a sky blue Under Armor shirt. She thought he looked amazing in it. But lots of guys had blue Under Armor shirts. Matthew wouldn't be out kissing some other woman. "It couldn't have been Matthew." She finished with the wax and tossed it onto Dylan's bag.

There wasn't much else to be said. Dylan stood up, grabbed his board, and motioned to her foot. "Don't forget to attach the leash to your ankle. Let's hit the waves."

Rainey followed Dylan out onto the water. She was a little nervous. On top of not having surfed in a few months, now she was distracted. *There's no way Dylan saw Matthew kissing another woman. Matthew wouldn't do that.* When they were about hip height in the water, Rainey put the board in the water and hopped on. She settled her body on her board by moving side to side, making sure she was steady. Dylan was already paddling ahead. She figured he was angry with her for not believing him about Matthew "tonguing" some other girl. *What a disgusting thing to say.*

The waves were choppy. Rainey tried to get herself into the mood. It was nice to be on the water. The Pacific was cool, but the warm sun on her back took the chill away. She paddled behind Dylan until they got to the right take off spot.

"This will give you a nice gentle warm up." Dylan motioned toward an approaching wave rolling toward them. "Drop in." Dylan paddled toward the area and began to roll with the wave. In only seconds, he was on his feet, riding the small wave.

Rainey watched a few sets roll in and mapped out her location by sizing up the landmarks on the beach. She knew they weren't far out, but she didn't want to get thrown off course. She caught the wave and steadied herself to her feet.

It was a smooth wave. Rainey steadied her arms and tried not to think about anything but the waves. The wind in her hair and the sound of the waves blocked everything else out. It was a good moment.

When she reached the shore, Dylan was waiting for her, ready to give her a high five. "That was an epic wave."

Rainey licked her salty lips and smiled. "That was awesome!"

Dylan touched her slender shoulder. "You're a natural." He turned back to the water and watched as another surfer rode toward the shore. "This is a good day. Lots of clean waves."

Rainey followed Dylan back down the beach where they'd left their stuff. She wanted to get a drink before heading back out.

"So, why did you show up today?" Rainey asked and set her water bottle back on her towel. "I mean—you haven't been around in over a month."

Dylan studied the waves for a minute. "I've missed talking to you. When I saw Matthew with that blonde chick, I thought maybe things were over between you two."

Rainey shook her head. The blonde chick thing had to drop. "Dylan, you must have seen someone that looked like Matthew. I know he wouldn't be out kissing another girl."

Unexpectedly, Dylan reached his arms toward Rainey and placed one hand on each of her shoulders. "Look, I know what I saw." He stared into her blue eyes and studied her face. "I wouldn't make that up. The guy's a cheating jerk."

His warm hands on her shoulders made Rainey nervous.

"Do you have any idea how jealous I am? I see you with that guy, holding his hand, laughing with him, sitting with him at the coffee shop—I've even seen you kiss him, but you never even gave me a chance." He took a step closer to her and licked his lips. "For three years I've been here for you—waiting for that moment when you'd wake up and look at me the way you look at him."

Rainey stepped back and shook her head.

Anger flashed in Dylan's eyes. He stepped away and picked up his board.

They both attached their leashes and walked toward the water.

This time, Dylan was determined to head out further and catch a larger wave. Rainey paddled behind him, trying not to lose sight of him in the water. He'd never taken her out so far before. Was this his way of dealing with his frustration?

They passed another surfer setting up for a smaller wave, but kept going.

A large wave was approaching her and she knew she'd have to duck dive—a trick Dylan taught her to pass underneath a rolling wave with her surfboard. She steadied her board perpendicular to the wave and waited until the edge of the oncoming water was about two feet away. She was nervous as the wave approached. She grabbed the rails and leaned forward, putting the force of her weight on the front of the board to push the nose underneath the wave. She dove beneath the wave and surfaced on the other side, successfully avoiding a thrashing.

"There's a good one coming," Dylan yelled. "I'm gonna take it!"

Rainey watched the horizon. She tried to gauge herself with a landmark, but they'd gone even further than she thought. Dylan was in the zone. He watched as the waves approached. Rainey wondered what he was trying to prove. Should she head back to the shore?

He yelled something to her but Rainey could barely hear him. She watched as he caught the wave and was quickly out of her sight. Rainey watched the next oncoming wave rolling in. It seemed bigger than the last. She got herself into the proper position to catch it, faced the nose of her board toward shore, laid down and began to paddle.

In only moments, Rainey was on her feet riding the largest wave she'd ever been on. It was a different feeling—terrifying and exhilarating all at the same time. The water began to curl around her and Rainey felt like she was alone with God in the silence of His raging sea. It was a personal and soulful experience, harnessing the water's tremendous power and experiencing the rush of the ocean. Her heart raced with the intensity of it; she'd never taken on such a wave. She tried to steady herself on her board, but it wanted to pull into the wave. Suddenly, the exhilaration turned to fear and she cried to God.

Make it stop, Lord... please just get me through this thing...

Before Rainey could react, she lost her balance and found herself under her board with a wave pummeling her into the sand below. Salt water burned her eyes and she swallowed mouthfuls of water with no way to spit it out. Her arms flailed as she attempted to pull herself out from under the powerful current. She managed to surface for a gasp of air, but another wave pushed her back under and the board hit her in the head.

The world went black.

***

Rainey! Rainey! Can you hear me?

There was a voice in her head. Or was it real? Rainey felt someone's lips on hers. Breathing—she could feel someone breathing. Her chest heaved and she turned to spit a mouthful of water onto the sand. She took a deep gasp and felt her head pulled into someone's arms.

"I can't believe you tried to ride that monster wave! What were you thinking?" Dylan brushed her hair away from her face. "Are you okay? Can you hear me? Rainey…"

Rainey looked up and blinked a few times.

"Is she alright?" Someone asked.

"I think she'll be fine."

"Do you want me to call 911?"

"Rainey? Are you okay?" Dylan shook her lightly.

"What happened?" It seemed like the thing to say at the moment. Rainey was trying to figure out why she was lying on the beach with Dylan bent over her.

"You about drowned out there. That was a sick wave!"

She rubbed her head. It ached.

"You were knocked out." Dylan wiped the sand off her face and unattached her board from her ankle. It was rubbed raw. "I seriously thought you were dead."

Those last moments before everything went blank were beautiful. She'd never seen anything like it. In that one single moment the world was blocked out. It was just her and her Creator in the crest of that wave. But then everything went dark. She couldn't remember how she ended up under the water.

"Let's get you back to my place." Dylan tried to get her to stand up. "Can you walk?"

Rainey blinked. "I think so." She was still very disoriented. Her lips tingled. *Did he give me mouth-to-mouth?*

Dylan steadied her and looked into her eyes. "Rainey. Can you balance yourself?"

Rainey nodded.

He carried the boards and walked beside her. Thankfully, Dylan's apartment was closer to the beach than Rainey's. She walked, feeling slightly dazed, not knowing what to say because there didn't seem to be any words just then.

She needed to stop a few times and recover her balance. Should she be walking? Should Dylan take her to the hospital? She felt the lump on her head and wobbled along behind him. "I'm really dizzy."

"We're almost there."

Dylan ran ahead, set his boards by the door, and ran back to help her inside. "Let's get you inside and decide if you need to go to the hospital."

Rainey let him lead her inside. She heard him swearing about something while he led her to the futon couch by the window. The apartment was a mess. Did Dylan usually keep his place so trashed? Why were the drawers all opened in his desk? Why was his lamp on the floor?

"Someone broke into my apartment!" Dylan punched the wall and swore again.

Rainey leaned back on the futon and closed her eyes.

"Let me get you some ice." Dylan walked toward the refrigerator.

Rainey heard a commotion and opened her eyes. Her head was still swimming but she blinked to focus on a man holding a gun toward Dylan. Dylan walked backwards toward the living room with his arms in the air. "Look, dude, take what you want, man. I just need to take care of my friend."

Another man stepped from Dylan's bedroom, carrying a laptop.

Dylan seemed to recognize the man. "You're the dude that stole my phone!"

"About that…" The other man motioned toward a chair and told Dylan to sit. Carlos steadied his gun while he pulled the phone out of his pocket. "You've got some interesting numbers here."

A look of concern crossed Dylan's face.

"I especially like this text, *Update on the boyfriend. It looks like he's got another girlfriend.*" Carlos glanced up at Dylan. "I like the reply, *Talk to Rainey. See if they broke up.*"

Dylan glanced quickly at Rainey and back to Carlos. "Look—I don't want any trouble. I'm just a kind of an overseer."

"Overseer?" Carlos pulled the ottoman closer and steadied his gun on Dylan.

Rainey's head spun with confusion. Who were these men? Why were they holding a gun at Dylan? She tried to sit up but the larger man pushed her back against the futon and sat down beside her. A threatening glare and a well-aimed Glock told her not to move.

"So this is Rainey?" Carlos took a few steps toward her. "You don't look like you're a very good overseer. She appears to be hurt."

"She almost drowned. We were surfing. Look, what do you want? I don't have any drugs."

"I don't want any drugs, Dylan." Carlos read the man's stolen driver's license. "I want to know where her parents are."

"I don't know where they are. I just text her mom a couple times a week and send pictures. That's all."

"I don't think so." Carlos motioned for the other man to hand him the laptop. "You've got secret files on this computer that you need to open up for me."

Dylan clenched his jaw. "Would you just lower your freaking gun? I'm in swim trunks dude, I'm not gonna fight you."

"Tell me about your job, Dylan."

Dylan glanced at Rainey. She was obviously in pain. Her eyes were shut as if she was trying to sleep. "Her mom hired me three years ago to keep an eye on Rainey. She paid my college and housing, plus a little more. I just watch out for her, that's all."

Rainey opened her eyes. Was she hearing right? Dylan worked for her mother?

"We want to know where they are, Dylan."

Dylan was quiet for a moment, as if trying to assess the situation. "Information like that isn't free, Mr…"

"Call me Carlos." Carlos lowered his gun and studied Dylan for a moment. "This is Rod. Are you telling me your allegiance is only as deep as your pocketbook?"

A bitter expression crossed Dylan's face as he studied Rainey. "I have no other attachment to her."

Those words were obviously in reference to her not returning his feelings. "Dylan don't…" She tried to sit up.

Rod pushed her back on the futon.

Dylan turned away from her.

"Name your price." Carlos nodded.

Dylan spouted off a number.

Rainey trembled. It all seemed unreal. She could hardly think with the throbbing in her head, but she understood what was going on. Dylan was selling her parents out. He knew where they were. How was any of this possible?

Dylan motioned for his computer. "I need to see some proof of payment before I give you their location." He opened his laptop and pulled up his banking information. "You can make the deposit right here."

Carlos glanced at the name on the account. "Marcus Rauch." He glanced at Dylan. "Is that you?"

"It is."

"You're German?"

Dylan shrugged. "My bank thinks I am. Make the deposit and the information is all yours."

"I don't have access to those kind of funds. It's going to have to be approved."

Dylan grabbed a clean t-shirt from the arm of his chair. "What do we got to do?" He shoved his feet into a pair of flip-flops.

"Bring her." Carlos motioned toward Rainey.

Dylan hesitated. "Why do you need her?"

"What's that to you? You work for me now. Let's go."

The four of them headed out the door toward a dark green SUV parked outside Dylan's apartment. Rod shoved Rainey in and climbed into the driver's seat. Dylan climbed in beside her with his laptop in his hands.

Questioning eyes turned to Dylan. "Why, Dylan?"

"Call me Marcus." A German accent Dylan never used before came from his lips. "And maybe, just maybe, if you would have returned just a little bit of my affection, things might have gone differently."

"You've been my friend…"

"Shut up back there." Rod pointed his gun at Rainey.

Rainey's head ached and she closed her eyes to keep out the sunlight. She felt sick to her stomach, but was too afraid to express her discomfort. Why was this happening? Dylan was really Marcus and he worked for her mom? Why? Why would she pay some guy to look out for her after cutting her off five years ago?

"Where are we going?" Dylan asked.

"San Francisco."

Chapter 7

"I think we got it." Trey heard Carlos' voice on the other end of his cell phone.

"Got what?" Trey was driving back to the campus from his weekend at the FBI office.

"The location of Rainey's parents. Where are you? I want you to meet us at the wharf."

"I'm just driving back from Santa Monica. You're in San Francisco?"

"We just left Malibu. We've got Rainey with us."

Trey was quiet for a moment. This wasn't part of the plan. Once they got a location on Rainey's parents, they were going to head to San Francisco and meet with Enrique to plan out the next step. Why did they have Rainey? "Why do you have the girl?" He tried to hide the concern he felt.

"I'll explain when we see you. Grab a few things. You might not be home for a while. We'll see you in about six or seven hours."

Trey glanced at his phone when Carlos hung up. This was not the plan. He grabbed his other phone and called Tiffany. "Change of plans." He explained what he knew.

"Try to stay in contact."

Trey glanced at the cop behind him in his rear view mirror. He could easily break the speed limit and flash the patrolman his FBI badge, but Trey didn't feel like messing with it. He made his way to his apartment and loaded up a duffle bag with all he'd need for a trip—including his gun. A well-hidden compartment in his duffle bag would conceal his badge, extra cell phone, credit card and several large bills.

He decided to swing by Rainey's apartment to see if Clarissa was all right. Had Rainey been taken from their apartment?

Clarissa was on the phone when Trey knocked at the door. She greeted him with a smile and waved him inside. "I gotta go. Rainey's boyfriend just showed up." She chuckled.

"Hey, Matthew. What's up?"

"I haven't been able to get a hold of Rainey. Any idea where she is?"

"She went surfing with Dylan." Clarissa walked to the table and held up a note in Rainey's handwriting. "Said she'd be back before dark." Clarissa studied Matthew's expression. "Don't worry. There's nothing between them. Rainey's been friends with Dylan since their freshman year. Can I get you something to drink?"

Trey shook his head. "No. But thank you." Trey caught sight of Rainey's purse sitting on the table. "Does she have her cell phone with her?"

Clarissa flung open Rainey's purse and pulled out the pink iPhone. "Nope. Guess that's why you couldn't reach her.

"Any idea where Dylan lives?"

"He's got a sweet place right along the beach. I don't know the address. It's along a row of nice houses and condos. Shore Road, I think."

Trey tucked the information away in his memory. "Thanks. If she gets home soon, have her call me, okay?" Trey was anxious to go. San Francisco was a six-hour drive and he had no idea what Carlos and his men might do to Rainey.

He hurried down Rainey's apartment stairs and hopped into his Jeep. He tried to remember Dylan's last name. "Tiffany." He had his phone on speaker as he sped away. "She was with some guy named Dylan, a surfer. I guess he lives on Shore Road. That's all I got right now."

"Alright. Keep us posted as best you can."

Trey promised he would and made his way north.

***

"I'm going to be sick." Rainey finally spoke up. "Please pull over. I'm going to throw up." She bent over in her seat and held her stomach.

68

Carlos glanced in the rear view mirror and assessed the situation.

"She's probably got a concussion." Dylan sounded unconcerned. "She got hit pretty hard by the board."

Carlos pulled over and let her open the door. "If you try to run we'll blow you so full of holes you'll be throwing up in a hundred directions."

Threats meant nothing at that moment. Rainey was sick and the thought of running was the furthest thing from her mind. Everything was so confusing. She'd fallen asleep in the car, but wasn't sure how long ago that was. It was already dark outside. Wasn't it only around five?

Carlos gave her time to empty her stomach on the side of the road. He turned away and made a sound of repulsion.

"Can I have something to drink?" Rainey asked in a weak voice as she climbed back into the car.

"We'll be stopping for food soon." Carlos locked the doors and pulled back onto the highway.

Rainey closed her eyes. A picture of the wave ran through her mind. She was alone in that very quiet place. God was there with her. The smell of salt water and the cool breeze of the ocean blew across her skin. She could see the wave—it was like a giant tunnel of blue and foamy white. Ringing in her ears replaced the quiet and Rainey returned to the present to listen to the conversation between the two men in the front seat and Dylan.

Was Dylan really selling her parents out? Why would Dylan know where her parents were but she didn't? Who was this man? *Marcus... Marcus... what did he say his last name was?* Rainey couldn't think.

"I just spoke to Enrique. He agreed on the amount. We'll be at the wharf in two hours. He'll want the location down to the very latitude and longitude and if you try to pull something on him, expect a very short trip to San Francisco."

"I've got their precise location."

Dylan don't give it to them. Rainey knew that whatever it was these people wanted with her parents' location it wasn't good. *They didn't trust me with their location but they gave it to this traitor?*

Carlos pulled into a drive-thru and ordered food for himself and the other guys. Rainey wanted to ask for a bottle of water, but heard him order her a soda. She was too tired to ask him to change it. It didn't matter. She just needed something to wash away the vile taste in her mouth.

***

It was dark on the wharf and Rainey's eyes shifted nervously about as they led her toward a large yacht at one end of the dock. The vessel was well lit and Rainey glanced at her captors thinking that since she could obviously identify her abductors they would likely never let her live.

Dreams for her life flashed through her mind. Matthew—she would never have a future with Matthew now. Of course, she didn't know if they ever would have had a future, but it was certain they wouldn't now. What would he think when he realized she just disappeared? Would he search for her? She glanced at the boat. *He'll never find me.*

She staggered as she walked. It felt strange to be on her feet again. The movement of the dock made her dizziness worse.

"Keep up." Rod grabbed her arm and practically dragged her along.

It was cool on the boat. Rainey shivered as they led her into a nice-sized living room area, surrounded by windows on three sides.

"You made pretty good time." A tall, slender man in his mid-fifties rose from a white leather sofa and welcomed them into the room. Smoke floated in the air above his cigar.

Rod shoved Rainey onto a large, overstuffed chair. She blinked her eyes against the throbbing in her head.

"Is Mr. Smith here yet?"

"No. He should be shortly." Carlos motioned toward Dylan. "Take a seat."

"You must be Dylan." Enrique reached out a well-manicured hand and shook the surfer's hand firmly. "So you've made a deal with us, is that right?"

Dylan nodded. "I named my price."

"And you have no loyalty to this family?"

"There is absolutely nothing tying me to Rainey or her

70

parents." Dylan glanced at Rainey for just one quick moment. "I can give you their coordinates, Margaret's email address and you already have her phone number."

Enrique studied Dylan curiously. "You've worked for her for how long?"

"Three years. I've been Rainey's shadow for three years." There was bitterness in his tone.

"Hmm." Enrique glanced at Rainey. He motioned Dylan toward the table. "Take a seat. I'll make the deposit."

Rainey closed her eyes while the men made their transaction. The numbers seemed to whirl through her head. Every once in a while she'd drift off to sleep and wake up wondering where she was.

"Did you really need to rough her up?" Enrique rose from the table while Dylan double checked his account.

"We didn't rough her up. She hurt herself surfing today." Rod said.

Enrique walked to the chair where Rainey was half asleep. "A beautiful young lady." He knelt down and gently moved a hair away from her face. "Carlos, take her to a cabin. Lock her in. There's an empty room at the back."

Carlos nodded. He helped her to her feet and walked her to an empty room. Rainey sat on the edge of a small bunk bed and watched him pull the door closed behind him.

***

Trey glanced at the clock on his console. They were at least two hours ahead of him. He tried to still the unsettling thoughts that ran through his mind as he considered Rainey in Carlos' custody. Why did they take her? Would they hurt her?

As he neared the bay area, he phoned Carlos for a description of their meeting location. Carlos explained they would be meeting on a yacht and may be gone for several weeks. He told Trey where to park his car so it wouldn't get towed. Trey phoned Tiffany and gave her what limited information he had. He warned her that he would be going into deep cover from this point on.

"I'm not sure what kind of cell phone reception I'll have. Only message me in an extreme emergency."

"We'll let you act first. Find out whatever you can about Enrique. And be careful."

Trey asked her to check on his car if he wasn't back in three weeks. He hung up the phone and reached for the Starbucks he'd bought at the last exit. *This might be my last cup of good coffee for a while.*

Why did it have to be a yacht? It would be far more difficult to get away from these people on a yacht. What if they hurt Rainey? Would he be able to hide his feelings well enough to keep them from growing suspicious? Was he that good of an actor? What were his feelings for Rainey?

Trey thought about Friday night. It seemed like so long ago. Meeting her Uncle Jack was supposed to be the ticket to more information about Rainey's parents. Instead it turned into a preaching service aimed at Trey. Jack was an odd bean. After a busy weekend of digging and investigating, Tiffany and Trey were completely convinced that Jack had to be Rainey's biological father. But it was clear that she didn't know.

There are so many secrets in Rainey's life.

Trey wondered how Rainey would feel when she realized he worked for Carlos. She would hate him for sure. Was there a way he could tell her he was FBI? No. It would be too risky. It would be more natural to let her hate him. *Wouldn't she hate me either way?* Trey thought about their long, intimate kisses. *I'm sure there won't be any more of those.*

The thought of Rainey's soft, tender lips did something in Trey's heart. He did his best to fight his attraction to Rainey, but she was beautiful inside and out. It was difficult to disconnect his heart from his mission in this particular undercover job. She was a real person... a real person who cared about him.

What have I done? Trey found himself speeding, trying to get to her.

Chapter 8

"We expected you sooner." Carlos watched Trey as he headed up the plank.

"Traffic was bad and I wanted to get my stuff." Trey held up his duffle bag.

Carlos nodded and motioned for Trey to follow him.

"Tell Frances to pull out of port." Trey heard a man call out an order. "You must be Mr. Smith." Enrique held out his hand to shake Trey's. "What should I call you?"

"Call me Matthew." Trey returned the handshake.

Enrique studied the younger man keenly. "May I inspect your bag?" Enrique held his eyes steady on Trey.

"Absolutely. My gun is in there. But it's not loaded."

Rod made a move toward the bag but Enrique dismissed the request. "No need." He waved off Rod. "This man is not hiding anything. At least not in the bag." Enrique motioned toward an empty seat on the white leather sofa and sat across from it.

Trey sat down and did a quick assessment of everyone in the room. He recognized Rod as the man wearing the Steelers shirt on the dock the day he'd met Tiffany. Another man stood across the room with his arms crossed over his broad chest. Trey was sure he'd not seen this man before. He wore a gun on his hip and a look of mistrust in his eyes. Trey figured this was Enrique's bodyguard. Trey turned to the familiar face beside him. "Dylan—am I correct?"

Dylan reached out a hand to shake. "Ah, yes, I've seen you around campus. You're Rainey's boyfriend, right?" Dylan chuckled dryly.

Trey felt the antagonism in Dylan' gaze. "How is it we have the pleasure of you on this journey?"

Carlos poured himself a glass of brandy and took a seat near Enrique. "Dylan just joined our team. He worked for Rainey's parents."

"And he just sold us their location." Enrique motioned for Rod to bring him a drink. "Would you like something?"

"I just finished off a Starbucks," Trey said. "But I'd love a bottle of water."

"Get him a water."

Enrique's bodyguard brought Trey a glass bottle of sparkling water and Trey thanked him.

"This is Ian." Enrique motioned to the bodyguard.

Trey gave the man a nod. There was something intimidating about Ian's cold stare. He was a sizeable man, with a smooth dark head and eyes as black as night. "Finish the story."

Trey listened while Carlos filled in the details.

"So, where's the girl?"

"She's in one of the cabins. Unfortunately, she was injured surfing this afternoon. She appears to have suffered a concussion." Enrique took a sip of his drink and requested another ice cube. "When I say, 'on the rocks,' I mean more than one ice cube." His tone was cool and collected, but it was clearly a tone not to take lightly.

Rod was quick to add more ice.

"Has anything been done for her?" Trey leaned back and took a long drink from his water.

"I had one of my men bring her ice earlier. We should probably check on her."

"I'll check on her in a while," Trey said.

Dylan let out a sarcastic chuckle. "Oh, so you're going to act like you actually care about her?"

Trey crossed his arms and leveled his gaze on Dylan. "As opposed to you?"

"Touché," Enrique said.

"I knew you were playing her. I just didn't know your game." Dylan's eyes held something deeper than mistrust. Was it jealousy?

"You're just angry because I played her better than you did.

But it's all right—you had the missing link. I'd say you won." Trey attempted to keep it cool. He made a motion with his drink like a toast. "So where are they?"

Carlos motioned toward a map on the table in front of Enrique. "Dylan tells us they are in Santa Marta, Colombia."

Trey watched as Carlos placed his finger on the coordinates. "He gave us the exact location."

"So, as I see it," Dylan glanced around the room. "You should be dropping me off in Malibu in a few hours."

"That's not the way it works." Enrique took a sip of his drink. "You don't get off my boat until I know that what I purchased today is the real thing. Anyone can rattle off coordinates. I want to see her parents before you get off this ship."

It was obvious this wasn't the response Dylan was hoping for. "But I didn't bring anything. My apartment..."

"You can buy all new things with what I gave you today. However, you won't be cashing in until I am certain that you were not lying to me."

Trey set his water down on the coffee table and got up to stretch his back. "Why don't you take me to see Rainey?" he asked Carlos. "And show me where I'll be sleeping."

"Give him the room across from the girl." Enrique stood up with Carlos. "And Mr. Smith," he paused to study Trey further. "I look forward to having you work with me."

"Thank you, sir." Trey nodded and followed Carlos down the long ship's hull toward his room. He tossed his bag on the bed and stepped out while Carlos opened Rainey's door.

***

An overwhelming sensation of sunshine and saltwater filled Rainey's dreams while the feeling of surfing inside of a blue tube of water filled her senses with another place. A pleasant smile crossed her lips for only a moment until the touch of someone's hand on her bruised forehead pulled her from her dream.

Where am I?

"She has a nasty cut right below her hairline. We need to get more ice on it." Trey sat on the lower bunk beside Rainey and looked up at Carlos.

75

"I'll have Ian bring some down."

"Bring her a bottle of water, too." Trey reached for her hand after Carlos walked away. "Rainey…"

When his face came into focus, Rainey's lips curved into a smile. "Matthew?" She reached to his face with her free hand. "Is it really you or am I dreaming?

"It's me."

"How did you find me? Are we in heaven?" She glanced around the room, trying to remember where she was.

"You've had a nasty head injury, Rainey. Do you remember anything about it?"

Rainey shook her head and smiled into his eyes. "I missed you. Kiss me."

Trey licked his lips. He wanted nothing more than to kiss her. "I shouldn't…"

"Please." She pulled at his shirtfront.

Trey leaned forward and found her lips. His heart raced as he felt the tenderness and trust in her kiss.

"I was inside a wave today."

Her eyes were wide and her pupils dilated. Trey was certain she had a concussion.

"What was it like?"

"The water was all around me, like I was in a tunnel. It was all blue and white with sparkles of the sun shining through it. I could feel God there. It was intense. It was just me and God on the waves of the great big ocean He created. I've never felt anything like it in my life."

"It sounds beautiful."

Ian stepped in and handed Trey a plastic bag of ice and a bottle of water. "The men are playing cards if you'd like to join them."

"Thanks. I'll talk to Rainey a little longer and be up."

Ian nodded.

"You're not leaving me are you?"

Trey swallowed. "Not yet."

"Where am I?

It was clear that Rainey still had no idea what was going on. How long had she been this disoriented? Was she okay? Trey handed her the water and encouraged her to take a drink.

"Do you remember how you got here?"

"No. My head hurts."

Trey placed a tender hand on her head. "I know. Let's ice it. You have a nasty bruise."

"What happened to me?"

"You were surfing with Dylan today. Do you remember?" Trey helped Rainey lean back and placed the ice pack on her head.

"I remember the wave. It was amazing." Her eyes held a faraway look in them. "It was so pretty. It was all blue and white inside. I felt like I was with God." Her eyes beamed.

Trey was surprised to hear her repeating the same story. Did she not remember telling him about it a minute ago? He brushed her salty hair away from her face. "Do you remember who you are?"

"Rainey Meadows."

"Yes." Trey was trying to figure out what she did know without telling her more.

"I remember that I love you." Her lips curved into a smile.

Trey let his fingers tighten around hers and his heart beat just a little bit faster. "You've never said that to me before."

Rainey let out a chuckle. "I wanted to. But I wanted you to tell me first." She closed her eyes. "But it's okay. I know you love me. You're here…" Her breathing slowed down and Trey figured she was asleep.

This was not the reception he expected.

***

"She has no idea where she is?" Carlos sat across from Trey at the game table and twisted the top off a bottle of beer.

Trey shook his head. "Nor who any of you are. She has no memory of anything since she was in the wave."

"I wonder if seeing Carlos and Dylan will change any of that." Enrique played a card and slowly reached for his drink. Enrique was an intriguing man. Trey could tell the other men had a fearful respect for him. He appeared to be well-educated and was used to being obeyed.

"It must be some kind of amnesia," Trey said. "Sometimes a familiar sight or person will bring the memory back. We'll have to see." Trey glanced around the room. "Where is Dylan?"

"We gave him a cabin. He's gone to bed." Enrique cleared his throat. "I don't trust him."

Trey leaned forward, hoping Enrique would explain. Trey didn't trust Dylan either, but his reasons were different he was sure. How could Dylan make Rainey walk back to his apartment in her condition? Why didn't he call 911? Why would the guy sell out Rainey's parents?

"Anyone who is so unfaithful to his employer is not to be trusted." Enrique lit up a cigar and set it down in an ashtray. "He was bought out once, he can be bought out again."

"Are you sure his information is correct?" Trey asked.

Enrique shrugged. "It is the only lead I have so far."

"So, if Rainey does not remember anything, what are we going to do with her?" Carlos asked. "She is really no threat to us."

"I still want to keep her for leverage." Enrique tapped the ashes from his cigar.

Trey figured Enrique meant leverage for her parents. "And we don't know when she might get her memory back." Trey acted his part. "Most likely this is just temporary amnesia."

**

When Rainey woke up, she felt the sun streaming through her small porthole window. She tried to sit up but her head throbbed. She glanced around the room and tried to recall where she was. It was a small room, but everything looked new and well made. The bunk bed was white painted wood and the walls were soft gray. Clean medium gray carpeting covered the floor and a white dresser stood beside the window on the other side of the room. Nautical-themed pictures and decorations graced the room in a tasteful fashion that suited the furnishing.

Trey heard her stirring from the top bunk where he'd chosen to sleep. He climbed down and greeted her cautiously. Would she remember yet?

"Did you sleep in here with me?" Rainey reached for his hand.

Trey sat on the wooden bench beside her bed. "I did. My cabin is just across the hall, but I was worried that you might need help in the night."

"Thank you." Rainey ran her hand over the lump on her head. "Where are we? This isn't a hospital. I dreamed I was in a hospital."

"It's a yacht." Trey wondered if this would trigger a response. "Do you remember getting on a boat?"

Rainey shook her head. "No." Rainey reached for his hand. "Why are we on a boat? I don't understand."

Trey glanced toward the cabin door. What should he say? What would sound believable? "You were hurt pretty bad, Rainey. You appear to have amnesia." He ran a tender hand over her hair. "We're taking you to your parents."

Rainey's face grew concerned. "You won't like my parents, Matthew."

"It's okay."

"I don't even know where they live."

"You really don't know?" Trey studied her eyes carefully.

"No." Rainey spoke honestly. "So how can you know where to take me?"

Trey decided to give what portions of truth would best make this story believable. "Dylan knows where your parents live, Rainey. He works for your mom. She hired him three years ago to keep watch over you while you were away at college."

Rainey started to smile, as if she thought Trey was joking. "You... you're serious?"

"Yup." Trey meant every word of it.

"How did you find this out?" Rainey tried to furrow her eyebrows but it hurt.

"He came clean about it. It's a long story." Trey ran his fingers over her hand. "Are you hungry?"

"Not really. But I'd love to take a shower. My hair feels so sandy."

Trey understood. "There's a bathroom right there." Trey motioned across the room. "It's not real big, but there's a shower. I'll make sure there is soap and shampoo." He stood up to check the amenities. "I'll get some from my room." Trey stepped across the hall and brought back his shampoo, soap and razor. "I'll leave you to get ready." He helped her sit up.

"Do I have any clothes with me?"

Trey shook his head. "I can bring you a t-shirt to wear over your bathing suit. Your board shorts should be okay."

Rainey nodded. She looked confused. "Why did we leave without any of my things?"

Trey lowered his eyes. "We left in a hurry. You were hurt pretty bad."

Rainey accepted his explanation and watched him close the door. Everything was still so confusing.

***

Rainey was sitting on her bunk with her clean wet hair hanging around her shoulders when Trey returned. She gave him a wane smile. "You didn't tell me I looked like a raccoon."

Trey sat at the edge of her bed and ran a tender hand over her hair. "You look beautiful to me." He studied her face for a moment. "The bruises will fade. How was your shower?"

"It was nice. If my head didn't hurt so bad I might have stood under the warm water for hours."

"Do you think you can eat anything? Our captain has an amazing cook. He made some delicious bean and rice soup."

"I might try a little."

"That's good. Then you can take something for the pain. I found some ibuprofen on the ship. But I wouldn't want you taking it on an empty stomach."

Trey got up to get her soup and returned a few minutes later.

Rainey accepted the bowl and took a bite of the thick bean and rice soup. It was made with good ingredients and tasted better than anything she could have bought from a can.

It was obvious that she was tired. Her eyes were heavy and she leaned back on her pillow after she finished the soup. "How long will I feel this way?" She accepted the medicine Trey offered her and sat up to drink the water.

"Your brain needs to heal, Rainey. You just need a lot of rest."

Rainey nodded and laid back down.

"I'll check in on you later."

***

"Still no memory?" Enrique motioned toward an empty seat at the table and Trey took a seat across from Dylan.

Trey shook his head. "She doesn't remember anything from the time she went under the wave. I am curious to see how she will react to Carlos and Rod. If she doesn't remember them from Dylan's apartment, then there's no telling when or if she will remember."

"How do you know so much about amnesia?" Dylan crossed his arms and raised mistrusting eyebrows at Trey.

"I served some time in the military," Trey admitted. "You learn a lot about head injuries when you're in combat."

Dylan scoffed.

"This is new." Enrique interjected. "A hostage who doesn't know she is being held."

Trey explained to the others what he'd told Rainey. "I didn't know how else to explain why she's on a yacht. I say we take it one day at a time."

Dylan listened to the plan and glared at Trey. "This is ridiculous. Why not just tell her the truth and keep her locked up?"

Trey could read the suspicion in the other man's eyes. "It's best that we keep Rainey calm during this time. She's content with the explanation."

"Of course she is. She believes everything you tell her."

"It is far easier to control someone who trusts you than someone who does not." Enrique gave Dylan one long glance and motioned toward Trey. "She is welcome to leave her cabin when she is feeling well enough." He glanced at Trey. "We will see how she reacts to the other faces." He returned his gaze to the rest of the men. "If she does not remember the night she was abducted then we shall treat her as a guest."

***

Dylan stood in the doorway to Rainey's room and stared at the sleeping figure. He took a few steps inside and sat on the bench

81

beside her bed. Dark circles around her eyes were evidence of her injury. Dylan let his eyes roam over the slim figure under the thin blue blanket. He brushed her hair away from her forehead and glanced at her injury.

She opened her eyes and blinked a few times as Dylan's face came into focus. She smiled weakly and reached out her hand. "Hi, Dylan."

"I'm so sorry you got hurt." He took her hand and leaned forward.

"Did I tell you how beautiful it was inside the wave?" She smiled.

"No. But I saw you. You were amazing in there. How long did you ride before the water took you under?"

"I don't know. It was such a peaceful place." Her eyes were radiant.

Dylan looked away. "I'm glad you got to experience it."

"You always told me there was nothing like the inside of a wave."

"I didn't let you down, did I?" Dylan ran his fingers over her cheek. He glanced over his shoulder and noticed Trey standing in the doorway. Dylan looked up at the top bunk and back to Trey. "So you're sleeping with her, huh?"

"I slept on the top bunk last night to make sure she's okay."

"Isn't that sweet." Dylan's tone spoke volumes. He turned to Rainey. "Listen, I know Matthew told you I'd been working for your mom." His tone turned to honey. "I just want you to know, I'm sorry I deceived you."

Rainey looked confused for a moment and shook her head. "Oh, I'm so out of it I actually forgot. You work for my mom?"

"Your mom hired me to keep an eye on you at school. But Rainey, I still considered you a friend." He tightened his clasp on her hand.

Trey watched the interchange and crossed his arms. It was obvious he wasn't buying it.

Dylan turned to Trey. "You know, you really don't need to stand there."

"I think I do."

Angry eyes flashed at Trey and Dylan released Rainey's hand to stand up and face Trey. "Do you have something to say to me?"

"Outside. Not here."

"Oh… you have secrets you don't want to say around Rainey?" Dylan furrowed his brows and glanced at Rainey. "I don't see why we can't talk right here. You don't mind, do you, Rainey?"

Rainey glanced from one man to the other. She didn't seem to know how to respond.

"This is not the place." Trey opened the door wide and motioned for Dylan to follow.

"We'll talk more later." Dylan grabbed playfully at Rainey's toes through the blanket. She gave him a weak smile in return. The two men silently left the room and Rainey was left to her swirling thoughts.

***

Trey began walking toward the stairs to the deck but Dylan grabbed his arm. Trey turned and faced him. Both men were equally matched in height and build. Dylan sized up Trey with fire in his eyes. "You really think she's safer with you than me?" He gave Trey an angry shove.

It was obvious Dylan was trying to provoke him. Trey attempted to steady his temper. "Do I really need to answer that?"

Dylan shoved Trey again. "You've been playing her for the past few months and somehow I'm the one that can't be trusted?" He stepped closer to Trey's face. "I was working for her mom. You've been working for these guys."

"Yeah. And you just sold her parents out. That makes you a traitor." Trey wished he could throw Dylan on the ground and slap handcuffs on him.

The anger in Dylan's eyes intensified and Dylan made a few verbal threats.

"Not here." Trey turned to go but Dylan shoved him one more time.

Enough of this. Trey returned the shove with twice the force and Dylan hit the wall.

Dylan reacted quickly with a fist toward Trey's abdomen but Trey was quick to block the impact and grabbed Dylan's wrist. "You want this to get ugly?" He pulled Dylan's fist behind Dylan's back and spun him around into the wall. Dylan relented but the fire in his eyes burned intensely. Trey released the hold cautiously and backed away.

Trying to recover from his humiliation, Dylan straightened his shirt and breathed heavily.

Neither man seemed to want to talk first. Trey's muscles were tense with readiness. He watched Dylan with mistrust. "Why didn't you take her to a hospital?"

"She was fine."

"A person that has to be revived with mouth-to-mouth is not fine." Trey's eyes flashed angrily.

"Maybe I just wanted to feel those sweet lips you've been kissing." Dylan smirked. "It was kind of a let down."

"She was knocked unconscious with a surfboard, almost drowned, and you made her walk back to your apartment with you?" Trey couldn't imagine what kind of insensitive fool would make someone walk after such an accident. "You didn't know that her neck or back weren't broken. You should never have let her walk."

Dylan looked like he was going to attempt another punch but the readiness in Trey's eyes stopped him.

"I had my reasons."

Trey glanced down the hallway and tried to stifle his desire to thrash the younger man. "Yeah. You were afraid to take her to the hospital because they'd ask you questions—and you didn't want anyone to find out that you're not who you claim to be."

"It's more complecated than that."

"They wouldn't have asked you anything about yourself!"

"Look, I thought I could take care of it myself." Dylan clenched his fists. "Her mom never wanted much attention drawn to Rainey. It's complicated and I was doing my job." He crossed his arms. "Why do you care so much?" He stared at Trey for a moment. "Do you have feelings for her?" He narrowed his eyes and chuckle escaped his lips. "You do!" His chuckle turned to a mocking laugh.

It wasn't like Trey to get defensive. He was a professional. But Dylan had a way of getting under his skin. He resisted the desire

84

to punch Dylan square in the jaw. "I've had enough." He stormed up the stairs to the deck, hoping to find a place to think.

Chapter 9

"It's 3,750 miles from San Francisco to the Panama Canal," the ship's captain explained to the group of men sitting in the large living room. Frances was an older man. He wore a crisp white captain's jacket and matching pants. Thick gray hair pulled back in a short ponytail peaked out from his captain's hat. He pointed to a map in the middle of the table. "We should be able to make that distance in four days provided the water is relatively calm. Once in Panama, we will have to wait for passage. Usually this takes weeks, but Enrique has connections so we hope to get through within a week."

Enrique nodded. "I've made a few phone calls."

Trey listened as the travel plans were laid out.

"Could we have taken a slower form of transportation?" Dylan shook his head. "What kind of idiot takes a yacht?"

There was an uncomfortable silence at the table for a moment. Ian moved a hand to his gun. Trey wondered if this was going to be the end for Dylan.

Enrique motioned for Ian to relax, leaned back slowly in his chair, and reached for his unlit cigar. He snipped off the tip and breathed in the fragrance for a moment. The seconds ticked while he lit the cigar and watched a few streams of smoke drift up toward the can lights. "Interesting choice of words." He spoke calmly. "You're young—no?" He sized up Dylan and tapped his cigar on the ashtray. "Twenty-two. Twenty-three perhaps. Youth often feels the need to have everything now." Enrique took several puffs of his cigar and studied it for a moment. "I believe you have missed the understanding of something called patience."

"I have patience." Dylan was quick to say. "I've followed Rainey around for three years."

Enrique's lips curved into a slim smile at Dylan. "Three years is nothing to a patient man." He took another puff from his cigar and let the smoke swirl in his mouth before blowing it into the air. It curled and danced in the soft breeze coming in from the opened window.

"Please continue, Frances." Enrique returned his gaze to the captain.

Frances nodded. "We are almost to San Diego. I was planning to stop while we are still in U.S. waters and gather fuel and a few more supplies."

"If you have needs, tell them to Carlos," Enrique spoke to the group. "He and a couple of the others will be going ashore for a few hours."

"Can I go?" Dylan asked.

Enrique glanced at him and blinked. He chose to ignore the question. "Find out what Rainey needs." He glanced at Trey. "If you need to go ashore to make purchases, you may go with Carlos."

Trey nodded. He hated the thought of leaving the boat with Rainey still on board. But he knew she would appreciate some more appropriate clothing.

The meeting only lasted another half an hour. Before leaving, Trey stopped to talk with Enrique alone. He was concerned that Dylan might attempt to communicate with Rainey and give away their plan. Enrique agreed. He handed Trey a master room key and recommended they lock her in. Trey was more than pleased. He made his way to Rainey's room and knocked.

"Hey." He walked to her bedside and sat down. "How you feeling?"

"Better." She smiled and reached for his hand. "I wondered where you were when I woke up."

"We were having a meeting up top. The captain is going to be stopping in San Diego for a couple hours to get gas and supplies. I'm going on shore to shop. What all do you need?"

"I wish I could go with you." Rainey said.

Trey shook his head. "You need to lie still." He placed a gentle hand on either side of her face and kissed the crown of her head. The feel of her soft hair on his lips only made him wish he could stay. "Your brain needs rest. The least amount of movement you can make, the quicker you will heal."

Rainey rattled off a small list of personal supplies and then Trey asked her clothing sizes. "I'll try to get something you'll like." He leaned forward and kissed her tenderly on the lips.

"I love you, Matthew." Her huge blue eyes rested trustingly on his.

Trey glanced away for a second and tried to still the quickening of his heartbeat.

"It's okay." Rainey said softly. She reached her hand to his shaven face and smiled. "I shouldn't have rushed my words."

Trey closed his eyes. *Why do I feel so guilty?* He opened them to find Rainey watching him. "You're beautiful, Rainey." He spoke softly. Her innocent eyes seemed to pierce his soul. "Inside and out. You're the most amazing woman I've ever met." Trey felt suddenly nervous. This wasn't acting anymore. "I've never said 'I love you' to a woman before." He swallowed. Why was he being so vulnerable? "I want to. I just don't want to hurt you." *Too late for that... you're going to hurt her. This whole thing is going to hurt her.* "I'm sorry." Trey was apologizing for far more than not returning her words.

"It's okay." Rainey reached for his hand. "I'm glad you don't take the words lightly."

"I should go."

"Matthew." She stopped him before he could stand up. "Did you bring a Bible on board?"

"I'll pick one up while I'm in San Diego."

***

They'd chosen to get a large rental van to pick up supplies. Ian sat in the back seat and Trey looked over Carlos' list. "Do you know your way around San Diego?"

"Quite well." Carlos swerved through traffic. "I used to live in San Diego. I'll drop you off at the mall while Ian and I get dry goods and groceries." He turned onto the interstate. "You got money?"

Trey nodded. "Enrique gave me cash." *It must be nice to have an endless supply of funds.*

"Get some ibuprofen at the grocery store," Trey instructed Carlos. "We're almost out and I think Rainey's going to need some more."

Carlos nodded. "You do know all this compassion you're showing her might be for nothing." He glanced quickly at Trey. "I do not know what Enrique plans to do with her once we find her parents."

"It's not humane to let her suffer." Trey glanced behind him to gauge Ian's reaction but got nothing from the blank-faced man in the back seat. "And it's much easier to negotiate with a live hostage than a dead one."

Carlos nodded. "There you are right, amigo." He glanced into the rearview mirror to switch lanes. "And for now you still have the affections of a beautiful woman. I am not sure your blonde girlfriend would approve of your assignment." Carlos chuckled.

"She's had plenty of her own." Trey thought about the many men Tiffany probably kissed in undercover work. His FBI boss didn't seem to have any problem thrusting herself on him on the pier.

Carlos neared the exit for the mall. "Grab a couple shirts for Dylan. We need to stop his whining."

Trey nodded. He wondered if he could find a shirt with "fool" written on it.

At the mall, Trey hopped out of the car. They would meet back up in two hours. He hurried inside and found a coffee shop. *First things first.* With a hot drink in his hand, he pulled out his cell phone and called Tiffany.

"Where are you?" Tiffany asked immediately.

"San Diego."

"We lost tracking on your phone. I was worried."

"Enrique's got a scrambler on the yacht. No internet or phones for anyone without his permission." Trey explained where he was and what he was doing. "Rainey's friend, Dylan, also has the alias, Marcus Rauch. Supposedly he's got a bank account under that name. See what you can find out on him. As far as where Rainey's parents are, Dylan claims they're in Santa Marta, Colombia. I don't have any more details. That's where we're headed."

"Colombia?" There was a pause at the other end. "Be careful."

Trey realized that Colombia was not in his jurisdiction and he would have little authority there if he ran into any trouble. But this was where the job was taking him.

"Got any ID on Enrique?"

Trey gave a detailed description. He took a long sip of his coffee. "Enrique wants to find Nash McCarness more than we do."

"We need to find him first." Tiffany's tone was serious. "If those two partner up or if one kills the other and takes over, we're back to where we started and this whole drug explosion continues."

Trey understood the seriousness of his mission.

"What about the rest of the crew?" Tiffany asked.

"Carlos seems to trust me. The captain is an older man named Frances. He seems harmless. Pretty much just drives the boat. Rod's a thug. He's the guy we saw on the pier that day. Right now I'm on his good side, but I don't think he trusts me. And Ian is Enrique's bodyguard. He walks around with his hand on his gun. I have no doubt he'd put a bullet in all our heads if Enrique told him to."

"How's the girl? Are they treating her well?"

Trey took a few minutes to explain the situation. "Dylan should have taken her to the hospital. Her concussion is serious. She has no memory of anything that happened from the time she almost drowned to when she woke up on the yacht." Trey told Tiffany that they were allowing her to believe she was a passenger not a hostage. "Of course, without a doctor, it's hard to know the extent of her injury, but I've been keeping her on bed rest. Just pray for her…"

"Pray for her?" Tiffany repeated sarcastically. "Since when do you ask me to pray for people?"

Trey shook his head. He glanced around the mall and rolled his eyes. "I don't know what I meant… I've been hanging around Christians for a few months. It's what they do."

An awkward silence followed. "Okay… Um. Its not really what I do, but… I'll keep it in mind."

Why did I say that? Trey carried his coffee and his phone across the mall to a women's clothing store. "Look, I've got less than two hours to shop. Just call me within an hour and a half if you think of anything else I need to know."

"No problem."

"We'll be stopping in Panama. I'll try to call you then." Trey hung up and shoved the phone in his pocket. *Pray for her? Where did that come from?*

At the clothing store, Trey found an attractive skirt, similar to those he knew Rainey wore. He also found a pair of denim shorts and a few nice shirts that could be worn with the shorts or skirt. It took Trey the full two hours to find everything Rainey requested. The more intimate apparel was a bit embarrassing, although he knew it shouldn't be. He wrapped up his shopping visit with a quick purchase at a teen clothing store for Dylan. He figured trendy high school clothes were a good match for the man's maturity.

***

On his way to Rainey's room with her supplies, Trey passed Dylan in the hall and tossed him a bag. "Here—this should work for you."

Dylan glanced in the bag and mumbled something Trey chose to ignore.

Trey pulled out the key to Rainey's room and Dylan leaned against the wall and crossed his arms. "So did you lock it to keep her in or to keep me out?"

"You figure it out."

"What are you afraid I'm going to do? Tell her what you really are?"

Trey stopped before he opened the door. He had no patience for Dylan. "No. I'm afraid you'll do something even more stupid than not taking her to the hospital and ruin this whole mission."

Dylan took a step forward but Trey opened the door, stepped inside, and closed it softly behind him.

"How you feeling?" Trey wasn't sure if Rainey was awake.

She opened her eyes and stretched. "I'm good."

"I didn't mean to wake you."

"I wasn't sleeping. Just resting my head." She ran her fingers through her hair and moved over so Trey could sit on the edge of her bed.

"Are you ready to see my purchases?" Trey hoped she'd be pleased. It was his job to study people and he thought he knew Rainey pretty well by now.

Rainey sat up and Trey propped a pillow behind her. "It's like Christmas." Her eyes twinkled when he held out the first items of clothing.

"These are perfect!" Rainey held the shirts up to herself. "Matthew, how did you know exactly what I'd like?"

"Because it's stuff I like to see you in. Your style is you and I like it." Trey handed her a bag of personal items. "You can look through that stuff later. I also bought you a Bible." He handed her a leather bound study Bible.

Rainey glanced at it and held it against her chest. "Thank you." She reached a hand out for Trey.

Trey leaned forward and kissed her. He couldn't help it. It was so natural to kiss her now when she reached for him. "It would have been more fun shopping with you."

"How long do I need to be on bed rest?"

Trey lowered his eyes. "The longer you rest the better. From what I can tell, you have retrograde amnesia as a result of your concussion."

"What's that?"

"You've forgotten all the events following your injury for at least twelve hours."

Rainey folded the shirts in her lap. "Will I get my memory back?"

"You should. As you heal your memory should slowly return." Trey hoped it wouldn't be too soon. How would she handle the truth?

"I still don't really understand why we are going to see my parents." She lowered her eyes. "Have you been in contact with them?"

Trey shook his head. "Dylan has. It seemed like the right thing to do. We're done with school for the summer. You were injured pretty badly." Trey glanced toward the door, wondering if Dylan was out there listening. "You should have been taken to the hospital—but Dylan… decided on this route."

"Has anyone talked to Uncle Jack?" It was clear she was slowly gaining her ability to think logically.

Trey hated all the dishonesty in her time of need. "No. But we can call him when we get to Panama." Trey wasn't sure this was true, but it would at least give her hope. He stood up and ran his hand gently over her soft hair. "I'll talk to the owner of the yacht and get his opinion about when would be a suitable time to let you come up on deck and enjoy the sunshine."

***

A critical moment for Trey was introducing Rainey to Carlos and Rod. If they triggered a memory for her, it could change how Rainey would be treated on the ship. The men all agreed, as long as Rainey didn't recognize Carlos and Rod, they would play it off as if they were taking her to Colombia so she could be with her parents. Trey hoped for Rainey's sake she didn't recognize them.

Trey helped Rainey up the ship's stairs to the deck the next morning and walked her to a large, white deck chair. She was still wobbly on her feet and he helped her sit down on a soft, orange cushion.

"It's nice to breathe some fresh air." She leaned back and turned her face to the blue sky.

Carlos walked over to introduce himself. "Glad you're feeling better." He reached out to shake Rainey's hand. "I'm Carlos."

Without flinching, Rainey's face shone with a smile and she thanked him. "It's nice to meet you."

Rod was right behind Carlos and said hello.

There was no recognition in her eyes and Trey was relieved. He wasn't sure what they would have done to her had she remembered. It seemed unreal that she would have completely forgotten ever meeting these men. She spoke to them for a few minutes and they left to return to their responsibilities. Everything seemed fine.

Trey sat beside Rainey while the sun beat down on the deck of the ship. He handed her the new Bible and encouraged her to rest and read for a little while.

"This must be our special guest." Enrique approached before Trey had a chance to stand up. "So nice to have you on my yacht." Enrique punctuated his greeting by extending a large, well-manicured hand. Everything about him spoke of wealth and refinement.

"Thank you." Rainey accepted his handshake. "I haven't seen much of it yet, but my room is very comfortable and the deck is lovely."

It occurred to Trey that this man was as good an actor as himself. Rainey had no idea the man whose hand she shook intended to use her to blackmail her parents.

"I'm glad you like it. Have you had breakfast yet? My cook made the most delicious waffles. You must try some."

Trey rose to his feet. "I'll get you some." He took a moment while Enrique was talking to her to get Rainey's breakfast together. Dylan was unlikely to approach Rainey while she was talking to Enrique. Trey felt safer leaving Rainey alone with Enrique for a few minutes than he did leaving her alone where Dylan might find her. Trey hurried back with a plate of warm, fluffy waffles covered with maple butter, fresh raspberries and whipped cream.

"Perhaps you might enjoy the Jacuzzi tub while you are recovering, Miss Rainey." Enrique opened the invitation to her. "Please, make yourself at home." He waved his hand in the direction of the ship's pool.

"Thank you." Rainey watched Enrique walk away and turned starry eyes on Trey. "How in the world did you make these travel arrangements? This yacht is beautiful."

Trey cleared his throat. "I've done some work for the man." He glanced across the deck, hoping Dylan was nowhere around.

***

Rainey ate what she could of her waffles and let Trey take her plate to the kitchen. The view from the ship's deck was refreshing. She leaned her head back on the padded headrest and watched a few billowing clouds drift past as the yacht cut through the water at a steady pace.

She tried to read for a few minutes, but decided to wait for Trey. Her head still hurt and reading seemed to make it worse.

"Will you read to me?" She asked when he returned. She explained that her head still hurt and Trey gave her a pain reliever.

"Where should I read from?" Trey held the new Book in his lap.

"Why don't you read me one of your favorite passages?" Rainey leaned her head back and closed her eyes.

Trey licked his lips and opened the Bible. Flipping through the pages he glanced up at her and shrugged. "Why don't you pick?"

"How about 1 John 1:5-9?"

Trey tried to recall where 1 John was. He found the book of John and flipped past it a few times trying to figure out where 1 John could be. It took him a few minutes and he finally found it. "This is the message we have heard from Him and announce to you, that God is Light and in Him there is no darkness at all. If we say that we have fellowship with Him and yet walk in the darkness, we lie and do not practice the truth…" Trey let the words sink in for a moment. "But if we walk in the Light as he Himself is in the Light, we have fellowship with one another, and the blood of Jesus His Son cleanses us from all sin. If we say that we have no sin, we are deceiving ourselves and the truth is not in us. If we confess our sins, He is faithful and righteous to forgive us our sins and to cleanse us from all unrighteousness."

Rainey turned her face toward the water and let her eyes soak in the splendor of the rippling waves. "That was the verse that my friend Monique shared with me when she led me to Christ." Rainey turned to look at Trey. "When I first started going to the Christian school I really didn't understand what it meant to be a Christian. I watched how the others acted, I learned the Christian lingo and like a chameleon, I just blended right in. But Monique and Rebecca could see right through me." She smiled. "'If we say that we have fellowship with Him and yet walk in the darkness, we lie and do not practice the truth.'" She turned her blue eyes on Trey and seemed to look right through him. "I was a liar."

Trey felt suddenly uncomfortable. He knew he should show some form of excitement for her, thank her for sharing her testimony, or at least ask questions. But right now he wanted to get away from the accusation… was it an accusation? *Who is accusing me?* He felt like he was being called a liar.

"Did it make you angry?" he asked.

Rainey turned toward the ocean and considered this for a moment. "I think deep down I wanted to hear it. Do you know what I mean?"

"Not really."

"I knew that they had something that I didn't, but my pride wouldn't allow me to admit it. Until I realized that they could see right through my charade anyway…"

Trey turned toward the water. *Well I guess I'm a better actor than you were.*

Rainey was quiet for a few minutes. "Matthew…" She fidgeted with the fabric of her skirt. "I—I'm a little confused about this yacht and my injury and… why we're going to my parents. Did you tell me my mom wanted me to come when she found out I'd been hurt?"

Trey wasn't sure how Rainey arrived at this conclusion, but if it helped make sense of things for her, he'd roll with it.

Rainey furrowed her brows. She glanced off in the distance. "I'm surprised they want to see me."

Trey didn't know how to respond.

"Did you talk to them?"

"No." Trey leaned forward with his elbows on his knees. The warm sun on his face relaxed him in spite of his nerves.

Rainey showed a mixture of concern and confusion. "I know that God might have a plan in this. Maybe I'm supposed to see my parents again to talk to them about the Lord." She glanced into her hands. "Did Dylan arrange all this?"

Trey shook his head. "Not exactly."

"When did he tell you that he worked for my mom?"

Trey looked away. "It came out after you were injured."

"How did Dylan get a hold of you?"

Several good stories ran through his mind. *Liar…* "It's complicated."

"I'm glad you're here." She reached for his hand. "But how much do you know about my parents?"

How much do you know about your parents? Trey considered how to answer. "I know a little…"

Rainey's eyes moistened with tears. "Matthew, my parents are involved in some illegal things." She paused and tried to form her words. "They're ethno biologists. My mother specialized in botany. They are involved in plant cultivation. Plants used for drugs. I started putting things together when I was in high school and when I confronted them, they silenced me."

"How did they silence you?"

"They disappeared from my life and told me I was never to try to find them, nor talk about them. They told me it would be dangerous for me to ever attempt to reestablish my relationship with them."

Trey studied her intently. How could parents completely disconnect themselves from their child? As bad as his upbringing was, he couldn't imagine his parents ever cutting him off. "That's terrible."

Rainey nodded. "Uncle Jack is literally my only family."

Chapter 10

"I think we should go to Alaska," Jack pointed at the travel brochure he was looking at with his fiancée. They were making plans for their honeymoon and Jack threw out the coldest place he could think of because he knew Judy liked warm weather.

Judy knew he was playing with her but she raised her eyebrows. "It may actually surprise you to know that I've always wanted to explore Alaska."

Jack leaned over and kissed her. "Nothing you do surprises me."

The doorbell interrupted their conversation and Jack rose from the kitchen table. "You keep looking. I'll be right back."

Jack opened the door and let his eyes travel over his two visitors. A tall, blonde woman wearing a dark blue business suit, and a well-built African American man wearing a pair of Dockers, a gray dress shirt, and a purple tie stepped forward to meet him.

Tiffany Waterford tucked a short hair behind her ear and stepped forward. "Mr. Peterson?"

"Yes?"

"I'm Tiffany Waterford, FBI." She showed him her badge. "This is Officer Elm. May we come in?"

"I'm not in the habit of entertaining FBI agents." He made no motion to welcome them in. "How may I help you?"

"We're here to talk about your daughter, Rainey Meadows."

Jack clenched his jaw and glanced from one agent to the other. He paused to form his words. "What are you insinuating?"

"I think you know. Rainey's in trouble and we need to talk."

"Who is it, Jack?" Judy approached the door and sized up the two agents at the door.

"Tiffany Waterford, FBI." She showed her badge.

"I'm Vince Elm." The gentleman showed his badge.

Judy glanced at Jack. "Aren't you going to let them in?"

Jack stepped back and Judy motioned for them all to go to the living room. "Jack, what's wrong?" She sat next to him on the sofa and took his hand.

"It's about Rainey. They said she's in trouble." He turned to Tiffany. "I tried to call her three or four times yesterday but her phone goes right into voicemail. I just assumed she had her phone turned off. She's been wrapping things up with the school year. I knew a lot of her friends were leaving for the summer…" Jack's words trailed off.

"When is the last time you talked to her?"

"Friday. She was here with her boyfriend."

Tiffany glanced at Vince and back to Jack. "Mr. Peterson, may we be candid right now?" She let her eyes shift to Judy.

"Judy is my fiancée. She knows everything… Where is Rainey?"

"She's been abducted." Tiffany spoke gently, unsure how this older man would handle the information.

Jack's face turned white. "Dear Jesus…" he prayed out loud. Tears filled his eyes.

"One of our agents is undercover with Rainey. He's doing his best to look out for her." Tiffany assured him. "We've been conducting an investigation into her mother and Bradley Meadows. Of course, I assume you know their real names are not Margaret and Bradley Meadows…"

"Margaret Reed and Bradley Scott." Jack lowered his eyes.

"Yes. Are you aware of what they do, Mr. Peterson?"

"Minimally." Jack clutched Judy's hand. "Rainey told me what she suspected when she was in high school. Five years ago, Margaret told me they'd kicked Rainey out and planned to disappear. I confronted Margaret about Rainey's claims and she warned me that I was to live like I didn't know. For two years Rainey drifted around Europe living with the various missionary families she'd grown to know while attending the Christian school. Finally, three years ago I convinced her to move to the states and attend college. We've never talked about what her parents do… I never pushed for more and she assumed I didn't know."

"Does Rainey know she is your daughter?" Tiffany asked.

Jack shook his head. "I was married to Ruth when I got Margaret pregnant. At first, I wanted nothing to do with the baby. Margaret left the country angry and disillusioned. In time, my heart changed. I told Ruth about the affair and eventually, only through the power of Jesus Christ, Ruth forgave me and I found forgiveness in Jesus. I found Margaret and told her I wanted to make things right with the baby." He shook his head. "For the first few years, Margaret wouldn't even tell me if we'd had a boy or a girl. Eventually, I think because they needed money, she told me about Rainey. I flew to Spain to meet my little girl when Rainey was seven. They called me Uncle Jack and that's who I became."

"You say you gave them money?"

"Yes. She was living with Bradley and claimed they needed money to care for Rainey. I was more than willing to comply. I wanted to reestablish contact with my child. I got to see her for two weeks every summer. We usually met somewhere in Europe or South America, although sometimes they were in the United States. Ruth even found a place in her heart to love Rainey. Although, Ruth didn't live long enough to really get to know her. After Ruth died, I tried even harder to see my daughter. Every break I had at the University, I flew to whatever location I had to in order to see her."

"At the time did you suspect Margaret and Bradley of anything illegal?"

Jack shook his head. "They were like a couple of peace-loving hippies floating around Europe, the U.S. and South America. I had no idea they were cultivating hybrid varieties of cannabis and poppies. When Rainey was fourteen, I begged them to allow me to finance a proper high school education for her. I found the mission school in Europe and they allowed me to pay her way through. I can't begin to tell you the joy I found when I learned that Rainey put her faith in Christ."

Tiffany shifted her gaze to her notepad. "Why did you never tell her that you are her father?"

"That was the agreement I made with Margaret. I knew that as easily as they'd disappeared the first time, Margaret could

100

disappear again and I'd never see my child. It was better to see her as her uncle than to never see her again."

"When you suspected them of illegal drug production, why did you not turn them in?" Tiffany asked. "Wouldn't that have given you opportunity to take custody of Rainey?"

Jack was quiet for a moment. He glanced at Judy. "This is the part I was always afraid to tell you."

Judy's eyes were wet with tears. "I always knew there was more. If you need me to leave the room I will."

"I want you to know." He kissed her hand and turned his face to Tiffany. "When I finally realized what Margaret and Bradley were involved in I realized it was bigger than just a couple of hippies running drugs. They're involved in something big—much larger than anything I could simply turn into the police. Margaret told me that my silence would determine Rainey's safety." He shook his head. "I had no evidence. Not even a true confession. I had the suspicions of a high school girl who was drifting further and further from her mother and making accusations that could not be proven. They were living in South America and made it very clear to me that if I attempted to dig into Rainey's claims she would disappear."

"Do you know where Margaret and Bradley are living?" Tiffany asked pointedly.

Jack glanced at Judy and let out a heavy sigh. "I was told never to give out the information… for Rainey's safety."

Tiffany sat up in her chair. "This is for Rainey's safety." She leaned forward. "Mr. Peterson, I believe you. I believe everything you've just told me. But I need you to trust us. We need that information."

Jack pulled himself from the chair and walked to his computer. "Their location changes almost every year. Margaret only gives me access to the information in the event of an emergency." Jack pulled up the screen and opened a file. "They're in Santa Marta, Colombia."

Tiffany wrote down all the information.

"Is my little girl okay? Who is this agent? Where are they?" Jack just gave them all they wanted to know; now it was their turn.

"I'm afraid I can't answer all those questions."

Jack walked back to the couch and shook his head. "I just gave you the one piece of information that I was warned never to share and you can't answer my questions?"

Tiffany let out a sigh. "They're actually en route to Colombia now. I guess Margaret hired a young man named Dylan three years ago to keep an eye on Rainey at school. He gave the information to one of the groups we've been investigating and they decided to take Rainey as a hostage."

Jack shook his head. "Margaret never hired anyone."

"You might not have known about it."

"No. I'm positive. Margaret would never have hired anyone. She said it was imperative that all communication be cut off. She sends me their new locations when they move, but I don't even email her. She sends their location using the name of a deceased student through the alumni website. I check it regularly. That's how I know where they are."

"So you have no way of actually contacting her?"

Jack ran his fingers through his gray hair. "I can send messages to this deceased student. Look, I know she never hired this Dylan fellow. I've met Dylan. Rainey and him have been friends for years. You're saying he's in on this?"

"Evidently he knows where her parents live. He claims he works for her mom."

Jack shook his head. "And they're taking Rainey there as a bargaining chip?"

"I'm not sure."

Jack stood up and began pacing the room. "I don't know if Rainey's mom has enough loyalty to Rainey to bargain for her life." His eyes showed his fear. "I'm sure Bradley doesn't. He'd just as well kill her."

"We have an agent with her now. He will do everything in his power to make sure she is safe."

"As long as it doesn't interfere with your investigation, right?" Jack stopped pacing and glared at Tiffany. Jack was no fool. He knew if the FBI had a long time investigation going on, the life of one civilian would not be enough to risk what they considered the greater good.

"We've got a top agent with her and he actually cares about the outcome for her."

Jack narrowed his eyes on Tiffany. "Matthew Westerly?"

Tiffany closed her notebook and motioned for Vince that it was time to go.

"You don't want to answer." Jack stood in front of Tiffany. "I knew it. I couldn't find anything about Matthew on the Internet. No Facebook page. No Twitter. No record of him at a Christian school in Ohio. He's your agent, isn't he?"

"Mr. Peterson, we're not at liberty to disclose our agents."

"He was playing with her heart to find out where her parents are—wasn't he?" Jack's eyes began to burn with anger.

Judy stood up and placed a calming hand on his shoulder.

"Sir, I can promise you that Trey would never intentionally hurt your daughter."

"Trey." Jack repeated the name. "That's his real name, huh? How nice. I've never seen my daughter so crazy about a young man before. He played her well. Attended her Bible study, talked about God, met her uncle…" Jack put his face in his hands.

"Now at least we have a name that we can pray for," Judy said softly.

Tiffany took a few steps toward the door and stopped. "Mr. Peterson, I know Trey. He's a good agent and I know he would never hurt your daughter."

"Lying to her. Dating her. Winning her heart. How is that not going to hurt her?"

Tiffany didn't have an answer.

***

Dylan was glad to find Rainey alone at the pool. They were preparing to pass through the Panama Canal so Trey and the gang he apparently worked for were busy making plans. Dylan had not been invited. Over the past six days, her fake boyfriend thwarted every attempt he'd made to talk to her. Finally, he had his chance. She was wearing her bathing suit and a pair of new sunglasses. Dylan wasn't sure if she was awake.

"Hey, gorgeous." He sat down on the chair beside her and took off his t-shirt. "You awake?"

"Dylan." Rainey pushed her sunglasses into her hair and smiled. Her eyes were still bruised, but there was a sparkle in them again. "I was beginning to wonder if you'd left the boat."

"No. Just busy." He glanced at her tan legs and freshly painted toenails. "So Matthew bought you some nail polish, huh?"

Rainey smiled. "He did." She brought the sunglasses back down in front of her eyes. "I'm sorry. The sun still gives me a headache."

"That's okay." Dylan leaned back and closed his eyes. "Are you enjoying the cruise?"

Rainey turned to Dylan. "It's amazing. I don't know how this whole thing got arranged. But I'll be honest, I'd be having a lot more fun if I understood how you got my mother to want to see me."

Dylan licked his lips and let the sun warm his face. "Is that the story?"

Rainey was quiet for a moment. "What do you mean, 'story'?"

Dylan opened his eyes and looked around. They were alone. "I don't expect you to believe anything I tell you right now, since you know that I've been working for your mother these past three years and never told you, but your boyfriend isn't who you think he is."

Rainey sat up and turned to face Dylan. "What are you talking about?"

"Are you really that gullible? Think about it. Why are we on a multi million-dollar yacht headed to your parents? Do you really think it's because your mother was worried about you?"

Rainey felt her hands sweat and wiped them against her legs.

"Yes, this is about your parents but it has nothing to do with you." Dylan sat up and turned to face her. "You and I aren't guests on this yacht. We're prisoners." He softened his tone. "You don't remember the abduction? How they came to my apartment?"

Rainey shook her head. Dylan continued. "They threatened to kill you if I wouldn't disclose your parents' location." He reached a hand for hers. "I didn't have a choice. They were going to kill you."

"Who?"

"Carlos and Rod. I told them I needed to get you to a hospital. They didn't care. They held a gun to your head and would have pulled the trigger if I hadn't talked. I can't call your mom to

104

warn her that we're coming because Enrique, the one who seems to be in charge, has a scrambler on all electronic devices."

Rainey shook her head. "Why are you telling me all this? You're lying."

"Believe what you want. Your fake boyfriend seems to think it's better for you not to know." Dylan leaned in closer. "But understand, if you question him about it—you will be a prisoner. He might even kill you—and he'll definitely kill me."

"Not Matthew…"

"Don't be naïve. Remember me telling you about the woman I saw him with? The blonde? Do you remember?" Dylan placed his hands on her shoulders as if he was going to shake her.

Rainey thought about it for a moment. Before she went out to the water she and Dylan spoke. Dylan claimed Matthew kissed another woman. "You were wrong."

"No. You're wrong. And this fake boyfriend of yours works for Enrique and probably plans to kill you and your parents."

Steps could be heard walking up to the pool deck. Dylan quickly moved to a sunbathing position and closed his eyes. "Don't question him," he whispered.

***

Trey pulled a chair closer to Rainey and spread out a towel. "Enjoying the sun?" He leaned back on the chair beside her and put on his sunglasses.

Rainey rolled onto her stomach and turned her face to Trey. She was still reeling from her conversation with Dylan. *What should I do?* Dylan's claims seemed like foolishness. A look was exchanged between the two men, but she couldn't read their expressions. Was it hostility? She vaguely remembered an exchange of words between them when she was still out of it. For whatever reason, there didn't seem to be fondness between them. That was strange for Matthew. He got along with everyone. *Why doesn't he seem to like Dylan?* "When will we start going through the canal?" Rainey found something neutral to talk about.

"We plan to start though the canal tomorrow. Enrique said if any of us wants to explore Panama, we will be stopping there. Have you been to Panama?"

105

"No." Rainey closed her eyes. How could she act normal? She wanted to question Matthew. She couldn't believe Dylan's claims. *Why would Matthew invite me to explore Panama with him if I'm really a prisoner?*

"Perhaps the three of us could go together." Dylan glanced boldly at Trey.

Trey ignored the suggestion. "We can explore some shops. Maybe find you a comfortable pair of shoes."

"Don't we need passports?" Rainey asked.

"No. Since we are only disembarking from the yacht for the day, Enrique said he would give us valid tourists cards."

"Interesting." Dylan turned his eyes toward the pool. "I thought maybe he'd make us IDs."

"We did leave somewhat unprepared." Trey gave Dylan a heated glare.

"Won't we need a passport to enter Santa Marta?" Rainey asked. "I have a passport, but it sounds like you guys didn't bring it."

"It will work out." Trey closed his eyes.

Rainey felt awkward. She didn't like the questions hovering over her head. The whole thing of going to Santa Marta had seemed strange to her, but what else could she believe? She did have amnesia. Was it so hard to believe her mother hired Dylan to keep connected with Rainey? But why would Dylan make up such a story about Matthew? She knew Matthew. *You also knew Dylan...* She closed her eyes and pretended to go to sleep. She couldn't talk to Matthew with Dylan here. What if Dylan were telling the truth? Would Matthew really kill her? *No. Never. Matthew loves me.*

Chapter 11

The yacht began its passage through the Panama Canal sometime in the night. Rainey woke up when she felt the movement of the ship. She'd been dreaming. She was in a car... she was sick. There were men... men she didn't know. *Just pull over. I'm going to throw up...*

The full moon shone through her porthole and Rainey glanced outside to see the light dance on the water. Still unsettled from the dream, Rainey wanted something to distract her. Doing her best to find her way around in the dimly lit room, Rainey found her clothes and got dressed. Ready to take a moonlight tour of the ship while it slipped along the canal, Rainey tried to open her door.

Every night Rainey locked her door from the inside, but she'd never attempted to open it after going to bed. It was locked. Why would her door be locked from the outside? Who locked it?

She knocked on the door a few times but got no answer. A sudden feeling of being trapped clutched her throat. She knew Matthew was only across the hall. She pounded harder on the door. "Matthew!" She banged. "Matthew!"

In only a matter of moments the door opened and Trey stood in the doorway wearing just a pair of shorts. "What's wrong? Are you okay?" He was out of breath and his face showed alarm.

Rainey stared at him for a moment. Her fists were red from pounding and her heart beat fast. "Why was my door locked?" Her eyes showed a new kind of mistrust.

Trey stepped inside the room, pulled the door shut and locked it. "It's for your safety, Rainey." He attempted to place his hands on her arms but Rainey pulled away.

"How am I more safe locked inside a room?" Her eyes darted to the door. "Why did you lock it now?"

Trey moved closer to her. "I don't trust Dylan… Enrique gave me a key so I could keep Dylan out. It was not to lock you in."

"Why don't you trust Dylan?" She watched his face in the moonlight. "Didn't he come to get you when I was hurt? Isn't that how we're here on this ship? You're taking me to see my mom because I was injured, right? Dylan told you how to find her. Isn't that the story?"

"Rainey, listen…"

"No, you listen." She stepped back, suddenly afraid of this man she loved. "Am I prisoner?" She watched his eyes intently.

Trey delayed in answering.

"Who are you?"

"Rainey." He reached for her again.

"Don't touch me. You said you've done some work for Enrique. What kind of work?"

Trey ran his fingers through his hair.

"Dylan said that he and I are prisoners. He said you plan to kill my parents—and maybe me." She searched his face for answers. "Do you work for Enrique? Is this really about my parents?"

Trey let a slight moan escape his lips. "I'm not going to kill you or your parents, Rainey."

Tears welled up in Rainey's eyes. "It's all been a lie?"

"Let me explain."

"No!" Rainey stepped back and shook her head. "Leave me alone. Go away. Just go away!" Fear she'd never felt toward anyone before suddenly engulfed her. She backed away and grabbed the edge of the bunk bed for support. Her stomach wrenched as she looked at this man. Was this the man she dreamed about spending the rest of her life with?

"Rainey, please don't be afraid of me." Trey took a step forward.

"I don't even know who you are. Are you a hit man?"

He glanced at the door. "I can show you something." He made a motion for her to stay where she was and he hurried across the hall for his bag.

"I don't think I want to hear your explanation," she said when he returned. Her face was wet with tears.

108

"You've got to."

Rainey watched Trey unzip his bag and pull something from a compartment within the lining of the bag. He held up a badge and put his finger to his mouth. "Please, Rainey…"

Trey Netherland. FBI. Rainey's body shook with sobs and she took a few steps backwards and stared at Trey with pained revelation in her eyes. "You lied to me. You're a liar!" She clenched her teeth and moved to his face. "How could you?" She began beating Trey in the chest with her small balled up fists. "How could you?"

Trey grabbed her wrists. "Shhh… Rainey stop." His tone was soft and controlled. "You can't yell like this. Please."

Rainey felt her knees weaken. She just wanted to sit down. *Dear God… I feel like I'm drowning again. Please help me…*

Trey helped Rainey to the edge of her bed and knelt down in front of her. "I'm not here to hurt you. I'm here to help you." He tried to run his hands along her arms but Rainey slapped him.

"Don't ever touch me again." Fire burned in her eyes. "At this moment I don't care who you work for. You lied to me." Tears threatened to quench the fire. "You spent almost two months pretending to be my boyfriend—for what? What were you trying to find out?"

"This is big, Rainey."

"So it's about my parents. Dylan was right."

"But Dylan doesn't know that I'm FBI." Trey spoke in soft tones. "I don't trust Dylan."

Rainey clenched her jaw to control her emotions. "Yeah, well, I don't trust you."

Trey closed his eyes and released a steadying breath. "I'm deep undercover, Rainey. If Enrique or Carlos or any of those men find out I'm FBI, I'm a dead man."

"And me?"

"I don't know what they'll do to you. I didn't know they planned to take you. I think it was because you were in Dylan's apartment when they cut him the deal."

"What deal?" Rainey didn't know what to believe.

"They paid him for your parents' location."

Rainey shook her head. "He said they were going to kill me."

Trey shook his head. "I wasn't there. But I do know Enrique

109

has a large amount of money ready for immediate deposit into Dylan's account once he verifies the location of your parents."

This was too much for her to handle. Rainey felt suddenly tired. "Just leave." She shook her head.

"No." Trey reached for her hand.

"I told you, don't ever touch me again."

Trey pulled back his hand.

"Let me ask you this." She looked at his eyes in the moonlight. "Did you kiss some blonde woman on a pier outside of Santa Monica?"

Trey swallowed hard and lowered his eyes. "Yes."

Rainey sat up straight and waited for him to continue.

"She was another agent—my boss actually. We were being watched by one of Enrique's men. We had to play it off like she was my girlfriend." Trey glanced up at Rainey. "It was the only way to make sure we didn't blow my cover."

Rainey almost expected Trey to lie about the blonde. She licked her lips, wondering if it was really that easy for him to throw his affections around. "So I was just part of your undercover job." It hurt to even say the words.

Trey reached for her hand and stopped himself. "I'm actually relived that I can be real with you now. I didn't want to have to lie."

"Let me guess. You did a profile on me and learned what I liked—a strong Christian man, stable, fun, adventurous, a lover of the outdoors, friendly. You studied me well and became the perfect man for me."

Trey turned around, sat on the floor and leaned against her bunk. "Pretty much."

Rainey nodded. "I might have known. I think Uncle Jack saw through you."

"He probably did." Trey closed his eyes.

Rainey was quiet for a long time. Tears coursed down her face and she laid her head on her pillow to cry. She was emotionally drained and her heart, so full of love for this man only an hour before, now felt shattered and broken.

***

110

Trey sat beside her bed for a long time. He could hear her stifled sobs and felt the bunk shake with her body. A numb sense of loss encased his heart. He felt like he'd lost a real friend. *She really loved me.* He longed to turn around and wrap his arms around her. He ached to feel the soft innocence of her lips on his. *Don't ever touch me again.* Her words echoed in his ears.

How were they going to play this off now? When she didn't know, she was safe. Why did Dylan tell her? Did he have genuine feelings for her or did he have another motive?

Trey stood up and returned his badge to the secret compartment in his bag. It was well designed. Even someone searching for a pocket would likely miss it.

He returned to his room long enough to gather his remaining things. He couldn't leave Rainey alone any more. She knew too much.

As tired as he was, Trey knew he'd never get back to sleep. He made a pillow out of one of his shirts and lay on the floor beside her bed. He didn't want to climb the bunk and risk waking her after she'd finally fallen asleep.

What was going to happen tomorrow? They'd be in Panama City. Would it be wise for him to leave the ship with Rainey? Maybe they could talk. Maybe he could help her escape? Even as the thought entered his mind, Trey knew he couldn't do it. They were this close to Nash McCarness. If he blew his cover now, they might never stop the man.

Trey stared at the ceiling. Strange shadows streamed through the window. *What about Rainey? I can't let them hurt her.* His stomach tightened. *I've already hurt her enough.*

By the time the sun was completely up in the sky, Trey knew they were close to Panama City. In an hour or so they would be docking and he and Rainey would be free to explore. He hurried and showered, put on a pair of casual shorts, a t-shirt and a pair of comfortable shoes. Rainey was still asleep so Trey locked the door and slipped upstairs to learn what he could about the day's plan.

"Ian said he heard yelling in Rainey's room last night." Enrique looked up when Trey entered the room. "What was going on?"

"She had a bad dream." Trey sat down across from Enrique; glad the man couldn't see the scratches and red spots on his chest

111

from the angry thrashing Rainey gave him the night before. "I plan to stay in her room tonight to make sure she's not regaining any memories." Trey's eyes traveled to the other side of the room and noticed Dylan, who glared mistrustfully at Trey and got up to leave.

"Do you have any reason to believe she is regaining her memory?" Enrique lifted a glass of orange juice to his lips. "We cannot risk her attempting to escape."

Trey shook his head. "The twenty-four hours following her accident appear to be erased from her mind." One of Enrique's staff set an omelet and a bowl of fruit on the table in front of Trey.

Enrique motioned for a refill on his coffee and leaned back in his chair. He watched as Dylan passed and exited the dining cabin. "Dylan says he wishes to go into town with you and Rainey this afternoon." There was a question in Enrique's tone.

"That's not what I want." Trey watched as Enrique's servant filled Enrique's coffee mug. "I'll take some too." He motioned toward his cup. "I don't know what Dylan's game is, but I don't want him saying anything to Rainey." Trey reached for the creamer and added enough to his coffee to turn it beige.

"I think he is jealous of you." Enrique took a bite of his omelet. "Rainey looks at you as a woman in love. Dylan looks at Rainey with lust."

Trey nodded. Enrique was a good reader of character. *I hope he can't read me that well.* Trey did his best to appear loyal to Enrique. While the wealthy drug lord was fair to those he trusted, Trey knew the man was capable of killing someone he didn't.

"Perhaps I shall encourage Rod to go into Panama City with Dylan." He turned his eyes toward the door where Dylan made his exit. "I have no doubt that Dylan will return. Unless of course the coordinates he gave me are wrong."

Trey took a long sip of his coffee and wondered how he was going to convince Rainey to leave the ship with him.

***

The room was empty when Rainey woke up. She glanced around and saw Trey's bag and a few of his things scattered about the room. Memories of the night ran through her mind and refreshed the pained feeling in her heart. *Matthew isn't real.* It was still hard to come to grips with. She leaned back on her pillow, thinking about the relationship she thought they had. *Was all that just a show?* The long, intimate talks, the Bible study, the hikes, roller blading, the way his lips felt on hers. It hurt too much to think about.

She quickly took a shower and changed into one of her new outfits. The door was locked from the outside but Rainey turned the inside bolt as well. *You lock me in. I lock you out.* Turning her eyes to Trey's bag, Rainey decided to take a look at who he really was.

The bag was full of clothes—all of which she'd seen him wear at least once. Her eyes lingered on his blue Under Armor shirt. *Is this the one Dylan saw him wearing when he kissed that woman?* Rainey felt Trey's gun at the bottom of the bag. She pulled it out, almost afraid to touch it. It was a Glock. It meant nothing to her but she'd heard these were powerful guns. Setting the gun aside, Rainey searched for the secret compartment. She knew it was here, she'd seen Trey pull his badge from it. *This is ridiculous.* Rainey resorted to emptying his entire bag and feeling along each inner seam. The bag was lined with enough reinforcement that it was impossible to feel where the objects were hidden. She could only search where she thought the compartment should be.

A click of the lock brought Rainey's head up and she watched Trey walk in to see her with the contents of his bag scattered on the floor.

"I hope you plan on folding all that when you put it back." Trey closed the door and bolted it.

"How did you open the door?"

"I have a key." Trey held out the master key.

Rainey stood up with his bag in her hand. "Where is it?"

"What?"

"The secret compartment?" She held the bag out to him and shook it for him to take it.

Trey took the bag and knelt down on the floor beside his stuff. "That's why it's called a secret compartment." Trey began folding his clothes and placing them inside the bag.

Rainey stood there for a moment, frustrated with his composure and unwillingness to show her the compartment. She bent over, grabbed Trey's gun and pointed it at him with a trembling hand. "Show me."

Trey sighed and reached for the gun. "It's not loaded." He pulled it from her hand, turned it over and showed her that the magazine was not in place. "See... no ammo."

Rainey stormed to her bed and sat down while Trey repacked his suitcase.

"We're going into Panama City today."

"I'm not."

"Yes, you are." Trey folded a gray t-shirt and put it in the bag. "And if you want to survive this boat ride you're going to pretend you like me."

Her eyes burned with disgust. "I'm afraid I'm not able to play people the way you are."

Trey pulled his identification and his cell phone from his secret compartment but Rainey missed how he did it. He inserted a loaded magazine into his gun and put it behind his belt. "Now it's loaded. But you do realize that if you aim it at me again, I can arrest you."

Trey zipped his bag and approached Rainey. "I'm being serious, Rainey. Hate me as much as you want, but if Enrique sees it, you will no longer even feel like a passenger. The only reason he's given you the freedom he has is because he thinks you can't remember anything and that you're in love with me."

"I'm supposed to just act like nothing happened?" Rainey glared at him.

"That's right." Trey reached for her hand—his strong, muscular arms, smooth tan skin, and his broad chest stood right in front of her.

Rainey stared at him for a moment. *And of course he's wearing that amazing cologne.* She turned away. She promised herself she wouldn't let him touch her ever again.

Trey grabbed her hand and pulled her to her feet. "I'm here to protect you."

Rainey pulled her hand away. "Then you shouldn't have played with my heart."

***

Rainey wasn't sure how she did it, but she managed to walk off the ship with her hand in Trey's. Dylan was nowhere around, but

Enrique talked to Trey for a few minutes before they left the ship. She saw Trey show Enrique his gun and heard him tell the man that he didn't want to be out there unarmed.

Enrique and Ian sat down at a table and began discussing something about Panama City. They planned to conduct business in town and had several things to do in a short amount of time. "Be back by eight." Enrique called out to them before they disappeared.

The feel of Trey's hand in hers was like a bittersweet taunting of something she had but was never real. She loved the feel of his hand but she hated it too. As soon as they were away from the ship she pulled her hand away.

"Does it repulse you that much?" Trey put his hands in his pockets and walked beside her with no show of affection.

"Yes." Rainey kept her eyes straight ahead. "Why are we out here? Why not just stay on the yacht?"

"I need to make a phone call for one. I also figured you could use a break from the boat."

"All I need a break from is you." Rainey took a few steps ahead and crossed her arms.

Once they were out of the harbor, the city of Panama encroached upon them quickly. Trey caught up with her and grabbed her arm. "You're walking with me."

Rainey flung her long hair behind her shoulders and let her eyes travel to the large buildings and crowds of people. Cars were everywhere but seemed to have no order. A loud honk and the squeal of breaks followed by a few angry Spanish words told Rainey that she wasn't the only person in a bad mood today.

Trey stopped someone on the sidewalk and spoke fluently in Spanish, asking them to direct him to the nearest shopping area. Rainey stared at him for a moment. She'd lived in enough Spanish speaking countries to know that Trey's dialect was good.

"Did they teach you that at Quantico?" Her blue eyes flashed.

"That and foster care. Come on." Trey pulled her along with as much warmth as she was showing him.

All the sweetness and warmth they'd shown one another for the past two months seemed to have been washed away. Rainey didn't know what to do with her raw emotions. How did she expect him to act this morning? Had she given him any reason to believe she wanted him to be friendly? It was better this way. "Just sever the arm. Then there's no more pain."

"What?" Trey furrowed his eyebrows.

Rainey turned away. "I didn't mean to say that out loud."

Trey was quiet for a moment. "Even when you sever a limb, you can still feel it."

"That's only if you have feelings." It felt good to slam him right now. Rainey hoped something she said would actually hurt him. *But that's implying he actually has feelings.*

Trey rounded a corner and brought Rainey along. They were only a block away from the shopping area. "You didn't eat breakfast. Are you hungry?"

"No."

"Well, we'll get some coffee then. I've got to call my boss."

"Oh, is this the one who shoved her tongue down your throat? Or was it you who did it to her? I can never keep up with you special agents and your love lives." It felt good to use Dylan's crass description.

Trey cleared his throat. "I'm not even going to comment."

They crossed a busy road and Trey slowed as they approached an outdoor café. "Let's stop here." Trey opened a small gate that cut off the restaurant from the sidewalk. Flowerbeds and small potted trees decorated the patio, while upbeat instrumental music played softly in the background.

Rainey followed Trey to a small, round table covered with a red and white checked tablecloth, and listened while he spoke to a waitress in perfect Spanish. He ordered a coffee for them both and requested a breakfast menu. Rainy turned away. Who was this man?

Trey pulled out his phone and made the call he told her he needed to make. "Tiffany, we're in Panama City." He paused while Tiffany spoke. "How did that go?"

Rainey wished she could hear the voice on the other end. Did he have feelings for this woman?

Trey got up and walked away with the phone when the waitress approached. Rainey thanked her in just as perfect Spanish as Trey used. The waitress offered her a variety of pastries and Rainey chose one that looked delicious and asked for fruit.

She watched as Trey walked around the edge of the café, talking in muffled tones.

Her coffee was good. Rainey took a few long sips and let her eyes roam over the foreign city. It was warm and the sun was high in the sky. She could not see the water from the downtown area, but a combination of contemporary and historical buildings gave Panama City a unique skyline. Palm trees lined the street and Rainey noticed a water fountain in front of a nearby hotel. The atmosphere would easily appeal to tourists.

Trey returned and sat across from Rainey.

"Nice of you to involve me in the conversation." Rainey crossed her arms.

"Do you want to call Jack?" Trey let her sarcasm bounce off his chest.

Rainey stared at him for a moment. "Really? Can I?"

"He would probably love to hear your voice. Tiffany saw him two days ago. He was extremely worried."

Rainey reached for his phone and dialed Jack's number from memory. She stood up and gave Trey an artificial smile as she walked away.

"Uncle Jack!" She could not contain her excitement at hearing his voice.

"Rainey? Are you okay?"

"I'm in Panama City." She glanced over at Trey who was watching her closely.

"Thank God you're alright."

"He lied to me." Rainey turned her back on Trey while tears filled her eyes.

"I know." Jack paused for a moment. "But right now, you've got to trust him."

Rainey wiped her face. "You knew, didn't you?"

"I suspected that he wasn't all he professed to be." Jack clarified. "But I only questioned his testimony. I never suspected this. I never questioned his feelings for you."

Rainey clutched the phone. "It was all an act."

Jack was quiet for a moment. "Maybe."

"What did you tell the FBI?"

"Everything I knew. I know where your parents are."

"Dylan told Enrique where they are. That's where they are taking me."

"Rainey." Jack's voice grew suddenly firm. "I don't believe your mom hired Dylan."

"She must have. How else would he know?"

Trey tapped Rainey on the shoulder and motioned for her to wrap it up.

"I don't know. But be careful. I don't trust him." Jack's warning came through clear.

Rainey took a few steps away from Trey and told Jack she had to go.

"I love you," Jack said with a tremble in his voice.

"I love you, too." Rainey closed her eyes and wished she could hug him. At least she knew who Jack was.

She hung up the phone and handed it to Trey. "You didn't tell me I had a time limit."

"I have to be careful charging this phone. Enrique doesn't know I have it." Trey checked his battery strength, put the phone in his pocket and sat down. "Your pastry looks good." He pushed the plate toward her side of the table.

Rainey sat down and ate a few bites. She didn't feel like talking to Trey. There was nothing to say. She didn't know this man. Wrapping her fingers around her coffee mug, Rainey turned her face away to avoid looking at him. *Why is this happening? Matthew was just a lie.* Rainey swallowed back the lump in her throat and took a sip of her coffee.

"We have about five hours to explore Panama City." Trey interrupted her thoughts. "Do you need any more clothes?"

Explore Panama City with this man? Rainey stared at the water fountain in front of the building next door and tried to suppress her emotions. "What would you do if I just took off right now?"

"Alone?"

"Yes."

"I'd follow you."

Rainey narrowed her eyes and set down her coffee mug. Anger, hurt, and disbelief competed for her emotions. It was unbearable. She stood up and pushed in her chair. "Don't forget to pay the bill." She walked through the metal gate and out onto the sidewalk. She knew that Trey would only be a few steps behind her, but it felt good for just a moment to be alone in the crowd.

118

Trey hurried the waitress down and handed her more than what he knew the small meal would cost. He was glad that along with the Balboa, the U.S. dollar was accepted tender in Panama. Rainey was serious. He had to catch up to her before she disappeared in the crowd.

He caught a glimpse of her almost a block ahead. He hurried through the throngs of shoppers, keeping his eyes on Rainey in her teal green skirt and white blouse. "Rainey!" he called to her. He didn't expect her to actually stop for him—he knew she was upset. Could he blame her?

In only a moment Rainey disappeared into a store. Trey thought he knew which one and opened the door. In his best Spanish he asked the merchant if a woman fitting Rainey's description was there.

"She is very beautiful," Trey explained in Spanish. "She's tall and slender with long dark hair, a white blouse, and a teal green skit. Have you seen her?"

The woman motioned toward the back of the store and Trey saw Rainey looking through a dress rack.

Rainey glanced up, unconcerned. "There's a men's shop next door, why don't you go there?" She turned around and approached another clothing rack.

Trey walked to the back of the store and reached for her arm. "I'm not amused."

"Wow, you seem annoyed." Rainey let him drag her from the store. "That wasn't exactly the emotion I hoped to draw from you. But at least it's something." She snatched her arm back and stood up to her full height. "I wanted to shop there."

"You drew too much attention to yourself." Trey glanced around. "The men from our ship could be around, you know. They don't need to see us fighting."

Rainey's eyes flashed indignantly. "Oh. Well maybe you should teach me how to fake a kiss."

Trey shook his head. He'd never seen this caustic side of Rainey. "Is this what I did to you?" His tone softened. This wasn't the Rainey he knew. Where was her heart? He stared into her light blue eyes and thought about the sweetness he knew was hidden

119

behind them. He missed her. "I'm sorry Rainey." Before she could resist him, he pulled her into his arms and placed his lips on hers.

The kiss only lasted a few seconds, but Rainey stepped back with tears in her eyes. She glanced around to see who might have witnessed them. "How dare you?"

"Rainey…" Trey reached for her hand, but she was already two steps ahead. "I'm sorry." He caught up to her and walked at her pace while she deliberately ignored him.

Chapter 12

Dylan was not amused by his Panama City companion. Not only did they provide him with a babysitter, they gave him the man who'd stolen his iPhone and beat him up only a few weeks ago. The two men had nothing to say to one another.

There was little Dylan hoped to accomplish while in town. His only goal was to make a phone call and he couldn't do that with Rod trailing along beside him.

They walked along the city sidewalk, stopping in at a few stores while Dylan made a couple purchases. He made note of the location of Rod's gun when the man bent over to pick up a Balboa off the ground. *It figures the man would stop to pick money up off the street.*

Although Dylan knew he'd met his match last time he'd fought this man, the last time Dylan was caught off guard. Dylan wondered the best way to catch this man off guard.

"How about a little tequila?" Dylan motioned toward a bar across the street. He had no idea if this man would drink with him or not, but it was worth a try.

Rod nodded. "Sounds good to me." He walked with Dylan and held up his currency. "The first one's on me."

The two men shared several rounds before Dylan detected a change in Rod's behavior. The man was becoming more relaxed and willing to talk. "Take a look at those two beauties." He motioned toward a couple women across the room.

"You must be seeing double because I only see one beauty. The other one looks like she chases parked cars." Dylan motioned for the bar tender to pour them another shot.

Rod laughed at the joke. "Fine, I'll take that one." He waved toward the women.

They approached and Dylan smiled. This might be the distraction he needed.

Neither Dylan or Rod spoke Spanish, but the women understood the word tequila and were willing to be treated to a drink. They sat and drank with the men for a couple rounds, flirting and making hand motions to communicate for over an hour. Dylan stopped drinking, but made Rod think he was well on his way to intoxication, while Rod really was.

Dylan noticed that the women didn't appear to be drinking either. He observed, more than once, the 'car chaser' poured out her drink under the table and asked for more. She was all over Rod, running her hands over his chest and eventually moved in for a kiss. It was then he noticed the other woman put something into their drinks. *These girls are hoping to knock us out—probably to rob us.* This was better than anything Dylan could have conjured up himself.

The other woman spoke affectionately to Dylan and held his drink up to his lips. Dylan moved it aside and pulled her to him for a kiss instead. She returned the kiss and said something in Spanish.

Rod downed the shot his 'date' gave him and his head began to wobble.

Dylan pulled his date onto his lap and held his drink up to her lips. "Do you actually speak English?" he whispered in her ear. "Because if you do, I saw the whole thing, and I plan to smash both of your heads into the table in about ten seconds."

The woman hopped up from his lap and knocked his drink from his hand. She said something to her friend just as Rod's face landed on the table. "Thank you for your help, ladies." Dylan watched them walk away.

In only a second he pulled Rod's wallet, gun and cell phone from his pockets and slipped out of the bar. *That was really too easy.*

***

"I've been trying to get a hold of you for over a week." Dylan recognized the voice on the other end of the phone. "Where are you and whose number are you calling me from?"

122

"I'm in Panama." Dylan began. "And we should be there in a few days." Dylan walked along the crowded sidewalk, watching his back in case any of the others from the yacht were around. He explained the situation in detail. "They're going to use her as a bargaining chip."

"That will never do." The voice on the other end spoke sharp. "Kill the bargaining chip."

"That's what I thought." Dylan leaned against a building and watched people pass by. He tried to think of the best way to kill Rainey with Matthew constantly on guard. He noticed the two women who drugged Rod walk into the bar across the street and an idea crossed his mind.

"Can we reach you on this phone?"

"No. Enrique has the whole yacht on a scrambler. I'll try to call you when we get into Santa Marta."

Dylan hung up and walked across the crowded street into the bar. He scanned its occupants for the familiar faces. They were about to hurry away when he approached, but he called them back and waved Rod's wallet in their faces. "Wait. I'd like to make you a deal."

***

It was just before eight when Dylan stumbled on board the yacht with one strong arm practically dragging Rod on board.

"We almost left without you." Enrique didn't even look up when Dylan helped Rod into a chair.

"But you wouldn't have. Would you?" Dylan smacked Rod a few times in an attempt to revive him.

"What happened to Rod?"

"Two women drugged our drinks. Thankfully I saw Rod pass out before I drank all of mine. I was only out for about an hour." Dylan sat down and opened a bottle of water. "They stole our stuff."

Rod moved his head around a few times. "Just one more kiss—come on."

Enrique shook his head. "Take him to his room." He motioned for Ian. "Sober him up with a cold shower."

Dylan leaned his head back on the comfortable sofa and closed his eyes. He didn't want to appear overly sober. "Where are Matthew and Rainey?" he glanced up and looked around.

"They've been back for an hour. We were waiting for you." Enrique motioned for the captain to be notified and crossed his legs. Lighting a cigar, he watched Dylan curiously. "Did you have a nice afternoon on shore?"

"Until we were drugged. They stole the new clothes I bought."

"Hmm." Enrique took a long drawl from his cigar. "You should know better than to talk to strange women in bars, especially in foreign port cities. Perhaps now you will be wiser."

Dylan shrugged. "I think a cold shower sounds good to me too." He pulled himself up from the couch and stumbled toward the door.

***

Rainey wished there was a way to block Trey's presence from her mind. She sat with her legs crossed on her bunk with Trey above her in his. She knew he was awake because she heard him turn the pages of whatever he was reading. Every sound he made was a reminder of his presence in her room. She leaned back and closed her eyes, remembering how she'd treated him throughout the day.

After his kiss in Panama City, Rainey did her best to completely ignore Trey the rest of the day. She shopped with him and let him make the few purchases she wanted, but avoided all eye contact and touch. Only as they approached the ship did Trey force her to stop and listen while he lectured her on the importance of maintaining their show of affection while on the yacht.

"Enrique will notice if something is wrong." Trey held her arm tightly to keep her from walking ahead. "I'm warning you, unless you want to be treated as a prisoner, you've got to act like my friend."

Rainey had let him hold her hand as they boarded the ship. They greeted Enrique and Rainey yawned a few times, expressing how tired she was.

Trey told Enrique they planned to turn in early and hurried them to her room. She knew Trey was trying to protect her. But to

124

what end? Trey's real purpose in this undercover job was to find her parents and stop whatever drug trafficking ring they were part of. *I'm just a pawn. I mean nothing to Trey.* Rainey knew there were no guarantees she would get out of this alive. *If I weren't so mad at him maybe I'd ask him about his game plan.* Her Uncle Jack told her to trust Trey. *How can I trust him?* Rainey felt a lump rising in her throat. She thought about how rude she was to Trey once they reached her room.

"You're not sleeping here." She had said as soon as they reached her door.

"Yes, I am."

Rainey snatched a clean pair of shorts and a t-shirt from the dresser and stormed into the bathroom. She took a very long hot shower and spent an unreasonable time getting ready for bed, just in hopes of annoying him.

"I used up all the hot water." Rainey smiled to herself when Trey walked into the bathroom.

Trey ignored her and took his cold shower. He walked out wearing a pair of shorts and dug his comb out of his bag. Rainey turned away. "You could wear a shirt."

Without a word, Trey climbed up the bunk and started reading.

Rainey listened as he turned pages, reflecting on the conversations they'd had in Malibu about books they enjoyed. Was any of that real? *Why God? Why did he have to win my heart? Why was I such a fool?*

***

Margaret Reed rubbed her fingers over the papaver somniferum plant and gently touched the smooth white seedpod. A very gentle scratch on the pod released a thin milky substance containing the alkaloids codeine and morphine. She touched the substance and touched it to her tongue.

"How are the poppies?" Bradley walked into the greenhouse and greeted her with a mug of coffee. He set the mug down and attempted to shoo a fly away from his face.

"These are beautiful." Margaret's eyes glistened with a kind of rapturous high. Without a stitch of makeup, Margaret was an attractive middle-aged woman. Long brown hair, peppered with gray, hung down her slender back. Her attractive pink lips curved into a smile. There was something about plants that thrilled her— especially plants that could be used for so many purposes. "We need to test the percentage of morphine in these plants. If 12% is the average, I'm hoping we've cultivated something that can produce at least 18%."

"That's asking a lot."

"We've been working on this for years, Bradley." Margaret pushed a hair behind her ear and walked toward him.

"But Nash will be happy with 15%."

Margaret accepted the coffee mug and took a sip. "This is good."

Bradley sat across from her and took a sip from his own mug. "I sweetened it with stevia." He leaned back and ran his fingers through his thick dark hair.

"I can tell. I like it." She breathed in the flavors of her fresh Colombian coffee and smiled. "Anyone who hasn't lived in Colombia has never really tried coffee."

The steamy warmth of the greenhouse was more like a sauna and the coffee only added to the heat. Bradley suggested they take their drinks to the veranda. "I don't know how you stand this heat. Vanessa probably has breakfast ready."

Margaret brushed the dirt off her skirt and followed Bradley into the house in her bare feet. She was hungry, but it was easy to forget to eat when there were so many beautiful plants to care for. "Who called earlier?"

"It was Nash." Bradley's expression grew serious.

"Is something out of harmony?"

"We may have visitors."

Margaret took a seat across from Bradley on the veranda.

Vanessa walked out with two bowls of fresh fruit and yogurt. The young servant wore her hair high on her head and bowed as if she were serving royalty.

"Thank you, Vanessa." Margaret spoke kindly. She turned to Bradley. "What kind of visitors?"

"A drug runner from the states." Bradley crossed his arms. "Evidently, he wants to meet us." He watched Margaret closely to gauge her reaction. "Nash wanted us to know because they might make some false claims about Rainey."

"False claims?" Margaret held her spoon steady and waited for Bradley to continue.

"They might claim that they have her in order to get us to bargain with them."

Margaret set her spoon down. "Do they have her?"

"No." Bradley steadied his eyes on Margaret. "Nash assured me. He has a man on the boat undercover. Rainey is not there."

"How can we be sure?"

"Have peace. Good thoughts." Bradley reached for Margaret's hand.

Margaret nodded. "I know. I've just taken on negative energy. I can feel it."

"Do some yoga later." Bradley placed a comforting hand on Margaret's.

Margaret nodded and did her best to eat the delightful breakfast but she was distracted. Bradley had business in town that afternoon and offered to take Margaret with him.

"I think I'm going to try to take a chemical reading on that papaver somniferum." Margaret took a sip of her orange juice and pushed the empty fruit and yogurt bowl away. "But can you stop by Helena's store and buy some goat's milk soap? I'm almost out."

Bradley promised he would.

Margaret returned to the greenhouse to work until she knew Bradley was gone. She brushed the dirt off her hands and walked upstairs where their one computer sat at their rarely used desk. Margaret hated computers more than she hated cellular phones. She felt that too much exposure to electronic devices destroyed the harmony between mankind and nature.

But this afternoon, Margaret wanted to check her alumni messages. She logged into her old college website and pulled up the name she'd been using for the past five years. *Tanya Hardesty has one new message.*

"Rainey is in trouble. The FBI are there to help. Work with them—it's your best bet." There was a phone number attached to the message and Margaret wrote it down with trembling hands.

***

127

Rainey sat beside the pool with her Bible on her lap. She'd found it at the foot of Trey's bed that morning but decided not to ask him if he'd been reading it.

They were through the Panama Canal now and making a steady course toward Colombia. Rainey wondered if Trey had a plan for when they arrived. She figured that she was the bait to catch her parents. What she didn't know was what Enrique wanted to do with them. Did he plan to kill them? Did he want them to work for him?

Dylan approached her while she was sitting on a pool chair and she glanced around quickly for Trey. It wasn't like him to leave her alone very long.

Dylan spread out his towel on the chair beside her and laid on his stomach. "Where is your bodyguard?"

Rainey considered jumping into the pool. She didn't want to deal with Dylan right now. She took a sip from her water bottle and stood up to stretch before getting in the water.

"I take it you don't want to talk."

"There's nothing to say."

Dylan reached for her arm. "We used to be so close." His blue eyes seemed to question hers.

Rainey sat back down and faced her old friend.

"One word from you, Rainey, just one word, and you know I would move heaven and earth to be with you." His hand still held her wrist gently. "I could get you off this yacht and we could escape all this."

Rainey shook her head. "You know I can't." She lowered her eyes. "I don't have those feelings for you, Dylan."

"I was right about Matthew, wasn't I?" He studied her face intently, seeming to search for her reaction. "It shows in your eyes. You're sad."

Rainey shook her head. "It isn't that."

"I don't believe you." Dylan moved his hand to her fingers. "Then what?"

Rainey wondered what it was about Dylan that her uncle didn't trust. So what if he worked for her mother? Didn't that mean that her mother trusted him? Dylan had been looking out for her for three years. Didn't that say something?

"Your silence is telling." Dylan interrupted her thoughts. "It's okay. I already knew. Now you do. What gave it away?"

"My door is locked."

"Yes. He does that to keep me out."

Rainey glanced at the sky. So much blue. Why did the sky have to be so glorious when everything else hurt so much?

Dylan glanced at Rainey's water bottle. "Can I have a sip?"

"Sure." Rainey leaned back on her chair.

"You love him, don't you?" Dylan sat the bottle beside her and joined her in watching the sky.

"I did."

Dylan was quiet for a moment. "Now you know how I felt about you." He glanced at her.

"No, Dylan. Don't compare this." She shook her head. "I never led you on. I was always honest with you about my feelings."

Dylan watched Rainey reach for her water bottle.

"I never pretended to be somebody I wasn't." She took a sip. "I was honest with you. I told you that more than anything I wanted a man who loved the Lord with all his heart." She glanced into her hands. "You told me you didn't share my beliefs."

"So, if I would have lied like Matthew did, you might have loved me?"

"Oh, Dylan." Rainey placed a hand on his arm and shook her head.

They were both quiet for a few minutes. Rainey took a few more sips of her water and found herself growing slowly relaxed. Dylan watched. "Come on, finish your drink and we'll take a swim."

Rainey did as she was told and stood up. She felt strange. Blinking a few times, Rainey wondered why the pool seemed to be floating above the ocean.

"Remember how we used to do those dives into the pool on campus?" Dylan grabbed her arm and tried to sound like his old self.

"Yes. You were crazy."

Dylan laughed. "Let's do it." He hurried to the diving board and motioned for her to follow. "I'll go first." He walked to the edge and did a quick bounce and dove into the pool. Once in the water he called for her to jump in. "The water is warm!" He swam to the edge, and pulled himself out, watching as Rainey stepped onto the diving board. She was unsteady on her feet.

Rainey tried to remember the dive. She walked to the edge of the board and blinked a few times. One bounce. Two bounce… Rainey lost her balance, slipped off the diving board, and hit her head on the way down.

Dylan grabbed his towel. "You never loved me."

Chapter 13

Trey was glad his meeting with Enrique was finally over. He told Rainey he'd meet her at the pool at least an hour ago. He thought he heard voices on the upper deck and hurried up the stairs to make sure Dylan wasn't filling her head with more twisted truths.

"Rainey?" He saw movement in the water but where was she? A body floating toward the top was all he saw. Trey threw down his towel and jumped in. It was Rainey.

He had her out of the pool in moments and began performing mouth-to-mouth. "Rainey! Rainey!" He shook her body, listening for her breath to return.

A mouthful of water sputtered from her lips. Rainey was alive but unconscious.

Trey laid her head back on the towel and called over the deck for help.

"What happened to her?" Carlos and Rod were at the pool moments later.

"I don't know. She was in the water, unconscious." Trey was beside himself. He knelt by Rainey and smoothed the hair away from her face.

Enrique was poolside a few minutes later and looked down at Trey and Rainey. "What happened?" He questioned Trey.

"I'm not sure. I found her in the pool. She's breathing but she won't wake up. We should get her to a hospital."

Enrique licked his lips as if he were considering the options. "If she dies we lose our bargaining chip."

"How close are we to a hospital?" Carlos asked.

"We're right above Cartagena," Enrique said. "But we could be in Santa Marta in a couple hours."

"We might not have a couple hours. Can Francis get us into port?" Trey rubbed Rainey's fingers and tried to revive her. "Come on, Rainey. Wake up."

Enrique studied Trey and motioned for Carlos. "Tell Francis to get us into port in Cartagena immediately."

Carlos nodded and hurried away without question. Trey turned to Enrique. "Thank you."

"I believe your undercover job with this young lady has become personal." Enrique's tone was not rebuking. He turned to Rod. "Help Matthew take Rainey to her room."

Rod grabbed Rainey's towel while Trey lifted her gently in his arms and carried her like a precious, broken doll, down to her room. Rod opened the door and offered to get anything they needed.

Trey knelt beside her bed and bowed his head.

***

The Hospital Universitario de Cartagena was not far from the port. Carlos had phoned ahead to make them aware they would need an ambulance. Trey climbed in beside Rainey. Enrique planned to send someone by in a few hours to hear how she was doing.

Rainey's soft eyelids barely moved as they rushed her through the emergency room doors and down the hallway. Trey tried to protest when they refused him admittance to the hospital room. He paced the floor and watched the clock. What kind of hospital was this? Why were things taking so long?

After what felt like eternity, a doctor walked from the room and motioned for Trey. "I am Dr. Alberto Hernandez," the older Colombian man started to talk in very broken English but Trey stopped him and spoke Spanish.

"She has a concussion. And because, as you said, she was still healing from a recent concussion the risk factor is very high," the doctor began. "She is still unconscious. Her brain swelling, although not as bad as it could be, is reason for concern."

Trey licked his dry lips. "Is she awake?"

"No. But I think the reason for that is that there were traces of clonazepam in her blood."

Trey didn't need to be told what clonazepam was. As an FBI agent, Trey was familiar with many of the drugs used to create unconsciousness in individuals. "How is that possible?" Trey shook his head. "She was swimming." He tried to recall if he noticed a second towel.

The doctor held up the chart. "It was there. I assure you. And I believe it's the clonazepam that is keeping her unconscious. She should be coming out of it soon."

"May I see her now?" Trey glanced toward the door.

Dr. Hernandez nodded. "We will be monitoring her for change. I don't know what to expect when she awakes."

Trey followed the man into the room and saw Rainey lying lifeless on the bed. He hurried to her side and reached for one of her hands. IVs stuck out from her arm and Trey tried to be careful not to bump them.

One of the nurses brought a chair closer to him and Trey sat down wondering how in the world Rainey could have been drugged. *You were on a yacht with drug dealers. Is it really so hard to believe?* Trey considered the options. Enrique had no incentive to drug Rainey. She was going to be his bargaining chip when they met her parents. What about Carlos? Why would Carlos harm Rainey? Trey tried to recall who came when he called for help. *Where was Dylan?*

"Señor," a nurse called to him from the doorway. "You have a friend here to see you."

Trey stepped out into the hallway and found Carlos and Ian waiting for him. "Enrique wants to know how she is."

Trey told the men exactly what the doctor said. "Who would have access to clonazepam?" Trey asked.

Carlos was quiet for a few minutes. "I wonder if that is what the women used in the bar who drugged Rod and Dylan while we were in Panama."

Trey listened while Carlos explained the condition Dylan and Rod were in when they arrived back at the yacht.

It was possible. "But how would Rainey end up getting drugged?" Trey paced the room and softened his voice when a nurse walked passed. "Where was Dylan when Rainey fell in the pool?"

"I assume he was down below in his cabin. I will question him."

"Tell me if you find anything out." It felt strange giving an order to a drug lord but Trey knew Carlos didn't take it personally.

***

Several hours passed before Rainey regained consciousness. Trey was beside her in seconds when he heard her stirring. "Rainey? Rainey? Can you hear me?"

Rainey's soft blue eyes fluttered opened and closed a few times while she adjusted to the bright lights over her head. She glanced around the room and back at Trey.

The doctor hurried in and checked her vitals. He spoke softly to her in Spanish and Rainey nodded softly as if she understood.

"She's cognizant. That is good." Dr. Hernandez checked her IVs. "Nurse, more fluids, quickly."

Trey reached for her hand and squeezed it. "I was so worried."

She stared at him blankly and back at the doctor. A questioning look of concern spread across her forehead. "Where am I?" she asked in Spanish.

"You're in a hospital in Cartagena," Trey answered in English. "Do you understand me in English?"

Rainey nodded. "Who are you?"

"I'm… Matthew." Rainey's blank expression confirmed his fears. Trey glanced at the doctor with concern. "She asked who I am." He returned to Spanish.

Dr. Hernandez began asking her general questions about herself to which Rainey had no answer. Concern spread across his face and he motioned for Trey to follow him. "I'd like you to see the MRI."

Trey followed the doctor to another room where he pulled up the images of her brain. "This is her new injury. It's fairly small. But here is the injury she incurred prior to today's accident. As you can see, the trauma here is far worse. I believe the new trauma aggravated the old one. This is bad. You said she had partial amnesia before?"

"Yes."

"Had she regained any of the memories?"

"She had a memory that came in the form of a dream a couple days ago. But I'm not sure she recognized it as reality."

The doctor scratched his chin. "She needs complete calm. She's going to be here for a while."

Trey paced the room and ran his fingers through his hair. "Her life could be in danger beyond this head injury." Trey glanced toward the door. "I have reason to believe someone tried to murder her. I don't want to risk her being found."

Dr. Hernandez glanced over Rainey's file. "Give me a new name." He set the file down on the paper and picked up a pen. "We will change the information in the computer."

Trey racked his brain. "Call her April Netherland."

Trey helped him with the spelling. "Make sure no one calls her Rainey. If anyone asks for Rainey Meadows, notify me immediately." Trey patted his pockets. "I don't even have my phone." Trey needed to get back to the yacht to get the rest of his belongings.

***

Rod found Dylan in Rainey's bedroom digging through Trey's bag. "What are you doing?"

Dylan stood up and carried the bag to Rod. "Interesting bag. I've never actually seen anything like it." He opened it and motioned toward a simple seam. "Looks normal doesn't it?" He pushed it and pulled it back, opening a small compartment.

"What's in it?"

"Nothing." Dylan looked up. "Anymore." He tossed the bag on the floor. "Makes me wonder what was in the bag." Dylan crammed Trey's stuff back inside and zipped it shut.

"Enrique wants to talk to you." Rod pushed the door opened and motioned for Dylan to follow.

"But I have something else to show you." Dylan motioned toward the bunk. "Close the door. This is really interesting."

Rod glanced over his shoulder and shrugged. He closed the door and took a few steps closer to Dylan.

Dylan picked up Rainey's pillow, slipped Trey's gun behind it and fired at Rod. The man fell to the ground with a look of shock on his face.

135

"Sorry about that, friend. You did make a great drinking buddy." Dylan fired another shot, stepped casually over the body and locked the door behind him.

Armed with Rod's old gun and Trey's Glock, Dylan made his way down the hallway, opening doors to see who might have heard his shot. Sound on the steps alerted him and he ducked behind a door. Ian walked past and Dylan steadied Rod's gun. With one well-aimed shot, Ian fell to his death.

Carlos was at the door to Enrique's large meeting room, on guard against whatever attack they were under. Dylan could hear their voices and knew Carlos was on the other side of the thin, wooden door. He smiled to himself. *What kind of drug lord doesn't have reinforced doors?* He pointed the Glock to the door and blew holes in the wood. A moan on the other side was enough to convince him he was safe to enter.

With a hard kick and both guns in position, Dylan fired and shot the gun from Enrique's hand. Enrique clutched his hand and rose quickly.

"That's the fastest I've ever seen you move old man." Dylan stepped over Carlos' body and steadied his gun toward Enrique.

Enrique raised his hands. "So it was you."

"Did you really have to think about it?" He motioned for Enrique to take a seat near Dylan's computer, which still sat on Enrique's desk, awaiting his deposit into Dylan's account. "But just so you know, your buddy, Mr. Smith, is really FBI." Dylan pulled Trey's badge from his bag and slapped it down on the table. "Trey Netherland." Dylan read the name on his identification. "And look, he has a cell phone. Open it. I believe he's made calls. One while we were in San Diego and again while we were in Panama. Unfortunately, he neglected to notify them that we arrived in Cartagena. Which means, the FBI is probably watching for us in Santa Marta."

Dylan motioned toward the computer. "Now. I did my job. I told you how to find Rainey Meadows' parents. I need you to complete that transaction."

Enrique held Trey's identification card in his hand and read the name. It was obvious that he was surprised. Dylan figured Enrique did all kinds of background checks on Mr. Smith, whoever

Enrique thought that was, which would have ensured him that his new agent would be one of his best.

"Hurry up, old man." Dylan motioned toward the computer.

Enrique turned on the Internet and opened Dylan's computer. The bank window was still opened but the account information needed to be re-entered. Dylan spouted off the numbers for Enrique to enter. When the name Marcus Rauch showed up on the screen, Enrique turned to Dylan. "So are you Marcus Rauch?"

Dylan grinned. "Among other people." He glanced over Enrique's shoulder at the information on his computer screen. "Hurry up. Transfer the money."

Enrique scratched his chin and cleared his throat. He never did anything quickly. He entered the numbers into the computer and glanced at Dylan. "Shall I hit send?"

"No. That's not necessary." Dylan fired his gun at Enrique and watched the old man fall off the chair. "I want the pleasure." Dylan sat in Enrique's chair, positioned the mouse, and hit accept. He waited for less than a second.

Account information denied. Information incorrect.

Dylan's eyes grew wide and he turned to Enrique, whose hand was on his chest. The drug lord's breathing was slowing, but he had a slim, knowing smile on his lips. "You have missed the understanding of something called patience."

Dylan grabbed Enrique's shoulders and shook him. "The numbers! What are the numbers?" But it was too late. Enrique was gone.

Dylan felt like throwing his computer across the room. Anger mounted and he clenched his fists to stave off the rage. *Idiot! What an idiot!* He paced the room trying to figure out his next course of action.

The amount of money he'd gathered from Trey's duffle bag would hold him over for a while, and once he finished his job for Nash he would undoubtedly see a significant deposit into his account. *But what a waste… the old man played me.*

With the scrambler turned off on the ship, Dylan picked up Trey's cell phone and glanced through his recent calls. Undoubtedly, his most recent call was to one of his FBI buddies. Dylan glanced over the murder scene on the yacht and dialed up the most frequently called number in the past few days.

137

"Where are you?" A woman's voice met Dylan on the other end of the line.

Dylan grinned. "I'm afraid I've made a terrible mistake." His tone dripped with sarcasm. "I got carried away with my gun. Everyone on the ship is dead. Just arrest me. My career is over."

"Who is this?"

"Oh, come on. Don't you think I sounded like Trey? Kind of whiny and nasally."

"Where is the owner of this phone?" Tiffany kept her tone steady.

"You mean, Trey Netherland?" Dylan repeated the name on Trey's identification card. "Maybe I killed him. You'll want to get out here and ID bodies." Dylan hung up the phone and left it lay on the counter. He was sure they had a tracking device on it and would be here in no time. With a quick search for any more cash lying around, Dylan grabbed his computer and slipped off the yacht unnoticed.

***

The scene at the yacht caught Trey off guard. Local police officers stood guard while a few familiar FBI agents walked around the deck with Colombian authorities. Trey approached the boat and was immediately stopped. "I'm with them." He pointed to the agents on the yacht, but wearing casual shorts and a t-shirt he wasn't surprised they didn't believe him.

The local police approached the members of Trey's FBI team and eventually he was permitted access to the yacht.

"What happened?" He walked into the main room and found Tiffany standing over Enrique's body.

Tiffany's face showed relief. "We thought you were dead. We were about to search the water." She shoved a blonde hair behind her ear.

Trey couldn't hide the surprise on his face. "Who did this?"

"Now that I know you're alive, I'm hoping you can help us put this together. We still haven't found any identification on these men and the ship is registered to a business out of the Netherlands called 'West Coast Compilations' whatever that means.

"That's Enrique." Trey motioned to the body near the desk. "The man at the door is Carlos."

One of the other agents began writing everything down.

"There are two more bodies downstairs." Tiffany motioned for him to follow. "Where is Rainey?"

Trey began explaining the events of the past several hours. "She has no idea who she is." Trey told her the doctor's diagnosis. "They don't plan on releasing her for a while. Two concussions in less than two weeks can be very serious." Trey stopped and softened his tone. "I feel certain it was attempted murder." Trey told Tiffany about the drug found in her blood.

"That means, most likely, whoever killed the men on this ship intended on killing her too." Tiffany chewed on her lower lip. "We've located her mom. But we haven't made contact. I was hoping Margaret would respond to a message we sent her through Jack Peterson, but she hasn't yet." Trey and Tiffany passed a couple agents on the stairs. "Margaret and Bradley aren't the big players in this game. If we could get one of them to lead us to McCarness, we might be able to cut them a deal."

Trey and Tiffany stopped near Ian's body in the hallway. "That's Ian." Trey shook his head at the sight. He also identified Rod's body lying dead on Rainey's floor. Trey found his bag with its contents carelessly thrown about and opened his secret compartment. He let out a heavy sigh. "Whoever did this has my badge, and my ID."

Tiffany turned from the body to look over Trey's shoulder. "You didn't have it on you?"

"I didn't have time when Rainey got hurt." Trey dug through the bag a little more. "They've also got my gun."

Tiffany sighed. "I understand you were deep undercover, but Trey, someone's out there with your badge. This is not good."

Trey sat down on the bunk and leaned his head into the railing. A sickening feeling crept into his stomach.

Tiffany crossed her arms. "Alright, listen. He used your phone to make a call." Tiffany gave him a synopsis of the conversation. "You know who's dead and who's missing." She opened her arms up and waved them in the air. "Who did this?"

"Dylan." Trey was sure. It made the most sense.

"We checked into that guy. Dylan Daugherty is a fictitious name and so is Marcus Rauch—although we found a Swiss bank account under Marcus' name."

Trey didn't want to think about the possibilities of Dylan walking around carrying an FBI badge. *His FBI badge.*

"I need to get back to the hospital. Rainey's there alone and she doesn't know who she is. What if Dylan shows up?"

Tiffany nodded. "You get back to the hospital."

Trey tossed Rainey's clothes into his bag and grabbed her Bible from the nightstand.

Tiffany watched Trey zip up his bag and carry it out of the room. He stopped and turned. "Do you have my phone?"

"It's in evidence. I'll bring you a new one at the hospital."

Trey nodded. He wanted to hurry.

***

Margaret Reed walked down the stone-lined sidewalk to her friend's bread shop. A warm ocean breeze caught her long, straight, brown hair and she tucked it behind her ears. Bradley was still at his meeting, but she couldn't think to work. She pulled a piece of paper out of her skirt pocket and read the number Jack gave her. *I want nothing to do with the FBI.* She let out a heavy sigh. Did they really know where she was? Were they watching her now? *My plants. Who will care for my plants?*

A silver haired Colombian woman greeted her as soon as she walked through the door to the bread shop. Margaret glanced at the bread display behind the counter.

"Buenas tardes, Margarita." Rosa pulled a loaf of bread from her brick oven and set it on the clean, marble countertop. "You just missed the crowds. I must have had fifteen customers in fifteen minutes."

Margaret let the smell of fresh baked bread fill her senses. "That's a good problem to have."

"What can I get you today?"

"I would like another loaf of that stone ground multi-grain bread."

Rosa grabbed the last loaf and placed it in a brown paper bag. She quoted the price and Margaret handed her a couple bills.

140

"Bradley loves this bread. He ate almost the whole loaf last time."
She took the bag from her friend. "It was wonderful with honey on
it."

Rosa studied Margaret for a moment and walked around the
counter. "Are you well?" She placed a hand on Margaret's.

Margaret gave a wane smile. "My karma isn't good today, is
it?"

Rosa made a face. "You and your karma. I'd say you need a
few hours of prayer." She tightened her grasp. "What is it? I see you
three times a week and usually you are so happy."

Margaret shook her head. "My life is all about secrets, Rosa.
I wish I could tell you."

Rosa placed a soft wrinkled hand on Margaret's face. "I will
be praying for you."

Margaret didn't put much stock in prayer but thanked Rosa
anyway. She tightened her grip on her bag of bread. "I need to go.
Bradley should be home by now." She left the store with a heavy
heart.

The usually pleasant walk home was consumed with the fear
that she was being watched. She hurried down the street, glancing
over her shoulder every so often to see if there were any unfamiliar
eyes on her.

Bradley was in the flat as soon as Margaret entered. "We
have to leave." Bradley didn't even greet her. "The FBI is involved."

Margaret didn't tell Bradley she already knew. "What about
the plants?"

"We need to gather the hybrid plants. The rest will be
burned."

"No, Bradley. We can't burn them." She dropped the bag
with the bread and placed her hands on Bradley's chest. "We can't."

"Any plant related to drug production that we don't bring
must be destroyed." Bradley bent over and picked up the bag. "Pack
quickly. Nash will have a vehicle here shortly to pick us up."

"Have you heard any news about Rainey?" Margaret
followed Bradley through the living room to the kitchen.

Bradley's back was to Margaret. He licked his lips and
closed his eyes for a moment. "No. I think they were only bluffing—
probably to try to get to us." He turned around and faced the slim,

nature-loving woman before him. "Get your things together. I'll take care of the plants."

Margaret protested. "I've got to say goodbye to them." She grabbed Bradley's arm. "Are you sure we've been found?"

"Nash's source said the FBI are in Cartagena right now. They could be here any minute."

Margaret gave a reserved nod and sucked in a deep, renewing breath. "I knew this day was going to be a bad one. I found a dead butterfly on the veranda this morning."

***

Dr. Hernandez greeted Trey as soon as he returned to the hospital. "A man came looking for Rainey Meadows while you were gone." The doctor pulled Trey to the side and spoke softly. "None of the staff here have even heard of her. It was easy to convince him that there was no patient here by that name. We told him to try one of the other hospitals."

"What did he look like?"

The doctor sized up Trey. "About your height and build, blonde hair, blue eyes, strong chin, like yours. He had a tattoo..."

Trey nodded. "That's the man. We can't let him find Rainey."

"We will do our best to protect her," the doctor promised.

Trey considered having the police guard Rainey's door, but that would be like hanging a sign that said 'this is her' over the room. It was best to treat her as a normal patient and do their best to find Dylan. "How is she?"

"Quiet. Her vitals are good. She said her headache is minimal. We have taken out most of her IVs. I have left one in to make sure she is getting fluids. She has not wanted to eat or drink anything yet." The doctor shrugged. "All of this is normal."

Trey held up his bag. "I have some of her things in here, including her Bible. Maybe something familiar will help."

Dr. Hernandez agreed and patted Trey's arm. "See if you can bring her comfort."

Rainey was sitting quietly on her bed when Trey walked into the room. She gave him a blank smile as if she remembered him from earlier but didn't really know him.

142

"I brought some of your things." He sat down and unzipped the bag. "Do you recognize this skirt?"

Rainey shook her head. "It's pretty though."

Trey pulled out another article of clothing he'd seen her wear since he bought it. She shook her head. "Do you remember Uncle Jack?"

"No."

Trey tried a few more names. "You've got to remember Clarissa. She's your college roommate."

Rainey sighed.

"Here's your Bible." He handed it to her. She looked at it blankly and shook her head. "I don't recognize it."

Trey hoped that at least she would have smiled at the Bible. Wouldn't she have found some kind of comfort in it? "I know it's not your old one. The one you've got all marked up back home. But you've enjoyed this one too. Why don't you read it? You love the Bible."

Rainey glanced at the Book in his hands. "What's it about?"

Trey stared at her for a moment as if he couldn't believe her question. "The Bible?" How could she not remember the Bible? He watched for any kind of reaction. "It's about God and Jesus and… a bunch of people." He explained as best as he could.

Rainey leaned back on her pillow and closed her eyes. She looked like she was about to cry. "I don't remember ever reading it."

Trey zipped up his bag but kept the Bible in his lap. "Do you want me to read it to you?"

"No."

Trey stared at her for a moment. "Why not?"

She opened her eyes and shook her head. "I'm tired. I just want to sleep."

Trey let her sleep. For the first time since he'd met her, he wished she would let him read the Bible to her.

Chapter 14

Dr. Hernandez let Trey know that he was leaving for the night. "Dr. Jacobson will be in to check on her later. You'll like him. I told him that you are family so the next shift will not give you any trouble about staying with her."

Trey nodded.

"We will have to move her out of emergency care tomorrow morning. I will be here for that."

It was late and Trey was tired. The room was not as well equipped as hospital rooms in the United States. It was almost impossible to rest on the hard wooden chair beside her bed.

The sound of shoes in the hallway pulled him from his drowsiness. He pulled the curtain around Rainey's bed to ensure her privacy in case it was someone looking for her.

"Trey?" Tiffany called at the door.

Trey got up and walked to the hallway.

"It took us five hours to get through all that stuff." She shook her head. "I couldn't get away until we got all the documentation we needed. The Colombian police plan on taking over now." She sighed. "We've got a search going on for Dylan and I got you a new phone. Your old one is in evidence." She handed Trey another smart phone. "Don't lose this one."

Trey sighed. "How about a gun?"

"The Colombian government doesn't just hand out guns to FBI agents. It might take me a few days. I've also got a call in to get you a new identification card." She handed Trey a small wad of bills and an American Express. "This should hold you over. I doubt you'll be able to use the American Express without ID, but hopefully I'll have your identification card within a day or two." She looked around the hospital corridor. "How is she?"

"She seems to be doing okay except she has no idea who she is or who anyone else is." Discouragement showed on Trey's face. "I've run through everything I know about her. She doesn't remember the Christian school she attended, her family, her college." He shook his head. "She doesn't remember anything."

"The poor girl." Tiffany took a few steps toward Rainey's hospital room and glanced in. "You've got the curtain pulled."

"Dylan was here earlier asking about her. My guess is he's searching all the area hospitals and when he doesn't find her by the name Rainey Meadows, he's going to search harder."

"What name did you give her?" Tiffany asked.

"April Netherland." Trey watched to see how his boss would react.

Tiffany raised a curious eyebrow. "You gave her your last name?"

"It was the first name that rolled off my lips.

"Interesting." Tiffany glanced at her smartphone and jotted down a few notes. "We'll get a description of Dylan out to every hospital within a fifty mile radius."

Trey nodded.

"We're headed back to Santa Marta tomorrow." Tiffany softened her tone. "I was hoping Rainey's mother would have called by now. Maybe she didn't get the message."

"Seeing a truly familiar face, like her mother, could help." Trey crossed his arms and leaned against the doorframe.

"Are you coming with us tomorrow?"

Trey shook his head. "I want to stay with Rainey."

"We can get someone else to pose as her family."

"No. I need to be the one."

Tiffany studied Trey curiously. "You're not getting personal, are you? You know this isn't your fault."

"That's not it."

"Okay… personal in another way?" She crossed her arms.

"What do you mean by that?" Trey wasn't sure what Tiffany was saying. Was she accusing him of having feelings for Rainey?

"Relax, college boy." Tiffany placed a playful hand on his chest. "You don't have to get defensive." Her red lips curved into a smile.

Trey glanced down at Tiffany's long, painted nails and shook his head. "I'm the only familiar person around right now. I need to be here."

"No problem. She's still your case. I'll be by as soon as I get your new ID card."

"And my badge?"

"You're either going to have to get it from Dylan or wait until we get back to the States."

***

It was early morning when Trey heard a nurse walk into the room. He'd pulled his chair up close to Rainey's bed in the night and slept with his head on her mattress while sitting in the uncomfortable chair.

The nurse clicked her tongue a few times and shook her head. "That is no way to sleep."

"Unless you want to bring another bed in here, it is the only thing I can do." He answered in Spanish.

She glanced over Rainey's chart. "We will be moving her upstairs this afternoon. There are more comfortable guest chairs up there."

Trey was thankful for that. "How about showers?"

"This is not a hotel you know." She checked Rainey's IV and vitals.

Rainey woke up while the nurse was working on her and Trey stepped out to stretch his legs. He checked his phone but there were no calls. It was good to have a phone again.

He was tired and hungry, but he wanted to wait until Dr. Hernandez arrived to get any food. He didn't know these new nurses and couldn't risk leaving Rainey alone.

When Trey returned to her room, Rainey was sitting up with her head turned toward the window.

"It looks like a beautiful morning." He let his eyes travel to the window and noticed the blue sky.

Rainey shrugged. "I can't see much."

"The doctor said you'll need to be on bed rest for a couple weeks." Trey sat in the chair near her bed. "But I hope we can get you out of here before then." Trey let his eyes rest on hers. It pained him to see her lying in a hospital bed. He searched her face and wondered when the light would return to her eyes.

"Do I have any family looking for me?" Rainey studied Trey curiously.

Trey wasn't sure how much he should tell her. The doctor said Rainey was to be kept calm. "Neither of your parents know about your injury yet." Trey was honest. "We are trying to reach your mother."

Turning her blue eyes toward Trey, she watched him for a moment. "Who are you... in my life I mean?"

That was a difficult one. Who was he in her life? Trey studied her soft facial features, her long brown wavy hair, her eyes the color of the sky. *At one time she told me she loved me. She loved Matthew. Not me.* Trey reached for her hand and held it gently. "We're good friends."

She glanced at him but did not pull her hand away. It was strange. Just a few days ago she told him to never touch her again. Was he wrong to hold her hand? Was he just taking advantage of her ignorance? Trey felt her cold fingers and wrapped them in his warm ones. It felt good to touch her hand again. Could he ever regain her trust? Maybe he could start over. Let her meet him for the first time—let her see the man he really was.

"I know you told me your name, but I can't remember it right now." She watched him curiously.

Trey wondered if this were some kind of test. How should he reply? *The truth. Tell her the truth.* "My name is Trey." He smiled. It felt good.

***

Dylan stood in front of the mirror in the small hotel room and studied his new hair color. He picked up Trey's identification card and studied his hairstyle. A pair of scissors and a little snipping did wonderers to transform Dylan's carefree curls into the sophisticated style in which Trey wore his hair. They had similar hair. With a few alterations, Dylan was impressed with how well he'd matched Trey's look.

It bothered him to admit that he and Trey had similar features. They both shared a strong chin and were built very similar. *I never wanted to look like that man.*

For two days Dylan was forced to hide in his hotel room. Nash told him to lay low. There was a search going on for him. While his boss was glad Dylan took out Enrique and his top men, Dylan still needed to find Rainey. Undoubtedly, she was with Trey.

After a clean shave, Dylan ran his hand over his face. "I'm Trey Netherland. FBI."

***

Rainey slept most of the day. Trey slipped out to get dinner, leaving her in the care of Dr. Hernandez. For some reason Trey trusted the insightful doctor. It impressed Trey how willing the man was to use a different name for Rainey. Dr. Hernandez seemed to understand the real threat to her life.

The town around the university hospital was cheery. Small, well-kept houses and businesses, landscaped with colorful flowering bushes and trees, stretched out along the busy streets. Trey had slipped out a couple times over the past couple days, but was careful never to be gone long. Even though he trusted the doctor, Trey realized the friendly staff at the hospital would be no match for an armed man with a vendetta.

Trey stopped at the same restaurant he'd gotten his dinner the evening before. A familiar face greeted him and Trey ordered a quick bite to go.

"Would you like your coffee the same way you ordered it yesterday, señor?" The man behind the counter asked.

"Yes, please." Trey watched the man stir cream into his coffee cup and wished there was a way to get a few pumps of mocha in the coffee. "Thank you." Trey took the to go cup and paid.

He walked the tree-lined street back to the hospital, careful to keep his eyes out for Dylan. It wasn't a long walk, but Trey hated being away at all. He glanced at his phone and saw that he'd received a text from Tiffany.

"I'm at the hospital. Where are you?"

Trey texted a quick reply that he would be there in a few minutes.

Trey carried his food and coffee to Rainey's room. She was still asleep.

"Your friend Tiffany is here." Dr. Hernandez motioned toward the visitor's waiting room.

"Thank you." Trey sent her a quick text that he was there.

Tiffany met him at Rainey's door. "Let's take a walk."

"Can I eat first?" Trey couldn't explain the weariness he felt. "She's sound asleep."

Tiffany sighed. "There are some tables outside." She motioned for him to follow.

Trey carried his food to a patio just outside the first floor of the hospital. Tiffany gave him a few minutes to get some food in his stomach. "You're like the walking dead."

Trey nodded.

"And you need to shave." She touched is face playfully.

"I know." Trey felt the scruffiness of his face and took a bite of his burrito.

"Rainey's mom and Bradley Scott are gone." Tiffany waited for his reaction.

"She never contacted you?"

Tiffany shook her head. "Margaret replied to Jack using her alumni email. He notified me this afternoon. She told him she wasn't going to fall for his trap. Apparently, she doesn't believe Rainey is in trouble and said, 'nice try.'"

"She thinks Jack was lying to her?" Trey took a long sip of his bitter coffee.

"Yes, and now she and Bradley have gone into hiding."

"Does Jack know that Rainey is hurt?" Trey asked.

"We told him that she had been hurt but that she was under your care and that her identity needed to be kept a secret until we could secure her safety." Tiffany reached over and grabbed one of Trey's nacho chips. "He wanted to come see her but we told him that wasn't possible at this time."

"Dr. Hernandez hopes that Rainey can be released in about a week. He's monitoring the swelling in her brain. He doesn't want her to leave until he's comfortable that the swelling is almost gone."

"I'll let Jack know."

Trey asked for Jack Peterson's phone number. "I can keep him updated on her progress." The thought occurred to him that Jack probably hated him. "Do you have any idea where Rainey's mother went?"

"None. They torched the plants and their flat is clean. Their maid said they dismissed her Tuesday afternoon and she hasn't seen them since." Tiffany reached for another chip. "They knew we were coming."

"Do you think Jack's message spooked them?"

"I don't know. Jack's message gave no indication that we knew where she was. It was left wide open for her to make the move. I think they got a tip."

"And nothing on Nash?" Trey pulled his chips away from Tiffany. "This is the first meal I've had all day you know."

Tiffany shook her head. "I can send another agent over to help you. Why don't you let us get you a room at the hotel?"

Trey considered the option. "Maybe." He finished his coffee and stood up. "We should get back upstairs. Dr. Hernandez gets off soon and I don't want to leave her alone."

"Has she remembered anything?" Tiffany stood up with him and grabbed his empty burrito wrapper.

"No. And thanks." He appreciated Tiffany cleaning up after him.

Pausing at the door to the hospital, Tiffany turned to Trey. "You're not letting yourself fall for this woman are you?"

Was she really asking him this? Trey raised his eyebrows and crossed his arms. "Define fall."

Tiffany took a few steps away from the door while someone walked past. "Her parents are involved in drug trafficking, you know."

"But she's not."

"Are you purposely evading the question?"

"You never defined fall. And anyway, why does it matter? She has no idea who she is and once she remembers, she'll hate me again." Trey pulled the door opened and motioned for Tiffany to walk inside. "Let me know if you find someone who will watch her through the night. I'll take you up on the hotel."

Tiffany promised she would. "You should have your new identification card by tomorrow."

Trey watched her walk away and made his way back to Rainey's room. She was still sleeping when he sat beside her on the chair. He studied her delicate features framed by soft waves of brown hair. The bruises around her eyes were evidence of her second concussion, but they didn't detract from her beauty. Now that he knew her, Trey was sure nothing could detract from her beauty. It radiated from the inside. *Am I falling for this woman?* Trey wasn't sure how to answer. *She loves Matthew. Not me.*

***

Trey had another miserable night's sleep in Rainey's hospital room. The emergency room nurse was right, the chairs were better in this part of the hospital, but they weren't the same as a bed. He walked around the room, trying to work the kink out of his neck.

"Morning." Rainey's soft, groggy voice called out to him.

Trey was at her bedside immediately. "Hey." He gently brushed her hair away from her face and smiled into her blue eyes. "You're awake."

Rainey smiled. "I feel rested."

"Good. How's your head?"

Rainey blinked a few times. "It doesn't hurt this morning."

Trey breathed a sigh of relief. "Do you want me to call for your breakfast?"

Rainey shook her head. "I'm not really hungry." She shifted her position on the bed and tucked a hair behind her ear. "Did you sleep well?"

Trey glanced at the padded vinyl chair across the room. "Not really." He grinned. He dragged the chair closer to her bed and sat down. This was the most coherent he'd seen Rainey since her accident. "Would you like me to read to you?"

Rainey reached for the bottle of water beside her bed. "Sure."

Trey grabbed the Bible from his bag and started flipping through the pages. "How about 1 John 1:5-9?" Trey remembered the verses Rainey chose for them the last time they'd read together. "You once told me these verses mean a lot to you."

Rainey shrugged. It was obvious she didn't recognize the reference.

Trey lowered his gaze to the Book and began to read. "This is the message we have heard from Him and announce to you, that God is Light and in Him there is no darkness at all. If we say that we have fellowship with Him and yet walk in the darkness, we lie and do not practice the truth." Trey glanced at her to see if she recognized the words. "But if we walk in the Light as he Himself is in the Light, we have fellowship with one another, and the blood of Jesus His Son cleanses us from all sin. If we say that we have no sin, we are deceiving ourselves and the truth is not in us. If we confess our sins, He is faithful and righteous to forgive us our sins and to cleanse us from all unrighteousness."

"Those are beautiful words." Rainey smiled. "Can you keep reading?"

Trey glanced back down and continued reading. "See how great a love the Father has bestowed on us, that we would be called children of God; and *such* we are. For this reason the world does not know us, because it did not know Him."

"Stop there." Rainey raised her hand. "Where was that?"

"1 John 3:1."

Rainey sighed. "The world does not know us." She chuckled. "I don't know me." She closed her eyes. "I just thought that was interesting. Please keep reading."

Trey read. He read all of 1 John, he even went back and read the first part of 1 John so that they could say they read the whole book. While he read, Rainey would stop him from time to time to ask him what he thought something meant. Trey had to confess sometimes that he wasn't sure.

In the early afternoon, Dr. Hernandez came in and told Rainey he wanted her to sit up and take a short walk around the hallway. One of the nurses came and assisted the doctor while they made sure Rainey wasn't going to lose her balance. Rainey seemed happy to be up. Trey was sure she must be tired of being stuck in a hospital room. He sure was. Trey stood up and stretched his own legs, using this opportunity to walk around the room and let his eyes rest from reading.

He was glad they had Rainey up and walking around. He wasn't sure how long the doctor would insist on keeping her in the hospital, but Trey was anxious to see her safely back in California. *Will she be any safer in California?* With Dylan still out there, Trey wasn't so sure. *Dylan tried to kill her. Wouldn't he try again?* Trey shuddered at the thought. Dylan knew too much about her. He knew her friends. He knew her interests. *We have to catch Dylan to keep her safe.*

Rainey was smiling when she returned to the room. "Thank you, Dr. Hernandez." She let the man lead her back to the bed. "It felt good to be up."

Trey tried to push Dylan from his mind and sat beside her on the chair. "You look refreshed."

"I would like to see her up walking around a couple more times today," Dr. Hernandez said.

"I'll walk with her." Trey turned to the doctor.

After the doctor left, Rainey asked Trey to read to her again. Trey was glad she was regaining interest in the Bible. They read and talked together the rest of the day.

It was close to dinnertime when Rainey grew tired. Dr. Hernandez offered to keep an eye on Rainey while Trey got something to eat.

"You need more than dinner." The doctor placed a comforting hand on Trey's shoulder. "You should rest."

Trey glanced over his shoulder at Rainey. He was tired. A long hot shower and a whole night's sleep in a bed would be wonderful. Trey hoped Tiffany would send an agent over to stay with Rainey soon.

***

How many hospitals can there be in Cartagena? Dylan adjusted his tie and walked into the University Hospital. He approached the registration desk and pulled out his badge. "I'm with the United States Federal Bureau of Investigation. We're in search of a missing person. Do you know if any of your patients are U.S. citizens?"

The gentleman behind the desk raised his eyebrows over his glasses. "We are not at liberty to give out patient information."

Dylan had heard this line before at the previous two hospitals. He glanced at the man's name badge. "Well, Jorge. "He

153

pulled out a small pile of bills and waved it in front of the man behind the counter. "Perhaps you need some convincing."

Jorge glanced around to see if anyone noticed the attempted bribe. He snatched the bills and motioned for Dylan to glance at the computer screen. He began to scan the list of patients. "This gentleman is from the U.S." He pointed to a name and glanced at Dylan.

Dylan shook his head. "We are looking for a woman."

Jorge continued scanning the names. "April Netherland." He glanced at Dylan for a reaction.

A sinister grin spread across Dylan's lips. *Netherland...did he really have to make it so easy.* Dylan pointed at the screen. "That's her. What is her condition?"

Jorge shook his head. "It said she was admitted with a head injury. I don't know anything else."

Dylan reached into his pocket. "Can you find out?"

Jorge glanced at the money. "Come back tomorrow." He took the money. "I'll learn what I can."

Dylan was pleased. This was better than he hoped.

***

Vince Elm cleared his throat and pulled Trey from a restless sleep. "Trey."

Trey blinked a few times and turned to Vince.

"You look like death warmed over." Vince handed Trey a hotel room key. "Tiffany said you need to go sleep for about twelve hours."

Trey looked at the clock. It was almost eleven. He hated to leave Rainey without telling her where he was going, but he knew he needed a good night's sleep. "If she wakes up, tell her I'll be back."

Vince grinned. He wasn't used to seeing Trey so concerned about a woman. "Tiffany said you had it bad. I didn't believe her."

Trey stood up and stretched. "Call me if there are any problems."

"I got this." Vince took Trey's seat. "Get some sleep." He watched Trey reach for his duffle bag. "And shave."

Trey rolled his eyes and walked from the room. He was so tired he wasn't sure he had enough energy to walk across the street to the hotel. He glanced at the key. *She actually got me a room.*

The hotel was nice. Trey took the elevator to his room and walked dreamlike to the room number on his key. He stepped inside and breathed in the clean smell of hotel. *A bed and a shower—I must be in heaven.*

***

"She's got amnesia. Doesn't have a clue who she is or who anyone else is." Jorge explained. "They've got someone sitting with her round the clock."

"Where is her room?"

"Second floor. She's in recovery. They're monitoring the swelling in her brain."

"Do you know how long they plan on keeping her?"

Jorge raised a finger for a moment when someone approached the counter. He answered the man's question and turned to Dylan. "At least a week."

Dylan tapped his finger on the desk impatiently. "Do you know who they've got watching her?"

Jorge shook his head. "Look. I know you're FBI, but I can't help you any more. People start wondering when you ask too many questions. I need this job."

"No problem." Dylan nodded and handed Jorge a few more bills. "I appreciate the information you gave me.

He ran his fingers through his brown hair and stepped out the doors. This would require some planning.

***

It was never easy starting over. Margaret walked into the empty greenhouse and glanced at the empty pots. Her few survivors sat near the window, ready to propagate and test for composition.

Jack's reply on the alumni email upset her. He assured her that his concern for Rainey was not a set up. *She's in a hospital with a concussion. The FBI is not using her as a bargaining chip. They are trying to get her to safety.*

155

Margaret didn't know what to believe. Without a doubt the FBI wanted to contact her to make a deal. This wasn't the first time they'd gotten close to her and Bradley. However, they'd never used her daughter before. What if this was real?

Bradley wouldn't listen to her concerns. He told her that they'd washed their hands of Rainey. "She wanted to live her own life. Let her go."

"But what if she's really in danger? What if our daughter is truly in a hospital with a serious head injury?"

Bradley's response had been unsettling.

"Your daughter." He crossed his arms. "Don't blame me for that child of yours. I did my part to provide for her, but I am not her father."

Margaret's eyes still burned with the pain of those words. Bradley was the only father Rainey knew. She thought he was her father. She called him her father.

Attempting to pull herself from her negative thoughts, Margaret made herself busy rebuilding her plant population. The hybrid poppy seeds were ready to plant in the new pots. It was sad to lose all the cannabis plants back in Santa Marta, but she was glad her specially cultivated poppies survived. Provided this new variety of poppies produced, they would see an abundance of seeds, ready to sell and distribute around the world.

Their new home was more private than the last. They were closer to the beach and didn't share a building with any other residents. The small stucco house was cozy. Margaret only regretted leaving her maid behind. It would take forever to find another servant like her. *Vanessa was such a good cook.*

She walked to the window and looked out at the ocean. This house reminded her of one they'd lived in while Rainey was young. The child practically grew up on the water—until she went off to that Christian school. Margaret was convinced the Christian school ruined her daughter. *Why would anyone want to be bound to the laws and restrictions of Christianity? There is so much peace and harmony in nature.* Margaret couldn't imagine finding anything more harmonious than the oneness she found soaking in the splendor of a newly blossoming flower or the melodious sound of a bird. If by her contributions to science she could take nature one-step further in

156

the evolutionary process, Margaret was convinced she would reach her higher self and find the fulfillment of her soul.

***

Trey was a little anxious when he woke up. It was almost one in the afternoon. *How long did I sleep?* He pulled himself from the comfortable queen sized bed and took a quick, refreshing shower. He'd received a text from Vince telling him that things were fine, but Trey hurried with only a quick bite to eat and a cup of coffee so that he could get back to Rainey.

"You look better." Vince stood up when Trey walked through the door.

Rainey's eyes were bright and she greeted Trey with a sunny smile. "You look rested."

"I was beginning to wonder who had the concussion." Vince winked at Rainey. "I'll come by later to take the night shift." He waved at Rainey before he left the room.

"Your friend is very nice." Rainey watched Trey open a bottle of water and pull the chair closer to her bed. "Are you going to read to me again?"

Trey grinned. He was glad she asked. It bothered him when Rainey woke from her coma with seemingly no interest in the Bible. She needed to have interest in the Bible. That was Rainey. "Where do you want me to read from?"

Rainey took a deep, refreshing breath. "What do you mean where?"

"What book?"

"The Bible."

Trey laughed. "I know. I mean, which book of the Bible." Trey wondered how she could have forgotten the way the Bible was laid out. "There are 39 books of the Old Testament and 27 books of the New Testament. All together it makes up the Bible." Was he really explaining this to Rainey?

"Oh." Rainey nodded. "I think I understand." She chewed on her lower lip. "Well, I liked the books you read yesterday."

"Do you remember what any of them were called?" Trey tried to get Rainey to pull from her memory.

"Genesis and John. Right?"

157

"1 John. But yes." He studied her face. "Did you have a favorite?"

Rainey considered this for a moment. "I liked it all. But I really liked when we talked about it. You explain things really well."

Trey tried not to chuckle. Was he really teaching her the Bible? "Okay. Well, let's read something else from the New Testament." She had no idea that it was just as new to him as it was to her. Trey chose the book of John and started at the beginning.

Trey read for several hours. Sometimes one of the nurses stopped in and listened. Several of the nurses spoke English, but Trey even translated verses a few times.

Dr. Hernandez stopped in to tell Trey he would be leaving for the night. "I've scheduled her for another MRI tomorrow to see how her brain is healing."

Trey nodded. Things were quieting down in the hospital as evening was approaching. One of the nurses brought a plate of food to Trey when they brought Rainey her meal.

"His devotion to you is lovely." She said to Rainey and handed Trey a cup of coffee to go with his meal. "If you need anything, just call for me."

Trey thanked her and watched her walk from the room.

It was the first time Trey and Rainey had taken a meal together in a long time. Trey remembered their dates back in Santa Monica. Rainey was about to take a bite of her baked yam when Trey suggested they thank God for their food.

"Okay." Rainey almost seemed embarrassed. She put down her spoon and watched Trey.

Trey closed his eyes and bowed his head. This time he was going to pray as Trey, not Matthew. He thought about it for a moment and realized the day Rainey almost drowned on the ship he'd prayed as Trey. It was a real prayer and God answered it. Rainey was okay. She was alive. Had he ever thanked God?

He realized Rainey was still waiting for him so he cleared his throat. "God..." there was a holiness in the Name he'd never felt before. This was real. He reached for her hand and entwined her fingers in his. "First I want to thank You that Rainey is okay. Thank you that she didn't drown. You did that... and I hadn't said thank You yet. I'm sorry." Trey glanced up for a second and noticed Rainey's eyes were still on him. He closed them again and continued. "Thank You for all You've done and for this food. In Jesus' name, amen."

Rainey echoed his amen.

Trey released her hand and shrugged. "I'm sorry if I rambled."

"No… it's fine. Don't apologize." Rainey let her eyes linger on him for a few seconds before she began to eat.

They were both quiet. Trey was deep in thought.

Rainey glanced up shyly at Trey after a few minutes and watched him until he noticed her eyes on him.

"Is everything okay?"

Rainey nodded. "You seem to know a lot about me." She set down her fork and took a drink of her water. "I know this might sound strange but—am I a Christian?" Tears welled up in her eyes as she asked.

Trey was struck by her genuine concern. *How do I answer this? What do I know about Christianity? Of course she's a Christian. I've heard her story. I know how and when she got saved. But she doesn't remember."*

"Let me ask you this question, because I think you need to reach deep within your heart and find this answer." He set his plate aside and leaned forward. "Remember that verse from Romans that we read earlier today, 'that if you confess with your mouth Jesus as Lord, and believe in your heart that God raised Him from the dead, you will be saved.'" Trey tried to remember exactly where it was, but couldn't.

Rainey nodded.

"Have you done that?"

Rainey chewed on her lower lip and moved her food tray away. "Have I confessed Jesus as Lord?"

Trey nodded. "And do you believe in your heart that God raised Him from the dead?"

Rainey swallowed hard. "I do believe that God raised Him from the dead." She squinted her eyes and stared at the light for a moment. "And I think I've confessed that Jesus is my Lord. I feel like I have."

Trey's lips curved into a smile that radiated from his eyes. He nodded. "You have. I've heard it. I've heard your testimony. You told me how you put your faith in Christ. But I wanted to see if you could remember on your own."

Tears coursed down Rainey's eyes. "I'm glad."

Trey reached out and wiped a tear from her face. Her eyes seemed to glow with renewed hope. It was like some of her joy had returned. "So am I."

"Can you remind me how I became a Christian?"

Trey relayed the story she'd shared with him on the yacht and refreshed her memory of the verses from 1 John they'd read the day before. Rainey listened rapturously, as if she was hearing the best story of all—the story of God working in her life.

"When did you become a Christian?" Rainey asked Trey after he finished answering all her questions about herself.

Trey sobered. A voice in the hallway saved him from having to answer. *Vince is here.* Trey glanced up and smiled at his co-worker.

"How's it going?" Vince greeted them both. "Resorting to hospital food, huh?" He glanced at Trey's empty plate.

"It's far better than starvation." Trey rose to his feet. He placed a hand on Rainey's feet beneath the blankets. "We'll talk more tomorrow."

Rainey nodded. "Thank you."

***

Trey walked across the street to the hotel with a heavy heart. Rainey's question plagued him. He was almost glad for Vince's interruption. How could he explain to this woman who barely understood her own relationship with God that he wasn't a Christian; that until he'd played the part of Matthew Westerly, the idea had never crossed his mind. "I've done too many bad things." Trey pushed the elevator button and waited patiently. An elderly couple stepped off the elevator when the doors opened and Trey stepped on.

As tired as he'd been the night before, Trey wasn't nearly as tired tonight. Part of him wished he could have just stayed. *If it wasn't for that question.*

A nice hot shower and clean sheets calmed his troubled spirit and Trey found himself asleep before he could put many more coherent thoughts together.

160

***

Rainey watched Trey walk away with mixed emotions. She knew he needed rest. It was obvious that he felt better after a good night's sleep. But she missed the security of his presence. Although she couldn't remember him, there was something safe and familiar about Trey that she liked.

Vince was nice. He felt more like a security guard than her friend. But Rainey knew that for whatever reason, Trey didn't want her left alone.

Reclining her head back on the pillow, Rainey tried to pull something about her life from her memory bank. Vague snippets of things would pop in her mind if she relaxed and let herself daydream, but Rainey wasn't sure if those were real memories or just stories her mind was making up.

She saw a little girl sitting on the beach. The girl dug a hole in the sand and found a large, smooth piece of colored glass. She held it up to the light and reveled in the translucent color.

"It's called sea glass." A tall, slender woman with long brown hair told her. "Let's see if you can find more. We can put it in a jar on your dresser."

Rainey could see the little girl digging all around, looking for these precious stones called sea glass. Every once in a while she'd squeal with delight and hold up another piece of colored glass. "Look at this one, Mom!"

Rainey opened her eyes. *Is that my mom?* She tried to picture the woman in her mind but the whole memory seemed so foggy. *I'll ask Trey. Maybe he knows what she looks like.* It seemed odd to need someone else to tell you what your own mother looked like. *Where is my mom? He said they were trying to get ahold of her.* Rainey tried not to let the absence of family make her feel alone. *Trey said I'm a Christian.* Rainey smiled at the thought. It felt good to know she was a child of God.

It was quieter without Trey. Vince brought his own reading material and seemed content to entertain himself. Rainey knew she needed the sleep. She wanted to make sure she was rested so that she would be awake when Trey came back.

161

Chapter 15

Trey woke up earlier the next morning than he had the day before. He hurried and grabbed a muffin, orange juice, and a cup of coffee from the hotel café. He texted Vince to let him know he was on his way.

"Up before noon this time… good job, lol," Vince texted back.

Trey crossed the street and caught the tail end of a conversation Rainey was having with Vince about whether he was a Christian.

"I got saved when I was about twelve." Vince leaned forward in his seat and spoke with enthusiasm. "I know I should get back in church. I just got so busy." He shook his head.

"Too busy for God?" Rainey asked innocently.

"Sounds pretty bad, doesn't it?" Vince glanced up when he saw Trey enter the room. "I know it's a bad excuse. I need God in my life again." His eyes misted.

Trey was surprised by Vince's transparency.

"My dad is a Baptist preacher," Vince confessed. "I ought to know better."

"Well it's never too late to get back on track." Rainey reached out and grabbed Vince's hand. "Last night, Trey was reading to me about the prodigal son and how when his father saw him coming back, he dropped everything and ran to his son, and even had a party for him."

Vince nodded. "Trey was reading that to you, huh?" he glanced over his shoulder at Trey and winked. "I didn't know you were a Christian."

Trey lowered his eyes. "That's not what she said." He cleared his throat. The memory of 1 John flashed through his mind. Trey was done lying about being a follower of Jesus Christ.

"You're not a Christian?" Vince wanted to clarify.

Trey felt Rainey's eyes on him. "No."

Vince stood up and placed a hand on his shoulder. "Well, you need to fix that."

Rainey was quiet and her eyes expressed emotion.

Trey felt suddenly awkward. "How did last night go?" He changed the subject.

"It was good." Vince shrugged. "I think I slept a few hours on this chair. But I'm ready to head to bed for real now." He gave Rainey a friendly handshake. "It has been a delight talking with you."

Rainey thanked him.

"And I'll see you both tonight." Vince gave a slight bow and walked from the room.

Trey sat down and found Rainey watching him closely. He could almost feel the question burning in her eyes. *I read her the Bible. I talked to her about Jesus. I talked about her own testimony. But I'm not a Christian.*

"I had something that felt like a memory last night." Rainey started in, surprising Trey that she wasn't going to push him about his lack of a personal relationship with God.

"What was it?"

Rainey relayed the story to him. "The little girl called the woman 'mom.' I wondered if that was my mom."

"I've never actually met your mom," Trey confessed. "But I can't imagine such a vivid image would not have been a memory. I mean, you did grow up near the ocean so it would make sense that you would hunt sea glass."

"The sea glass felt so real—like there really was a little jar filled with different colors of smooth glass. I can almost see it."

Trey watched her reflective expression.

"I feel like sea glass should be something I like." She smiled. "Doesn't that sound funny?"

"No. It makes sense. You're trying to piece yourself back together."

"It's like a puzzle. Except, I don't have a picture to know what it's going to look like."

Trey studied her lovely face and wondered at the feelings welling up inside him. "It's a beautiful puzzle."

Rainey's eyes twinkled. She cleared her throat. "I meant to ask you something last night." She chewed on her lip for a moment. "When you prayed, you thanked God that Rainey didn't drown." She glanced toward the door. "It felt like you were talking about me… but everyone calls me April." There was questioning in her eyes.

Trey realized his mistake. In his desire to protect Rainey from anyone searching for Rainey Meadows, he avoided the use of her real name and the hospital staff only knew her as April. Would it hurt her to know her real name or would that put her at risk? Would knowing why they'd given her a fictitious name add stress to her during this time of healing? He would talk to Dr. Hernandez about it later. Trey was done lying to Rainey, but wanted to expose her to the truth in stages she could handle. "April showers bring May flowers…" Trey recited the little poem. It was how he came up with the name April.

"So April is rainy..." She seemed to get it.

Trey wished he could just explain it. *She's been lied to way too many times.*

Rainey glanced at the Bible on the table beside her bed. "Are you ready to read to me?"

Trey was glad for the distraction. "Absolutely. Where should I start?"

"We still have a few more chapters from John to read." Rainey suggested they start where they'd left off.

Trey began reading from John 15. Rainey listened intently to each verse. He got to verse 13 when Tiffany walked in. "Greater love has no one than this, that one lay down his life for his friends."

Rainey noticed Tiffany before Trey did. He turned around and greeted his boss.

"I didn't realize I was late for Bible study." There was mischief in her eyes.

Trey stood up to introduce her to Rainey. "This is Tiffany."

Tiffany approached Rainey uncomfortably and shook her hand. "Hi." She sized the younger girl up with her eyes. "Um, Trey,

I have your card." She turned around to face her fellow agent and handed him his new identification card. "Don't lose it this time."

"Any news on my other one?" Trey realized this answer might require a walk down the hallway.

"No news at all." Tiffany shrugged. "Kind of hitting brick walls all over the place." Trey was noticeably disappointed. "Give me a call when you get back to the hotel tonight." She took a few steps backward toward the door.

"Will do." Trey watched his boss make her exit and slipped his new ID card into his pocket.

Rainey seemed to be waiting for an explanation but this fell under the same umbrella as why she had a fictitious name. He wasn't sure she should know about the FBI investigation and his stolen belongings. It could potentially open Pandora's box.

Dr. Hernandez arrived just as Trey was about to continue reading the Bible. "Are you ready for your MRI?" The older gentleman had a way of making an MRI sound like a trip to Disneyland.

Trey squeezed Rainey's hand and ensured her that he would be waiting for her. "You'll be alright."

***

Trey was almost asleep in the chair when they returned Rainey to her room. "How was it?" He sat up and blinked a few times in an attempt to wake up.

"It wasn't too bad." She leaned back on her pillow and took a sip of water. "Dr. Hernandez said he was going to review it and come talk to you about it in a little while.

Trey nodded. He took a few sips of the bitter coffee one of the nurses brought him earlier and tried to get past the fact that not only was it black but it was cold. "When we get home, I'm taking you to a nice little coffee shop where we can enjoy a couple of hot mocha drinks with plenty of milk and whipped cream."

"Tell me about home." Rainey closed her eyes.

"You love the outdoors," Trey began. "We used to hike together." Was it wrong to share these memories? They were so fresh in his mind. Trey wanted her to remember them. But would he ever be able to tell her the truth? How would he explain to her why

165

they'd taken those hikes together? It was part of his job. *She'll hate me all over again.* Trey gazed into her trusting eyes and thought about her reaction to him when she learned he was undercover. Was there any way to tell her without making her hate him? Why did it matter?

***

"The MRI is good," Dr. Hernandez stood by the scan and showed Trey the picture. "It shows that the swelling in her brain has reduced greatly." He pointed to the places on the MRI that indicated trauma. "Just a week ago this whole area showed significant swelling."

Trey couldn't read an MRI but trusted the doctor's diagnosis. "She's asking a lot of questions. When can I be honest with her about her name and what happened to her?"

The doctor took a moment to consider this question. "Soon. But I feel it is best to let her start figuring things out. Don't rush her. You haven't told me very much, but I've gathered by your level of protection that there is some real concern for her life. You mentioned attempted murder." Dr. Hernandez shook his head. "That could be very frightening. I'm not sure she is ready to know."

Trey nodded. *So the secrets must continue.* "When will she get her memory back?"

"It's hard to say. Most people do get their memories back in situations like this…" The doctor's words trailed off.

"But?"

The doctor shrugged. "There is always the risk that she won't."

Trey sent up a quick, silent prayer. "I can't imagine how terrible it would be to lose all your memories."

"Her situation is pretty severe." Dr. Hernandez sighed. "Some of it might be tied to the stress she was under at the time of the trauma."

Trey considered her situation at the time of her last accident. "Rainey was under a great deal of stress at the time."

Dr. Hernandez gathered the MRI images together and placed them in a large manila envelope. "Well, all the talking and praying and Bible reading you are doing with her is very healing. Don't stop." He patted Trey on the shoulder. "I honestly think Rainey will be ready to go home in four or five days." He stopped and pointed at Trey. "Provided you make sure she doesn't over do it at home."

"I'll baby her."

"I believe you will." The doctor nodded.

***

It was well after midnight and Rainey had been asleep for a while. Stretching his back in an attempt to return feeling to his legs, Trey glanced at his phone. *Why would Vince not answer his texts?* Trey got up and walked down the hallway. The nursing staff was always scant at night. Trey phoned Tiffany and asked her if she'd heard from Vince.

"Not since earlier today. He assisted us this afternoon with the computer files we uncovered on Enrique's yacht. Maybe he fell asleep in his hotel room."

Trey shrugged. "Well, I think I'll just pull up a chair next to her bed and use her mattress as my pillow."

"She should be fine you know."

"It's not worth the risk. Not with Dylan still out there." Trey walked back to Rainey's room.

It was in the early morning hours before Trey was finally able to sleep. Every sound in the hospital seemed to wake him up.

Rainey woke up before Trey did. His head was on the mattress while his body was contorted quite uncomfortably on the hospital room chair. He sensed her motion and blinked a few times.

"Good morning." Rainey said sympathetically.

Trey moaned. "Hey." He sat up and tried to work the kinks out of his neck.

"Did Vince not show up at all last night?"

"No."

"Are you okay?" Rainey watched Trey walk around the room a few times to get the blood circulating in his legs.

"I will be. At least I've had two nights of good sleep under my belt." He grinned.

"Good morning." Dr. Hernandez knocked on the doorjamb and stepped inside. "Did you sleep here again last night?"

Trey shrugged. "My night shift didn't show up."

167

Dr. Hernandez glanced over her chart. "It looks like you slept through the night." He smiled at Rainey. "No painkillers. That's good."

Rainey nodded. "I haven't had a headache in a few days."

The doctor asked her a few questions about her memory and how she was feeling. Trey looked like he was about to fall asleep in the chair again. "Why don't you go get something to eat and maybe a glass of orange juice," he suggested.

Trey nodded. He felt comfortable leaving for a few minutes now that Dr. Hernandez was back. "Would you care if I ran across the street and took a quick shower?"

"Not at all. I'll keep an eye on her." Dr. Hernandez walked to the door. "I'm on this floor all morning."

Trey watched the doctor walk across the hall. "Will you be okay?" He reached for her hand and sat at the edge of the bed.

"Of course I will." She smoothed an unruly hair away from his face. "You look so tired."

The feeling of her hand on his face stirred up feelings in his heart. He swallowed. "I don't like being away from you."

"You're so sweet." She gazed in his eyes for a few minutes. "Did I..." she stopped herself and stifled a laugh.

"What?"

Rainey blushed. "It's a strange question."

"I can handle strange questions. But I might give you a strange answer." Trey replied playfully.

Rainey let out a sigh. She looked as if she was afraid to ask. "Did I ever kiss you?"

The question caught Trey off guard. He lowered his eyes and pictured her lips on his. The memory made him smile. "Yes."

"I thought so." Rainey tucked a hair behind her ear.

"Did you have a memory?"

Rainey shrugged. "I wasn't sure if it was a memory or a dream."

Trey held her hand tighter. "For me, it's both."

***

Rainey watched Trey slip out the door with the feeling of his hand still on hers. She closed her eyes and remembered her dream.

168

They were on the beach. She could picture his face and the feelings in her heart. *Was I in love with him?* It was a strange thought. No… not him. Rainey couldn't place it. For some reason her memory of Trey's kiss felt more like a story than the image of her mother and the sea glass. Why was that?

One of the nurses brought Rainey her breakfast and tidied up the room. She was a different nurse than Rainey was used to. She introduced herself and told Rainey she'd just returned from maternity leave.

"I had a little girl." She pulled out her smart phone and showed Rainey pictures. "Her name is Gloria after my mother."

Rainey glanced at the photo of the lovely Latina baby. "My mother thought I should name her Maria, after myself." The young nurse chatted on. "But I thought that would be confusing. If my husband calls for Maria I wouldn't know who he is talking to."

It was entertaining if nothing else and Rainey was glad for the distraction. The room didn't feel as lonely while this woman was talking.

***

Dylan watched Trey cross the street to his hotel. *It's about time.* He shook his head. *Does that man ever leave Rainey alone?* He straightened his tie and glanced in the rear view mirror at himself.

Once he was sure Trey was in the hotel lobby, Dylan stepped from his car and walked to the entrance to the hospital. Rainey's room number was still fresh in his memory as he pushed the elevator button to her floor.

"I'm here to see April Netherland." Dylan approached the nurse's station with a look of genuine concern on his face.

Maria glanced up from her computer where she'd just added her baby to the screen saver. "Are you family?" She'd been instructed to ask.

A smile crossed Dylan's lips. "I'm her husband." Dylan showed the nurse Trey's identification card.

"Oh." Maria's eyes lit up. "Oh, of course. She is in room 203."

Dylan thanked her and began walking toward the room.

"May I help you?" Footsteps approaching from behind him caught Dylan off guard.

"I am on my way to meet with April Netherland."

Dr. Hernandez sized Dylan up curiously. "How do you know Ms. Netherland?"

"This is her husband." Maria approached from behind and placed a hand on Dylan's shoulder.

The doctor did not look convinced. "Gracias Maria." He dismissed the nurse but held Dylan's eyes. "I was not made aware of a husband."

Dylan pulled out Trey's identification card and quickly showed it to the doctor. "I'm Trey Netherland."

Dr. Hernandez shook his head. "You are not Trey Netherland."

Dylan slipped the identification card back into Trey's wallet and put it in his pocket. "Perhaps you and I should talk."

The doctor glanced down the hallway. He did not wish to have this conversation publically. "Come to my office."

Dylan followed the doctor, keeping his eyes opened for other hospital staff. He'd not anticipated an informed doctor.

Dr. Hernandez walked the imposter to the end of the hallway and opened his door. Dylan followed him inside and the doctor motioned for him to take a seat. "Would you care to tell me the nature of your visit and why you are claiming to be Trey Netherland?"

Dylan opted not to sit and quickly weighed his options. "This is truly unfortunate." Dylan pulled gun with a silencer from his suit pocket and shot Dr. Hernandez before the man could react. "I really didn't want to have to kill you." Dylan stood over the doctor's body. Convinced that he was dead, Dylan searched Dr. Hernandez's pockets for his keys.

Sounds from outside the office startled him for a moment. Dylan waited, listening for any movement outside. As quickly as he'd entered, Dylan opened the door and slipped out, locking the door behind him.

It was still early, but more nurses began arriving in the halls. Dylan hurried past them with his head bent low and found his way to room 203. He glanced inside and saw Rainey with her face toward the window.

"April." He spoke softly, almost tenderly.

She turned to look at him but her face showed no recognition.

"It's me, darling." Dylan hurried to her side and grabbed her hand. "You're alive! You're really alive!"

Rainey let him clutch her hand but it was clear she was not comfortable with this display of affection. "Do I know you?"

Dylan did his best to force tears to his eyes. "It's true then. They told me but I didn't want to believe it."

Rainey pulled her hand away slowly.

"Darling, I'm your husband."

***

Rainey wasn't sure what to think. The man sitting on the edge of her bed showed her his identification card with the name Trey Netherland. Netherland was the name on her chart. Could this really be her husband? But what about the other man named Trey? What was his last name? She wasn't sure she'd been told.

"I... I don't understand."

"I don't expect you to." Dylan looked around the room for Rainey's clothes. "Darling, you've been discharged today. I have a car waiting outside. Perhaps when you get home things will look familiar."

Maria knocked on the door and smiled at the couple. "I'm sure you're happy to see your husband." She gushed pleasantly. "I didn't mean to interrupt. I just needed to see if April needed anything for pain this morning.

Rainey shook her head. "No. I'm fine." *The nurse knows about my husband? Why didn't Trey ever tell me?*

"Alright. Well... I will leave you two alone." She stepped out and closed the door.

Rainey's eyes darted from the door to Dylan and she furrowed her eyebrows. "Dr. Hernandez didn't tell me I would be leaving today—and what about the other man named Trey? I don't understand."

Dylan pulled back her blankets. "April, don't do this to me. Please get dressed." He handed her a skirt from the bag and a white blouse. "The doctor wanted to surprise you. We hoped the surprise

171

might pull you from your amnesia. Sometimes shock works that way."

"Do we have children?"

Dylan laughed. "Now that would really shock you, wouldn't it?" he laughed. "No. We haven't started a family yet." He held up the skirt. "Now get dressed."

Rainey rose gingerly from the bed and carried the clothes to the bathroom. Even if this was her husband, she didn't know him.

She stepped out of the bathroom in her skirt and blouse. Dylan's eyes drank in her figure. "I missed you." He pulled her into his arms and kissed her forehead. "I will explain more later. But we must hurry. Our car is waiting outside."

Dylan clutched her hand and practically dragged Rainey out the door and down the hall. She glanced around nervously, wondering if she would see the other Trey. Why was this man rushing her so? Should she say goodbye to the doctor? She felt suddenly afraid.

They hurried onto the elevator and Dylan kept his head low.

"I feel like I should talk to the doctor first. Did he give you any directions for me?"

"Of course. I talked to him this morning." Dylan led her from the elevator and directly to his car.

Rainey felt herself ushered into the passenger seat and glanced over while this man climbed in beside her. There was no sense of familiarity. Wouldn't her doctor have reintroduced them? "I'm not comfortable with this. I'm sorry." She reached for the door but Dylan grabbed her hand.

"It's not a choice you have, dear." Dylan backed up the car and pulled away quickly. "I'm your husband and in this country, wives respect their husbands."

Rainey put on her seatbelt and glanced over her shoulder at the disappearing hospital, while a vision of a very different Trey lingered in her mind.

Chapter 16

Trey didn't mean to be gone so long. After the long hot shower, he'd only meant to lie down for a few minutes. He realized he'd been away from the hospital for a couple hours. He put on a fresh pair of shorts and a clean t-shirt and walked across the street, hoping Rainey wasn't worried.

It seemed strange to Trey that there would be commotion when he got off the elevator. The second floor was usually such a peaceful place. The sudden realization that there were police officers at the nurse's station caused alarm. Trey hurried his steps past the officers toward Rainey's room. Was she okay? *Dear God, is Rainey safe?* The room was empty.

"That's him! That's the man!" Maria yelled from down the hall. "He's in her room!"

Trey turned around to see two armed officers hastening toward him.

"Hold it right there!" Trey started to reach for his FBI identification but the officer ordered him to put his hands in the air.

Trey obeyed. "Where is she?" He was more concerned with locating Rainey than why these men were shoving him into a wall. "Where is Rainey?"

One of the officers pulled Trey's ID out of his pocket. "It's him." He handed the card to Maria. "Is this the man?"

"Yes! He showed me the very same picture just a couple hours ago." Maria took a few steps back and glared at him hatefully.

"Trey Netherland. You're under arrest for attempted murder and kidnapping."

Trey shook his head. "You've made a mistake! I'm FBI. I'm here to protect Rainey. Where is she?" He pulled himself free of the hands that tried to cuff him. "I'm FBI!" One of the other officers knocked him to the floor with a metal rod. Trey attempted to resist but found a gun pointed at him from a third officer. Before he knew it, metal cuffs were placed around his wrists and he was being yanked from the floor. "Ask Dr. Hernandez... he can tell you. He knows me... Ask one of the other nurses..." Trey found himself being ushered down the hospital corridor while a million questions ran through his mind.

***

"Why did you try to kill Dr. Hernandez?" A Colombian police officer stood over Trey in the poorly lit interrogation room.

Trey was handcuffed to a table and sat on a cold metal chair. He still ached from being thrown to the floor and struck with a metal rod in the hospital and his mind whirled with questions that no one was answering for him.

"Why have you arrested me? I didn't try to kill anyone. Dr. Hernandez encouraged me to return to my hotel at seven a.m. I walked across the street to take a shower and took a quick nap. Please tell me what happened to Rainey Meadows. She was registered as April Netherland. Her life could be in danger."

"Your life could be in danger if Dr. Hernandez dies." The officer slapped the table.

"I never did anything to Dr. Hernandez. I don't know what you're talking about."

The policeman shook his head and walked about the room in frustration. "We have it on video. You've been identified by witnesses. You and Dr. Hernandez walked into his office at seven-twenty. You shot him. Then you kidnapped Ms. Netherland—or whoever she was, claiming she was your wife."

Trey shook his head. "You're wrong! I'm an FBI officer! Call my superior!"

The Colombian officer placed both of his hands on the table and leaned so close to Trey that he could feel the man's breath. "This is not the United States of America. You might have full immunity in your country to kill whomever you please, but in Colombia, you die for that."

"I didn't try to kill anyone!"

The officer slapped Trey hard across the face with the backside of his hand. "We also don't have the same laws about how we treat common criminals."

Trey wiped the blood from his lip with a trembling hand. In the pandemonium of his arrest, he still hadn't processed what might have happened to Rainey. She was missing. They thought a man posing as her husband kidnapped her. Trey Netherland. *I'm Trey Netherland.* Trey closed is eyes. *But Dylan has an identification card with my name on it.* Trey racked his brain for how such a mistake had been made. "Listen, was the man in the pictures a blonde man with blue eyes? I know who it was…" Trey tried to steady his voice. "The man you're looking for goes by the name of Dylan, he also goes by Marcus Rauch. Both of those names are aliases. Talk to my boss. Her name is Tiffany Waterford. We've been searching for Dylan for almost two weeks."

"Enough!" The Colombian officer slapped the table. He walked to the door and ordered that Trey be placed in a cell.

***

As uncomfortable as it had been sleeping on the hospital room chair, there was nothing worse than the hard, dirty mattress in the Colombian jail. At least in the hospital he was with Rainey. Where was Rainey?

Trey's body ached with discomfort and his stomach growled with hunger. Without his phone, Trey had no concept of time, but he was sure it was at least midnight.

He'd tried to sleep a little, but his mind was filled with thoughts of Rainey. Where was she? Was she frightened? Had Dylan killed her? Where was Tiffany? Why was he still in jail?

Trey got up and paced the dark cell for the hundredth time. The unknown was worse than anything.

Trey was no stranger to the fact that countries such as Colombia had very different laws from the United States when it came to crime. Surely it could easily be proven that he was nowhere near Dr. Hernandez when the man was shot. The doctor would know it wasn't Trey. Was the doctor going to live?

Hours passed. Trey's mind reeled. He felt like he was going to go crazy being trapped in a cell while Rainey was somewhere out there with no idea who she was.

Oh God, Trey dropped to his knees in the dark, dirty cell. *God, please help her!* His nerve-wracked emotions overtook him and Trey began to shake with tear-filled sobs. *Please protect her God. Please don't let that man hurt her.*

***

Trey sat on his bunk with his back to the wall, sick with emotion and hopelessness. If he'd ever felt like he was going to lose his mind, Trey was convinced it was now. Footsteps in the corridor echoed against the concrete walls. A few cat calls and course words followed. Escorted by a Colombian guard, Tiffany was stopped outside of Trey's cell and waited while they unlocked it for her entry.

"Trey." She stepped inside and held both of her hands on her face. She didn't look like the triumphant boss who just put the Colombian police in their place by telling them what a mistake they'd made. This was the look of genuine concern.

"What happened?" Trey didn't even have the energy to stand up.

Tiffany sat beside him and glanced through the bars at the guard. "They've drawn up charges against you. Evidently the nurse who was on duty saw a man fitting your description, carrying your identification card, claiming to be April Netherland's husband. She saw him walk with Dr. Hernandez to his office and return a few minutes later alone. She saw the man with Rainey in room 203 and left them alone. Fifteen minutes later you were both gone and no one could find Dr. Hernandez. He was found thirty minutes later locked in his office. He'd been shot. He is still in critical condition."

Trey shook his head. "It was the perfect crime."

"There is no perfect crime, Trey. We know who did it."

"But how did he make himself look like me?" Trey was almost too tired to think.

"He must have colored his hair. You're both built the same."

176

Trey looked up. "But he has tattoos."

Tiffany raised her eyebrows. This was new information to her. "Where?"

"One is on his arm. The other is on the back of his neck. It's a seagull." Trey leaned his head against the wall. "It's too late for Rainey isn't it? He's probably killed her by now." Trey's eyes filled with tears.

Tiffany placed a hand on Trey's arm. "We don't know that."

"He was going to kill her before. Why not now?" Trey covered his face with one of his hands.

"Let's concentrate on getting you out of here. Then we'll work on finding Rainey."

Trey's head shot up. "No! Find Rainey. I'm fine!"

"You're in a Colombian prison. That's not fine." Tiffany glanced at the guard. "I've only got a few more minutes. They're convinced it's you. The tattoo might help. Have you got anything else?"

Trey thought for a moment. "Dylan has blue eyes. Not as blue as Rainey's. Hers were blue—the most beautiful blue I've ever seen."

"Stop it!" Tiffany ordered him. "Trey, we don't know that she's dead. Snap out of this. If she is alive, she needs you to help find her. Let's get you out of here before the Colombians trump up worse charges and keep you under lock and key the rest of your life," she whispered. "They seem to be reveling in the fact that you're an FBI agent. I think they've watched too many American cop shows and have this idea that you're some corrupt rogue agent whose been getting away with murder back home and will finally come to judgment in Colombia of all places."

Trey shook his head. "Why did I go back to my hotel?"

"If you hadn't you might be dead right now. Dylan still has your gun remember?"

Trey blew out a heavy sigh. "Have you found Vince?"

Tiffany shook her head slowly. "No. We haven't found him. It doesn't make sense."

"Unless Dylan got to him first."

"But where is he? We'd at least find a body if Dylan killed him."

"Times up!" The guard called to Tiffany.

She reached into her purse and pulled out a package of mints. "I know it's not much, but at least it's sugar." She clasped his hand. "I'm not going to stop until we get you out of here."

Trey nodded in spite of the hopelessness he felt.

"And we are looking for Rainey. We'll find her."

***

Rainey woke to the sound of birds chirping outside her window. She opened her eyes in the strange new environment. The feeling of someone beside her on the bed startled Rainey. She'd gone to bed early the night before and no one was beside her then. She glanced over and saw the strange man claiming to be her husband, sleeping on the other side of the bed. Slipping from beneath the sheets, Rainey hurried to grab the skirt and shirt she'd worn the day before.

When they arrived at the place her husband called 'home sweet home,' none of it looked familiar. Their house was a large bungalow behind an even larger estate on several acres of land along the ocean. She remembered hearing him say they lived in Santa Marta, and that he worked for the man who owned the mansion.

The inside of the bungalow was decorated with expensive, high quality furniture. Her dresser contained several articles of clothing that her husband said were her clothes. None of them looked familiar and none of them felt like her style.

She grabbed a fresh pair of underclothes from the dresser and hurried to the bathroom to take a shower, careful to lock the door behind her.

Dylan was awake when she stepped from the bathroom. She smoothed the wrinkles from her skirt and brushed her long hair with the brush she found on the dresser.

"Why are you wearing that skirt again? I thought you'd be happy to wear one of the outfits you haven't seen for a while."

Rainey lowered her eyes. How could she explain that they didn't feel like her style anymore? "I guess right now I just want the familiar."

"Well, perhaps your wedding ring will feel familiar." Dylan rose from the bed and pulled a diamond ring from the top drawer of his dresser.

He was wearing a pair of shorts but no shirt and Rainey felt suddenly embarrassed. She noticed his tattooed arm and the strength of his chest. He approached with the ring and slipped it on her left finger. It was slightly loose.

"You must have lost some weight in the hospital."

Rainey's eyes took in the lovely cut of the large diamond. The ring was stunning but it didn't feel like hers.

Dylan pulled her into his arms and pressed his lips against hers. Rainey pulled herself away and stepped back.

"What's the matter?" Dylan's eyes flashed. "I'm your husband."

Rainey twisted the ring around her finger nervously. "I… I don't remember you, Trey." It felt strange calling this man Trey. Where was her friend, Trey? "Please be patient with me."

"But maybe my kisses will help you remember." Dylan took a step closer to her, but Rainey recoiled.

Dylan was obviously frustrated. He shot her a look of disappointment. "This is not the reception I expected from my wife."

Rainey's eyes moistened with tears. "I'm sorry. I just don't remember you. I don't remember this place. I don't remember anything." She held her face to her hands.

Dylan placed his hands on her shoulders to comfort her, but the closeness of this shirtless man made her uncomfortable.

"Where were you while I was in the hospital? I asked Trey…" she lowered her eyes. "The other man, Trey, if I had any family. He never mentioned you."

Dylan released his touch and let out a sigh. He walked to his side of the bed and pulled a t-shirt over his head. "Alright. I didn't want to have to tell you. I thought maybe the amnesia could be a fresh start for us—maybe we could move forward in our marriage and forget the past."

Rainey sat on the edge of the bed and watched Dylan pace the room.

"You were having an affair." Dylan sat on the other side of the bed and looked into his hands. "That man, who called himself 'Trey' at the hospital… it was him. But his name isn't Trey. He's Matthew. Your boyfriend."

Matthew? Rainey remembered him calling himself Matthew when she first met him. Did he fabricate the Trey story to try to win

179

her heart? Rainey felt sick with the thought that she was having an affair. *What kind of terrible woman am I?*

"You left me a couple months ago. I didn't even know you'd been hurt until a few days ago. I arranged to take you from the hospital quickly to avoid any confrontation with Matthew. He doesn't know I have you." Dylan turned to Rainey and reached across the bed for her hand. "I wanted this chance to win your heart again."

Rainey shivered. Had she really been so fooled by this man in the hospital? An affair? She shook her head with shame. *Matthew confessed that he was not a Christian, but what about me? What kind of Christian woman am I if I was having an affair?* It was all too terrible to think about. Rainey leaned over on her pillow and let her tears fall.

***

"They sprouted!" Margaret hurried into the kitchen and found Bradley enjoying a cup of coffee. "The poppies! They sprouted!" She handed him a small pot with two fragile leaves sticking out. "They're so delicate." She stared at them. "You know what this means?"

"Your hybrids are not infertile! We will be able to propagate them." A smile spread across Bradley's face as he held the little pot in his hand. "Poppies producing the highest levels of morphine and cocaine that's ever been seen. You will go down in history!" Bradley set the plant down, scooped Margaret up in his arms and twirled her around their kitchen. "We've got to tell Nash. He'd better offer us a good deal."

Margaret picked up her plant and held it to the light. "It's a dream come true! None of my other hybrids would reproduce. It's almost overwhelming." She motioned for Bradley to follow her to the greenhouse.

Once inside, Margaret pointed to the hundreds of little poppy sprouts all over the room. Her face glowed rapturously. "A room full of baby plants." She let her eyes travel from pot to pot. "My own little contribution to the evolutionary process. Can you feel it? Can you feel the karma?"

180

Bradley chuckled and ran to his tall, slender partner. "I can feel your karma." He kissed her lips and let out an excited whoop. "This means millions—no billions of dollars! We can retire wherever we want. We can own a greenhouse ten times this size."

"We can buy an island." Margaret let herself dream with him.

"I still have the picture of that island you showed me ten years ago." He took her hands and danced around the greenhouse with her. "When do you think we should show Nash?"

"Let's give the plants at least a week to really take off."

Bradley's face beamed. "I can hardly wait a week."

"I know. But right now they look like little green sprouts. In a week they will be taller and show the distinct slender stem of a young poppy. If we're going to request numbers in the billions we'd better have something solid to show for it."

***

Rainey found a quiet place to sit and read in the garden behind their bungalow. She still had very little energy and after her emotional talk with Dylan, she didn't feel like sitting in the strange house with her husband. Dylan wanted to show her affection. He wanted to hold her hand and kiss her, but she'd made it very clear that she needed time. Rainey hoped he would understand. If they indeed were separated before her accident, he would have already experienced an absence in physical intimacy with her. Surely he could be patient as they worked to get to know one another again.

Rainey couldn't come to grips with the story he'd shared with her. An affair. It seemed like a terrible nightmare. She closed her eyes and recalled the dream she'd had about Trey… or Matthew… just a couple nights ago. They were standing on the beach watching the sun set along the coast and he kissed her… very gently. It was such a beautiful, innocent kiss. But now she knew it couldn't have been beautiful or innocent. It was the kiss of an adulteress woman.

Dylan had no idea the impact his story would have on Rainey. Any joy she might have felt at finding her true identity was turned bitter by the reality of who she really was.

Great tears coursed down her face. She was torn between the friendship she'd developed with the man she knew as Trey and the total absence of feelings for this man she now learned was her husband. Part of her wanted to talk to Trey. To ask him why he lied to her. Why did he read the Bible to her every day and talk to her about God if they were both living in sin? What kind of terrible, deceptive person was he? *What kind of terrible deceptive person am I?*

Rainey buried her face in her hands. *God, please forgive me. I'm so sorry! Please wash me white as snow.*

***

"Get up. We're moving you." Trey heard the voice before it registered. He'd finally drifted off into a fitful sleep and now he was being woken up.

Trey pulled himself from the bunk and walked to the door. Was Tiffany here? Had she gotten him released? "Where are we going?"

"They're moving you to a maximum security prison." The guard motioned to Trey with a gun.

"Did Dr. Hernandez die?" Trey didn't understand.

"Don't ask questions." The guard shoved Trey with the gun.

Strange faces watched him as he walked past. Rude comments and sneers echoed down the halls. Trey was ushered into another room where one of the officers who'd interviewed him the day before handed the guard a paper and waved them on.

"Wait." Trey stopped and turned to the man behind the counter. "Where is Tiffany? Where are my things?"

"You don't get any 'things' in a maximum security prison." The officer hissed. "Get him out of here."

In less than ten minutes, Trey found himself on a bus with bars on the windows headed away from Cartagena and deeper into the heart of Colombia.

Chapter 17

"We've been invited to have dinner with my boss tonight." Dylan found Rainey sitting beside the pool, still wearing her skirt, but with her toes dangling in the water.

Rainey looked up and forced a smile. "What should I wear?"

"You have many lovely outfits. Have you looked through them?"

Rainey nodded. She had. Nothing in her wardrobe felt like her. This skirt felt like her. "Are those all the clothes I have?"

Dylan blew out a frustrated sigh. "Actually no. You took all your favorite clothes with you when you ran off with Matthew."

"I see." Rainey lowered her eyes repentantly. *Then I deserve to wear what I have.* "I'm sorry. I will find something."

Dylan sat beside her and took off his flip-flops so that he could dangle his feet in the water with her. "We used to do this in college you know."

"We did?" It was the first time Dylan mentioned something from their past that wasn't about her affair. "Where did we go to school?"

Dylan glanced at the water glistening on the pool. "Hawaii." He turned to her with a winning smile. "We met there."

"Really? I can't even picture Hawaii in my mind." She closed her eyes to see if she could pull out the memory.

"You were a design major. You've always been artistic." Dylan continued. "And we loved to surf together."

"Surfing..." with her eyes still closed the word surfing did something in her mind.

"Can you see it?" Dylan was cautious.

"See what?"

Dylan let out a breath. "The waves. I wondered if you could see the waves." He pulled himself from the pool and massaged her shoulders. "Listen, maybe tomorrow we can go out shopping and find you some clothes you like."

Rainey hated to admit it but that idea made her feel better. Everything in her drawers seemed so provocative. She wasn't sure she could explain it. Dark colors, low necklines, and very short shorts. The idea of wearing any of those clothes almost embarrassed her. *Am I really so fashion conscious that I can't be versatile? I must have liked those clothes at one time or I wouldn't have bought them.*

"For tonight, just wear your artsy flowy skirt. I don't care."

***

Dinner in the mansion was a bit intimidating and felt sudden. How was she supposed to suddenly walk back into her old life and feel normal?

Nash McCarness met Dylan and Rainey at the door and welcomed them inside. "April, it's so good to have you back." The man reached to shake her hand and used his other hand to pat her back.

Nash was a handsome, middle-aged man with light hair, blue eyes and a distinct square jaw. He wasn't much taller than Rainey, but his presence felt large. He motioned for them to follow him into the dining room where he said the chef was almost ready to serve them.

"One of the joys to living right behind my house—I can see when you're about to arrive." Nash laughed.

"How long have we lived here?" Rainey asked shyly. She felt foolish asking such questions, but she hoped Nash would understand.

"Oh, what would you say?" Nash glanced at Dylan. "A few years?"

"Two." Dylan nodded. "We moved here right out of college."

Nash agreed. "That's right." He turned to Rainey. "Would you care for some wine? I have a 1987 merlot that I thought you both might enjoy." He motioned for a servant.

"No, thank you." Rainey shook her head and held her hand over the glass when the servant approached with the bottle. "I'm still trying to gain my memory back. I don't want to do any thing that could hinder it." She chuckled nervously hoping she hadn't offended her husband's boss.

Dylan and Nash talked for a few minutes about a car that Nash recently acquired and hoped to rebuild. Rainey gathered from the conversation that Nash collected antique cars. Dylan seemed to understand all the technical car terms, but Rainey tuned it all out.

Her eyes roamed the large dining room. Four great windows took up one side of the wall and she could almost see their house behind the gardens. It impressed her how well kept the gardens were. Was her husband Nash's gardener?

The house itself was a bit too flashy for Rainey's taste. A large, gaudy chandelier hung over the glossy black dining room table and white, fabric chairs stood around the table, seeming to just tempt someone to spill something on them. She almost chuckled at the thought.

Underneath the table was a thick burgundy colored carpet. She was told to remove her shoes when they entered the house, so she could feel the carpet's plushness beneath her feet.

Nash's taste in décor seemed to run in the lines of Mediterranean Modern Extravagance if there was such a definition. The paintings on the walls were large and colorful. They depicted scenes of scantily clad dancing women and what looked like contemporary expressions of the ocean and the mountains. None of the paintings were clear enough to completely understand. It wasn't Rainey's taste in art.

She noticed a small cat staring at them from the entrance to the dining room, but it took a few minutes for her to know if it was real or not because it barely moved.

"So Charlemagne has finally graced us with his presence." Nash glanced in the direction of Rainey's eyes and nodded to the cat. "He is a remnant of my ex-girlfriend. I only keep him so that I can rub in the fact that he still lives in the house and she doesn't.

Rainey wasn't sure how to take Nash's humor.

"How was your first night home? I'm sure you two had much to catch up on." He gave Dylan an insinuating grin.

Dylan's expression communicated frustration. "I think April and I need some time to reconnect." His blue eyes flashed accusingly at Rainey.

Dylan's irritation was not lost on Rainey. The arrival of their meals was a welcome distraction. A soft-spoken Colombian woman served the meal and both Dylan and Nash began eating right away. Rainey remembered Trey's simple prayer before their meal together a few days ago. Was it real or was he just playing a game?

"This is amazing." Dylan took a bite of his prime rib. "I haven't had cooking this good in a while."

Nash began talking about the quality of this particular cut of meat and how much he'd paid per pound. He was sure very few locals could afford such premium cuts. Rainey found the conversation shallow and dull. She ate quietly and listened to their discussions while trying to figure out what she'd seen in her husband. *Surely there must be something. Why would I have married him?* She recognized that he was handsome. There was no doubt that his muscular chest, blue eyes and strong arms were attractive, but so far she'd not seen anything in his personality that attracted her to him.

As good as the food tasted, Rainey had still not regained her appetite and pushed her freshly steamed carrots around on the plate.

"I'm hoping to hit some waves this weekend." She heard Dylan say. "If April is up to it she can join me." He gave her a hopeful grin.

"Do I know how to surf?" It sounded like a crazy question.

"Like a pro—and I'm sure it's like riding a bike. You just get back on and it will all come back to you."

"Will Dr. Hernandez feel I am ready?" Rainey was almost certain he would say no, but she didn't want to start out the rebuilding of their marriage by turning her husband down on yet another thing. Her unwillingness to show him affection was obviously a sensitive subject for him and Rainey wasn't sure how he'd feel about her turning down something as simple as surfing.

"I'll give him a call." Dylan promised. "I was reading the surf report and there are supposed to be some killer waves next week."

Nash chuckled. "You can keep your waves, I'll stick with vintage automobiles."

186

What's my hobby? The thought popped in Rainey's mind. Hearing Nash talk about cars and her husband talk about surfing opened up a new kind of emptiness in her heart. *I don't know who I am…*

She grew suddenly weary and wanted to go back to their house. This was the longest she'd been awake in a while. She glanced at Dylan. "Would you be offended if I went home now? I'm so tired."

"That's fine." Dylan shrugged and took a long swig of his wine. "You hardly ate anything though."

"I still don't have my appetite."

Dylan rose to help his wife from her chair and reached to give her a kiss. Rainey avoided his lips and his kiss landed on her cheek. She turned to Nash and thanked him for the delicious dinner and slipped away, glad to escape the tiresome experience.

***

Nash watched Rainey walk across the gardens through the large dining room window and turned to Dylan. "She's gorgeous. I'll give you that." He grinned at the younger man. "But it's obvious that she's not in love with you."

Dylan crossed his arms. "It takes time. I'm a stranger to her."

"Was she that quiet when you knew her as a college student?"

"Not at all. She was cheerful and fun. We used to surf together, grab coffee, walk the beach." Dylan shook his head. "She was a little too much into the God stuff, but I could hang with it most of the time. I'd just let her ramble and give her an interested nod now and then."

"But she never fell for you, did she?"

Dylan picked a piece of meat out of his teeth. "Was she supposed to?"

Nash chuckled sarcastically. "No. That would have seriously hindered your mission."

"I did what I was supposed to do. She would have drowned if that FBI agent hadn't found her."

"But she didn't drown and now you're trying to convince her she is your wife. I can't help but wonder if she injured your pride somewhere—perhaps you wanted her to fall for you and she didn't."

Dylan rolled his eyes. "That's ridiculous."

"So why tell her she's your wife?"

Dylan narrowed his eyes. "You're the one that told me that since she survived her accident we would take advantage of it and hold her hostage in case her mother considered backing out of the deal. It's a lot easier to keep a willing hostage." Dylan remembered the conversation he'd had with Enrique. "It is far easier to control someone who trusts you than someone who does not." He repeated the other man's words exactly.

"But does she trust you?" Nash glanced at the window.

Dylan was getting defensive. "She will."

"I think you're trying to prove something. I think it bothers you that this FBI guy came along and won her heart while you couldn't even turn her head." Nash wore a grin.

"I will win her heart."

"To what end?"

Dylan stood up and threw his napkin on his plate. "You do realize, Dad," he said the name bitterly. "That if it wasn't for me, Enrique and his men might already have descended on your master gardeners and offered them a deal they couldn't resist. You also realize that if it weren't for me, you'd likely have the FBI knocking at your door. I don't need this!"

Nash laughed at the younger man's tantrum. "You've never liked it when you couldn't get what you wanted—even when you were a kid." Nash tapped his wine glass with his ring and watched his son pace the room. "I have a feeling that Rainey Meadows was more than just a 'job' to you. Am I right?"

Dylan's eyes flashed angrily. "You have no idea! I was her friend. I spent time with her. I taught her to surf. I bought her birthday presents. But she never noticed me. That FBI jerk comes along and suddenly she's floating around in a love bubble! What does that stiff-necked moron have that I don't?"

"Maybe he's a better actor." Nash finished his wine. "Do you care for her, son?"

Dylan crossed his arms and turned toward the window. "I saved her life on the beach and then I tried to kill her on the yacht."

He turned back around and stared at his father. "I don't know how I feel about her." He shook his head. "I think if she would have loved me everything would have been different."

***

It was obvious they had no idea Trey was fluent in Spanish. Trey woke up to a conversation centered on him. Prison initiation for the U.S. FBI agent would put him in his place. Trey heard the plan clearly. Every day he would be expected to fight with four inmates until he worked his way through all the prisoners. Pretending he was still asleep, Trey couldn't see the faces that went with the voices. Their conversation made it clear, some of these prisoners hated people from the U.S. worse than they hated the police.

"I give him two days," one of the voices said.

Another man chuckled and used some choice swear words to describe the condition Trey would be in after he was done with him.

"Wake him up," the man who Trey figured must be the leader ordered.

Trey took a few jabs to the shoulder and pretended to be roused from his sleep.

"Hey gringo, get up," one of the men said in broken English.

Trey opened his eyes and found a small group of men standing around him.

"Time to make friends."

A couple men laughed.

Trey did a quick visual assessment in attempt to gauge the attitudes of the various men. "I'm Trey," he said in his best Spanish. "But I assume you already know that."

The men gave one another curious glances.

The obvious leader approached with a dark, sinister glare and explained the rules of the game. "You start with Don Paul." He motioned to a large Latino man with tattoos covering his body, from his bald head to his ankles. "Then you will fight Cameron." A slim, fit young man stepped forward and smirked confidently at Trey. "And if you have energy for more, you will take on Roberto and Juan." He spit something out of his mouth onto the concrete floor. "Together."

Trey nodded. He understood. This initiation apparently had no rules. If he could survive he'd get to move on to the next day and the next round of prisoners. With this group of men it was best to show no fear and muster all the strength he had to survive.

"We fight outside." The leader motioned toward the door.

By listening to various conversations as they walked, Trey figured out that the leader's name was Rodriguez. He spoke very little, but he seemed to control everything.

Trey clenched and released his fists as he walked and tried to mentally psych himself up for his first match. He was hungry and tired, but he couldn't allow himself to think about it. He had to survive. This was for Rainey.

Stepping into the sunshine, Trey glanced up at the blue sky and thought about Rainey's eyes. He licked his dry lips and readied himself for battle.

The fight began at Rodriguez's call. Don Paul moved in like the giant going after the Israelites. Trey knew he was out-sized, but he hoped his quick movement and military training was enough to defeat this giant.

All the cheering went out to Don Paul, but Trey figured out after the first few punches that the big guy had little agility. Their fight lasted almost five minutes with Trey dodging swings and making swift, clean jabs. He finally gained the upper hand by jumping on the other man's back and putting his neck into a sleeper hold. With no way to breath, the giant fell and Trey stepped away the victor of his first fight.

Rodriguez watched Trey's moves and observed Trey's victory with little more than an amused sneer. He motioned to Cameron and the younger man made his entry.

Trey had Cameron beat for size, but Cameron was equally quick on his feet and hard with his punches. Trey found himself on the ground more than once and could not say the same for Cameron. He needed to change his moves. Cameron had studied him and knew what to expect. Pretending to be winded, Trey took the defensive and began swift, military moves on the confident young prisoner and finally took the upper hand.

This fight was active. Their combat took them all over the prison grounds and wore on both of their energy. Trey finally defeated Cameron by lying on the ground and giving one powerful unexpected kick that took the younger man over the edge and crashed him into the ground.

Trey thought he detected a few words of approval, but the response from Rodriguez redirected their allegiance. The leader gave Cameron a swift kick in the ribs and told him not to show himself again.

Roberto and Juan were the tag team brutes. Trey leaned over with his hands on his knees and tried to catch his breath before his next attack. Blood streamed from his lip and his ears were ringing. He was running low on steam but he had to survive this.

The thought of asking God for strength crossed his mind. *Why would You help me fight?* He spit blood from his mouth and closed his eyes for a moment. *When did You ever defend me? You helped Rainey... but where were You when I was a child?* Trey clenched his teeth and readied himself for the attack.

Both men moved toward him at the same time. Trey used both fists to strike them in their faces and the fight began.

Trey was too tired and weak for such an unfair match. In only minutes, both men had him on the ground and were taking turns sucker punching him. Trey could only bury his face and steady himself against the abuse.

Finally, Rodriguez called them off.

Trey lay on the floor with his back on the ground and his face to the sky wondering why he'd even tried.

"We will see you tomorrow." Rodriguez spat and the crowd walked away.

***

The bungalow was quiet when Rainey finally woke up. She wasn't sure how she'd slept so late. The sun was high in the sky and her husband was nowhere to be found. She quickly showered and dressed and made her way to the gardens. The variety of flowers and fauna was breathtaking. Rainey walked around, exploring the property, wondering if she used to walk around this same way before she lost her memory.

As she neared the boarder of the property, Rainey noticed darkly clad men with machine guns. It startled her at first. The men appeared to be guarding against intruders, not the residents. As she approached one of the men he greeted her. It wasn't exactly a friendly greeting, but it wasn't intimidating.

"Hello." She returned his greeting in Spanish.

"You sound like a Colombian." This time he smiled. "I'm Pedro."

"April." Rainey introduced herself. "Where is Trey?" She asked.

Pedro shook his head. "I am only a guard. I don't answer questions." He seemed apologetic.

Rainey shrugged. "Thank you anyway." She took a few steps toward the house and turned around. "Do you remember much about me? Before I lost my memory I mean?"

Pedro shook his head. "I am sorry, señora."

Rainey thanked him again and walked away. It was good to be outside, enjoying the fresh air, but Rainey never felt so alone. She was almost back to the bungalow when Dylan approached.

"You're finally awake." He greeted her and glanced at the skirt she wore for the third day in a row. "I promised you a shopping day, did I not?"

"I would love that." Rainey hoped her husband wasn't offended that she was being so picky about her clothes.

"I'll be ready to leave in about twenty minutes." Dylan glanced at his cell phone. "Does that suit you?"

"Yes." Rainey smiled to show her appreciation but her husband didn't show the same positive response. She wondered what was going through his mind. It would have to be difficult to bring an adulteress woman back into his life only to find that she was unwilling to show warmth toward him.

There was very little for her to do to get ready. Rainey wondered if she had a purse, but couldn't find one. After exploring the bungalow, Rainey found it strangely void of anything that might be unique to a woman. Apart from the clothes, which she didn't like, there was nothing that felt personal. *Where are our wedding pictures?* It all felt empty. Perhaps her husband got rid of her things when she left him. Maybe he destroyed the pictures. She might have wanted to do the same.

"April?" Dylan called from the door.

Rainey hurried from the bedroom and walked outside with him. "Did you bring my Bible home when you picked me up?" she

192

asked. "I haven't been able to find it."

"I thought it was in with your belongings. I'm sorry." Dylan opened the car door for her. "We can buy you a new one."

Rainey sat beside her husband and watched out the window to see if she recognized the scenery. Santa Marta was a lovely coastal town. Rainey realized there were several other nice sized villas tucked away along the ocean. As they neared town, Rainey noticed several shops and cafés. Dylan parked the car and suggested they take a walk.

"There's a nice art community here," Dylan explained. "Some of these shops are probably more in line with your style."

"Have I been here before?" Rainey asked.

Dylan nodded. "Many times." He walked beside her and reached for her hand. "At least you can hold my hand, right?"

With his hand wrapped in hers, Rainey could feel her diamond press against her finger. She glanced down and wondered if she had ever grown used to the feeling. They passed several small stores, a café, and a pawnshop.

"This is a fine shop." Dylan pointed to an expensive clothing store with several short, slinky skirts and tight fitting blouses on headless hot pink mannequins.

Without even going inside, Rainey instinctively knew it wasn't her kind of store. She shook her head and Dylan let out a frustrated sigh.

They walked along the stone lined street and Rainey found a unique clothing store that caught her eye. "Can we go in there?" She motioned to the store and Dylan shrugged. "Whatever you want."

It was the perfect store for Rainey. She found unique clothes that were both modest and stylish.

Dylan sat in a comfortable chair and read an English newspaper while Rainey shopped. He paid for her purchases and carried them to his car. Rainey would have enjoyed the shopping trip more if her shopping companion weren't being so aloof.

"Are you ready for lunch?" He glanced at his watch and told her it was after two thirty.

Rainey suggested a little bread shop she'd noticed earlier. "The sign said sandwiches and homemade bread."

Dylan was willing. For some reason he was more reserved than yesterday. Rainey wished she could ask him about it, but felt certain it had more to do with her affair than anything. How could they possibly heal in a marriage where she'd committed such a heinous act and had no memory of it?

They stepped into the bakery and Rainey reached for his hand, hoping she might encourage him. Dylan raised his eyebrows and tightened his hold.

"How can I help you?" A silver haired Colombian woman asked. She stopped for a moment and stared at Rainey for a few seconds. "Do I know you?"

Rainey's eyes grew wide. Finally here was someone who recognized her. "Yes. You probably do. I mean, maybe." She turned to her husband. "Would I know her?"

Dylan placed a hand on Rainey's shoulder and massaged it gently. "My wife is recovering from amnesia."

"Oh, my dear child. I am so sorry. I'm Rosa." She stepped from behind the counter. "I'm not sure I do know you. I actually believe you look like a younger version of a dear friend of mine." She reached her hands out in a very familiar way and touched Rainey's hands. "You're features are very lovely and unique." She smiled. "And those blue eyes are stunning."

Rainey appreciated the woman's warmth.

"We wanted to order a couple of sandwiches." Dylan pointed to the sign over the shelves of fresh baked bread. He didn't seem as impressed with Rosa's warmth as Rainey was. "I would like the ham and avocado on wheat."

Rosa was quick to prepare their meals. She chatted about the coming rain that they were forecasting. "We need the rain of course. But it's not good for tourism." She handed Dylan his sandwich and quickly took Rainey's order.

Rainey noticed that Rosa's eyes lingered on her several times as she made the sandwich and again as they sat at the small table just inside the bread shop. Rosa appeared to want to talk to her, but was obviously resisting. Perhaps she felt, as Rainey did, that Dylan did not welcome Rainey making friends with shopkeepers.

***

Trey leaned back on the hard prison bunk, dreaming of a beautiful place. He was with Rainey. She knew his name and they

194

were free. *Rainey... Where are you?* Trey rubbed his temples and massaged the bruise on his jaw. His head ached from today's initiation fights. He clenched his fists and tried not to let himself grow angry at the injustice. He'd been in the prison for almost a week. Every day started the same. They woke him up to fight and he spent the rest of the day recovering. Today he'd won all three fights. He wasn't sure how he did it. The two who fought together weren't in sync with one another. They seemed more interested in watching how Trey would defend himself against the other and it opened them up to defeat. Yesterday, he'd been caught off guard by his attackers and lost two of the three matches.

It was obvious that Rodriguez did not appreciate it when Trey won. The leader seemed to give an additional lashing to those who lost, but no one dared cross him.

As they usually did, the other inmates left him alone after the fights. They seemed to sense his need to recuperate.

Between the terrible food, uncomfortable bed, and the abuses he was suffering, Trey wasn't sure how long he'd be able to hold out at this prison. His body ached and he felt helpless to defend himself against this insane injustice. When would Tiffany get enough proof to get him out of this place?

During the afternoon, most of the inmates enjoyed the sunshine or played games together in the cafeteria. Trey had no desire to fraternize with these men. They were ruthless and with each passing day, his anger toward them mounted. *Maybe that's why I fought so well today.* Trey opened his eyes and stared at the cracked concrete ceiling.

It had been a long time since Trey felt this kind of anger. He knew it wasn't good for him. He'd spent years as a child trying to stuff this feeling. Now it was the anger that seemed to be keeping him alive.

What am I becoming? Trey turned his head and glanced through the bars at a couple other inmates in nearby cells. *I'm becoming like them.* Trey blew out a steadying breath. Each day Trey felt like he was sinking more and more. *It's only been a week... what will I become if they never let me go?*

"You know that eventually they will break you down." The voice of an elderly man spoke softly from beneath his bunk.

Trey didn't have enough energy to roll over to see who'd spoken to him.

"Rodriguez doesn't like you and he likes you even less because you win." The old man stood up and looked toward Trey's bunk.

"So what am I supposed to do? Lose?"

"No." The old man shook his head. "You die when you lose."

Trey eased himself into a sitting position so that he could better see the man behind the voice. He remembered hearing that this was David, one of the oldest men in the prison. "Then there truly is no hope." Trey's jaw tightened and he turned toward the cold stone wall.

David pointed up. "You will only win by His strength."

Trey cleared his throat. "God?" He almost laughed. "God doesn't help me."

"Only because you don't allow Him to."

Trey laid back down on his bunk and covered his head with the pillow.

"I know this." David pulled the pillow off of Trey. "Walk with me outside."

"I can't." Trey closed his eyes.

"You can. You must." David stared at Trey for a few minutes waiting for him to respond.

"Fine." Trey slipped from the bunk and followed the old man toward the outside doors where the prisoners were permitted to sit on picnic benches and enjoy a few minutes of sunshine.

It was the first time Trey really noticed David. The man looked to be in his mid sixties. His deep-set eyes were dark brown and his hair was almost white. There was something in his look that gave Trey the feeling that David was at peace with his life.

"Alright, you dragged me out here. What?"

"I was like you."

"When?"

"Many years ago, when I first came here." David sat down on the picnic bench and rested his forearms on his thighs.

"And what do you mean exactly?"

"I was angry and I tried to fight the fight by myself."

"You don't know what you're saying old man." Trey crossed his arms and sat beside David with enough space between them to block David out if he needed.

"I do. The initiation tradition has been going on for over thirty years. Rodriguez has only been the top man for about five years. He is the only one I have ever known to make the full round. He has fought every man in the prison. Many of them make it only as far as the fight with Rodriguez. Those who survive, live."

"That's insane."

"But it put him on top." David shook his head. "He kills who he wants to kill. I guarantee he will not give his position away. You intimidate him because you are good. If you lose you may die, but if you continue to win you may die. Your situation is hopeless apart from God."

"God?" Trey shook his head. "I already told you. God doesn't help me."

"Do you believe in God?" David's eyes shone with a softness Trey didn't see from any of the other men in the prison.

Trey thought about the verses he and Rainey studied together about nature declaring God's glory. "Of course I believe in God."

"That is good." The older man smiled. "There is a verse that says it is good that you believe in God, but even the demons believe and tremble." David leaned forward and steadied his eyes on Trey. "Just knowing God exists isn't enough."

"Look, I already know I'm not a Christian. I recognize that." Trey wasn't sure why he was wasting his time with this. "But I have my reasons."

"Trey," the man used his name for the first time. "God sent His Son to pay the price for your sins and all you have to do is accept that gift. What reasons would you have for turning that gift down?"

This conversation was getting frustrating. Trey shook his head and turned toward the prison wall where two security guards stood, armed with machine guns.

"You are angry with God. Am I right?" David continued.

Trey ignored the question.

"Something in your life hurt you. You're angry because you felt God should have helped you. He should have stopped the bad thing from happening…"

197

"Enough!" Trey slapped his hand on the table.

"I am right aren't I? I can see it."

"You know nothing." Trey got up and walked away.

Chapter 18

Rainey sat by the pool reading her new Bible. It was good for something in her life to feel familiar. She read from the book of John and remembered it. She'd read these verses just a couple weeks ago with Matthew. She had forced herself to start calling him Matthew in her mind. The memories of those days reading the Bible with Matthew in the hospital were bittersweet. She loved the hours he read to her from God's word. It was that which sustained her during those first days of not knowing who she was. But learning that Matthew was a man she had an affair with soiled the whole beautiful picture.

Once again Rainey bowed her head and asked for forgiveness for the sin she had no memory of committing. The guilt she felt consumed her some days, especially as she saw her husband pulling away from her more and more.

Why was she so resistant to his affection? His few attempts at kissing her over the past week did nothing to help the situation. He complained that she did not return the kiss. One morning he asked if he repulsed her.

"Does the feel of my lips on yours disgust you? My own wife won't kiss me!"

Rainey felt terrible. She tried to return the affection, but it was forced. She felt nothing for this stranger who was her husband. She asked him for time. "I want to please you, but I don't even know who I am. Please be patient with me."

At the mention of patience Dylan flew off the handle and left. He'd been gone since last night.

Rainey finished her Bible reading time with prayer and made herself a quick lunch of fruit and granola. She took a stroll in the garden and watched the sky with concern. Dark clouds moved quickly across the sky, absorbing what little blue sky there had been this morning. They'd had rain a couple days during the week, but people were saying that a big tropical storm was expected soon. Rainey hoped it wouldn't be too bad.

With little to do around the property but read and swim, Rainey had taken to weeding the garden the past couple days. She enjoyed the quiet and it gave her mind something to do. She was surprised that she actually knew the names of many of the flowers in Nash's garden. A row of Birds of Paradise ran just behind a grouping of smaller flowers that Rainey didn't recognize.

The sound of a car horn pulled Rainey from her work. She looked up to see her husband pull through the security gate with his surfboard on top of the car. Rainey began to walk toward his car. He must have done some early morning surfing. He parked closer to the main house so he didn't see Rainey approaching. From a distance she could see that he'd lightened his hair… he was blonde. She stopped when she saw him open the door for an attractive woman wearing surf shorts and a bikini top. The woman stepped out and wrapped her arms around his neck. She was laughing about something and he pulled her to himself in a very familiar way.

Rainey couldn't watch it. She turned around and hurried back to their bungalow with tears in her eyes.

***

"You work for me. You do not set your prices." Nash leaned back and crossed his arms. "I don't know what made you even think you could try to negotiate with me about the price."

Bradley leaned forward on the patio chair and pointed an angry finger at Nash. "Margaret has been working endlessly for years on this project. You know it is worth billions!" He waved his hand in the air. "And yet you insult us by telling us you'll be giving us a one hundred thousand dollar bonus?"

Nash rose from his chair. "Don't point your finger at me." He glared down at Bradley. "Margaret wouldn't have even had a place to work on her project if I didn't provide her with the greenhouse. I provide you with the lab and the equipment. I even pay for your home. You are my employees and Margaret's hybrid poppy is my investment."

Margaret didn't like the disharmony going on in her home. "Men, please. This doesn't have to be a yelling match. What can we accomplish with angry words?"

"That poppy is our plant. Not yours." Bradley challenged Nash. "And if you won't pay us what it's worth we will find someone who will!"

A sarcastic smirk crossed Nash's face and he calmly sat down and rested his arms on the mosaic tile table and shook his head. "Oh, Bradley, Bradley, Bradley." Each time he said the man's name it was punctuated by a condescending shake of the head. "You should know better than to make threats to me."

Bradley's jaw flinched. "I'm tired of being your hired hand."

"Well, that's what you are." Nash crossed his legs and reached for the glass of lemonade in front of him. "That's what both of you are." He glanced at Margaret but she gave no reaction. "I don't have partners in this business."

"Then we're done with you." Bradley stood up from his chair.

Nash didn't move. He took another long sip of his lemonade and glanced at Margaret for a moment. "Is this how you both feel?"

Margaret didn't like the conflict but she had dreams and as long as Nash controlled their every move, they weren't free to embrace them. "I stand behind Bradley."

Nash shook his head and moved to the edge of his seat as if he were about to stand. "Then I suppose you don't care what we do with Rainey." He glanced at Margaret knowingly.

"Rainey?" Margaret's face changed. "What are you talking about?"

Nash rose to his feet. "We have Rainey." He grinned. "And you have my plants. So, if you refuse to give me my plants, we will kill Rainey."

"No!" Margaret jumped to her feet. "You can't…"

Bradley grabbed his wife's arm and attempted to stop her from making any deals with Nash. "What's that to us?" His eyes shot to Nash. "We washed our hands of her years ago."

"Did you now?" Nash didn't sound convinced. "Did you, Margaret?"

"Leave her out of this. She's done nothing wrong."

Nash laughed. "She's been in it all along. I've been watching her these three years while she was away at Pepperdine and more recently when she was taken by one of my competitors, who I believe hoped to make a deal with you." He glanced from Margaret to Bradley. "I could go home and put a bullet in her head right now, since she doesn't matter to you…"

Margaret was beside herself. She fell to her knees and grabbed Nash's pant leg. "No, don't kill my girl!" She bent her head and buried her face in her hands.

Nash only laughed. "I'll let you two talk it over and make a decision. For now, I'll let her live." He stepped back and shook his head. "Margaret, I didn't know you cared this much."

***

"We are not compromising, Margaret!" Bradley paced the living room carpet and turned to give her an intimidating glare. "We've worked for this for way too long. You can't let your attachment to Rainey interfere with your dreams. You've compromised too much for that illegitimate child! I told you when we met that you should just have an abortion."

Margaret couldn't believe Bradley was saying this. Didn't he grow to love Rainey with time? When she decided to keep her baby, Bradley promised he'd help take care of her. "How can you say this? You love Rainey."

Bradley stopped his pacing and put his hands on his hips. "I liked that cute little brown haired thing with curls she used to be. I could tolerate her. But then she changed. I can't stand that right wing puritan do-gooder she's become. She's not my child. She never was."

Margaret shook her head while tears coursed down her face. Hearing these words was too painful.

"We need to walk away." Bradley's tone was unmoving. "Take the plants and what seeds we have, and let Nash do what he's going to do." Bradley shook his head. "I'm not giving up my fortune for your mistake."

Margaret buried her face in her hands.

"I've spoken to two other drug runners who were prepared to make an offer if Nash wouldn't come through for us." Bradley cleared his throat and turned his back on the crying woman. "I'm going to make an appointment with one of them for later this week."

"You can't!" Margaret begged. "She's my daughter."

"That's the point. She's *your* daughter."

***

"It's sprained." David ran his fingers over Trey's aching wrist and made an assessment. "I don't feel any breaks."

Trey leaned back on his bunk and moaned. This was the worst fight he'd had. Rodriguez decided that it would be more challenging for Trey to take on all four men at once. The fight only lasted ten minutes. *Ten long minutes.*

"He will only make it harder for you." David wrapped both of his hands around Trey's swollen wrist and closed his eyes.

Trey wondered if David was praying for him.

"I have already told you what you need to do." David sat down on the bunk below.

"And I have already told you there is nothing in it for me. God has never been there for me and I'm certainly not about to cry out to Him now."

"Then you will never know the blessings He wants to shower upon you." David shook his head somberly.

Trey closed his eyes. His wrist ached and the muscles in his body screamed. The initiation practices of this prison were torture. Would Tiffany ever get him out of this place? She'd been by the prison yesterday to tell him she was still working to get him out.

"What are they doing to you, Trey?" She had asked with genuine sympathy in her voice. "You look terrible."

"Thanks." He just loved her encouragement. He had only been able to see her from the other side of the glass, but he figured she was talking about his bruises.

"You look different. Your eyes… they're angry." She had put her hand on the glass as if she wished she could touch him. "Don't let them destroy you."

"Tell me what happened." David pulled Trey from his thoughts.

Trey was quiet. Tell him? Was this man serious? How many times in life had Trey tried to tell someone what was happening to him and they didn't believe him or they just moved him around into another bad situation? What good was it to drag out painful memories and tell this old man who would only try to shove God down his throat?

Silence crept into the dirty cell.

"The Lord is my Shepherd, I shall not be in want." Trey could hear David softly repeating Psalm 23 from the bunk below. "He makes me lie down in green pastures, He leads me beside quiet waters…"

Trey closed his eyes and felt tears stinging his eyes.

"…and lo even though I walk through the valley of the shadow of death, I will fear no evil, for Thou art with me. Thy rod and Thy staff they comfort me…"

"Please…" Trey's strained voice attempted to silence the older man.

"You prepare a table before me in the presence of my enemies. You anoint my head with oil. My cup overflows. Surely goodness and mercy shall follow me all the days of my life and I will dwell in the house of the Lord forever."

Trey could hardly contain his emotion. Anger mixed with fear and exhaustion threatened to drive him out of his mind. "Why are you doing this to me?"

David stood up and turned to face Trey. "Because I believe the Lord is calling you and you need someone to show you how foolish you are being to resist."

"I already told you I'm not interested."

"You think the hell you lived in as a child was worse than the hell you will experience for eternity if you reject the gift He is offering you?"

"You have no idea!"

"Then tell me."

Trey climbed down from his bunk and sat down beside David on the bunk below. "You want to hear my story?"

David folded his hands and leaned onto his knees. "I have wanted to hear your story from the day you arrived. I saw the hurt in your eyes then. But it has only grown and become more and more ugly. You do not look like the same man today that you were when you arrived… and yet you are because it was there all along, you just didn't allow others to see it."

Trey blew out a heavy sigh. "Alright." He leaned against the wall. "I don't remember a time when my father and mother weren't fighting." Trey forced out the words. "My dad was an alcoholic and my mother was addicted to drugs and other men. Often times my father would abuse us in his drunken fits of anger. Other times, he'd ignore us for days. My mother left my father when I was eight and we moved in with one of her boyfriends."

As the memories rushed in, Trey had to fight harder to hide his emotions. "Then life got even worse." He sucked in a trembling breath. "That man abused me mentally and physically… and sometimes other ways." Trey glanced at David to see what kind of reaction he had. "Thankfully it didn't last very long. One of my teachers finally believed me and I was taken away from that situation. But foster care wasn't perfect either. I lived with some nice people, but they didn't love me." He shook his head. "Eventually my father regained custody of me and I spent a couple years with him until I joined the service to pay for college."

"How were those years with your dad?"

"I was an angry, rebellious teen. My father had gotten his life back together. He'd given up alcohol and even started going to church, but he could never repay what he took away from me."

"How did you end up an FBI agent?" David asked.

"College and the military gave me confidence. I did very well in school and excelled in the military. I was encouraged to consider joining the FBI, so I went to Quantico and dedicated myself to taking down criminals."

"You didn't try to kill that doctor, did you?"

"No." Trey shook his head. "Dr. Hernandez was helping Rainey. He's a good man."

"Rainey?"

Trey explained the details to David. "I know it was Dylan who tried to kill the doctor but I don't know what he's done with Rainey. As long as I am in here, I can do nothing to help her… if she's even alive."

David was thoughtful for a few minutes. "You said Rainey is a Christian."

"Yes."

"Then no matter what happens to her, you can have faith that she is well. Whether in the body or out—she is with the Father."

Trey blinked back more tears. "I don't want her to be dead."

"You love her very much." David placed a comforting hand on Trey's arm. "Tell me, how would Rainey tell you to handle the situation you are in?"

Trey sighed. "She would tell me to turn my life to Jesus."

David nodded.

"But can't you see? Where was God when I was a kid? Where was He?"

David got up slowly and walked to the other side of the room. He opened a small box under the rickety old table in their room and pulled out a well-worn Bible. Carrying the Bible back to the bunk, David turned the pages and found one verse. "Read this for me." He held the Bible out for Trey. It was in Spanish, but Trey had no trouble reading the two small words found in John 11:35. "Jesus wept."

In those two words, Trey finally broke down and let the tears course down his face. He shook his head and wiped his cheeks. "Why? Why did He weep and yet not do anything for me?"

"We have choices in this world, Trey." David glanced at the Bible in Trey's lap. "God created us to love Him. But real love must always be a choice. If God did not allow man to choose, then our love for Him would not be genuine. If every time a person sinned they were zapped into dust, it is true, many people would not sin. But it would still not be a choice. Their obedience would be motivated by fear. God wants our obedience to be driven by genuine love for Him, Our Creator, Who gave everything for us, Who wants to shower you with blessings… Who wants to help you in this terrible situation you have found yourself in." He patted Trey's arm. "You may have learned to hide the hurt from your past, but it is still there. God wants to wash it away. He wants to heal you with His love."

Trey lowered his eyes to the Bible in his lap. He thought about the hours he'd read the Bible to Rainey. He knew those words were special. He knew God had been trying to get his attention. Did

206

it really take him getting beaten up every day for almost two weeks for him to realize he couldn't do it without God?

"What do I need to do?"

Suddenly transformed into a sanctuary of the Most High, the little jail cell in Colombia became the place of healing for Trey. He laid his life at the foot of the cross and put his faith in the Creator of the Universe.

Chapter 19

The storm clouds swirling over the ocean were nothing like the storm clouds raging inside Rainey. She watched from the window in the bungalow while her husband drove away with the woman he'd brought home from the beach. They'd spent most of the day in the villa. At dusk he'd taken the woman to the pool where they swam and drank pretty little alcoholic drinks until dark. He seemed to expect Rainey to stay away as he exploited his little affair right under her nose.

Rainey was torn between tears of rage and tears of sorrow. Was this man really her husband? How would she be able to face him upon his return?

It was late when Dylan opened the door to the bungalow and found Rainey sitting on the sofa with a tear-stained face. His expression was not in the least repentant as he walked past her to the refrigerator.

"How could you?" Rainey steadied her tone but felt her blood boiling.

Dylan downed a half bottle of beer and laughed. "How could I what?" He grabbed another beer and carried them both to the living room. Taking a seat in the leather recliner across from her, he kicked up his feet and finished the first bottle of beer.

"That woman. Is she your girlfriend?"

Dylan let out a sarcastic chuckle. "I just met her last night. We just had some fun together."

Rainey could only imagine what kind of fun he had. "How can we ever hope to have a real marriage again if you're bringing home strange women?" Tears welled up in her eyes and threatened to spill down her hot face.

Dylan popped the top off the next bottle of beer. "Calm down woman. We don't have a marriage anyway."

"I told you to give me time. I want to be a good wife…"

Laughter gushed from Dylan's lips. "Forget it. I'm tired of pretending." He took a sip of his beer. "You're not my wife."

Rainey shook her head. "I want to work on it, Trey. I want to make it work."

Dylan stood up and carried the empty bottle to the trash. "No, stupid. You're not my wife and I'm not Trey." He drank from the second bottle and opened the fridge to see what there was to eat. "Do you want a beer?"

"No." Rainey stood up and followed him to the kitchen. "What do you mean? If you're not Trey, who are you and who is Trey?" Her mind reeled with questions. Why was her whole world dependent upon the word of everyone else?

"Trey was that guy who watched over you like a hawk while you were in the hospital." He leaned against the counter. "I'm Dylan and your name is not April Netherland. Believe it or not we were friends for about three years. At least I was hired to be your friend. Biggest waste of three years of my life." He shook his head. "But hey, it paid for college."

Rainey watched Dylan turn around and begin assembling a sandwich from the ingredients he'd pulled from the refrigerator. She walked to the other side of the counter and watched Dylan. "I don't understand."

"Of course you don't." Dylan licked the mayonnaise off his knife. "That's what's made this whole thing so much fun." He shrugged. "You're like a book with blank pages. I can write whatever I want on them." He took a bite of his sandwich. "But I can't change what the book is made of." He grabbed a plate and carried the sandwich back to the living room. "You're a wreck. You can't even find it in your heart to love me when I give you all this!" He waved his arms around the beautifully furnished bungalow. "Or when I spend a couple thousand dollars buying you a bunch of modest, artsy, earthy kind of clothes that make you look like some kind of conservative, tree hugging, backpacker. I don't know." He shook his head. "You'd look ten times better in a bikini. Did you see

that girl? Her body was nothing compared to yours. But you hide it."
He shook his head. "At least she shares the love." His lips curved
into a sarcastic sneer. "I bought you a dresser full of gorgeous
clothes and you wouldn't even wear them."

"You bought all those?"

"Of course. I thought I'd spruce up your wardrobe. But you
liked that stupid skirt Trey bought you."

Trey bought the skirt? Rainey lowered her eyes. "Why did
you bring me here?"

"Actually, you're a hostage." Dylan took another bite of his
sandwich. "Now that you actually know, we're going to have to keep
a closer eye on you."

Rainey shook her head. "Hostage? I don't understand." She
racked her brain. *Who am I? Where do I belong?* "Is that man, Trey,
my husband?" Her eyes widened with fear. Where was he? Did the
real Trey care where she was?

"No." Dylan spoke through a mouth full of food and rinsed
it down with his beer.

"Who am I?"

Dylan shook his head. "I'm not telling you." He stood up and
carried his plate to the kitchen counter. "You're on your own now."
He grabbed a few things from the bedroom and carried them to the
door. "Don't try to leave. Those guards out there, they will shoot to
kill."

"Where are you going?" Rainey stood up and fidgeted
nervously with her hands.

"The main house. My dad should be home soon."

***

Alone in the bungalow Rainey wasn't sure if she should be
crushed or relieved. If she wasn't married to that man then she never
committed adultery. It was a strange sort of relief. But now the
feeling of being alone was even stronger. If she wasn't April
Netherland, who was she? Why wouldn't he tell her? Why was she a
hostage? Could she really not leave this elaborate compound if she
wanted?

She grabbed a throw pillow and wrapped her arms around it.
Where was the real Trey? She closed her eyes and allowed herself to

210

imagine his face again. She had tried to force his image from her mind when she believed herself to be married to another man. Now she was free to think about him again.

God, where is Trey? Please help me find him. She remembered him telling her that he wasn't a Christian. She prayed God would help him turn his life to Jesus. *Be with Trey wherever he is and please, help me find out who I am.*

***

Nash was furious when he found his son crashed out on the sofa in the television room. The huge television was on, but Dylan was asleep.

"What in the world are you doing?" Nash kicked Dylan's feet. "There's gonna be a tropical storm in less than six hours and you're sound asleep with a bag of chips and a bottle of beer! I figured you'd have men out there boarding windows and tying everything down."

Dylan sat up and scratched his unshaven face. "Why are you chewing me out? I didn't know!"

"Did you check your phone?"

"Seriously, Dad. You knew I was going surfing yesterday. I just got home this morning."

"Your phone?"

"Man…" Dylan got up and grabbed the empty bag of chips to throw it away. "I must have left it at Megan's hotel."

"Megan?" Nash crossed is arms.

"Yeah. Some chick I met surfing yesterday. I'm done with Rainey. Tie her up and lock her in the bungalow. She's a prude. I'm done babysitting her."

"Well right now we've got to get the house ready for tropical storm Iris." Nash picked up the phone and started calling out orders to his employees. "I don't care if you're up all night, this house better be buttoned down so tight that a tornado couldn't lift it."

***

Trey knew it was morning, but something was different. A prison guard walked past and banged a metal rod on the bars. "Wake up. Tropical storm." He continued moving down the hall.

Trey sat up and blinked a few times. He could hear the winds outside.

David pulled on his shirt and glanced down the hall. "They're going to take us all down to the cafeteria." He tossed Trey his shirt. "Get your clothes on."

"Why the cafeteria?"

"It doesn't have any outside walls. They can keep a closer eye on everyone. It's where they always send us when there is a tropical storm."

Trey wondered what this meant for his morning fights. He hurried to get ready and walked into the hallway behind David. Crowds of prisoners were being ushered into the cafeteria, talking about what was supposed to be one of the worst tropical storms in years.

"I called my wife yesterday," one of the men was saying to another man. "She said they were talking about evacuating parts of Santa Marta."

"They always do that," the other man replied cynically. "The people on the news need to have something to talk about. Santa Marta doesn't get hurricanes and the most we're going to see is a few trees and electric lines down."

Armed guards lined the walls while prisoners took seats around the large room. They were being heavily watched in the event of a riot. Any display of violence was going to be nipped in the bud quickly. It was strange. There was about to be a tropical storm and Trey was truly thankful. It looked like he was going to get a day off from fighting.

David seemed to be reading Trey's thoughts. He placed a tan, wrinkled hand on Trey's back and let out a low chuckle. "Strange how God works, isn't it."

"This doesn't mean we won't be on again tomorrow."

"Do not worry about tomorrow." David nodded. "Be thankful for today."

Trey rubbed his tender wrist and said a quick thanks to God.

***

"The tropical storm is almost to Santa Marta." Bradley knocked on their bedroom door and found Margaret still in bed. "They say it will hit here next."

Margaret pulled herself from the bed and ran her fingers through her hair.

"You need to take care of the plants. I'll make sure the lab is secure."

Margaret contemplated his words. The thin, timid woman was not without a temper. She'd thought all night about how to take care of the plants and this might be her opportunity.

She and Bradley had not spoken since the day before. Margaret had nothing to say to him. He had bad karma.

After he slipped from the room to take care of his responsibilities, Margaret packed a small suitcase and carried it outside to the greenhouse.

The winds were picking up outside. A greenhouse would be a terrible place to spend a tropical storm. Bradley expected Margaret to load all the plants into boxes and take them to the safe room in the house.

He wants me to take care of the plants… I'll take care of the plants… She walked to the first little pot and pulled out the thin green seedling. She held it in her hands, inspecting the intricate little white roots and slender leaf stems. It was beautiful. She loved her little plants. *But I love Rainey more.* One by one, Margaret walked through each row, each pot, and destroyed every young plant in the greenhouse. When she finished she wiped her hands on her long skirt and walked to the mother plant. She still needed this. It was her bargaining chip. All her work, all her research, and all the time it took to cultivate the perfect poppy… she would give it up for Rainey.

When she finished, she grabbed the plant and her one bag and walked outside to the street. She was done. *Goodbye Bradley.* The man who never married her, who never loved her daughter, she was done with him.

Neighbors were working to secure windows and doors while Margaret headed toward a pay phone where she could call a taxi.

*** *

213

The wind howled and rain pelted like broken pieces of glass against the side of the bungalow. Nash's workers had secured most of the windows, but the rains started before they got the bedroom window covered. Rainey sat in the living room clutching a pillow while the lights flickered off and on and the wind ripped through the house.

It was frightening being alone during the storm, but Rainey felt a strange sense of something familiar about the storm. Had she been in a tropical storm before? She closed her eyes as she often did when she tried to picture a past experience. She was young… they were living on the beach somewhere. She saw that woman again— the woman with the long hair. Rainey was crying while the storm raged on outside but the woman she called mom held her close and comforted her. "This is just mother nature's way of cleansing us," was her mother's response.

Rainey opened her eyes. It was a memory. She was sure of it. Even though she didn't know her name and didn't know the woman in the memory, she was sure she had a memory.

She reflected on the memory she had shared with Trey. The same woman helped her find the sea glass. *It has to be my mother.*

As the storm raged on, eventually they lost power. Rainey made herself a light dinner and walked into her bedroom. Flashes of lightning tore through the dark sky. Rainey sat on the edge of the bed and glanced at the dim outline of her dresser. She'd put most of her new clothes away after she and Dylan went shopping the week before. Dylan took the others away. She wasn't sure where. He'd made other cutting comments about her dislike for his taste when he'd emptied the drawers.

She was incredibly glad he wasn't her husband. But Rainey still didn't know why she was here and if she were truly a prisoner. If she was, shouldn't she try to escape?

Rainey wouldn't even know where to go. She leaned back and closed her eyes.

***

When the brunt of the storm was over, the prisoners were escorted back to their rooms and the cells were locked. The guards wanted to assess any damage to the property. While the prison was not as close to the shore, the high winds and lightning were still able to produce quite a bit of damage.

As Trey was about to enter his cell he felt a strong grip on his arm. "Don't think that just because you didn't have to fight today you got a day off," Rodriguez spoke threateningly in Trey's ear. "Tomorrow you will make up for today. Expect to fight eight men." Rodriguez punctuated the end of his sentence by shoving Trey into the metal bars leading to his cell.

David caught the interchange and shook his head. "Do not fear tomorrow."

Trey blew out a sigh. "Be thankful for my day of rest."

"Yes." David nodded. "I have learned to be content in whatever circumstances I am."

"That's from Philippians." Trey recognized the verse.

"Just remember, God took care of you today. He will take care of you tomorrow. Be content in that."

Trey would try.

It was difficult to sleep with the threat of an eight man attack looming over his head. Trey woke several times in the night and tried to give it to God. He wished he could think of a way to escape, to hide from the men. Even in his best condition, Trey knew he couldn't take on eight men. Was this Rodriguez's way of killing him? Maybe this was it. Maybe this was why God made sure Trey finally surrendered himself to Jesus. Maybe Trey would be going Home soon. If he knew for sure that Rainey was already there, Trey didn't think he would mind. But if she was alive, Trey was determined to find her.

***

Margaret stood on the balcony of her hotel room and looked at the downed trees and flooded roads in the early morning light. Last night's storm left serious damage. It was hard not to wonder how Bradley had fared the strong winds and rain. Surely the anger he was feeling towards her right now was worse than the tropical storm. Several times in the night Margaret woke up wondering if she'd made a mistake. It had been over five years since she'd seen her daughter. Why was she willing to give up so much for the child who threatened to turn them in if they didn't stop? Her own child, willing to report her... It was Rainey's threats that turned Bradley against her. He would never have kicked her out if she hadn't made those threats.

The gray clouds outside only added to the gloominess Margaret felt inside. She turned from the balcony and walked to the precious plant that sat on the table beside her bed, the one remaining plant—the object that represented her life's work. Was she willing to surrender it for Rainey? Was there any doubt?

Margaret grabbed her sweater and zipped her bag shut. Grabbing the plant she made an early departure. She couldn't travel around town carrying her fragile plant everywhere she went. It was too risky.

Rosa's bakery was only a few blocks from the hotel. Margaret pulled her scarf close to her face and hurried toward her friend's bread shop, hoping it would be open. This area of Santa Marta still had electricity so Margaret was fairly confident.

"Good morning, Rosa." Margaret smiled when she saw Rosa's silver-haired bun bent over the brick oven.

"Ms. Margaret!" Rosa closed the oven door and walked around the counter to greet her friend. "I have not seen you in a few weeks. Where have you been? I was afraid you'd found a new bakery."

Margaret shook her head. "You've still got the best bread in Colombia." She was glad Rosa was so welcoming. "We moved unexpectedly."

"Are you back for a visit?"

"Actually," Margaret glanced around to make sure the previous customer was out of the store. "I have a favor to ask of you."

"A favor for my favorite customer?" Rosa's glowing face showed a willingness to be of any help she could.

"Yes." Margaret held up her precious plant. "I need you to plant sit for me."

Rosa glanced at the lovely poppy plant and back to her friend. "A flower?"

"It's a very valuable flower, Rosa. But I need someone to keep it for me for... at least a few days, but maybe longer."

"I would love to. But I don't have much of a green thumb."

"Just water it and give it sunshine. It should be fine."

Rosa lifted the pot from her friend's hands. "I have a nice large windowsill beside my pantry." She walked to the window behind the counter. "Would this be suitable?"

Hidden in plain sight. "Perfect."

"I will try to phone you if I will be longer than a week."

Rosa waved it off. "A plant is no hindrance. Please feel free to leave it here as long as you like." She touched the delicate dark orange pedals. "Is everything alright, Ms. Margaret? You still look sad."

Margaret wondered how Rosa read her so well. "I hardly know." She shook her head.

"I will pray that Jesus will wrap His arms around you and that you will know His love and experience His peace."

They were nice religious words to Margaret. "Thank you, friend."

Without another word, Margaret slipped out of the store, leaving her billion-dollar plant in the care of a baker.

***

Morning came too early and Trey was pulled from his fitful sleep by security guards telling the prisoners to awake and prepare for the chain gang.

"We have a city to clean up." The prison guard announced as he banged on their bars.

Trey was ready in a few minutes and walked with David toward the exit. It would be the first day he'd been out of the prison walls in over two weeks. He opened his eyes wide and took in the sights and scenery as the prison bus took them toward the city.

Trey's legs were chained together and he awaited his partner. He hoped they would be chaining him to David. He thought he could handle a whole day working beside David. They could talk and keep their minds off the labor. But Trey's heart sank when he saw the prisoner he would be linked to all day.

Rodriguez wore a cocky smile when they attached his chain to Trey.

The men were assigned various areas along the road to either clear debris or dig out the drainage channels. Trey and Rodriguez

217

were put on digging duty. Armed with two shovels, the men were directed to a portion of the road, which was nearly washed out from the storm.

Trey said very little as they began their mission but Rodriguez seemed determined to antagonize Trey and remind him of the beating he was going to receive the next day.

"Don't think you are getting out of another day of initiation. Now you've got twelve men to fight."

The hours were long working beside Rodriguez. Trey tried not to think about what it would mean to fight twelve men. Would he have to fight them all at once or would he have opportunity to fight off each one individually?

It was hard work digging out the flooded road. Trey resolved to give it his best so that he could show himself strong. Both men were wet with sweat and the fine mist of rain that broke out every once in a while.

The sky still showed signs of another storm brewing, and they were told to work faster to prevent further flooding.

An area of severe washout in the road took Trey and Rodriguez to an area beside a grouping of small shrubs and underbrush. Rodriguez worked with his shovel aggressively. Trey tried to keep his distance in spite of the chains that bound them together.

"Try to keep up, gringo." Rodriguez glared at Trey.

Trey worked hard, in spite of the pain in his body from weeks of physical abuse. As Rodriguez hurled toxic insults at him, Trey did his best not to let the same feelings of hatred rise in his heart that he'd allowed before. It was difficult. *God why? Why did you allow them to chain me to the one man out of all the prisoners who would provoke me most?* It felt like a cruel joke.

Once, during their shoveling, Rodriguez hurled a pile of mud and sand at Trey as if it were an accident. He laughed as Trey wiped the dirt from his eyes. Guarded by men with machine guns, Rodriguez would have been a fool to try to start an actual fight. But hour-by-hour, Trey felt the punches.

As they worked closer and closer to the brush, Trey picked up a strange smell. Not quite the same musky smell he'd noticed from the snakes he'd seen in North America, but he felt instinctively that it was a snake. He slowed his shoveling and let his eyes scan the area. Rodriguez was busy with his shovel and only glanced at Trey once to swear at him for stopping. Trey started back into the shoveling but the smell concerned him. He slowed again and watched for movement in the underbrush.

Then he saw it. The large brown Equis snake was only inches away from Rodriguez with its large venomous fangs exposed and his body ready to strike. In a matter of seconds, Trey's mind raced with how to respond. This could be it… if Rodriguez was bitten the endless abuse could stop. The Equis snake was deadly… Trey shook the vengeful thought from his head, shoved Rodriguez away with all his strength and used his shovel to quickly decapitate the snake.

A guard was quickly upon them as Rodriguez recovered from his fall in the mud. Trey was about to face a harsh rebuke from shoving Rodriguez to the ground when the guard saw the dead snake. He pointed at it and called for another nearby guard.

After brushing the mud from his hands and knees, Rodriguez stared at the dead serpent and back at Trey. Rodriguez hadn't quite recovered from the shock.

"That's an Equis. Muy peligro. Very deadly," one of the guards said to Trey. "They are a type of pit viper. You just saved his life."

Trey blew out a trembling breath thankful the snake hadn't struck during his moment of mental decision-making.

A few sets of chained prisoners came over to take a look at the snake. "He's at least six feet long," one of the men pointed out.

Another prisoner gave Trey a pat on the back. "Not bad, gringo."

"All right, enough looking at the snake. Get back to work," a guard called out.

The crowd broke up and Rodriguez flung the dead snake away with the head of his shovel. He was uncharacteristically quiet as they continued to work.

Trey put his back into the shoveling and tried not to think about what other venomous creatures might be nearby.

As it neared 7:00 pm, the men were called back to the bus. Each prisoner handed in their work tools as they were unchained from their partner and stepped into the bus. Trey looked for David but took a seat beside a window and turned to watch the sky. He wasn't sure where Rodriguez went and he didn't know how to take the man's reaction to the potential snake attack. He'd been quiet ever since the kill.

The return trip was longer than the bus ride to the worksite. Everyone was hungry, wet and dirty. Trey was anxious to get a shower, even if it was just one of several cold-water shower spigots lined up on a wall. His face was still caked with dirt and he couldn't stand his own smell. He'd take his shower while the other men ate.

It was late when he finally lay down on his hard bunk and closed his eyes.

**

Rainey stayed in the bungalow most of the day. She stepped out for a short while to walk around the grounds. Tree limbs, leaves, and broken flowers lay scattered about the garden. It was a shame to see all the damage.

The electricity was still out in the area and judging from the tangles of power lines hanging from the trees, Rainey guessed it would be a few days. She wondered where Dylan was.

As she walked the grounds, she met one of the security guards with his gun strapped across his back. Instead of guarding, he was working to clear the driveway. He glanced up as she approached. "Where are you going?"

"I wanted to take a walk." Rainey looked toward the security gate and saw that it was unguarded.

"No one leaves the compound."

Rainey noticed a tone of unfriendliness in his voice. "I won't be gone long."

"No one leaves the compound." He reached behind his shoulder to get a hold on his machine gun.

It didn't seem real to her. Was she indeed a hostage? She wasn't locked in a room or bound with a rope. *But I am in bondage to my lack of identity.* Rainey knew that without knowing who she was or who they were, she was of very little threat to them. What she didn't know was how valuable she was.

"I just want to take a walk."

"Maybe you aren't hearing me correctly."

Another guard approached. "Is there a problem here?"

"Our guests wishes to take a walk."

Rainey recognized this new guard as one who'd been friendly to her in the past. She remembered his name was Pedro. She smiled. "I won't be gone long."

"I'm sorry señorita. The boss says you stay in the compound." Pedro dismissed the other guard with a nod.

She glanced toward the house and back to Pedro. "Am I a prisoner?"

Something Rainey thought might be sympathy shone in Pedro's eyes. "I am only a guard. I do not answer questions."

Was this his standard answer to everything? "Please, Pedro. I don't understand."

Pedro glanced around and sighed. "We have been ordered not to allow you to leave. Any attempts are to be reported to Señor McCarness."

Rainey watched a pick up truck drive past with piles of debris from the grounds. "Why?" She returned her eyes to Pedro.

"I am only a guard."

"So you don't know?"

Pedro shook his head. "I only have my orders. You should go now." Pedro turned from her.

"Pedro." Rainey touched his shoulder. "Am I in danger?"

Pedro sighed. He turned around and studied Rainey's questioning blue eyes. "Do you understand where you are?"

Rainey shook her head. "I have amnesia. I don't know anything."

"Señor McCarness is not a man to anger. He and his son make their own rules. I don't ask questions and I don't cause trouble. I suggest the same for you."

Rainey wasn't sure how to respond. Who were these people? "Thank you."

He nodded. "I am sorry." There was something in his eyes that made Rainey think Pedro knew more than he was saying. Was her life in danger here?

She returned to the bungalow and tried to remember— anything.

Dylan stopped by sometime after dusk. Rainey could hardly see with only the dim light from the outside. They'd removed the boards from her windows, but with the cloud cover outside, the bungalow was dark.

"I was told you tried to leave earlier." There was nothing warm in his tone. "I told you yesterday that you are a hostage. I've ordered the guards to treat any attempt you make to leave the compound as a threat and to shoot first, ask questions later. Do I make myself clear?"

Rainey licked her dry lips and nodded. She could barely see his face.

"I asked you a question." He approached her in the dark room and grabbed her wrist. Rainey tried to back away, but Dylan only tightened his hold.

"I'm sorry. Yes, I understand." Rainey wasn't used to this side of Dylan.

Dylan released the hold and shoved her out of his way. "I need a few things from the bedroom." He disappeared to the other side of the bungalow and she moved to the shadows where she hoped he would miss her when he left.

"Remember what I said about the guards," Dylan threatened her once more before walking out the door.

Rainey watched him leave and sank into a chair in an exhausted state of discouragement.

Chapter 20

Trey was surprised to wake up on his own without the threatening crowd of prisoners forcing him into another fight. He sat up and noticed David pulling a shirt over his head.

"What time is it?"

"Breakfast." David turned around and tossed Trey his shirt. "And you wonder how you were left to sleep so late. Am I right?"

Trey pulled on the shirt and climbed down from the bunk. "That's exactly what I wonder. They didn't drag me outside to fight today. I was supposed to make up for two missed days." Trey wondered if they were just going to wait until after breakfast— maybe give him the chance to gain a small amount of energy.

"I was told the fights were done." David motioned toward the cell entrance. "Rodriguez said you passed."

Trey walked beside David to the prison cafeteria. There were no leers from angry prisoners as they walked toward their table. Trey didn't know what to think.

"God gave you a miracle." David leaned in and spoke softly. "God controls the weather, He controls the beasts of the ground and you chose to act upon what you knew was right in the eyes of your Savior. He has blessed you for it."

"This is about the snake?" Trey whispered.

David nodded. "They have all been talking about it. Rodriguez never expected you to save his life." There was pride in David's eyes. "You passed an even greater test than the test of physical endurance. You conquered with love."

"I hardly love the man," Trey confessed. "I even took time to think about it before I killed that snake."

"But you did it." David nodded. "It is doubtful that many of these men would have done the same for Rodriguez and he knows it."

Trey breathed out a relieved sigh. "So the fights are over?"

David nodded. "Now you can just live as a prisoner."

Trey would never have thought that living as a prisoner would be a better option for anything, but after two and a half weeks of daily beatings, it felt like a Sunday afternoon stroll.

***

Rainey pulled the tightly crammed backpack over her shoulders and took a long sip of her bottled water. She glanced out her window and scanned the compound for guards. They were still without power and Rainey was sure if she ever was going to try to escape, this was her best opportunity. What did she really have to live for anyway?

She'd packed her favorite new clothes and her Bible and said a quick prayer for safety.

Opening the door to the bungalow, Rainey crept through the shadows, avoiding any place that was not shrouded by trees and plants. The walk across the driveway toward the security gate was going to be her biggest challenge. Rainey held two large rocks in her hands and crept past the gardens surrounding the villa. Everything was dark. Not even a candle flickered inside.

A security guard passed by the back of the house and Rainey held her breath while he passed. Once she reached the part of the driveway that was closest to the security gate, Rainey threw the first rock with all her strength to the other side of the yard.

"What was that?" one guard asked the other.

"I don't know. Go check it out."

Rainey recognized Pedro's voice. She waited while the first guard crept carefully toward the source of the sound. Rainey swallowed hard and threw the other rock into the bushes on the other side of the driveway.

Pedro stepped down from the gate shed with his gun pointed toward the bushes.

As quietly as she could, Rainey crept past the guard station and quietly forced open the electric gate a couple feet. The power failure served to not only keep the compound dark, but also forced the guards to change the function of the gate to manual.

Rainey hurried past the driveway and pressed her body against the stucco wall in front of the compound. Her heart was beating so fast, Rainey thought surely someone could hear it. Doing her best to stay in the shadows, Rainey slunk along the wall toward her freedom.

"Why is the gate opened?" Rainey heard Pedro call to the other guard.

"It wasn't open a minute ago." One of the guards stepped outside and began walking in the opposite direction of Rainey's course. Rainey ducked behind a bush and tried to quiet her heartbeat.

"I'll head this way." Pedro carried a flashlight through the gate and began scanning the area for any movement.

As Pedro's flashlight illuminated the area, Rainey hid deeper behind the shrub. She was still several feet away, but he was coming her direction.

Her heart sank when Pedro's light illuminated her face in the dark. He looked as surprised as she did.

"What are you doing here?" he whispered and glanced up the road to see if the other guard were nearby.

"Please Pedro..." her eyes pleaded with him.

Pedro started to point his gun toward her and glanced back up the road. The other guard was nowhere to be seen. "Go." He lowered the gun and turned his flashlight away.

Rainey wished she could hug him. "Thank you," she said so softly she barely heard herself. In a matter of seconds she was hurrying along the dark sidewalk toward freedom.

***

Rainey walked all night. She was exhausted, but this was a matter of survival. It was difficult to know how far she'd gone, but Rainey had a picture in her mind of the town she'd gone to with Dylan. She remembered a pawnshop and she hoped she would be able to sell her diamond ring.

She had to get money and the ring was the only thing she could think of. It occurred to her that Dylan forgot the ring when he'd made the announcement that their marriage was a fraud.

A few familiar sights stuck out to her as she walked, and as the sun began to peek over the hills, her surroundings were becoming clearer.

What would Dylan and Nash say when they realized she was gone? Would Dylan think to look for her in the small shopping community he'd taken her? Rainey had no idea where else to go.

The sound of birds seemed to bring the morning to life. Rainey was weary, but she was still able to find pleasure in their song.

It was still too early for the stores to open when Rainey reached the familiar street where she'd shopped. She walked along the stone road toward a small round picnic table in front of a closed café. It felt good to finally sit down for a few minutes. She folded her arms on the table and rested her head for a moment. *I just need to close my eyes for a few minutes. I won't fall asleep...*

The wave was beautiful. Unlike anything Rainey had ever experienced. She could see it curl over her head as she rode the board across the water. The sound of the world seemed blocked out and there was nothing but the color of water reflecting the sun, herself and God. *God was there...* She could see herself talking to someone. He was concerned about her.

"Kiss me." She heard herself ask.

The feeling of his lips on hers pulled her from her sleep. She opened her eyes with a start and looked around as if someone were standing there with her. *It was so real. Was that a memory?* She tried to recall the face. *It was Trey.* Her lips curved into a smile. *I knew we kissed.* She chuckled. She remembered asking him about it in the hospital.

Why are my memories only coming to me in my dreams? Rainey blinked a few times and looked around the shopping district. She wasn't sure how long she'd slept, but judging from the people walking past and the movement in the stores, Rainey guessed she'd been asleep for a couple hours.

The pawnshop was right where she remembered it. It was good to remember things, even if they were only new memories.

Walking inside, Rainey was greeted by a friendly bald man who looked old enough to be her father. He placed his hands on the counter and asked if there was anything he could do for her.

"I have a ring I'd like to sell." She pulled the ring from her bag and handed it to him.

The man pulled out a hand loupe and studied the diamond under a light. His eyes were wide and he stared for several minutes, turning the diamond in various directions and making soft sounds that expressed his pleasure. He glanced up at her with the ring still in his hand. "I don't know when I've seen a diamond so clear." He studied her curiously. "Where did you get this?"

Rainey lowered her eyes. "My ex-husband." It seemed like the best explanation she could give.

"Well, I'm sure you know the value of this ring."

Rainey had no idea what the value of the ring was, but she nodded.

"I can only give you half."

"I understand." Rainey squared her shoulders. "I just want to get rid of it."

The man glanced through his loupe and shook his head. "I just like looking at it."

Rainey couldn't say she felt the same way. "Not me." She sighed.

"I don't have this kind of money in the store. I will have to give it to you tomorrow." He handed her the ring. "Please come back. I want the ring."

"Tomorrow?" Rainey felt suddenly concerned. She couldn't wait until tomorrow.

"I am sorry." The man was genuinely bothered that he couldn't secure the ring now. "I will have to talk to my banker."

Rainey did her best not to look desperate. Did the man really not keep a few thousand dollars in his store? She thanked him and promised to return in the morning.

Stepping back into the sunshine, Rainey realized she didn't even have enough money to buy breakfast. Where would she sleep tonight? Had she just gone from one bad situation to another?

The smell of bread caught her senses, reminding her that she was hungry. Would it be presumptuous to ask the woman at the bread store to allow her to buy a few pieces of bread on credit? Tomorrow she would have money for sure.

Rainey sucked in a shaky breath and walked the few stores down to Rosa's Bakery. The bell over the door rang as she walked inside. Her mouth watered when she saw the loaves of fresh baked bread sitting under the glass.

"Señorita Bonita!" Rosa called out as soon as Rainey caught her eyes. "You have come alone this time. Where is your very handsome husband?"

Rainey took a breath to steady her emotions. She didn't realize how emotional she was, probably because she was tired and hungry. She wasn't even sure she should ask. It was nice that the woman remembered her, but would she think it odd to sell a few slices of bread on credit? Rainey cleared her throat. "This may sound strange, but I don't have any money on me right now. I will tomorrow and I'm very hungry."

Rosa studied Rainey curiously. "Dear child, are you asking for a piece of Rosa's homemade bread?"

"I'll pay you back. You have my word." Rainey steadied her gaze on the older woman and swallowed back the thirst in her throat.

"Silly child." Rosa took her hand and walked her to the small café table beside the window. "Sit right here and I will cut you a thick slice of my pineapple bread. I just made it. I wanted to try it myself. This is the first time I've ever made it." Rosa walked behind her counter and cut two thick slices of the steaming bread. Rainey caught the scent across the room. Then Rosa poured two glasses of fresh goat's milk and carried it all to the table.

"We will enjoy our little snack together." She reached for Rainey's hands again. "Shall we thank the Lord for His provisions?"

"Of course!" Rainey couldn't believe her ears. This woman wanted to pray with her.

"Sweet Lord Jesus," Rosa's prayer began in a tone of immense respect and love. "Thank You for bringing me a friend this morning. Dear Lord, thank You for this food, this day, and Your great love for us through Your Son, Jesus, in Whose name we pray. Amen."

Rainey brushed away her tears as she said amen. "Thank you." She forced back a trembling sob.

The cold, refreshing milk paired perfectly with the steaming pineapple bread. Rainey ate the bread so quickly she was almost embarrassed.

"Tell me, child. Where is that ring that glistened from your hand the last time I saw you? You seem sad."

Rosa's boldness caught Rainey off guard. It was not surprising that Rosa noticed the ring the last time Rainey was here. The sweet older woman had taken both of Rainey's hands in hers. But how could she read Rainey's emotions? "It's a long story."

Rosa glanced around the store. "I have no customers right now. Would you like someone to talk to?"

Rosa's kindness was Rainey's undoing. Before she knew what hit her, tears poured from Rainey's eyes in a shower of sorrow. "I'm so scared."

"Come child." Rosa moved to the door and locked it, turning her open sign to the closed position. "Let's not talk here." She took Rainey's hand and led her through the kitchen to the back of the store where a door opened up into a house.

Rainey's eyes traveled around her new surroundings. It was a cozy little house behind the store. Rosa walked her to a small living room and opened the blinds to the back patio. Outside there was a small fenced in garden overflowing with flowers. Rainey sat down and felt the woman's hand on her back.

"Here—we can talk here."

"But I don't want you to lose business," Rainey sniffed.

Rosa handed her a handkerchief and patted Rainey's leg. "My Father owns the cattle on a thousand hills. He will provide for me. Now, what is troubling you so?"

Rainey explained as far as her memory would allow and ended with her current situation. "I have no idea who I am or where I came from. I don't know how to find Trey. I don't even know the name of the hospital."

"Was the hospital in Santa Marta?"

"I don't know."

Rosa's soft wrinkled hands held Rainey's comfortingly. There didn't seem to be much else to ask. Everything Rainey knew about her life could be told in five minutes. "I don't even know why I was being held hostage. Trey never told me anything about my parents. I don't think he knew them. I'm not sure how I knew Trey. He told me I'd been in an accident and had amnesia." Rainey buried her face in her hands while her shoulders shook with sobs. "I have no one. I'm alone. I have no money, no family, and I don't know who I am."

"This is a very strange story indeed." Rosa closed her eyes for a moment. Rainey was sure the older woman was praying.

"You are a follower of Jesus, are you not?" Rosa asked.

"Yes. I am." Rainey wiped her face with the handkerchief. A small smile tugged at her lips. "Trey told me how I became a Christian. He actually knew my testimony even though I didn't. I was so scared that it wasn't real because I couldn't remember it. Then Trey reminded me that the Bible says if you believe in your heart that God raised Jesus from the dead and if you confess with your mouth, Jesus is Lord, you will be saved. I guess the only thing I do know about my life is that I am His."

"If you know that, nothing else really matters." Rosa comforted Rainey. "Child, if you are His, then you are my sister." Rosa's full lips curved into a smile. "That means you are family. You always have a home with family. You are a child of God. You are not alone."

Rosa pulled Rainey into her arms and held her while she cried.

It took Rainey a few minutes to get her emotions together. "You will stay with me as long as you need to. This is your home." Rosa held her hands.

"I can't..."

"Why?" Rosa's clear eyes dared Rainey to come up with an excuse. "Where else will you go?"

"The man at the pawnshop—he will pay me for my ring. I can pay you."

"I do not want your money, child. But I will keep you as long as you need me."

Rainey didn't know what to say. A feeling of relief flooded her whole body.

"My husband is working at the print shop today. We own the little print shop across the road from the bakery," she explained. "He will be delighted to meet you." Rosa stood up and reached for Rainey's hand. "Let's go upstairs and I will show you your bedroom."

Rainey felt like this was a wonderful dream. She picked up her backpack and followed the sweet older woman up the smooth wooden stairs to the second floor.

"Gabriel and I share the room at the front of the house. We like to look over the street. That way he can keep an eye on the print shop." She motioned to the other two rooms. "You may either have the room at the back of the house—it used to belong to my daughter, Bella. Or you may have Stephen's old room."

The idea of seeing the amazing garden at the back of the house every morning appealed to Rainey more than anything. She followed Rosa into the room and took in a delighted breath.

The stucco walls were neatly stenciled with delicate lavender flowers. Soft, colorful rugs covered the tile floor and a cozy, white metal bedframe with a thick mattress stood beside the window.

"It's perfect!" Rainey set her bag on the floor and almost started crying again.

"Child. You need to rest." Rosa walked toward the bed and pulled the quilt back. "If you wish to bathe, the bathroom is between your room and Stephen's old one."

"Thank you!" Rainey found herself in Rosa's arms again and wondered if her own mother hugged her like this.

***

"What do you mean she's gone?" Nash looked up from his desk and glared at his son.

"She's gone. That's what I mean." Dylan answered back defensively. "She took most of the clothes I just bought for her and she's no where to be found. We've spent hours searching the grounds."

"How did this happen?" The steady coolness of Nash's tone was a little unnerving to Dylan.

"We've been without power for two days. My guess is she made the most of the opportunity."

"The woman doesn't even know who she is. Why would she leave? Didn't she think she was your wife?"

Dylan sat down beside the desk and crossed his legs in front of him. He chewed on his lip for a moment trying to think of the best way to explain what happened.

"It was that woman you met surfing, wasn't it? Did Rainey find out about her?"

"Look, I couldn't live like her husband, okay? You called it! There was no chemistry. She was a frigid prune. She wouldn't even kiss me." Dylan shook his head. "It wasn't worth it. I just fessed up."

"You fessed up? Meaning you told her she wasn't your wife?" Nash clarified.

"Yes. Okay. What's the big deal? It was my idea to tell her she was my wife anyway."

Nash took a deep breath and exhaled. "And I liked the idea because it kept her content. Why couldn't you have just played the game a little longer?"

Dylan stood up and crossed his arms. "I was sick of it!"

"Do you have any idea what this means?"

Dylan sat back down and ran his fingers over the leather office chair. He did know what it meant. It was made very clear to him just how instrumental Rainey was to his father's investment. Margaret and Bradley were making extreme demands and Nash needed Rainey to control them. Without Rainey, there was a risk that someone else would get their hands on the plant that could change the future of morphine and cocaine.

"How could you be so irresponsible?" Nash slapped the table.

"I told your guards to keep an eye on her. They were the irresponsible ones."

Nash was too furious to argue at this point. He tightened his jaw and turned his chair toward the window.

"I'll keep looking." Dylan realized this mistake wasn't as forgivable as a wrecked car or a speeding ticket. His dad was beyond angry. "She can't have gone far."

Nash turned the chair toward his son. "Find her." The man's eyes were cold as ice. "Don't come home until you do."

Chapter 21

Tiffany sat on one side of Dr. Hernandez in a brightly lit hospital room filled with bouquets of flowers and get-well cards. His wife sat beside him with her hand in his while two Colombian police officers stood by listening to his story.

It had been a rough three weeks in the doctor's life. He'd sustained a serious injury and almost died more than once. With many prayers and much attention from a caring hospital staff, he was finally out of danger and on his way to recovery.

With a sharp mind, the doctor was finally given the opportunity to share the events that made him a patient in his hospital.

"You are absolutely sure the man who shot you was not Trey Netherland."

"I know this. Trey was at the hospital with Rainey every day. We talked many times. I would know his dark brown eyes and friendly smile anywhere. The man who shot me may have had hair like Trey's, but he was very different. His eyes were gray blue and he had a tattoo on his neck. I would say he was younger than Trey, maybe by a few years."

Tiffany handed the doctor a photograph of Dylan. "Do you know this man?"

"That's him!" Dr. Hernandez didn't blink. "That's the man who shot me. His hair was darker when he came. I believe he was trying to look like Trey."

One of the Colombian police officers nodded. "He showed Trey's identification to the nurse. He must have planned the whole thing. Officer Waterford told us that Trey's identification and badge were both stolen from a recent crime scene." The officer looked at Tiffany. "It looks like your agent is innocent."

Relief spread across Tiffany's face. "I've been trying to tell you that for three weeks."

They continued their questions with the doctor and walked to the hall with Tiffany. She was noticeably upset with them.

"You've held an innocent United States FBI officer in a federal Colombian prison for three weeks. I want him released immediately."

"Yes, señora," the lead officer said.

Tiffany made a phone call to let the other agents on her team know the good news. Vince Elm would be anxious to hear that Trey was going to be set free. After not showing up to relieve Trey at the hospital, it was found that Vince's brake lines had been cut and he'd had an accident. He sustained a few bruises, but he was doing fine and was back on the case.

"I will be going to the prison today to pick him up," she explained. Tiffany had no idea what kind of condition Trey was in by now. He had been very worn down when she last saw him.

***

Trey played a jack of spades on the ten and trumped his opponent. Don Paul tossed down his cards and shook his head. "You won that one."

"Wait a minute!" Cameron slapped a king on top of Trey's jack and scooped up the cards. "I had not made my play yet. Nice try, gringo." There was a friendly smirk on the young prisoner's face.

David sat nearby and chuckled at the end to Trey's winning streak. "Be careful, Trey. Cameron cheats." He joked.

"Trey Netherland." One of the guards approached. "Get your stuff. You're free."

Trey sat there for a second trying to process what the prison guard just said.

Don Paul let out a roar. "Look at you, gringo! A free man!"

Rodriguez looked up from a nearby chair and almost grinned. "You heard him, gringo. I would be running through those gates."

Trey stood up and glanced quickly around the room. "Good game." Cameron shook his hand.

"Come on." David put a guiding hand on Trey's shoulder and they walked toward their cell.

"I owe you so much." Trey stopped inside the cell and turned to David. "I wish there was a way I could get you out of here."

David's lips curved into a smile. "I can leave whenever I want."

Trey furrowed his brows. "What?"

"My sentence was over ten years ago," David said. "I'm here as a missionary."

David's words were still not registering. "You're not a prisoner?"

"I was. I served a twenty-year sentence. But during that time an old man, just like me, told me about Jesus. He was here as a missionary too. He was getting up there in years and died around the time I was released. I decided to take his place."

"You chose to stay?" It was almost unreal to Trey.

"Compelled to stay really. I'm here serving my Savior." The light in his eyes glowed radiantly. "I asked to have you in my cell. I knew you needed to hear the message of salvation. I could see the hurt deep in your eyes even before they started beating you up every day."

Trey's eyes were moist with tears. "You saved my life."

David shrugged. "I helped. God saved your life." He placed a hand on Trey's slim, muscular shoulder. "Now you get out there and tell people about Him."

Impulsively, Trey reached forward and hugged the man. He didn't care what the prisoners thought. David was a man after God's own heart and Trey loved him.

"I will." Trey stepped back after the hug. "And I will be praying for you."

"I plan to start working on Rodriguez now. Pray that goes well." There was a twinkle in his eyes. "I would say after you killed that snake for him, he is a bit more humble."

Trey could see that. Even though Rodriguez hadn't said much to him since the incident, the man had changed. He'd called off the initiation beatings and ordered the other men to leave Trey alone. That was a huge change.

Trey grabbed the few things he had around the cell and was about to walk out when he saw Rodriguez walking down the hall toward him. David gave Trey a nod.

"So they found out you were innocent." Rodriguez stopped and sized up Trey.

Trey nodded. He wasn't sure what he should say. He didn't expect Rodriguez to come say good-bye.

"I never thanked you." Rodriguez looked around a few times and back at Trey. "You saved my life." He shook Trey's hand. "I don't know why you did it. Thank you."

Trey steadied his gaze on the hardened convict. "David can explain to you why I did it." Trey turned to glance at David. "Listen to him. He's got an awesome truth to tell."

Rodriguez turned toward David and nodded. "I would like you to tell me."

***

Tiffany didn't waste time in the prison. She watched Trey sign the papers and hurried him to her car.

"Any news about Rainey?" Trey wanted to know immediately.

"Not yet." Tiffany shook her head. "We haven't given up." She was quiet for a moment. "I'm so sorry Trey. Three weeks in a Colombian prison must have been a living hell."

Trey let his eyes roam the parking lot and the trees beyond. The sky was blue with white billowy clouds drifting slowly past. He breathed in the beauty of it with a new kind of appreciation. "It wasn't easy, I'll tell you that."

"You look... you look better than the last time I saw you." She unlocked the doors and they both climbed into the SUV. "And I don't mean just happier because you're free. I mean..." she turned to him and really studied his face for a moment. "Apart from the fact that you're thin and incredibly toned—you look peaceful."

Trey sat back on the soft passenger seat and blew out a sigh. "Tiffany, I'm better than I was before I went into this prison. In fact, I'm better than I was when I first came to work for the bureau." He turned to look at her and found her eyes still on him. "Are you gonna start this car?"

Tiffany laughed. "Yes. But I want to hear what happened to you in there. I thought for sure they were going to kill you."

"So did I." Trey leaned his head back comfortably and began to tell the whole story to his boss.

It was a long drive back to the hotel where the FBI had set up camp. Tiffany was quiet for much of the drive. "I have to admit, that's an amazing story." She parked the car and turned toward Trey. "So that old man, David, he decided to stay in a federal prison to tell others about Jesus."

Trey nodded. "He knew that my hurt was deeper than the bruises I got every morning. He said he saw it when I first showed up."

"I usually don't put a lot of stock in people's religious experiences," Tiffany confessed. "In fact, when you were reading the Bible to Rainey every day I thought you'd gone a bit off the deep end." She shook her head. "But, you're different. I can see it. You have a light in your eyes." Tiffany was reflective for a moment. "And the storm and the snake all happening right after you..."

"Gave my life to Christ," Trey finished the sentence for her.

"Yeah." She nodded. "That's pretty cool."

Trey was glad she saw it that way. "You know this means I'm going to start preaching to you about Jesus, don't you?" he teased her.

"Yeah, yeah, you and Vince together now."

Trey was anxious to hear what had happened to Vince. Tiffany explained how the brake line was cut and Vince had an accident.

"He's fine now. Although he sounds a lot like you, saying Jesus got him back on track that day while he was trapped in the car.

Trey was glad to hear it. It would be good to have a Christian friend in the bureau.

***

Margaret glanced at the slip of paper in her hand. She'd never phoned Nash McCarness. Bradley always did all the paperwork and business dealings. It took a little bit of sneakiness on her part to find the man's number in Bradley's cell phone before she left, but she did it and now she was going to attempt to contact the man.

The phone only rang a couple times and she heard the familiar voice at the other end.

"This is Margaret Reed." She held her voice steady. "I'm ready to make a deal with you."

Nash listened closely as Margaret explained that she'd destroyed all the seedlings and had in her possession the hybrid poppy he so earnestly desired. "I want my daughter set free. You can have the plant."

"A simple trade?" Nash couldn't believe how easy this sounded.

"Yes. I've left Bradley. He's not involved."

"And the money?" Nash clarified.

"I don't want your money." Margaret clutched the pay phone in her hand and watched people walk past her on the sidewalk. "It was never about the money for me."

Nash was silent for a few moments. "I need some time to consider," he finally said.

"Time? Why do you need time? Is my daughter okay?"

"Your daughter is fine." Nash fixed his tone. "I just need some time."

Margaret wanted to protest, but she knew there was no arguing with Nash. She didn't want to argue. She just wanted everything to be all right.

"Call me in two weeks," Nash said coolly.

"Fine." Margaret listened for the click on the other end of his phone. She hung up the receiver with a trembling hand and brushed away hot tears. *Two weeks? Why is he making me wait two weeks?*

***

Rainey pulled a steaming hot loaf of wheat bread from the stone oven and set it on the counter. The perfectly baked loaf filled the bakery with a mouth-watering smell.

"That is beautiful, Margaret," Rosa said, using the name she'd given Rainey the day she'd first stumbled into the bakery over a week ago.

"You remind me of my dear friend, Margaret," Rosa had explained. "So the name fits you."

Rainey wasn't sure how she felt about being called Margaret, but for some reason the name had a pleasant, kind of familiar sound to it.

"Remember that tonight is my little Cassandra's fifth birthday party," Rosa interrupted Rainey's thoughts and smoothed another round loaf of bread onto a stone.

"Are you sure I should come?" Rainey carried a bowl to the sink and began washing it. "I'm not really family, you know."

Rosa clicked. "Now stop that. My Bella insisted that you come. She and Stephen both love that you are staying here and have been helping me at the bakery."

"I don't know that I've been much of a help."

"You have been a wonderful help, child." Rosa set the baking stone into the oven.

Rainey finished washing the bowl and dried it. She set it on a clean shelf above the baking counter. "I do have a nice little present for her." She smiled.

It was good to have her own money to buy things. Rainey could still hardly believe how much money she'd gotten for the ring. When she'd returned to the pawnshop the day after she arrived, the man handed her seventeen thousand dollars and apologized that he was not able to give her more. "In the United States you would have gotten much more for the ring," he told her. "But in Colombia this is a fair price I believe."

Rainey didn't argue. She never expected that kind of money for the ring. Seventeen thousand dollars would go far in Colombia. She tried to get Rosa to take some, but the dear lady refused. "You keep your money. I have plenty."

Rainey was looking forward to the birthday party for Cassandra. She'd met Bella and her family at church on Sunday morning and they were all very pleasant. Stephen worked at the university so Rainey hadn't met him yet, although he planned to attend the party.

"You did not need to buy Cassandra a present." Rosa clicked again.

The door opened and a customer walked in. Rosa left Rainey to wait on the customer by herself while she continued making bread.

At the end of the workday, Gabriel walked across the street from the print shop and asked the women how long they would need to get ready.

"I just need to close the blinds and lock the front door." Rosa walked to the window. "Oh, and I should water the plant."

Rainey walked to the tall slender poppy flower and touched its tender pedals. "Be careful not to over water it. Poppies don't like too much water." She wasn't exactly sure how she knew that, but there was something familiar about the poppy. *Maybe I had a garden.* Rainey remembered her surprise at how many of the plants she could identify in Nash's garden.

Rosa touched the soil. "Well, I watered it yesterday. Maybe I shouldn't water it today."

Rainey stuck her fingers in the dirt. "It's a lovely flower." She admired the way the floppy pedals caught the sunlight.

"Thank you. It belongs to my friend, that's why I have to be extra careful. I would feel terrible if it died under my care."

***

Cassandra's fifth birthday party was a new experience for Rainey. The beautiful little Colombian child's eyes were aglow with excitement as her father hung a giant butterfly piñata in the tree and motioned for Cassandra's group of little friends to gather around.

"Cassandra, you go first." Bella placed a blindfold over the child's eyes.

"Let's all count while we spin her around," Cassandra's father told the children. Ben was a loving father and showed almost as much enthusiasm about the party as the children did.

Rainey watched the festivities with pleasure. She took a few sips of her fruity lemonade and sat on a patio chair near the tree.

"Mother tells me you are her adopted daughter." Stephen pulled up a chair next to Rainey's and reached out to shake her hand. "I am Stephen," he said in English.

240

Stephen was tall and slender with thick dark hair and a pair of attractive wire rimmed glasses. When he smiled, a dimple shone on his left side and his eyes sparkled almost as much as Rosa's.

"Yes. That's what she has told me too." Rainey spoke back in perfect Spanish.

"Ah, you are from Colombia. I thought my mother said you are from the United States."

Rainey chuckled. "No. I am from the U.S. However, I lived in Colombia when I was a child." Rainey blinked a few times as it rolled off her tongue. *Where did that come from? Did I live here?* She tried to remember. *Colombia... yes. I did live in Colombia.*

"Are you alright?" Stephen noticed that Rainey seemed somewhere else.

Rainey explained her situation. "I surprised myself by my answer. But now I remember. I lived in Colombia for a while."

"It must be strange not to have all your memories." Stephen leaned to the side and studied her attractive face.

Rainey sighed. "It is. I don't even know my name."

"I think Margaret is a lovely name." Stephen bit on his lower lip with his eyes on Rainey's figure and then turned his eyes to his niece. "She's having a wonderful time, no?"

The children were all laughing as Ben put on the blind fold and let them spin him around. "I think so." Rainey was completely oblivious to this man's attention.

"Mother said you bought her a lovely doll."

"Yes. They were selling it at the children's store down the road from the bakery. I couldn't resist it."

"There you are." Rosa hurried toward Rainey and grabbed her hands. "I want you to help me get the cake ready. You helped bake it, you know."

"Now, Mother," Stephen argued. "Let the woman rest. We were having a pleasant conversation."

"Which is exactly why I am taking her away from you." Rosa eyed her son. "Margaret is a Christian. You know how I feel about being unequally yoked to an unbeliever." She turned her eyes on Rainey. "My son is not a Christian."

"Who said anything about a yoke? I'm just talking to her." Stephen laughed at his mother.

241

Rosa clicked her tongue. "I saw the way you were looking at my girl. You give your heart to Jesus and then you may come courting."

Rainey almost fell off her chair. Courting Stephen was the last thing she would have thought of. He had to be at least fifteen years older than her.

"Let her decide, Mother."

Rainey tried to hide the smile that threatened to take away his dignity. "I agree with Rosa. I wish to find a man who loves Jesus with his whole heart."

Stephen let out a disappointed moan. "Alright. I see where this is going."

"Papa and I will keep praying, my boy." Rosa patted his shoulder and walked away with Rainey.

***

Dylan wasn't sure he wanted to answer his cell phone. A call from his dad was not usually a good thing anymore. He'd been searching for Rainey for over two weeks. Without any new information concerning Rainey, Dylan almost expected his father to put a target on his head.

"You don't have to tell me that you still haven't found her," Nash said when Dylan answered.

"Then why are you calling?" Dylan leaned his head back on the cheap hotel pillow and stared at the stained ceiling above him.

"I got a call from my jeweler today." Nash was cryptic. "You didn't tell me you neglected to get the ring back from the girl."

A choice expletive escaped Dylan's lips and he punched the bed. "I forgot all about the ring."

"You're clumsy, son."

"How did your jeweler hear about the ring?" Dylan didn't understand where this was going.

"Another jeweler brought it into his store yesterday. Evidently this jeweler bought it from someone who bought it from someone else who bought it at a pawnshop. The jeweler brought it to Julio to get a price on it and Julio recognized the ring."

"It changed that many hands?" Dylan could hardly believe it turned up after all that.

"She must have sold it for a song," Nash said. "Although, you've got to hand it to her, it was a brilliant idea."

"Which pawnshop?" Dylan knew where this was going.

"I don't know. It's switched hands too many times to be sure."

"Did you get the ring back?"

Nash let out a shallow growl. "No. My jeweler told me it would cost me a hundred and fifty thousand dollars to get the ring back!"

Dylan cringed.

"Start questioning pawn dealers. There has to be a trail and we will find her."

***

"Trey, you should really go back to California with Justin and Kaityn. We're going to have to start looking at new angles in this case and we can't stay in Colombia forever."

Trey shook his head. "No. I'm staying."

"You need some time off. The director ordered it."

"I'll take my time off here then." Trey was being stubborn about this. "Rainey is out there somewhere and might still not know who she is. I have to find her."

Tiffany lowered her eyes. She'd already told Trey that the likelihood that Rainey was even still alive was growing thinner. Over a month in a hostage situation usually didn't end well for the victim.

With all Trey just went through in the Colombian prison, Tiffany hated to give him different orders. He wanted to be here. Most likely he really would stay if she forced him off the case.

"Alright then. We just got a lead this morning that a man fitting Dylan's description went to a pawnshop and questioned the owner about a diamond ring. The pawn dealer said the guy threatened him. Told him if he knew something and didn't tell him that he could kiss tomorrow goodbye."

"I want to talk to the pawn dealer." Trey stood up.

Tiffany shrugged. "I figured." She gave Trey the address. "You and Vince go. Call me if you get anything."

Trey let Vince drive. He still found himself growing weary later in the day. But this new lead encouraged him. They drove to the pawnshop on a very shady side of town and locked the doors to the car.

"You're the FBI?" A short, elderly, Colombian man walked out from behind the counter. "I was threatened today. Threatened! Some blonde fellow comes in and tells me if I was the one who bought the ring I needed to tell him or he'd blow me to pieces."

"What did you tell him?"

"I don't have the ring. I told him no woman fitting his description has ever been in my store."

"Woman?" Trey clarified.

"Yes. The man said it would have been brought in by a tall, slender woman from the U.S. with long brown hair and blue eyes. Bluer than his, he tells me. He said she dressed like a hippie. I don't know what a hippie is, but I told him we don't get many women from the U.S. in our store. I don't think we get many nice looking women from the U.S. on this street. I told him this much and he thought I was being funny with him."

Trey looked at Vince with a glimmer of hope. "Did he say anything else?"

"No. I did not like him. He grabbed a pack of chewing gum from my counter and walked out without paying and told me to watch my back. I don't know what he means 'watch my back.' I cannot watch my own back—it's behind me."

Trey handed the old man a ten-dollar bill and said that should cover the gum.

"Thank you!" The man was genuinely appreciative.

As they walked back to the car Trey offered to drive. "You do realize what this means?" His eyes were alight with hope.

Vince nodded. "She's alive! And we get to tell Tiffany that's what happens when you have people praying for you."

"She must have escaped. But Dylan's on her trail."

"But we're on Dylan's trail now. Let's start hitting pawnshops."

Chapter 22

Margaret told the taxi to drop her off in front of the bread store. It was good to be back. She missed this quaint little pocket of small town right on the coast of Santa Marta. She paid the driver and hurried along the stone walk to the store. The familiar little bell jingled as she stepped through.

"Rosa," Margaret called to her friend.

Rainey was just carrying a handful of clean spoons to the sink when she heard the bells. She looked up and dropped the spoons. "Mom?"

Rosa was only a few steps behind Rainey and witnessed the revelation. She put her hand to her mouth and steadied her breath. "Of course…"

After Margaret recovered from her own shock she walked toward her daughter and pulled her into her arms. "Rainey…"

Rosa hurried to the door and turned the sign to closed. She watched the mother-daughter reunion with emotion in her eyes. "I knew that you were familiar."

Rainey stepped back and put her hands on her head. "I… I'm so confused. You are my mom. I know it. I recognize you from my dreams."

Margaret tilted her head to one side and studied her daughter's puzzled expression. "What's the matter? Of course it's me."

"Rainey has amnesia," Rosa explained. "Her memories are beginning to come back in little pieces and dreams. We did not even know her name until you just said it." She reached for Rainey's hands. "Does the name Rainey sound familiar to you, child?"

Rainey closed her eyes. She tried to picture the name in her head. "They're sea glass, Rainey. You can hold them up to the sun and it shines right through them in color…" Rainey's eyes filled with emotion. "I do remember." She nodded. "Rainey… Meadows?" It seemed to go together.

Margaret had no idea how much that new memory just meant to Rainey, but she nodded and wrapped her arm around her child. "My own little Rainey Meadows."

Rosa noticed a customer standing at the door looking in. "Why don't you two go on up to Rainey's bedroom and get acquainted again. Mr. Cardoon is at the door and wants his bread."

***

Margaret was not prepared for a daughter who had no memory. Apart from the memory of gathering sea glass together and the time they'd huddled together during a tropical storm, Rainey had no other memories of her family life. Rainey shared with Margaret all that she knew and it wasn't very much.

"Do you not remember your father?" Margaret held Rainey's hand in her soil-stained hands.

Rainey shook her head. "No."

"That's alright. Bradley doesn't deserve to be remembered." Margaret recalled the man's terrible words to her before she left. *He doesn't even think of you as his daughter.*

"Until I just now learned my name, the only thing I've known about myself is that I am a child of God," Rainey confessed.

"Of course you are. We all have god in us." Margaret touched a smooth pink crystal on her neck. "It took me many years to find my higher place of consciousness."

Rainey's eyes narrowed in confusion. "I don't understand what you mean?"

"We are all gods." Margaret waved her arms in the air and brought them back to her lap. "We are one with the universe. The trees, the sky, mother earth, they are all our family."

Rainey shook her head slowly. She had no doubt that this woman was the woman in her dreams. Margaret was her mother. But the stuff she was saying was craziness. "No. That's not true." Rainey didn't feel intimidated by this 'stranger' and wasn't afraid to explain

246

what she meant. She pulled out her Bible and opened it to Romans 1. She began reading the verses she remembered Trey reading to her in the hospital. She'd read them over many times since she'd been away from him. It helped her remember him better.

"What you are saying reminds me of verse 25," Rainey explained. "'For they exchanged the truth of God for a lie, and worshipped and served the creature rather than the Creator.'"

"So you are equating me with those who professed to be wise and became fools then, is that what I hear?" Margaret crossed her arms.

"I didn't write it," Rainey said unapologetically. "The Bible tells us that we are all sinners and separated from God. It's only because Jesus took our punishment that we can be in a relationship with Him."

Margaret's lips curved into a condescending smile. "Even with amnesia…" She placed a loving hand on her daughter's face.

"That's because of the Holy Spirit living inside of her." Rosa walked in carrying a tray with three glasses of fresh goat's milk and three slices of dark buttered bread.

"Dear Rosa, it figures you and my child would share this connection." Margaret moved over on the bed so that Rosa could sit down. "This is all her Uncle Jack's doing." Margaret added. "He wanted me to send her to a Christian school. He found this wonderful school for missionary children and told me that Rainey would excel there." She shook her head. "My darling child was never the same after four years there."

Rainey's eyes turned to her window and she held a faraway look. "Uncle Jack?"

"Yes." Margaret pursed her lips and sniffed.

Rainey closed her eyes for a moment. "Tell me what he looks like?"

Margaret began describing him in detail. "He has the same color eyes as you." She sighed. "They got him into trouble, that's for sure."

"And Uncle Jack is a Christian, right?"

Margaret let out a sarcastic chuckle. "That's what he tells me."

"I can see him. I think. Does he have a wife?"

"No. She passed away years ago."

Rainey opened her eyes. "I had this image of a man and a woman. She was a sweet woman, about your age. Does Judy sound familiar?"

Margaret shook her head. "But I haven't talked to him about anything personal in years." She took a few bites of the bread.

"How did I end up here?" Rainey shook her head? "Why were Dylan and Nash holding me captive?"

Margaret got up and walked to the window. She looked outside at Rosa's lush gardens. "I did not know you had such a haven behind your store." She spun around in her long denim skirt. "It's beautiful."

"Do you not wish to answer your daughter?" Rosa was no fool. She could tell Margaret was avoiding the question.

"I cannot say." Margaret's face grew serious.

"But that does not mean you do not know." Rosa leveled her eyes on Margaret.

"Mom, if you know please tell me. I need to understand why I'm in this situation. Where do I belong? Where is home?"

Margaret turned back to the window. "It's better for you not to know."

Rosa stood up quickly and objected. "Your child has been searching for answers for over a month. How can you withhold them?"

"The truth would be too painful." Margaret looked apologetically at her child.

"Please Mom!" Rainey pleaded.

"The truth shall set you free." Rosa clutched Margaret's hand. "You must tell her. Is her life in danger? Where are her friends? Where is Trey?"

"I don't know Trey." Margaret pulled the lace curtains in front of the window. "I need some time to think about things." She stood in front of Rainey. "Rosa is a good friend to have—stay with her. I will come back."

"Margaret, no!" Rosa hurried after Margaret. "You cannot just leave. This is your daughter." Righteous anger welled up in the older woman.

Margaret turned around at the bottom of the stairs. Her eyes were red with tears. "I just need time. Leave me be."

"Listen to yourself! Can you hear how selfish you are being? Your very own flesh and blood is upstairs trying to regain her memory and you will not help her. What kind of mother are you?"

"You have no idea the sacrifices I've made for my daughter!"

"Being a mother is all about sacrifices!"

Rosa tried to reach for Margaret's hand but Margaret pulled it away.

Rainey stood at the top of the stairs. "Mom…"

"Just leave me alone!" Margaret threw up a silencing hand and walked out the door.

***

Rosa half expected Rainey to be beside herself with grief after Margaret left, but when she walked up the stairs, Rainey was sitting on her bed looking out at the garden. All the natural mother instinct in Rosa welled up in her heart and she sat beside Rainey and pulled her into her arms. "Are you alright, child?"

Rainey appreciated the warmth of Rosa's embrace. After the hug, she smiled at the dear motherly woman and touched her silver hair. "Strangely, I'm alright."

Rosa waited for an explanation.

"I can't explain it really. I guess I feel like I don't really know her. I'm disappointed that she wouldn't tell me what was going on. I have no doubt that she knows. But I'm not really surprised." Rainey shook her head. "Am I a terrible daughter to feel this way?"

"No." Rosa shook her head. "Maybe you know something subconsciously that even you don't understand right now." She held Rainey's hands as she often did when they talked.

"How long have you known my mom?"

"She's been a customer of mine for about two years. She lived just down the road. We would often sit and chat over a cup of milk or coffee. I tried to talk to her about Jesus but she always changed the subject or talked about some of her strange beliefs in karma."

"Did she ever mention me in those two years?"

Rosa shook her head. "No. I didn't know she had any children."

"I never came to the store with her?" Rainey asked.

"No. The first time I laid eyes on you was when you showed up with that unfriendly man who claimed to be your husband."

"So, apparently I did not live here with her. Otherwise you would have met me at least once."

Rosa nodded. "Perhaps you have been estranged from your mother."

It sounded plausible.

"There is a mystery here, though." Rosa got up and gathered the glasses and plates left from their meeting with Margaret. "Why were you a hostage and why wouldn't Margaret answer your questions?"

Rainey shook her head. "At least I know my name now."

***

"Why does it feel like he's always one step ahead of us?" Trey followed Vince out of the pawnshop and climbed into the car.

"Probably because he is." Vince started the vehicle and pulled away from the crowded street, careful not to run into a man on a bicycle. "But at least we know we are still on the trail."

Trey nodded. "And if he's still looking that means he hasn't found her either."

Vince slowed the car to a stop and motioned toward a pedestrian. "I could really use something to eat," he said.

Trey pointed to a small restaurant that advertised fried chicken and fried plantains. "How does that place sound?"

After the pedestrians crossed, Vince pulled into a parking spot on the side of the road. Someone honked at him and said something unkind in Spanish.

"What did that dude just say to me?" Vince narrowed his eyes.

"You don't want to know." Trey led the way to the restaurant and they both ordered some fried food.

"I still can't believe you had to fight a bunch of prisoners every day for over two weeks," Vince said after they prayed over their food.

Trey took a bite of his plantain and thought about that experience all over again. "It was insane."

250

"But man, you're ripped now." Vince reached over and felt Trey's bicep. "There isn't much left of you but muscle."

Vince was right. Trey was always fit, but after his prison experience any remaining flab on his body was replaced with muscle from the constant fights. "I wonder how David is doing with Rodriguez. If that man got saved, it could potentially change the climate of the whole prison."

Vince cut the skin off his chicken and took a few bites. "So this passion that's driving you to find Rainey... is it because you just want to help her or is there more?"

It was a personal question and Trey wasn't used to personal questions from Vince. Trey pushed a sweet potato fry around on his plate. How could he answer that? He blew out a sigh. "I miss her like crazy. She's sweet and playful and smart." He looked past Vince toward the window facing the street. "She told me she loves me."

"So this is personal."

Trey nodded.

"Do you love her?"

"I've never said those words to a woman before." Trey took a sip of his iced tea. For some reason, Vince asking such a personal question didn't bother him. He glanced up and found Vince waiting for the answer. "Yes." He nodded. "I love her."

Vince grinned. "I thought so. I just wanted to hear you say it." He gave Trey a fake jab in the arm. "You know, women like to hear those words. My wife, she wants to hear it every night, whether I'm home or away, like I've been the past few weeks."

"Rainey was out of it when she said it to me. It was after she'd had her first head injury and remembered me. She admitted that she was hoping I'd say it first, but it just kind of came out." Trey smiled at the memory. "Of course, now that she has full on amnesia she probably doesn't remember."

"Then you can tell her first," Vince joked.

"That's funny." Trey shook his head with a smirk on his face. "But she needs to get her memory back. I want her to." His face sobered. "I know that means she'll remember the lies too, but maybe she'll give me a chance to explain. When she was in the hospital we were getting to know one another all over again and I loved it. I got to be myself with her. I didn't have to be Matthew."

251

"She's going to be really excited when she hears you got saved," Vince said.

"If we ever find her." Trey had a faraway look in his eyes as he stared toward the window.

Vince put his hand on Trey's arm. "We'll find her."

***

Vince and Trey spent the next two days driving the coast of Colombia questioning pawnshops. It seemed endless. There were even some pawnshops that were open 24 hours. Vince said he figured it was so people could go out, rob a tourist and take their goods right to a pawnshop and cash out immediately.

It was late when they finally decided to call it a night. "We'll hit up a few more places in Santa Marta tomorrow." Vince headed toward the hotel.

Trey closed his eyes and tried to think through the places they'd been. Barranquilla seemed to have an endless supply of pawnshops, but today they hadn't hit any shops where the store clerk remembered a blonde man asking about a ring, or a woman fitting Rainey's description selling a ring. Trey was convinced Barranquilla was too far west. "I think Santa Marta is a good plan."

"We've been to several in Santa Marta."

"And so had Dylan. I think Dylan knows something."

Trey was too tired to keep searching but he felt like today had been a wasted day.

At the hotel, Tiffany let them know that the lab reports were finally in. Fingerprints from Enrique's boat matched finger prints found in Dr. Hernandez's office. "Even the local authorities are willing to agree that Dylan is our man in both cases." Tiffany leaned back on the hotel chair and massaged the back of her neck.

Trey had a quick mental image of Dylan going through the daily beatings he'd endured in the Colombian prison. It occurred to Trey that he'd taken those beatings when it should have been Dylan all along. *Jesus took the punishment I deserve when He died on the cross for me.*

"We are going to have to wrap this case up pretty soon though." She glanced at Trey for his response. "The director said we've been out of the U.S. long enough on this case and that we need to back track to Southern California to see if we've missed anything."

"Rainey is not in California."

"I know. But we're not only searching for Rainey."

Trey didn't like that answer. He grabbed a bottle of water from the cooler and carried it to the room next door so he could get some sleep.

***

The small pawnshop along the quiet stone-lined street in Santa Marta was easy to miss, but as soon as Dylan saw it he remembered visiting these shops with Rainey. *Would she really have been perceptive enough to remember this place?* The pawnshop was so small that Dylan actually forgot it existed. Most of the shops along this street were upscale and drew more artsy tourists than those Dylan thought of as being the pawnshop type.

When he walked through the door a bell on the knob announced his entrance. Dylan was exhausted and sick of pawnshops. The man who greeted him wore a welcoming smile and it annoyed Dylan.

"I'm looking to find this woman." Dylan showed a photo of Rainey from his smart phone. "Did she come here selling a ring?"

The storeowner's expression said it all. Dylan realized he'd found his store. "I am looking for her, sir. She is my wife. I've got to find her."

It was obvious that the man was uncomfortable with this question. He rubbed his smooth head. "I gave her the best price I could for the ring. I explained to her that I could not give her its value…"

"This isn't about the money. This is about my wife." Dylan's face turned suddenly somber. "I love her. I've got to find her."

Once the pawnshop proprietor realized that it wasn't about how little he'd paid for such a valuable ring, he relaxed. "Well that's easy. She lives across the street and down about one block at the bread store. Rosa and Gabriel welcomed her in."

Dylan glanced out the window.

"They close early on Wednesdays because they go to church. Your wife goes with them. I see them walk past my store together sometimes. The bakery might be open for another hour or so."

It seemed too good to be true. He'd finally found the right pawnshop and the proprietor actually knew where she lived.

"I hope you will be able to work things out." The man seemed to think he owed Dylan some encouraging words. He had, after all, made a serious amount of money from the sale of that diamond ring.

Dylan glanced quickly around the store in search of security cameras. This man's shop seemed ill-equipped for highly valuable items. There were no alarms, no cameras, and only one man working the store. *Does it really have to be this easy?*

"You've been a great help." Dylan pulled out his gun. "Thank you." Before the man could react, Dylan shot him in the head.

Dylan walked to the door and turned the sign around to closed and stepped outside. Dialing his father's cell phone, Dylan stepped into an alley to make a phone call.

"I found her," Dylan said as soon as his father answered.

"Where is she?"

"In the little shopping district I took her to a few weeks ago. She sold the ring to the pawnshop owner here and moved in with the local baker." Dylan gave the details of the location and arranged to meet with Nash that evening to plan a way to recover Rainey the next day.

Chapter 23

Trey took a few gulps of the cold strong coffee he'd gotten from the hotel that morning and set the cup down in the console as he and Vince pulled up to the small pawnshop in Santa Marta. It was definitely the least expected location for a pawnshop. Trey's eyes traveled along the well-maintained street. Clean storefronts and restaurants spread down the road for several blocks. Nestled along the foothills of the mountains, the little street overlooked the beautiful coastline in the distance.

"After this, I want dinner." Vince walked ahead of Trey toward the door. He didn't notice the closed sign when he pulled open the door but Trey did.

"It says 'closed.'" Trey followed Vince inside. All the lights were on, but there was an eerie silence in the shop. "Hello?" Trey called out.

Vince saw the body first. "Man down."

Trey reached for his gun.

"He's dead." Vince looked up. "But his body's still warm."

"Our killer might still be close." Trey made a quick call to Tiffany and told her to notify the local police.

With their hands close to their guns, Trey and Vince did a quick scan of the pawnshop and slipped outside to check the neighborhood. Trey backed up against a building and focused on a man several doors down talking on his cell phone. With a quick gentle jab, Trey got Vince's attention. "It's him." Trey whispered.

Both men crept closer with their hands on their guns.

"Dylan," Trey called out when they were within earshot.

Dylan turned around and spotted Trey. He grabbed his gun and darted down a back ally. Trey and Vince were close behind. "Stop Dylan, I'm gonna shoot."

Dylan tossed his phone into a gutter, ducked behind a trashcan and fired a shot. It skimmed Trey's arm.

Trey dodged another shot, slipped behind a wall, and fired a shot toward Dylan.

Vince sent a deluge of shots in Dylan's direction as he ran toward a stone fence.

Dylan was growing bold. Every shot Trey made was followed by another from Dylan. Vince made a move to close in on Dylan and caught a bullet in his arm. Dylan stood from behind the can to finish Vince off but Trey fired two shots and took Dylan down.

"Vince, are you alright?" Trey ran to his friend.

Vince held his arm and blew out a steadying breath. "It's just a scratch." He glanced toward Dylan. "See what he knows."

Dylan reached for his gun as Trey approached. "Put it down."

A sarcastic smirk crossed Dylan's lips. "You're not gonna kill me. I know where she is." He coughed a few times and put his hand on his side where he'd been shot. His gun wobbled in his hand and he lowered it to his own head. "The guy in the pawnshop told me."

"Dylan don't." Trey's eyes pleaded.

Vince approached with his gun drawn. "Dylan put down the gun."

"You'll never find her." Dylan steadied the gun on his head and fired the shot.

"No!" Trey dropped his gun down and yelled. He ran his hands through his hair and paced the alley.

The sound of sirens filled the air and soon Trey and Vince were in the presence of the local police. Tiffany was not far behind. After they convinced the police that they hadn't just murdered this man, they were able to get Vince to a hospital. Trey's injury was much more minor, but Tiffany wanted to have him treated as well.

***

"We're close." Trey touched the bandage on his arm and paced the hotel room in front of Tiffany. "Dylan found her location. The man in the pawnshop told him where she was."

"And now that man is dead." Vince's arm was in a sling, but he was back from the hospital.

"Trey, you and I can head back to that pawnshop and see if he had anything in his records," Tiffany said. "Maybe talk to his son. The police said he had a son who also worked for him."

"I can go." Vince stood up from his chair.

"No, Vince. You need to take it easy for at least a couple days." Tiffany didn't give him an option. "Trey shouldn't even be working." She shook her head. "I'm only letting him help because I'm afraid he'd do something stupid like try to take this on by himself." She glared at Trey.

"Have they recovered the phone yet?" Vince asked.

"No sign of it. With all the water draining from these recent rains the phone is probably somewhere miles away from here in the ocean," Tiffany said.

"Okay, let's go." Trey ignored the glare and grabbed his gun.

"Local police wanted to question the family first. They're also trying to locate anyone associated with Dylan."

"Did he have any identification on him?"

"None." Tiffany typed a few things into her laptop. "Alright, let's go. Vince, take it easy."

Vince shrugged with his good shoulder.

It was only a twenty-five minute drive to the pawnshop. They met one of the local police there so they could investigate the property.

"Apparently keeping records isn't a high priority in Colombia." Trey spoke in English.

The Colombian police officer crossed his arms. "I speak English."

Trey shrugged and apologized.

"The man made a large deposit in his bank about two weeks ago." Tiffany found something in a record book and pointed it out to Trey. "That might have been when he sold the ring."

Trey's eyes widened. "That was a pretty substantial deposit."

"Here's the withdraw." Tiffany turned the pages back a few

days and pointed to an amount, which was significantly less. "If this is it he made a fair profit."

They continued to search the store for clues but came up empty. *Why do we keep hitting walls, Lord?*

***

Margaret sat alone in her hotel room and stared outside at the rain. Why did all of this have to fall on her shoulders? Everything was a mess. She was glad that Nash no longer had custody of Rainey, but what should her next move be?

That one plant was worth millions. She could be a very wealthy woman. But the satisfaction she thought she would feel from cultivating such a potentially high capacity drug-producing plant was not there.

The look in Rosa's eyes when Margaret left still haunted her. "Being a mother is all about sacrifices," the Colombian woman's words echoed in her mind.

But I made sacrifices. I have a doctorate in ethno-biology. The thesis I wrote for my doctorate placed me on the charts. I could have chosen fame. I could have aborted her. Instead I was a single mom. If Bradley hadn't been willing to support Rainey and me all those years, I don't know where I would even be today.

Margaret tried to think about where she really was today. She had a million dollar plant but nothing to show for it. Was it worth the risk to deal with these drug lords? Was this million-dollar plant going to better society or make it worse? She always wanted her life work to make the world a better place. Margaret had no convictions that drug use was bad. She and Bradley enjoyed the mind-altering experiences they found through drugs. Margaret felt it heightened her spiritual awareness.

But what do I have to show for my life? A daughter who doesn't know me? A man who is not my husband, a man willing to risk my daughter's life for money. Margaret walked to her bed and pulled back the blankets. It was late and she was tired. She promised Rainey she would be in touch with her soon, but Margaret wasn't ready to explain it all.

Rainey's mind was a clean slate. Free of any memories of the fights they had with her about drug production. Rainey had

258

threatened to turn her own parents in to the police. What kind of child would do that? But now her mind was empty off all of that. She was free from the memories of being kicked out of the only home she'd ever had. *But she's not free from the religion that caused us to make that choice.* Margaret sighed.

***

It was early Friday morning. Rosa heard the bell before Rainey, who was in the back room getting ingredients for a wedding cake they were commissioned to bake. The older woman looked up and immediately raised her hands in the air when she saw the gunmen. "The cash register is right there. There's not much but..."

"Down on the floor." The man interrupted through his black ski mask. "Hands on top of your head."

Rosa obeyed.

Rainey stopped cold when she walked through the pantry door and realized what she'd just walked into.

"That's her." One of the gunmen motioned toward the other.

Before she could turn to run, Rainey found herself pressed up against a wall with a gun against her back. In a moment her hands were bound and she was being dragged toward the door.

"No!" Rosa protested.

The man guarding Rosa pressed his foot against her back. "Shut up, old lady."

The men rushed out the door and threw Rainey into the back of a dark SUV. All three men climbed in and the vehicle sped away.

Rosa ran outside and watched the black vehicle disappear. *Rainey!* She ran across the street to the print shop and broke down in sobs in her husband's arms. "They took her! They took Rainey!"

***

Tiffany knocked on Trey's hotel room door. "Open up, Trey. We just got a call."

Trey glanced at the clock. It was after nine and he wasn't sure how he'd slept so late. Tiffany encouraged both Trey and Vince to get some rest the night before to recover from their injuries.

259

Trey pulled on a shirt and found Tiffany dressed and ready to go. "A woman at the bakery a block down from the pawnshop said her friend was just abducted." Tiffany leveled her eyes on Trey. "She said her friend was Rainey Meadows."

Trey's heart tightened in his chest. "Give me five minutes." Trey hurried, got cleaned up and met Tiffany and Vince in the lobby. "I thought you were ordered to heal."

"I'm not going to miss this." Vince walked beside Trey and they hurried to a car.

Tiffany hurried to the bread shop, where two Colombian police cars were parked out front.

"Rainey Meadows is the girl you are looking for, isn't she?" Officer Pablo Pérez met them just inside the door.

"Yes." Trey noticed the gray haired storeowner bent over at a table crying. An elderly man had his hand on her shoulder to comfort her. They were talking to another officer. Trey approached and listened as Rosa shared the events that occurred less than two hours ago.

"You have to find her!" Rosa clutched the officer's arm. "She was so scared. They had machine guns! Why did they take her?"

Gabriel pulled his wife close to his chest and comforted her. "We grew to love Rainey." He said to the policeman.

Trey was finding it difficult not to become emotional in all of this. "How did you know Rainey? he asked in Spanish.

Rosa looked up at him for the first time. She recognized him as a foreigner, but his Spanish was impeccable. "Rainey had been living with us for over three weeks. She was suffering amnesia and had nowhere else to go."

Trey nodded. "We've been searching for her for over a month. She was taken from The Hospital Universitario de Cartagena by a man known as Dylan."

Rosa nodded. "She told me as much. We only recently found her mother."

Tiffany's ears perked up. "You located Margaret Reed?"

"I didn't know her last name." Rosa glanced at Tiffany. "But she was a regular customer of mine for years."

"Where is she?"

Rosa shook her head. "I do not know. She left." Rosa's expression changed to one of frustration. "Rainey begged Margaret for answers but the woman only told us she needed to think about it and left. I was so angry. How could a mother do that to a child who has been searching for her identity for over a month?"

"Did she give any indication whether or not she would return?"

"She said she would return soon and I believe her. She left her plant here and for some reason Margaret has a strange attachment to her plant."

"What plant?" Tiffany knelt down to be closer to the woman who was still seated on a chair.

"It's over by the window. She called it her baby. I don't know. I just water it every few days and keep it in the sunshine."

Tiffany and one of the Colombian police officers walked to the window and inspected the plant.

"It's a poppy." The officer touched the pedals. "Used for cocaine and morphine. Let's take it in."

"No, wait!" Tiffany stopped the officer from grabbing the plant. "This is the key to finding Margaret. My guess is this plant is the link to finding Rainey." She turned to Trey. "This has to be it, Trey. All the other plants where we'd tracked Margaret and Bradley had been destroyed. This one plant must hold some significant value for it to be rescued."

Rosa glanced up at Trey. "Did I hear her call you Trey?" she asked.

"Yes."

Rosa bit her lips together and reached for his hand. "Rainey spoke of you often."

Trey swallowed hard. "She did?"

"Yes. You read to her from the Bible. You helped her find herself in God's Word and for that she holds you in her heart."

Trey sat in the chair next to her while she held his hand. "We prayed for you every night after our Bible reading," Rosa continued. "She said you had never found faith in Jesus."

"That has changed." Trey's eyes lit up in spite of the knots in his stomach. "I put my faith in the Lord just a few weeks ago."

"The Lord be praised." Rosa reached forward and put both hands on his face. "You are a handsome one. No wonder my Rainey could not forget you."

Tiffany began asking other questions and Rosa sat up and gave them the entire story of how she'd met Rainey, how Rainey came to have such a valuable diamond ring, and what kind of man Dylan had been.

"Rosa," Tiffany spoke gently to the older woman. "If Margaret shows up at your establishment, we don't want to miss her. Would you be willing to allow one of our officers to stay here until she returns?"

Rosa glanced at Gabriel and he nodded. "We will take Trey." Rosa reached for his hand again. "You can stay in our son, Stephen's, old room."

Arrangements were made for Trey to return with his things later that day. Trey walked back to the car with Tiffany and tried to still the trembling in his heart. "She was here all along. Just a few doors down from the shooting." He shook his head. "And Dylan knew. He knew he'd beat us to the punch."

"Dylan and whoever he works for have not won." Tiffany patted his back as they climbed into the car. "That plant is the key."

"Do you think it's Nash McCarness?" Trey asked.

"I have no doubt." She pulled away and hurried toward the hotel. "I'm going to call for the rest of the team to return to Colombia."

Chapter 24

Rainey sat with her back against the wall in a bedroom in Nash's villa. Her hands and feet were still bound and she couldn't get comfortable on the hard, wood floor. She glanced up when the door opened and watched Nash enter with an armed guard.

"I hope you are enjoying your accommodations." He walked toward her and crossed his arms.

"I liked the bungalow better." Rainey hoped she wouldn't get smacked for that.

"Then why did you leave?" Nash motioned for the guard to cut her zip ties. "I'm going to cut you free but if you attempt to leave this time, you'll be as dead as the two men on guard the night you left."

"You killed them?"

"They failed me." Nash paced the room. "I am simply awaiting a call from Margaret now." He turned to Rainey. "In case you haven't pieced it all together yet, Margaret is your mother."

Rainey lowered her eyes. She didn't want to tell him that Margaret stopped by the bakery only a few days ago. "Can you please tell me what this is about?"

"Margaret has something that belongs to me and I have something that belongs to her. Once we make the trade you will be free to go."

Rainey watched Nash pull a chair from the other side of the room and sit across from her. "Your mother is quite the horticulturist. She is a top ethno-biologist. She and her partner studied the connection between plants and mammals and cultivated a highly valuable plant."

Rainey remembered the poppy sitting in the window at the bread shop. *Is that the plant he's looking for?* They were right there… "Is this plant used for illegal drugs?"

Nash narrowed his eyes on her. "Ah, you're a bright girl. Have you been getting your memory back?"

Rainey shook her head. "Only snippets." She studied Nash. "Where is Dylan?"

The man's face sobered. "He was killed."

"By you?"

Nash shook his head. "Never. I would never have killed Dylan, as foolish as he may have been."

Rainey thought she detected some emotion in his voice. "What made Dylan different from Pedro and the other guard."

Nash glanced toward the window. "Dylan was my son." He sighed. "He was an idiot from the time he was a kid. Surfing was the only thing he could do well. He was crazy about you, you know." Nash turned his eyes on Rainey. "But he had no idea how to win your heart. I told him back when you were in college that he should tell you how he felt, he should romance you a little." Nash shook his head. "Dylan was just too moody. His emotions swung back and forth quicker than a pendulum on a clock.

Rainey sucked in a nervous breath. "We really went to school together?"

Nash nodded. "You went to Pepperdine University in Southern California. I sent Dylan there to keep an eye on you. With your mom and Bradley working on cultivating that plant for me I was worried that some other drug runner would set his eyes on them and try to get to them through you. I also didn't trust you. You'd threatened to turn Margaret and Bradley in when you found out what they were involved in."

Rainey closed her eyes and tried to picture it.

Nash watched her for a moment. "Are you falling asleep?"

Rainey opened her eyes. "No, I'm trying to remember. Everything you're saying sounds just a little bit familiar to me." She could hardly believe she was carrying on such a civil conversation with the man who'd abducted her. "Have my parents worked for you very long?"

"You mean your mom," Nash corrected her. "Bradley isn't your dad."

264

None of it made sense. "Who is Bradley?"

"As far as I know, Bradley and Margaret have a common law marriage. They've been together since you were a baby, but I don't think they're actually married. They came to work for me about seventeen years ago. You were a little kid. I remember you. Your parents were biologists studying the effects of various plants on the human mind. They'd done some work for other drug runners but I thought I could set them up to do something great." Nash flicked a piece of dirt out of his fingernail. "I financed their lab and their greenhouses and set them up with beautiful places to live. You benefitted from that too, you know."

Rainey didn't know. She had a few images of a house on the beach and playing in the sand, but it still hadn't materialized completely in her mind.

"Then one day your birth father got in touch with your mother and offered to send you to religious school in Europe." Nash shook his head. "Bradley told me about it. We'd grown to be somewhat of friends. Bradley's the one who told me you weren't his kid. You don't look anything like him. Bradley's got South American blood in him, your tan is just from living in the sun all the time."

"Where is Bradley?"

"He ran off after Margaret left him and I put a target on his head."

Rainey's eyes widened.

"He'd gone against our deal. That's what all this is about."

Finally she was getting the truth; the story Margaret wouldn't give her. She wasn't sure why Nash was telling her all this, but it felt good to finally understand why she was being held and why her mother had been so secretive.

"Do you really plan to let me live?" Rainey turned her blue eyes upon the man. She realized that because she'd seen his face she would be able to identify him. She was sure Nash would see her as a threat.

Nash rose from the chair and looked sympathetically at Rainey. "I told your mother she should give up custody of you when I first found out that you had a father in the U.S." He motioned to the security guard. "Get her some water."

The man nodded and slipped away for a moment.

"She didn't want to." Nash sighed. "It's never easy having children when you're lifestyle puts you at constant risk for crime investigations. I've had to move several times to get away from the FBI and other organizations. I'll probably have to move again now that Dylan went and got himself killed. If they find a way to link him to me I'm ruined." He glanced toward the door. "Running means leaving everything and everyone and starting over with nothing but your bank account and investment connections."

Rainey still didn't get her answer.

The guard returned with her water and handed it to Rainey. "So, is that a yes?"

"I can't make any promises." Nash gave her a nod and walked out the door.

Rainey closed her eyes and tried to find the memories that went with these stories.

***

The bells over Rosa's front door rang and she walked from the pantry into the shop. "Margaret." Her eyes grew wide.

Margaret looked as if she'd aged ten years. Her already slender face was gaunt and pale. She sat at the café table and asked Rosa for a glass of iced tea. "Do you have the plant?"

"That's your first question?" Rosa's eyes flashed angrily.

Trey walked out of the back and assessed the situation.

"Can you check that bread for me? It should be ready to take out of the oven."

Trey nodded. It was his job to appear like her employee and he'd done a pretty good job of it for the past two days. They were closed on Sunday and Trey hoped Margaret wouldn't chose to show up Sunday morning while they were all at church.

He'd enjoyed visiting a worship service in Colombia. The small congregation welcomed him. Rosa introduced him as her new employee. Several of Rosa's friends asked her about Rainey. Apparently Rainey managed to make friends in the little church. She had only been gone from Rosa's home for three days already people missed her.

"I decided to destroy it." Margaret laid her hands across the table. "I'm done."

"And what about Rainey?" Rosa got up to get the drink for Margaret.

"She is comfortable here. You would allow her to stay, wouldn't you?" Margaret called to her.

Rosa returned with three glasses of tea and invited Trey to join them while she locked the door and turned her sign to 'closed.'

Margaret didn't seem to understand why this handsome young foreigner was being asked to sit with them.

"This is Trey." Rosa introduced them. "He is in love with your daughter."

Trey wasn't sure how to respond to Rosa's bold introduction.

"He is here because Rainey has been abducted by your drug friends." There was an angry fire in Rosa's eyes.

It wasn't exactly the way he'd rehearsed it with Rosa. He told her he would cuff the woman and drag her off to the hotel. But the expression on Margaret's face told him she wasn't about to run.

"They took her again?"

"Yes. And maybe, just maybe, if you had told us what was going on, we might have been able to contact the authorities and prevented this from happening." Rosa slapped the table and almost knocked Trey's drink over. "Where is she?"

Margaret let out a trembling sigh. "Nash McCarness has her."

"You know Nash McCarness?" Trey spoke for the first time.

"Yes. I worked for him for close to twenty years."

"Where is he?"

Margaret narrowed her eyes on Trey. "Who are you?"

"Trey Netherland. FBI."

Margaret started to rise but Trey grabbed her arm. "We already know who you are Ms. Reed. We picked up Bradley Scott four days ago in Barranquilla. He'd been shot by one of Nash's men. He's recovering under FBI custody."

Margaret's eyes filled with tears. "I didn't mean for any of this to happen."

Trey steadied his gaze on Margaret. "Nash McCarness has Rainey. He wants the plant, doesn't he?"

Margaret nodded.

"What makes that poppy so special?"

"It's a hybrid that I developed. It took me years. Many hybrid seeds can't reproduce but mine can."

Trey still didn't get it. "A reproducible poppy? How did you do something special? God created reproducible poppies."

"This one has higher levels of morphine producing chemicals. It would be able to produce a far stronger product from very little substance." She began explaining the steps involved in producing cocaine and morphine from poppy plants. "I never meant to put Rainey in danger."

Trey told Margaret about Enrique and his attempts to use Rainey to get to Margaret and Bradley. "Your career choice put Rainey in danger years ago."

Margaret shook her head. "So what does this mean for me?"

"It means if you're willing to work with the FBI instead of against them, we might be able to reduce your prison time." He stared at this woman who bore a resemblance to the woman he loved and showed her his badge. "It means you are under arrest. You have the right to remain silent. You have the right to an attorney…"

***

Tiffany placed the wire on Margaret and watched as the woman covered it with her sweater. "Remember, make sure Rainey makes it safely inside the bakery before you hand him the plant. The tracking device in the soil will lead us straight to him."

Margaret nodded.

"You and Gabriel stay in the print shop," Tiffany said to Rosa. "You have our word that any damage that might occur will be covered by the FBI."

"We don't care about the bakery. We just want Rainey to be safe."

Tiffany nodded. "Let's get into place. Trey, control yourself. No hugging her until they drive away with the plant." There was a slim smile on Tiffany's lips. "Vince, you and Sam go on up the street to your car and I'll be with Justin at the coffee shop." She looked at the time on her cell phone. "He's supposed to be here in a half an hour and I don't want anyone around in case he shows up early."

"I can hear everything you say, Margaret." Tiffany pointed to her earpiece. "If anything goes wrong, we'll be there in a flash."

Margaret nodded nervously.

After everyone left the bread store, Trey walked away from the front door and watched Margaret. She'd made the phone call to Nash McCarness the night before and arranged for the trade, but how did she feel about it? Was she happy to rescue her daughter or disappointed that she'd be spending the next, who knew how many years, in a federal penitentiary? Trey knew which he'd pick. He'd walk right back into that Colombian prison for the rest of his life if it meant giving Rainey her life back.

"Do you really love my daughter?" Margaret asked from the table where she sat holding her plant.

Trey leaned against the counter and nodded. "Yes. I do. I love her very much."

Margaret turned toward him and studied him for a moment. "Tell me what she's like. I haven't had much of a relationship with her for many years."

Trey licked his lips. "She's warm and friendly. She's intellectual and loves the Lord…"

"You believe the way she does?" Margaret interrupted him. "Yes."

Margaret touched the crystal necklace and twirled the smooth rock around in her fingers. "I was never able to make much sense out of Christianity. It always sounded like a bunch of rules to me."

"Not at all." Trey felt suddenly sorry for this woman. "Christianity is about a God Who created us to know and love Him. That love compelled Him to send His own Son to die on our behalf. Jesus doesn't give us a bunch of rules. We obey Him because we love Him—just as an obedient child obeys their parent because they understand that the boundaries given by that parent are only set in place to protect them." Trey was kind of surprised he'd actually been able to articulate all those thoughts. They were true. He was more certain of his faith now than he'd been just a few weeks ago. His long talks with Vince every day while they drove around searching for pawnshops, and the things he'd learned in the Bible study he'd attended with Rainey back in California finally made sense.

Margaret took a sip of the iced tea Rosa gave her before she'd gone across the street. "That's a beautiful way to put it." She smiled at Trey. "You're a good man."

"No." Trey shook his head. "I'm a sinner just like you. I needed Jesus to wash away my sins just as much as you do."

"You're a cop. How bad can you really be?"

Trey shared with her about the anger he'd bottled from his difficult childhood. "It was Jesus Who washed away all the bitterness. He forgave me for years of hatred and resentment."

"Do you think God would forgive me?"

Trey nodded. "I know He would."

"Would Rainey?"

Trey thought about what he knew about Rainey. "Yes. Rainey would too." He glanced at the clock over the door. Nash could be here any minute. I'd better make myself scarce." He started to walk away and pointed up. "Ask Him."

"Ask who?"

"Ask God to forgive you. The Bible says, if we confess with our mouths, Jesus is Lord and believe in our hearts that God raised Him from the dead, we will be saved. It's that simple."

Margaret brushed away a tear and nodded. "Thank you."

***

"Come on. It's time to go." A security guard roused Rainey from her sleep. She sat up from the bed and smoothed her blue flowered skirt. She'd had several dreams in the night. The things Nash told her brought back memories and images of people who Rainey thought she knew. Last night she dreamed she was at college. It was a beautiful place overlooking the ocean. She remembered Nash called it Pepperdine. She had a vague image of Trey there. But it wasn't Trey. She was confused, even in the dream. She also remembered a roommate—a fun-loving friend whom she called Clarissa in the dream. Were those images really memories coming back to her?

Nash met her at the bottom of the stairs and tossed her a hairbrush. "Here, go get tidied up. I don't want her to think I abused you. You've got thirty minutes. There's a towel in the bathroom and a few of the clothes you bought when you were here the first time."

270

Rainey wasn't sure what this was about. Was her mother going to make the switch? Would Nash kill her and her mother before they could get away? Rainey took a quick hot shower and attempted not to let her fears overtake her. She put on a pair of denim shorts she'd left in the bungalow after her escape and a light blue knit shirt.

God please protect us.

She walked out of the guestroom bath and found Nash sitting at the table finishing his breakfast. "Hungry?"

"No." Rainey shook her head.

"You clean up nice." Nash wiped his mouth on a napkin. "Don't you want anything? I've got some fresh pineapple."

Rainey tried to keep herself from making some kind of sarcastic comment about whether this would be her last meal or not. "I don't have much of an appetite."

"Suit yourself." Nash shrugged. "Take her to the car."

"Wait." Rainey resisted the man who attempted to grab her arm. "What are we doing? What's going on?"

"We're taking you to the drop off and getting my plant."

"That's it?"

Nash chuckled sarcastically. "Yeah—your freedom for a plant. What a deal." Nash motioned to the guard. "Get her out of here."

Rainey sat in the backseat beside Nash while the driver headed in the direction of the bread store. Rainey recognized some of the sights out her window. With a gun pointed at her side, it was difficult to focus on the scenery, but Rainey did her best.

When they pulled up in front of the store Nash turned to her. "I hate it when the kids suffer for their parents' bad decisions." He shook his head. "Don't take any of this personally."

Rainey wondered what that meant.

He grabbed her arm and hid his gun under his suit jacket before pulling her out of the car. "Don't cause any trouble."

Rainey swallowed and let him lead her to the café table in front of the store.

"Take a seat."

Rainey obeyed. She looked up and saw her mother step from the store carrying the poppy.

"Good morning, Margaret dear." Nash greeted her.

"Good morning." Margaret set the plant at the table and placed a hand on her daughter's shoulder. "Water it three times a week and make sure it gets plenty of sunshine."

Nash grinned. "Feed her three times a day and make sure she doesn't talk."

Margaret was too nervous to respond.

Nash picked up the plant and walked toward the car. Margaret motioned for Rainey to follow her into the store. Rainey heard the car door close and glanced over to see Nash climb into his vehicle. She was only a few steps behind her mother when Nash lowered his window and pulled out his gun. Margaret saw the man aim it at Rainey. Without a second thought, Margaret dove onto her daughter just as the shot was fired. The bullet hit Margaret and Nash drove away.

***

Trey heard the gunshot and darted out of the store. "Rainey!" With both women still on the ground he wasn't sure who'd been hit.

Rainey sat up and saw Margaret lying beside her in a puddle of blood. "Mom..." she reached to touch the woman's face.

Margaret gave Rainey a wane smile. "I decided to do what Jesus did." Margaret's voice was barely audible. She reached to touch her child. "He died for me." There was a faraway look in her eyes and a look of peace washed over her face. In only a moment her hand went limp.

"Mom, don't die... don't die." Rainey clutched her mother's hand while tears streamed down her face.

Trey knelt beside Rainey and placed a comforting hand on her shoulder. He ached to pull her into his arms, to hold her close, to tell her all about the love he had for her. He longed to share with her the love he now had for their Savior. But at this moment, Rainey was lost in the final act of love her mother just showed her. "Greater love has no man than this..."

Rainey looked up with tearstained eyes and saw Trey for the first time. "Trey."

He pulled her to him and felt his heart well up with the realization that he never wanted to let this woman out of his sight again.

272

Tiffany approached from the street followed by several other agents. Time seemed to stand still while they worked to try to revive Margaret, but she was gone.

"She's dead." Tiffany glanced sympathetically at Rainey. "Get Rainey inside." Tiffany glanced at the body. "I'll have the local police here in a minute. We've got a track on the plant. Vince said he's still behind them but I need to be there for back up."

Trey reached for Rainey's hand and gently led her away from the body.

***

It was quiet in the bread shop and Trey walked with Rainey through the bakery to the back of the house. Alone for the first time in over a month, Trey pulled her into his arms for another long embrace. He breathed in the smell of her hair and felt its softness on his face. She returned the hug and trembled from the terrible events of the morning.

"Am I really safe now?" She turned her blue eyes to his.

"Yes. You're safe." Trey took both of her hands and led her to the couch.

Rainey sat down with his hands still clutching hers. "My mother is dead."

Trey wondered what was going through her mind right now.

"I don't know what to feel. I... I'm sorry for her. She's my mother. But I barely remember her." Rainey pulled her hands free and covered her face.

Trey did his best to console her and prayed that God would help him to comfort her.

"She said she was doing what Jesus did for her." Rainey looked up after a few minutes and wiped away her tears. "It surprised me. When she came to the bread store and we talked, she made it clear that she didn't follow Jesus. Had something changed?"

Trey shared with her their brief conversation about God. "Perhaps in those few minutes before you arrived." He was hopeful.

"Trey, how did you find me? I was afraid I was never going to see you again. I prayed for you. Rosa and I both did." Rainey reached for his hands again and held them. "We prayed that you would come to faith in Jesus."

273

"And I did!" Trey knew this would bring her joy. "I actually gave my heart to Jesus in a Colombian prison."

"What were you doing in a Colombian prison?"

There were not going to be any more secrets when it came to Rainey. She needed the truth; it was the only way she could ever really know him. Trey shared with Rainey everything that happened to him after Dylan took her from the hospital. He shared the events from his childhood that caused his anger toward God. Some of the memories were painful to recount, but he wanted Rainey to understand the wall he'd built up toward God. "David showed me the verse, 'Jesus wept,' and for the first time in my life I understood that God was there for me all the time and that He hurt when I hurt. David helped me realize that God wanted me to know Him and trust Him."

Rainey's eyes welled up with tears.

"After I gave my life to Jesus, God took over," Trey continued.

Rainey listened as Trey gave the details of his last days in the prison. "I've been praying ever since that God will get a hold of Rodriquez and do an amazing work in that prison."

"I can hardly imagine what you must have suffered those first couple weeks." She touched his arm tenderly. "I can see that you are thinner." She touched his face. "But I am so glad God used it and that you are His child now."

Trey loved the feeling of her hand on his face. "Have you regained any of your memories?"

"Believe it or not, my biggest revelations came the last few nights after Nash told me more about myself."

"What did Nash tell you?"

Rainey gave Trey the details and how they played out in her dreams. "I dreamed about a roommate. Did I have a roommate named Clarissa?"

"Yes." Trey smiled. She was remembering.

"Nash told me about a man who paid for my Christian school education. He told me the man is my birth father. He told me Bradley was not my dad." She shook her head. "In my dream yesterday, the man called Bradley, was my dad. That confused me."

"You dreamed it as you know it." *Rainey knows Bradley as her father.* Should he tell her? "There's a lot to tell you. I'm not sure

274

now is the time or place for all of it. Right now, my team is probably attacking Nash McCarness and his crew. The man is also suspected of gun running and murder. We've been trying to find McCarness for two years."

Trey gazed into Rainey's wondering eyes.

"You didn't tell me that you were an FBI agent."

"Dr. Hernandez didn't want me to tell you anything that might cause you mental stress while your brain was healing. I wanted to tell you." Trey reached for her hand and gave it a gentle squeeze. "There are a lot of things I want to tell you."

"How do I know you, Trey? I dreamed about you last night. Did we go to school together?"

Trey knew that he needed to tell her. He touched her face and remembered the feeling of her lips on his. Would she forgive him? Would she give him a chance once she knew about the lies?

His phone rang and Trey glanced down to see that Tiffany was trying to call. "I have to take this." He got up and walked across the room.

"We caught him! We've got Nash McCarness in custody and uncovered not only hundreds of kilos of cocaine and morphine, but just as we suspected, the man was running guns."

"Is the team alright?" Trey hoped his friends survived the raid.

"Sam took a bullet in the leg, but I think he's going to be fine. They've taken him to the hospital. The Colombian police were a huge help. They're working with us now. How is Rainey?"

"She's fine." Trey glanced at her and found her eyes on him.

"Can you and Justin get out here? I could use a couple more hands as we wrap this stuff up."

"Yeah." Trey hated to leave Rainey. But maybe it would be better for her to deal with the grief of losing her mother before he dumped everything else on her.

"They want me to get out to Nash's place. They made a huge bust." Trey walked to Rainey and reached for her hands. "Rosa and Gabriel can come back over now. You're safe with them."

"Will you be back?" Rainey bit her lower lip and stared into his eyes.

"Absolutely." He held her hand and walked back into the bakery. Margaret's body had been taken away and Justin was talking to Rosa, Gabriel, and a couple Colombian policemen outside.

"There is one thing I need to say to you right now, though." Trey stopped her before they reached the door. He pulled her closer and gazed into her eyes. "I love you." The words rolled off his lips and his heart beat just a little faster. He'd never uttered those words to a woman before. He meant it with all his heart, even though he was sure Rainey didn't have enough memories of him to understand how he could feel this way.

"I don't expect you to understand. To you I'm just a man you can only remember spending two weeks with in a hospital room. But there's so much more and I don't want another day to go by without telling you how I feel."

Rainey's eyes were moist with unshed tears. "I do understand, Trey. There is more. I have memories... even though they're very foggy. Something in my heart tells me that I've loved you for a long time."

Trey pulled her to him and found her lips.

***

It was late when Trey returned to the bakery. Rainey was up talking to Gabriel and Rosa when they answered his knock.

"Is everything wrapped up now?" Rosa asked.

"For the most part. Of course now begins the months of paper work and follow up investigations. But I've got the next four weeks off starting Friday."

"You'll be on vacation?" Rainey asked.

"It's more of a recovery leave. I spent three weeks in a Colombian prison so the FBI kind of owes me." He sat down. "I'm sure they'll be calling me every other day to make sure they have all their details right, but hopefully I can give them what they need in the next four days."

"You look tired." Rosa got up and walked to the kitchen. "I'm going to get you some milk and coffee cake."

Trey's mouth watered at the thought.

"Rosa found this on the table in the bakery after you left." Rainey handed Trey a napkin.

I believe. Trey read the two words.

"And she threw her crystal in the trash. I found it when I was cleaning up tonight," Rosa added. "That's significant. Margaret put a lot of stock in her crystal. What all did you say to her while you were alone?"

Trey shared the story.

"Praise be to God!" Rosa clasped Trey's hands and turned her eyes toward heaven. "Her words to Rainey make sense now. Margaret must have put her faith in Jesus just before she died."

Rainey had a peaceful look of joy in her eyes.

It was late when they finally went to bed. Trey prayed about the best way to tell Rainey the rest of the story. She needed to know the rest. She needed to know that he'd lied to her for two months while they'd lived in Malibu. She needed to know about Jack. But when would be the best time to tell her?

Chapter 25

Trey finished up the week and promised his boss that he wouldn't block her calls if she tried to reach him during his leave. Vince was also taking some time off, but wouldn't make the same promise.

"My wife told me I'm not allowed to talk to you while I'm on vacation."

Tiffany told him she'd find him if she needed him.

Vince took an earlier flight home while Trey and Rainey spent an extra day exploring Santa Marta.

Rainey asked a lot of questions as they explored a remote part of the beach and Trey answered what he could. She was beginning to put things together as he gave her details. "So, I'm a fashion design major?" She grinned. "What do I want to do with a degree like that?"

"You want to make modest yet fashionable clothing and sell it in your own store and online." Trey remembered clearly from their many conversations.

Rainey climbed onto a large rock and sat facing the ocean. "This place is beautiful." She watched the blue water as it crashed onto the shore. The mountains in the background made a beautiful frame for the lovely picture. Santa Marta was breathtaking. She closed her eyes and leaned back on the rock.

Trey leaned over and kissed her.

Rainey's lips curved into a smile. "You've kissed me on the beach before, haven't you?

Trey nodded.

She touched his face tenderly and gazed into his eyes. Trey prayed for an opportunity to talk. He needed to tell her everything.

"Let's go put our feet in the ocean." She slipped out of her flip-flops and ran to the edge of the water.

Trey was only a few steps behind her and stopped when he saw the expression on Rainey's face. "What is it?" He looked around, wondering if Rainey had just spotted a dead body or something.

"The waves... I rode in one of those waves." Her eyes were wide. "I could see the water all around me. It was like I was in a tunnel." The memory was coming back with a vengeance. "The sun sparkled through the tunnel and I could see millions of glistening stars in the sea of blue." She sucked in a deep breath. "And God was there."

Trey nodded. She was remembering... without dreams.

Rainey knelt down at the edge of the incoming tide and held her hands on her head. "I fell off the board. The water was crashing in on me over and over and I couldn't breath... then I was on the beach and Dylan was there. He rescued me." She took several steadying breaths. "We went back to his apartment and those men were there. Carlos... he was your friend..." She turned to Trey with questioning eyes. "All those men were your friends..."

"I was investigating them. I was undercover."

Rainey shook her head and closed her eyes. "Your name was Matthew." She looked up at him again. "We dated. You were an engineering major at the school. How can you be an FBI agent?" Suddenly things didn't make sense.

Trey knelt down and reached for her hand but she pulled it away.

"Who are you?" She searched his face.

Tears welled up in Trey's eyes. Was he going to lose her again? "Everything I've told you about myself since you were in the hospital in Cartagena is true. Everything... Rainey, I was undercover when I met you. I told you about it when we were on Enrique's boat. Do you remember?"

Rainey did remember. Tears filled her eyes.

"You told me you loved me on the yacht. Do you remember that?"

Rainey nodded.

"Rainey, you're the only woman I've ever loved like this. I started falling for you when I was undercover, but you didn't know the real me. I was so afraid you'd hate me when you learned the truth and you did. You told me you never wanted me to touch you again." Trey's voice shook with emotion. "It about killed me." He grabbed her hand and held it tight. "I don't want to lose you again, Rainey. Please forgive me for lying to you. The Truth found me out, Rainey. That Truth is Jesus. He's the Way and the Truth and the Life and He used all those lies and allowed me to get the tar beat out of me every day for two weeks to break me. I regret lying to you, Rainey. But I promise you that I've been honest with you ever since Jesus got a hold of me and if you'll allow me to, I'll be honest with you for the rest of our lives."

Rainey blinked back the tears that were running down her face. She couldn't wipe them away with Trey's hands clutching hers. "The rest of our lives?"

"I want to marry you, Rainey." Trey released his hold and wiped her tears for her. "I love you."

***

Rainey was quiet for a moment and watched a tear trickle down Trey's face. She was amazed that all her memories were back. Everything. Some of them were good, some bad. But they were back.

Trey sat beside her and turned his gaze to the ocean. Maybe to gather his emotions. Maybe to let her think.

All the dates she and Trey went on in California, their hiking trips to the mountains, their walks on the beach, the restaurants he took her to and the places they enjoyed coffee—it was all back.

He was Matthew then. He won her heart being Matthew… but not really. He was still Trey. The way he protected her on the yacht when he was undercover. That was Trey. The way he read the Bible with her and talked about what they were reading. That was Trey. Even when he was undercover he showed her glimpses of the man he is now. The stories he'd told her about his life were all lies… *part of his 'cover' I guess.*

She thought about the stories he shared with her after his conversion, about his real childhood. That was honesty.

His face was still toward the water. She could see the emotion in his expression. Was he praying right now?

Matthew wasn't truly a believer, but this man was. Trey was a new creation. He was a follower of Jesus Christ and Jesus forgave him and washed away all the lies. She stood up and reached for his hands.

He stood up and she started pulling him toward the water. "What?"

A smile crossed her lips. "Just walk with me."

Trey and Rainey walked into the ocean. Waves crashed against them as they stood, waist deep, in the water. "Trey Netherland, is Jesus Christ Your Lord and Savior?"

Trey suddenly knew what she was doing. "Yes, He is."

"Then I baptize you in the name of the Father and of the Son and of the Holy Spirit."

Trey let her gently dunk him into the ocean. When he rose from the salty water he let his eyes travel over the foamy white waves. Rainey smiled and reached for his hands. There was emotion in his eyes as he pulled her to him, wrapped his arms around her and kissed her.

A few tourists stood not far from where she'd baptized him and clapped. Rainey wondered if they knew what she'd just done.

"What made you do that?"

"Jesus washed away all the lies, Trey. He forgives you and I forgive you." She pulled him close. "I love you, Trey!"

Trey kissed her again.

"And yes, I will marry you."

***

Before they left Santa Marta, Trey made a few phone calls. He called his father and asked if they could get together soon. Without going into too much detail, he told his dad that he'd put his faith in Christ and wanted to tell him the whole story in person. He also apologized for the anger he'd bottled against his dad for all those years. Trey's dad was both surprised and overjoyed. Trey also planned to talk to his mother, but he wanted to do so in person. He could hardly wait to introduce them to Rainey.

Trey also made arrangements for Rainey's roommate, Clarissa, to be notified. She had reported Rainey missing after she'd not returned home, and the FBI contacted her to give her a brief explanation, but Trey knew Rainey's friend would be eager to know Rainey was safe. He was sure Rainey would fill in the details when they arrived home.

Trey also called Jack and arranged for him to pick them up at Los Angeles International Airport. Trey explained a lot to Jack over the phone. He confessed everything to the older man and asked for his forgiveness.

Jack cleared his throat. "Of course I forgive you. You already know what kind of scoundrel I was before God got a hold of me."

Trey was relieved by Jack's response. "You could see right through me, couldn't you?" he asked over the phone.

"Like glass." Jack chuckled. "I like what you said about God letting those men beat the tar out of you every day until you were finally broken for Him. You deserved it!"

Trey laughed. "Thanks!"

"We've been praying that you'd get saved. I'm glad God answered."

"Me too." Trey paused. "I haven't told her your secret though. I thought I'd leave that for you."

Jack was quiet for a moment. "Thank you."

"I want you to know that I've asked Rainey to marry me." Trey figured this might serve as a bit of a shock to Jack, but he wanted to make his intentions clear. "Because you are her father, I would be honored if you would give us your blessing."

There was a long pause on the other end of the phone and Trey wondered if Jack hung up. Jack cleared his throat and let out a long sigh. "As to my blessing… that I need to pray about. We'll talk when you get back in town."

Trey understood.

They took an early flight to Los Angeles the next morning and arrived in the late afternoon. As they exited the terminal, Rainey's eyes darted about excitedly looking for her uncle. Once she spotted the other couple, Rainey ran to them. "Uncle Jack! Judy!" She tried to pull them both into her arms. "It's really you!"

Jack kissed her on top of her head. "We missed you like crazy."

"Did I miss the wedding?" Rainey reached for Judy's hand and saw two rings.

"We just did a small wedding and decided to postpone our honeymoon until we knew you were safe." Judy placed her hand on Rainey's

They grabbed their bags and headed toward the parking garage. "We thought we'd take you two back to our place. Does that suit you?"

"Yes." Rainey wrapped an arm through Jack's with her other in Trey's and let them carry the suitcases.

"The two things I never wanted for my little Rainey was a cop or a convict and here you are dating both." Jack teased.

They piled their few bags in the trunk.

"Trey is not a convict!" Rainey scooted close to Trey in the back seat. "And when did you hear about that?" She leaned back and glanced at Jack in the rearview mirror. "Does he know about the Colombian prison?" She glanced at Trey.

"Wait till we get to the house and then I'll explain." Jack winked at her in the mirror.

***

Judy was happy to be hostess and carried iced tea to the living room where they could all sit and talk. She also grabbed a tissue box in case it got emotional. She knew Jack would cry.

"So, now you boys can tell me why you're being mysterious." Rainey took a sip of her tea. "It sounds like you talked about everything."

Trey glanced at Jack. "Do you want me to leave the room?"

"Of course not." Jack turned to Rainey. "Trey called to ask my blessing for him to marry you. He felt it was best to ask her father."

Rainey set her drink down on the coffee table and tried to process what he'd just said. "My father?"

Jack nodded. "Me."

"You're my birth dad?"

"Yes." Jack's eyes filled with tears as Judy predicted. She handed him the tissue box. "I'm sorry I never told you. At first it was me who didn't want you to know. I was married to Ruth. Your mother was one of my students."

Rainey reached for Trey's hand and tried to gather her emotions.

"Once I became a Christian, Ruth and I both agreed that you should know the truth. But your mother was insistent that we never tell. She promised to disappear with you if I ever did." Jack explained everything as best as he could.

"It all makes sense now." Rainey wiped away a tear and Jack handed her the box. "Bradley was never close to me. You've always felt more like a dad to me than Bradley did. But I hated to admit that because I didn't want to dishonor him."

"You're a good and faithful daughter." Jack said with pride. "You even honored a man who you only believed to be your dad."

"I always thought it was strange that Bradley was so willing to completely let me go from his life. When I threatened to turn them in, it was Bradley who told me never to come home."

Jack moved to the couch where Rainey and Trey were sitting. "But now you know you are home."

Rainey stared into the blue eyes that so perfectly matched hers and hugged her dad for the first time.

"And now we have to talk about this young man." Jack released his hold on Rainey to look at Trey. "He tells me he proposed to you and that you actually said yes."

Rainey glanced at Trey rapturously and clutched his hand. She was twenty-six and knew she didn't need her dad's permission, but it was important to both of them to have his blessing.

"They often say girls marry men like their fathers." Jack tilted his head and studied the two of them on the sofa. "Ironic, isn't it, that you want to marry a man who lied to you about his identity when you first met him? You can't get much more like your birth dad than that." His lips curved into a smile. "Trey told me Love found him out. I guess I can say the same. Love found us both out and set us free." He smiled at Rainey. "It's so good to have a daughter."

Rainey reached for his hand.

284

"Trey, you've shared your testimony with me, about how you got saved, and nothing could bring me greater joy than to have my Rainey marry a man who loves the Lord. But I've got one very important question for you." He leaned back against the arm of the sofa and leveled his eyes on Trey. "What does Jesus mean to you?"

Trey found he actually hoped Jack would ask him that question again. "Well you already know how Jesus got a hold of my heart. In order to open my eyes, God brought me to the place he brought Jacob, who was also a liar. God wrestled with me. Of course, in my situation he used a bunch of hostile inmates. But it worked. God opened my eyes to my need for Him and to the fact that He loves me. He delivered me from those who sought to kill me. He forgave me for my sins. He healed my hurts. He returned Rainey to me. He showed me that He was there with me all along. In all my sorrows, my hurts, my loneliness, Jesus showed me that He wept for me." Trey did his best not to need the box of tissues. "What does Jesus mean to me?" Trey steadied his gaze on Jack. "That's easy. Jesus means everything to me. I finally get it."

Jack's eyes lit up and he shook Trey's hand. "I knew that other answer you gave me was a crock of beans." He grinned. "Son, you have my blessing to marry my daughter. I couldn't be happier."

Trey turned to look at the woman he loved and reached to pull her into his arms. "I couldn't be happier either."